Once I had laid evidence to incriminate the one already guilty of five murders, I would leave the indisputable clue – a white kid glove, carelessly cast upon her body. The other thing, the one I abhorred, I would not now, due to a recent fortunate aberration in his procedure, be forced to imitate. He had always set his signature, a blood-bedewed rose, on the right breast or inner thigh of his victims ... always until the last. She was not thus mutilated, owing, a Scotland Yard detective told the newspapers, to the extraordinary resistance she had put up. Evidence discovered at the site of the murder suggested that she had wounded him and forced him to cut short his horrid work. Poor girl, how tenacious of life she must have been – a wonder to me, for her life seemed dreary enough: a shop assistant, her home and her future in the squalid East End, her fiancé a rough bargee. Be that as it may, Rose Doyle had done me a favour, had dispensed with that part of the deed I could not envision: myself kneeling over the lifeless but still fine body of Mari Prince.

*Also by Roberta Murphy
and available from
Mandarin Paperbacks*

The Enchanted

Roberta Murphy

NIGHT PLAYERS

Mandarin

A Mandarin Paperback
NIGHT PLAYERS

First published in Great Britain 1991
by William Heinemann Ltd
This edition published 1991
by Mandarin Paperbacks
Michelin House, 81 Fulham Road, London SW3 6RB

Mandarin is an imprint of the Octopus Publishing Group,
a division of Reed International Books Limited

Copyright © Roberta Murphy 1991

A CIP catalogue record for this title
is available from the British Library
ISBN 0 7493 0584 3

Printed and bound in Great Britain
by Cox & Wyman Ltd, Reading, Berkshire

This book is sold subject to the condition
that it shall not, by way of trade or otherwise,
be lent, resold, hired out, or otherwise circulated
without the publisher's prior consent in any form
of binding or cover other than that in which
it is published and without a similar condition
including this condition being imposed
on the subsequent purchaser.

To Dipu and Dinu

O Rose, thou art sick!
The invisible worm,
That flies in the night,
In the howling storm,

Has found out thy bed
Of crimson joy,
And his dark secret love
Does thy life destroy.

> William Blake,
> 'The Sick Rose'

He does not want to take your life,
just borrow it for the evening,
use you and return you,
call you back as you are leaving. . .

> John Morris,
> lyrics from 'Ladykiller'

Author's Note

In writing this novel, I tried as far as possible to maintain historical accuracy. Occasionally, however, I have altered facts to serve fiction. Wales did not play at Twickenham in 1913. That year, England and Scotland were the contenders, and the English team won the Triple Crown. I have also changed the date on which the match was played. Train schedules sometimes differ in the book from the real schedules to facilitate my characters' journeys. Mari and her fellow performers sing songs that were actually popular in other decades. And so on . . . The reader, I hope, will bear with these fabrications; without them, I could not have told the tale as I wished.

I would like to thank Dick Levinson, of the National Museum of Health and Medicine, for the enormous help he provided with my research. Thanks, also, to Edward P. Jones for his valuable advice and editing.

I

Mari: Friday Night

Stripped down to her frilly white knickers and *broderie anglaise* camisole, Mari Prince sits in front of her dressing-room mirror after the Friday night show at the London Palladium, brushing her auburn hair. She winces and swears each time the bristles catch in her tangled curls. 'Bloody mop,' Mari says to her hair. 'I've a good mind to have you shorn off, since you won't behave. Fetch a nice price, so long and so thick still . . .' she slips her hands into her hair and lifts it up and away from her face, as if she were showing it off to a prospective buyer at Madame Minette's Beauty Palace, '. . . and such a rare colour. How'd you like to be a dead thing, eh?'

Her choice of words is unfortunate, and Mari realizes it straight away. 'There I go again. Why did I have to say that? I'm wishing myself ill luck, I swear.' In the mirror, her face has turned sickly pale, as if the ill luck she fears has already visited her.

With shaky fingers she opens a drawer and rummages among diaphanous scarves and fishnet stockings, the props of her act, until she finds a pair of knickers much like the ones she is wearing. Wrapped in the knickers, like a babe in swaddling clothes, lies Mari's comfort, a half-full bottle of Beefeater's gin. She unscrews the cap and pours a generous swill into the white china mug from which, before she goes on stage each evening, she drinks strong tea, to charge her blood and pep her up. It's hard work, rousing an audience to frenzy, and vigour for the task doesn't come as naturally as it used to.

Mari sips the neat gin, shudders, and says 'Ahh' to her mirrored face. Holding the mug in both hands, she leans forward for a closer look at that face. Cleansed of stage make-up, it's nothing out of the ordinary, large-boned, broad of cheek and forehead, thousands like it in the mill town up North where she comes from. It's her hair, glorious though disobedient, that makes Mari unique.

No, tell the truth and shame the devil (so her father, a confirmed liar, counselled her), it's not just her fiery tresses that set her apart from those put-upon, down-at-heel mill girls. Now she has another distinction, one she could well have done without.

Her eyes, the colour of Marmite, and able, too, at certain moments, to suggest its melting consistency, assume a fixed aspect, as if her mirror, instead of reflecting the cluttered dressing room, had become a necromancer's window through which she views the future . . . though the horror it throws up, God knows, might make a clairvoyant's customer swoon.

She sees her white camisole, ripped and red, blood spurting from a gash in the cotton beneath her left breast. A hand swoops out of the air and tears away the remnants of the camisole, and she sees the wound itself, a great scarlet blot spreading its petals like a full-blown rose, the trademark of the Gardener. His introductory and only letter to Scotland Yard, sent after the discovery of his first victim and reprinted in the *Chronicle*, stated his intent: 'I will pluck the foul weeds from the earth and plant roses. I am the seed, the root, and the Gardener. I will transform Sodom into Eden.'

And Mari has become convinced she's high on the list of this fiend who stalks the West End streets and who, in the past six months, has totted up only one less victim than Jack the Ripper. How she came by this conviction, she can't fathom. Other women she knows, though equally vulnerable in age and situation (he favours youngish, unmarried females), don't share her fear. Take Doris, Mari's best friend. She's a bit more picky these days about who she goes off with after the show, but she hasn't let the murders alter or limit her life. For Mari, the killer has become an obsession . . . and it shows, in her eyes, in her gestures, in her conduct. If she's not careful, if she doesn't get a grip on herself, soon it will show in her act, where nothing and no one before – not even Antonio – interfered.

Have another go at the gin. Mother's ruin. But she is not a mother, and besides, she needs it to brave the dark streets. She lifts the hairbrush, removing from it a wad of hair which she tosses into the waste-bin. 'More coming out every night. I'll be bald as a baby's behind if I don't stop this malarky and get me a wig.'

Each time she goes on stage, Mari backcombs her hair until it flares like a bush on fire. She covers her face with ivory pancake make-up and wings her eyes with emerald shadow. Behind her lashes she sticks tiny silver sequins that glint and glimmer, witchlike. The make-up and the hair-style give her the supernatural appearance she needs for her magic act and offset her large breasts and her ample behind which, though men admire them, detract from the ethereal image she strives for behind the footlights. Like all the components of her routine, her appearance is the result of much thought, experiment and hard work. After all these years in music hall, she can still surprise her patrons and prides herself on that.

'They're a fickle lot, Mari,' Alf Ramsey, the Palladium manager, warned when he first engaged her fourteen years back. 'King Henrys, all of them. Stick you on a throne tonight and chop your head off in the morning. If you want to last in this business, you better be something of a Scheherazade . . . versatile and adaptable.'

Mari had never heard of King Henry – she knew only of Victoria and the Prince of Wales, Edward – and she wanted to ask if Scheherazade was as big a star as Vesta Tilly, but she didn't show her ignorance to Alf Ramsey, though she was only twenty-one then and just arrived in London. 'Don't worry about my head,' she told him. 'It's screwed on tight like the rest of me. I'm built to last, Mr Ramsey.'

She hadn't felt as cocksure as she sounded, but time has proved her right. While others have soared and plummeted, she's held a steady spot on the bill. In fact, since she changed her hair-style a year ago – by accident, not endeavour – she'd go as far as to say she's the one who packs them in. Alf thinks so. He treasures her. 'You're like India, love,' he tells her. 'The jewel in my crown. I'd rather have you than all the riches of Empire.'

Mari's hair-style has become her trademark. More than that – she believes it's the core of her magic. When she lets down her daytime chignon and teases it into a wanton aureole, an unearthly power seizes her. With the transformation of her locks comes a radical change in herself. No longer Mari Prince, toiling showgirl (underpaid for all her charisma), she becomes her stage persona – The Infamous Princess Marie, magician non-pareil, a sorceress more seductive than Circe. Every Friday and Saturday night she brings the house down with her prancing-dancing, singing-striptease conjuring. Leaping erect, the men applaud, stamp their feet, chant her name, bombard her with flowers.

The chorus girls swear it's Mari's body, and what she does with it, that excites the audience. 'Tits not tricks,' they say, half teasing, half nasty. 'It's not what you pull out of a hat but what they hope will fall out of your bodice.' Alf Ramsey calls it star quality. 'Pay those trollops no mind,' he says. 'You got star quality.'

Mari knows that Alf and the chorus are both wrong. What she has is magic, and like Samson's superhuman strength and Rapunzel's allure, it emanates from her hair. She knows her hair is charmed because when she hides it under a scarf, no one looks twice at her in the streets. And much as she had laboured to perfect her act since the day she joined the Palladium, she had caused no great stir until that night a year ago when, driven half out of her mind by a private catastrophe, she rushed into the theatre with minutes to spare, her chignon undone and herself in disarray, and having time only to slip into her costume, dashed on stage, her hair like a rain forest because she had run hither and thither in the fog, searching for a man who had vanished.

Funny really, Mari thinks, as she savours the bitter but bracing gin, how life can go on for years in a predictable way, so that a person knows, more or less, what each day will bring, knows by rote the signals that will guide her trek from getting-up time to bedtime, one day distinguished from the next only by minor hindrances, small pleasures. And then, suddenly, the wind shifts, the signals change, and you know you're on a different course, travelling toward something out of the ordinary, some grand and significant episode. Looking back, she can see how the first half of 1911, from January to June, had been a time when Fortune's fickle eyes had been turned on her, her hands scattering signals like meteors in Mari's path.

For Mari, Coronation year had begun badly. She suffered from a minor but chronic backache, bunions, and a depression, this last ailment brought on by the dreary winter weather, and by an upsetting incident on New Year's Eve. A man who had sent into her dressing room a bottle of champagne and a note penned in an elegant hand had taken her back to his rooms in Mayfair and there subjected her to a form of love-making that was more like rape. Had she been of smaller stature and slighter spirit, she might have been seriously hurt. As it was, she escaped into the freezing cold night with bruises, a torn dress, and his curses smarting her ears.

'This year's got off to an unlucky start,' she had told Mrs Perkins, her landlady, some nights later (when she could bring herself to speak of it) over a cup of tea in Mrs Perkins's parlour. 'He seemed a right enough chap . . . cultured, you know, in his handwriting and how he talked . . . but he could have done me a permanent injury—'

'Evil men are roaming about London these days,' Mrs Perkins said. 'It's all these foreigners coming over. If we don't put a stop to them, England won't be a fit place to live no more. Was he a Russian, Mari? Was he one of them Anarchists, do you think?' Mrs Perkins had been following the Siege of Sidney Street in the *Daily Chronicle*. 'The papers say Peter the Painter could've escaped that fire. There were three men in the house but only two bodies the police found. He could still be at large. There's a report he was spotted recently. At a music hall, Mari!'

'This chap was no Russian,' Mari said. 'He was as English as pork pie. An English gentleman, Mrs P.'

'Or disguised as such,' Mrs Perkins said, refilling Mari's cup. 'They found wigs on the premises, and if a man can dress up as a woman and get away with it, what's to stop him dressing up as another man, eh? I can't believe an Englishman would attack you. He was an Anarchist with a fake accent, is my belief.'

Everyone was talking about the Anarchists in January, Alf saying it could be bad for business, that bit about Peter being seen at a music hall; Doris joking that she wouldn't say no to a feller with a stick of dynamite in his trousers. Mari sees now that all the furore had been her first sign, the excitement stirred up in London an omen of the great adventure hurtling toward her at top speed in the shape of a dark-browed foreigner in a peaked cap, honey on his tongue and a stiletto in his pocket – a brimming, simmering lover coming to ignite a blaze that would outstrip the conflagration in Sidney Street and diminish the pyrotechnics of the Coronation.

The Coronation was the next signal. As the day drew near, a festive mood embraced the city and people forgot about the dark deeds of winter as decorations went up in all the streets. And Mari's depression lifted. She bought an elaborate hat and a stylish blue costume to wear on the Great Day and felt – she'd swear to this – a fluttering about her heart that was itself a sign of her own great day approaching, as if the flags and greenery adorning London had been put up in her honour, not the King's.

On Coronation Day she went with Mrs Perkins to see the procession. They stayed on for the illuminations, and Mari bought a souvenir biscuit-tin filled with Huntley and Palmer Royal Sovereign biscuits, each one stamped with a shortbread crown.

Later that night, as they ate the biscuits with their tea, Mrs Perkins said, 'Seems to me England's all right after all. And if we're all right, ducks, so must the rest of the world be, 'cause we're in charge, ain't we?'

Mari said, through a mouthful of shortbread and apricot jam, 'I can't speak for the rest of the world, but I feel all right. I really do. Like a person on the up-and-up's how I feel.'

Two days later Antonio made his flourishing entrance. When Mari brought him home from the picture palace, Mrs Perkins had taken to him at once. On being introduced, he had kissed her hand, flashed his black eyes, and said, 'You have the English grace I hear so much about but never before see,' and she had seemed instantly to shed her distrust of foreigners. 'He can stay as long as he likes,' she told Mari after a week. 'He's a proper gentleman. I've mixed with enough to know. And when he sings . . . why, it reminds me of Caruso. My late husband used to keep a regular box at the opera, did I tell you . . . ?'

All that summer – while their Majesties were fêted and dined throughout the kingdom, while a heatwave scorched Londoners, and the skies over Britain were stirred up with the great air races, the streets with strikers and rioters, seamen, dockers, railwaymen, miners coming out, famine and violence and spectacle vying for top billing in the extravaganza – Mari was in love and oblivious, her world no broader than the circle of her lover's arms, no occurrence more significant than their love-making, the voices that clamoured elsewhere muffled by his endearments, his jokes, the arias he sang while he shaved or bathed. She did not remark then his absences, his habit of leaving her for a day or an evening without explanation, except as a temporary, personal calamity. When he returned late at night and she said, 'Where were you?' his answer, 'With friends ... with old friends, *carissima*,' satisfied her, for soon she'd be in his arms, engaged in her own fireworks, her own heatwave, her private banquet. She did not then connect Antonio's disappearances with larger events ... indeed, she hardly knew or cared what those events were.

Less than a year after his entrance, he exited with just as much drama, vanishing, literally, from her side at the sound of a whistle piercing the night; and she had run in circles, not finding him but being found, instead, by a trio of policemen and a plainclothes detective who'd taken her to the station for questioning; and after they let her go, she had dashed to the Palladium and on to the stage, there to win acclaim, to bring the house down for the first time in her long career. That night she had given three encores. And it had to be my hair, Mari – dazed by it all – concluded later, for that was the only thing different. The only difference they could see, any road.

So the loss of Antonio, which she believed at the time she wouldn't survive, brought her good luck in another area of her life. Mari tips the Beefeater's and ponders this oddity for the umpteenth time. If she could make sense of the contradiction, she's convinced she could also make a life plan ... a thing a thirty-five-year-old woman sorely needs. But, as usual, when she remembers Antonio, nostalgia takes her by the hand and leads her away from the road of reason.

She shouldn't drink, she shouldn't reminisce, both wasteful occupations and tricky twins ... but she can't help it. Other pastimes don't attract her any more.

Sighing, sipping, Mari turns her attention back to her hair, which started all this. Putting down the glass she lifts the brush and tries to tame the riotous curls. She knows she will never wear a wig nor succumb to the scissors, a deed that ruined Samson and put a jinx on Rapunzel. In the mirror, as she works, she evokes a new scene: her homeward route. She studies it like a commander poring over a map of a battlefield – the gaslit alleys, the shadowy doorways, the dark corners she must pass before she's snug in her room. It's Friday night, the night the Gardener has chosen for his monthly sprees. It's the end of March, and no murder this month . . . not yet. Some say Rose Doyle, his last victim, is to be thanked for that. Dying, Rose put up such a fight that he was forced to flee without taking all of his customary pleasures. Some say she gave him such a fright he won't come out again. Mari is not one of these. An animal, once it has tasted blood, won't stop devouring.

Five victims since October, each of them plucked out of the night and the crowds – there's no safety in numbers – and dragged into a back street to be battered, mauled, murdered and then carved with his ghastly insignia, a rose – red and blooming indeed – on the inner thigh or on the right breast.

The police have no leads, though they suspect he's a gentleman, for one of the women was found with a white silk scarf knotted around her neck, a white kid glove picked off the bodies of three others. A gentleman . . . a toff . . . just the type Mari herself consorted with before she met Antonio and stopped all that. How many Friday and Saturday nights before Antonio did she accept offers from total strangers at the stage door? I'm lucky Antonio came, is what she thinks now, before I really paid. Thinking on what might have happened induces a violent shudder. Her hand slides down her hair. The brush snags and wraps itself up in a parcel of curls.

At the same moment a tall, wan-faced figure in black top hat and tails appears behind her in the mirror. With a small scream, Mari spins round, her arms locked under her bosom. She sees it's only Doris and her arms fall to her sides. 'Bloody hell,' she says softly, 'you gave me the fright of my life. What you want to come creeping in like that for, Doris?'

'*Me*, creeping?' Doris strikes a pose, her legs in black tights thrust apart, her hands crossed over the knob of her cane. It's a stance men find provocative, a hint of aggressive, androgynous sexuality in it, emphasized by the pseudo-male costume. 'I never crept in my life. Bit edgy tonight, aren't we?'

'Sorry,' Mari says. 'I didn't mean to snap. I thought you were someone else for a minute.' She looks at Doris's black satin waistcoat and silver-knobbed cane. A gentleman. Any girl could be taken in, especially one that was lonely – or a bit in need of the ready.

Turning back to the mirror, Mari tugs with both hands at the handle of her hairbrush. 'It's stuck to my head like a bloody leech,' she moans. 'I'll never get home at this rate. I'll miss the last tram and have to go in a taxi, and who knows who might be sharing it with me? There's something working against me, Doris. What can it be?' Her eyes fill up.

'Steady on, dearie.' Doris clicks across the room on her high heels and puts her hands on Mari's shoulders. 'An old hairbrush is nothing to cry about. You've been overdoing it again, haven't you?'

In the mirror, Mari looks up into Doris's kind face. 'Remember when Antonio was here? He used to brush my hair every night after the show. It wasn't a chore to him. He loved doing it.'

'He was a nice feller.'

'The best I ever had. I'll never find his match. Why'd he go and leave me like that, Doris? He never even said he was off.' He was in trouble, of course . . . but didn't he know she'd have hidden him, run off with him, done anything he asked . . . ?

'Don't ask me,' Doris says. 'Men are not natural stickers, that's all I can tell you.'

'I still dream about him,' Mari says. 'I still think I spot him in the street, or crossing the Square to get on a tram. I pick up my skirt and run to catch up – but it's never him really. Just some bloke who looked like him from the back.'

Doris sighs. She has heard all this before, many times. 'Haven't you got over him a little bit? It's been a whole year.'

'I started to look at other fellers again about six months back. Not with any hope, you know, but just wondering if . . .'

'So why aren't you still looking? What's stopped you?'

Mari's head droops. 'These murders,' she says. 'They scare me silly.'

Doris's hands grip her shoulders. 'I've told you, Mari, we're all scared about those. Every woman in London has got the wind up.'

'But you go with men, even so. Men you don't know from Adam. How can you?'

9

'Life must go on. You can't let one man, old flame or murderer, stop you from living.'

'But that's just what he does do,' Mari says softly.

For a moment both are silent. Then Doris says, 'Here, love, you know what you should do tomorrow? Give yourself a little treat. Get out somewhere. Go to Hyde Park and listen to the band. Lovely weather we're having for March. Get out in the sunshine. Don't stay in your room working on new routines . . . or opening a bottle of stout.'

Doris's words conjure up a pleasant vision. Mari sees herself reclining in a striped deck chair beneath a chestnut tree, a parasol in one hand, an ice-cream cone in the other, her foot tapping to the ta-ra-ra-boom-de-ay of a brass band. 'Will you go with me, Dor?'

'I can't, love. This feller I'm seeing has plans for us. I think he's gone on me, Mari.' Doris looks pleased. 'Two months and he hasn't even asked for my speciality, just the ordinary stuff.'

'I'm glad,' Mari says. 'I always told you that was dangerous. I'd never do it.'

Doris shrugs. 'They look at my costume and expect it. Not this one though. He's a decent type. Here, why don't you come to the Alhambra with us? I bet he can get you off with a pal. They always can, can't they?'

Under the flickering gaslight, and framed by her under-rolled platinum hair, Doris's face looks like a skull. The skin stretched tight over her high cheekbones seems to pull her blue eyes deep into their sockets. On her cheeks and mouth the bright red paint seems portentous – a warning of what can happen to women who live and work as she does.

'No, thanks,' Mari says. 'I have to get home. Will you help me get my hairbrush out of my hair?'

''Course I will. Have it out in a jiffy.' Doris's long red nails work dexterously. 'See, it's coming loose already. I know how to persuade obstinate doodahs. I've had plenty of practice.' She nudges Mari's shoulder and winks lewdly.

Mari drops the brush on the cluttered dressing table and searches out some hairpins among the jars of make-up. Placing them in her mouth, she begins to wind her hair into a fat chignon. 'I better get a move on,' she says between her teeth. 'I'm running late.'

'You got a feller waiting at home?' Doris arches a plucked eyebrow.

'A feller! Are you pulling my leg? Haven't you been listening?'

'You rush off so fast every night. Thought you might be shacking up again and keeping it quiet. Sorry.'

Mari slides in the last hairpin. She crosses to the wardrobe. The trouble with Doris is she's never had a serious love affair, so she can't understand the tenacity of Mari's heart. Not that she blames Doris; she doesn't understand it herself sometimes. Why must her heart cling to pain and feed (or starve) on memories? Why does it refuse to try again, balking at each new man Mari's eye proposes? Her own heart has become her enemy – a murderer just like the one on the streets – sucking her lifeblood like a vampire to feed its own longing.

'No wonder you're edgy,' Doris says. 'How can you do without for so long? It's not good for you, that.'

From the wardrobe Mari takes a cream-coloured taffeta blouse with leg-o'-mutton sleeves and a yoke of lace flowers. She fastens the tiny mother-of-pearl buttons that lie in pairs along the placket. 'So many,' Antonio said when he first undid her. 'It will take long.'

'Sorry,' she'd said, thinking he meant the buttons were a hindrance. 'I'd have worn something easier if I'd known–'

But Antonio had laid a finger on her lips and whispered, 'To see you piece by piece . . . it is so titillating. Like the dance of veils.'

He had often surprised her with long words he knew, words she'd never heard though she was the native English speaker.

'What does "titillating" mean?' she'd asked.

'It means I am filled with joy that soon I will see your beautiful tits.' And he had thrown back his head and laughed in that free, boisterous way that disconcerted her until she became charmed by it.

Ah, but he could be serious, too, and hold her to his chest, close as a Siamese twin, and say as he entered her, 'You are the wife of my heart, *carissima*, my bosom friend, the mate of my desire,' and on and on until Mari thrilled with pleasure. No wonder she can't give an eye to any Johnny-come-lately feller. It's like weaning a breast-fed babe on sugar-water.

'It don't make sense neither,' Doris is saying, 'going home on your own. A lot wiser, say what you like, to let a feller escort you—'

Mari steps into her herringbone skirt. 'I appreciate your concern,' she says, crossing to the mirror to powder her face, 'but I've no interest . . .' Suddenly, she has no patience either. 'Here, Doris, what about this beau you like so much? Is he going to wait all night for you?'

'I've said too much.' Doris moves to the door. 'I'm not poking my nose in, love, honest. You know best what you want.' She salutes, smacking the side of her hand against the brim of her top hat. 'Goodnight and God bless,' she says. It's how she always ends her act, though Alf Ramsey would like her to say something less proper, more *risqué*.

Mari gets up and puts on her coat. She fluffs out her tawny fox-fur boa, crams her costume (it needs mending) into a holdall, slings her bag over her shoulder, and steps out into the corridor. The janitor is already at work with his bucket and mop.

'Evening, Rudolph,' Mari greets him.

The janitor touches his temple. 'You're late, Miss Prince. Thought you'd gone, and my eyes had missed their treat.'

'I should be. Couldn't get myself together somehow. Did you . . . ?'

'I left your package in Mr Ramsey's office as usual. Got you some o' the cream tonight for a change.'

'Ta very much,' Mari says. 'I do appreciate the favour. Saves me stopping on the way home.'

Rudolph leans on his mop handle and tilts his head to look up at her. 'Glad to help out. Life ain't easy for a woman alone.'

'That's the truth,' Mari says. 'But two of those stouts inside me, Rudi, and I sleep like a baby.'

The janitor rubs his hand over his bald head. 'Fine woman like you shouldn't have to rely on booze for a good night's sleep. I wish I was twenty years younger. I used to know a better recipe.' He grins at her. 'Still know it, but I don't have the ingredients no more.'

'Get along with you.' Mari feigns shock. 'You make me blush. I bet you were a proper ladies' man.'

Rudolph dips his head. 'I had me successes, can't say different.'

'Lucky for me you're *not* twenty years younger. I can see you'd break my heart.' She lifts one gloved hand. 'Ta-ta now. Don't work too hard.'

At the end of the corridor, Alf Ramsey sits in his office which also serves as a storage room for disused props. Like a frugal housewife, Alf never throws anything away. Clothes-horses and hat-stands festooned with fake tiaras, feather boas, sequined tutus, gold lamé pantaloons, clutter the box-like room. Five cardboard palm trees hung with papier-mâché coconuts line the back wall. In the middle of this tawdry, glittering chaos, Alf sits hunched over a desk littered with papers, his head wreathed in cigar smoke.

Mari leans in the doorway and sings softly, '"Climb up the garden wall, and I will give you Persian tea" . . .'

Alf's head comes up and she glimpses the worry lines before his face breaks into a big smile, all his top teeth showing under a bushy greying moustache. 'Hello, my own darling.' His eyes eat her up.

'Hello, Ali Baba. How's business?'

Alf's smile fades. 'Not so hot, love.'

'What? I played to a packed house tonight. You must have raked in the shekels.' Mari tips her head to one side. 'You trying to put me off asking for a rise, Alf?'

'Tonight's Friday. We always have a full house weekends, but what about weeknights, eh?' The manager runs a hand through his hair. It's thick and black with a grey streak in front and grey sideburns. Very distinguished. 'It's these new picture palaces opening up like weeds, Mari. They're eating up my business. If things don't pick up, I'll be operating at a loss soon.'

'Oh,' Mari says. But she doesn't want to think now of the implications this statement holds for her. 'You're just feeling low with all those bills in front of you. Knock off for the night and go out on the town.'

'Is that an offer? Because if it is, I'll knock off right now.'

Mari leans against the doorframe and puts a hand on her hip. 'Here we go again,' she says to the air above her head. 'I can't come into your office without you start all that. Why, Alf?'

'Because I see that look in your eyes, love, and I know what it means. It's the twin of this one.' He points a finger at his own grey eyes, the message in them as easy to read as the show bills that paper his office walls, Mari's face smiling out of some of them. 'I'm a man without,' Alf's eyes say in big bold capitals.

Christ, Mari thinks, don't I hide it better than that? No wonder men stop me in the street. I'm a walking advertisement.

'And because you're a woman and women are changeable. One day I'll change your mind, Mari.'

Mari shakes her head. 'No chance.' She crosses to Alf's desk and reaches for the brown paper bag on the shelf above it. Another man might have taken the opportunity to feel her behind, but not Alf. 'I don't go with married men, and that's flat. Put a tanner on my tab with Rudi.' Slipping the bag into her holdall, she moves toward the door.

'To the best of your knowledge, you don't,' Alf says. 'But that's something you can't be one hundred per cent certain about, can you?' He puffs on his cigar. 'And suppose you have, Mari? Suppose some feller less honourable than me lied to you? Has it done you any harm?'

'I can't help what I don't know about,' Mari says, though his words sting. 'I do know about you. I know your wife as well.'

'Mary,' Alf says, the brief name falling heavily from his lips, 'wouldn't care.'

'I have to toddle,' Mari says, 'or I'll miss my last tram.'

'We're lonely people, you and me.'

Havana scent drifts under Mari's nose like a fragrant promise. It's a virile male scent, a guarantee of Alf's ability to warm, comfort and protect her. She leans against the doorframe for support as images rush into her head.

'You go home to a cold bed and me to a cold wife. It don't make sense.' He leans toward her, his elbows on the desk. His rolled-up shirtsleeves reveal strong, hairy forearms. Mari can imagine the rest. 'I think on you, Mari, lying back to back with my Mary. Have I told you that? I undress you, caress you. Countless times I've loved you in my mind. Don't that give me a right of some sort?'

Mari holds up her hand for him to stop, but it's a half-hearted gesture. She's felt so deprived, so hungry, since Antonio left.

As if he's a mind-reader, Alf says, 'I'd treat you right. I wouldn't do a bunk like that Eyetie, if that's what holds you back—'

Mari snaps out of her Alf-induced fantasy. 'Don't start on him,' she says. 'Don't run Antonio down. I won't stand for it.'

'Run him down? I gave him every chance, Mari. You know I did. Could have been the next Caruso, that feller. He had a good future and a good woman—'

Mari turns on her heel and flounces out of the theatre into the gaslit alley.

Alf's cigar has burned down to his fingers. He stubs it out in the ashtray.

2

Mary: Friday Night

I wake from a dream of Mari Prince and hear the grandfather clock downstairs strike ten. Lying alone in the canopied bed, I count the chimes. It is finale time at the Palladium. High-kicking, half-naked chorus girls prance across the stage. As the rumbustious music reaches a crescendo, the girls flip their backs to the audience, throw up their skirts and exhibit their behinds in flimsy frilly knickers, all the colours of a magician's rainbow.

My head throbs.

I sit up, fumble for matches and light the candle on the bedside table. I keep it there for the nights I can't sleep and must walk about the house to calm my nerves. These night tours have increased in frequency of late . . . since I discovered that Alf has taken a mistress.

'If you have insomnia, Mary, see a doctor,' he said, 'before it leads to other things. It will be cheaper in the long run.'

He thinks of his pocket, not of my health. Which is fragile, though it was not always so. Once I was robust enough. I fear I may not live long. I fear I may die by my Fathers' wills, or by my own hand, perchance, in that half-dreaming state in which I traverse the house at midnight and the hours beyond – when phantoms crowd to give me company, and wail in my ear, 'Why continue, Mary? What use? What purpose do you serve?' Sleepwalkers are prey to strange and insidious influences unknown to those who keep daylight hours.

'What I suffer from,' I told Alf, 'a doctor can't cure.'

'Oh, you've diagnosed yourself, have you?' he said. 'And what's your ailment?'

'Heart disease,' I said.

I rise from the bed, the brass candlestick in one hand, and cross to the window. Bereft of stars, the sky is black as a parson's coat.

My father was a North Country rector, with eyes and beard as black as his clothes, and dark looks always for me and for my mother. But he didn't keep a fancy woman. All his money went into a coffer, the key to which he wore around his neck, under his dog collar. My mother knew private shame . . . yes, I have witnessed that . . . but she could hold her head up in the town.

Mother, my heart cries.

I set the candle down on the little rosewood desk beneath the window, sit in the high-backed chair and reach for a sheet of notepaper, uncap the ink bottle and dip in the pen. I will begin my weekly letter.

'Dearest, beloved,' I write . . . she is the only one in all the world who cares about me now . . . 'Tonight, I dreamed again of Mari Prince. I dreamed that I stood at one end of a long dark alley. How I came there, I can't tell, or its location either. It reminded me of one of those noisome London back streets that branch off from Ratcliffe Highway, an infamous area indeed. If that's where I was, it was a fitting place to encounter Miss Prince.

'I did not see her at first. I saw only dark shapes in the alley, drunken men and women in lewd postures, and, at the far end, a bonfire whose leaping flames luridly lit the noxious passageway I was compelled to traverse. Imagine, Mother, the terror I felt, knowing I must pass among those rough and lawless creatures; I who in my waking hours, and in broad daylight, demur at venturing far even in my own quiet neighbourhood.

'Well, that is Alf's fault. He has made a recluse of me since we came to London. From the first he gave me no help, no companionship. How he changed once he had separated me from you and my own dear familiar countryside. He expected me to assume London ways, to go out and about on my own, to mix and mingle and make no demands on him. Those very qualities he professed to love me for he has sought to eradicate, transform: my natural reticence and modesty, my willingness to cast my fate with his, to become the tender clinging plant that wraps itself about the sturdy oak . . .'

I pause. I have digressed, and my mother knows all this. For upward of fifteen years, since I first arrived in London, a young woman not quite twenty-one, I have been writing home such letters.

I hated the city from the moment I stepped out at King's Cross and encountered the hubbub, the melee, the dirt and dust and infernal noise, the hawkers, the prostitutes, the urchins, the criminals (my purse snatched before we'd even had time to hail a hackney). True, Alf had rented a pleasant enough house in Putney, but only a stone's throw from those dreadful streets I'd seen through the window of the hackney; and I have felt, always, as if I dwell on the edge of an abyss. Besides, the neighbours pass remarks about me, offer me lip-smiles, and think me queer, aloof.

I miss my mother.

After my father's death, I would have left Alf, gone back to her. What a pleasant life we might have made, free at last of the tyranny that had made us conspirators, whisperers, hypocrites in our own home. But she forbade me. 'Henceforward, your place is with your husband,' she wrote. 'You must abide by the choice you have made.' I do not resent her harsh decree, though it came in response to a most desperate letter. All too well I understand my father's role in making her a woman unable to conceive of breaking the marriage bond, even when that sacred tie has become a fetter that chafes the nerves and rubs the heart raw. Besides, some things have changed with time. I have a mission in London now, and I could no more leave the city than a zealot could quit his cause. My mother is privy to my mission, and approves.

In the dark windowpane I meet my reflection, illuminated there by the flickering candle. Once I had a flowerlike face, delicate features, translucent skin. 'My white rosebud,' Alf used to call me when we courted, whispering in my ear, 'When you're mine, I'll make you bloom, Mary.' Now my skin is wasted, dark circles under my eyes. I see a spectre in the window glass, her dark hair a cape to hide her bony shoulders, the lawn nightdress hanging from her body like a shroud.

I am tall but not robust. I had the kind of beauty that requires nurturing if it is to thrive. He promised to cherish me, but he cast me off. I am a faded rose now, languishing on the stalk that offers no nourishment.

When he courted me, he was ardent enough. He adored me then. Once he knelt to kiss the hem of my dress and said, 'I worship the ground you walk on.' And my hand – he was forever lifting my hand to his mouth, pressing his lips against my fingers. I knew he wanted more. I saw how his eyes burned. But how *much* more . . . that I could not guess. He was a wolf in sheep's clothing, a devil in the bright garb of an angel, a robber disguised as a rescuer.

'I can't do it,' I said.

He said, 'Mary, you must.'

'I won't,' I said.

He said, 'You are my wife.'

'Give me time then,' I pleaded, and he gave his word. But one night not long after, he came into the bed and took me by force. Though I struggled and wept and begged, he would not stop, and I thought of my mother, and knew that if I did not prevent him, he would coerce me into those base acts my father thrust upon her. Tears and pleas would not restrain him. Men know no pity, driven by lust. I had to find a way to stop him for good. A frail and gentle girl, I had to fight him on his own terms, go against my nature, my sex, so that he would never again demean or harm me.

I had to put the fear of God into him.

As soon as he was done with me, his arms, that had gripped me like shackles, loosened, and I slipped away from him, out of the bed.

'Mary,' he said.

I heard pain in his voice. Sated, he was sorry, ashamed, perhaps, and would console me if I lay down again. My resolve wavered . . . I desired consolation. What creature does not? I stood on tiptoe between the bed and the door, torn two ways.

Then he said, 'Mary, it won't always be like that,' and I knew he felt no regret, no remorse. It was self-pity I'd heard in his voice, for he'd hoped to enjoy my body not battle with it; and, in his eyes, I'd denied him his entitlement.

'Do as I wish,' I have heard my father command my mother as he thrust her to her knees. 'I am your husband. You must pleasure me.'

Remembering the past, foreseeing the future, glimpsing the eternal pattern, I ran from the room, down the stairs to the kitchen. From the cutlery drawer I snatched the carving knife. How the sight of the sharp new steel thrilled me! What power flowed into my poor weak woman's body when my hand gripped the bone handle. Now I too had a weapon.

I raced up the stairs, my torn nightgown fluttering like feathers, a wren with the beak of an eagle. When I entered the bedroom, I thrust the knife behind me. I wanted to take him by surprise. The unprepared are most confounded, ambush the surest and deadliest strategy.

He lay on his back, naked. Black hair furred his chest and groin. Hide of a beast, to match his proclivities. The thing that had tortured me – the jackknife with which he had hacked and bloodied the doc, the burglar's crowbar, the hammer, the chisel – lay inert now, a snake in furze . . . the viper of Eden. My father preached that Woman brought Man to sin, but I say Eve was the victim, beguiled and coerced. For God, Satan, Adam are not separate beings but tripartite, the three faces of the male: tyranny, deception and lust, a triumvirate that rules the world and sends it swiftly to ruin.

I looked at the thing between his thighs and thought, one slice of the knife . . .

But my purpose was not to maim him, not to give tit for tat. No murderous intent possessed me at that time. I meant only to protect myself.

I approached the bed. He turned his head on the pillow and held out his arms. 'Mary,' he said, 'come here.'

And I sprang, the knife high in my right hand. His arms dropped to the bed, his face froze, all expression wiped from it, as if he were already dead. How temptation grappled with me then! For the first time in my life I knew the ecstasy and terror of supreme power. For one moment, I stood the equal of men and saw into their hearts and minds. Like Saint John the Divine, I had a revelation . . . and spurned it. His is not a vision women can nurture and thrive on. Or so I believed then, as I brandished the knife above my husband's – my assailant's – breastbone. All things change perforce, but then I was no murderer.

I brought the knife down, yes, but when its tip grazed the skin over his heart, I stayed my hand. 'Now, Alf,' I said, 'you will never abuse me again.'

I did not ask for his word on it. Promises from men are merely petals torn from the rose, baubles, bijoux they store in their hip pockets to pull out when the time is ripe.

'You will never,' I repeated, and stroked the skin a little with the knife tip.

He revived somewhat, sensibility returned to his features and mobilized them, but I saw no anger in his face, no fear, as I had anticipated. Instead, a look I have witnessed many times, before and since, when he comes in late at night from the Palladium, or when he lifts his head from the household and business accounts and runs his hand through his hair. Infinite weariness. Though I had not so much as nicked his flesh, I had penetrated to his core and his defeat was absolute.

'Put the knife away, Mary,' he said. 'From this time forward, I'll not lay a finger on you. I'll not have the stomach for it.' With the flat of his hand, he pushed the blade from his chest, turned to the wall . . . and slept. Or feigned it.

I turned from the bed to the door and went softly down the stairs, across the dark hall to the kitchen, and lit a candle and replaced the knife, and roamed the downstairs rooms, each step leading me farther from hope, shutting me off from mercy.

As I paced, a voice cried out, 'Ah, Mary! Mary, what have you done!' 'The irrevocable,' I answered it, and wrung my hands, and walked and walked, many miles it seemed, till dawn.

Alf rose early, as he always does. Washed and dressed and groomed, he came down to the kitchen, saw me still in my nightdress, my hair undone, my face, surely, wan and haggard, and said, 'A cup of tea, Mary, before I go?'

And this has been the tenor of our shared life for upward of fifteen years – he holds his distance, I hold my tongue, and we co-exist. So might we have continued, a married couple in a state of truce, into our dotage and until death parted us; never knowing the joy of some, but less wretched, too, I would hazard, than many – for I never raise my voice to him and he never lifts his hand to me, and how many husbands and wives can say as much? Ah, what might have been but was not to be! Is not this the saddest of human laments? An evil independent of my own devils rose up. Like the Whore of Babylon she came, with painted face and hair afire, a scarlet woman indeed, and she gave Alf the glad eye and thrust herself between us.

When I first met Mari Prince, years ago, I had no premonition that she would do me mischief. Misled by warm smiles and kind words, beguiled by the tricks of her trade, I trusted her, though I knew she was a loose woman and Alf licentious. Though we slept in a chaste bed, he had not kept celibate for fifteen years. Sometimes, as he lay down next to me, I smelled on his skin a lingering perfume, and other, fouler odours; but I learned to bear this . . . a woman picked up on the street for an hour or two, now and again . . . it sickened me but posed no threat. Mari Prince is different. Easily might a man become enamoured of her prodigality, her wealth of smiles, her voluptuous body, her mass of hair . . . a tangled web to lure and ensnare the sinner!

Well . . . I do not claim she is the devil incarnate, but she is an agent of wickedness, sent to torment me and ruin Alf. If I permit her!

She has not taken me into account in her schemes. She thinks me a poor, milksop thing with a will as slight and sickly as my body. But once I wielded a knife, fierce and implacable as an avenging angel, and I can do so again.

Vengeance is mine, saith the Lord.

Not His only, and not a male prerogative. Defiant, I snatch the sword from the hands of my fathers, my kinsmen, and with it I will wreak havoc. Yet for the moment, the pen must suffice. . . .

'Three or four hours must pass yet before Alf comes home. After business, he likes to take his pleasures, dining, drinking . . . and the rest. He takes his pleasures and never thinks of me, except to feel glad, perhaps, that he is far away from the venomous, contrary madwoman he must call wife.

'I can date the onslaught of my sickness almost exactly, to a Saturday night in June 1911, some days before the Coronation. The Palladium put on a gala performance in the King's honour (and in his absence, though Alf had sent an invitation). I had requested, with more spirit than usual, that Alf take me to see the show. At first, and as usual, he objected, tried to fob me off with his customary excuses: 'Now, Mary, you know how it will be, a lot of rowdies and ruffians coming in with the decent patrons . . . and I can't weed them out for your benefit . . . and you'll see and hear things unfit for a well-bred—'

'I've never complained,' I said, 'about anything I've heard or seen at the Palladium.'

'I know you haven't complained, Mary. I'm not saying you

have.' He had his watch out of his pocket and fingered it as he sat on the other side of the breakfast table, studying the links in order not to look at me. 'I'm thinking of the mental effect, you see. Dr Gibbons said, "Avoid excitement and crowds and unpleasant scenes." You know yourself that was his advice to us. And you know how you carry on for weeks after seeing the show at the Palladium.'

At that time I had just returned from a visit to you, Mother... my last visit to date, was it not? And I, all in turmoil from our painful parting, could not settle to the tedium of my London life again. So, weak and swayable as I was then, I had agreed to Alf's suggestion and was under this Dr Gibbons's care for 'a nervous condition'.

'I care nothing for the doctor's dictums,' I said, 'for I find them ill-founded. I intend to discontinue the treatment.'

'Now, Mary, that is not wise—'

'However—' and here I gripped my hands into fists, which he noticed; I saw his downcast eyelids flicker '—that is not the subject of discussion. I want to attend the gala performance at the Palladium. As your wife, I have a right, I think.'

'You will have to sit alone. I can't attend to you—'

'I do not require your attention. Place me in a box and I shall manage well, and neither swoon nor suffer a seizure from what I observe, I promise you.'

He had to acquiesce, Mother! When I demonstrate such fervour, I am stronger than he ... For I was schooled, was I not, by an Iron Master?

That night, the Palladium was decorated with wreaths of laurel and hung with great banners edged in purple and gold, bearing the profiles of His and Her Majesties (beautified beyond recognition, to disguise her pinched pallor and his obesity). Every turn included some homage to the royal pair. When it was her time, Mari Prince came on stage resplendent in a rhinestone tiara, her black magician's cloak edged in ermine, her gown ablaze with paste jewels. The audience gasped and applauded as she drew from her conjurer's top hat all the flags of the Empire strung together and led by the Union Jack. As the flags floated out over the auditorium, she sang a rousing chorus of 'Rule, Britannia', the audience joining in. Then before our very eyes, it seemed – but it was a trick of the light and her own dextrous hands – the gem-bestrewn dress wafted from her body and vanished into air and she emerged . . . naked, it appeared at first, causing a profound awed silence to fall on the masses who beheld this marvel . . . in fact, she wore a flesh-coloured but form-fitting costume which, though it covered all, revealed all in a most tantalizing and heart-stopping manner.

Recovering swiftly from awe, every man in the house was on his feet, and such a stamping and cheering and whistling filled the air you would have thought that England had won a new war at least. What imbeciles men are! What Philistines! Their admiration shows no seemliness, their gaze no deference. They must ever demean beauty in this way, reduce it to a burlesque, a pandemonium, and strip it of its pristine self to make it theirs, to make it less. As the curtains swung across the stage I saw, I swear, a look of shame on Miss Prince's face. The costume, I daresay, was Alf's idea.

Afterwards, there was a party behind-stage for the performers and the regular patrons – the well-to-do patrons whose goodwill Alf wished to retain for business reasons. That night all of these patrons had come without their wives, whom they had either left at home or swiftly dispatched there in a taxi after the show. I was the only married woman present.

I stood in a corner, melting and merging with the shadows in my dove-grey dress, holding in both hands, as if it were a goblet, the glass Alf had filled to the brim with champagne. 'Drink up then, Mary,' he said as he poured. 'Since you've come to the party, enjoy it.' Then he was off among the guests, urging food and drink upon them, throwing back his head to laugh at a patron's joke, patting the behinds and naked shoulders of his girls to commend them for their *joie de vivre*, so good for business!

I could not vie with them for his approval. I am no seductress, only Mary – pale and insignificant, and beset already that night (though I knew it not) by my demons. How they must have sniggered and snorted and pointed mocking fingers at me as I shrank in a corner, plain, undistinguished, while audacious images spun in my head like mythic beasts on a merry-go-round.

And where, all this time, was Miss Prince?

She appears now in the doorway, very late (too late to join the barter, for the men have all been claimed) and exceedingly regal, the Grand Empress of Byzantium, in a high-waisted black dress with a draped bosom and sweeping skirt, a style presently fashionable in Paris, so the Woman's Page of the *Chronicle* informs us. Though flowing, the dress also clings, artfully cut to show off her hips and thighs. In her massy auburn hair, piled up in waves and ringlets, she sports a single black aigrette fastened with a rhinestone clip.

We gasp, we stare, we suck in breath, our eyes rounded like telescope lenses, the better to see her.

Alf takes her by the elbow. 'Mari,' he says. She gives him a smile.

He leads her to the table to proffer food and drink, but as she crosses the room she sees me, shakes off his arm, and hurries to my corner, saying, 'Mary! Mary Ramsey!'

'How do you do?' I incline my head.

'How do I do? Why, that's a cold greeting for a friend! I'm glad to see you again! Aren't you glad to see me? Remember the high jinks we had in my dressing room a year back? I thought you'd come again, but you never did —'

Then Alf is beside us, putting a glass of champagne into her hand, saying, 'Mary's not much for socializing. She prefers a quiet life.'

I tilt my head to flash him a look, and he gives me a look back, dark, disgruntled, as if to say, 'See how you spoil things, Mary!'

But Mari Prince ignores my husband, her eyes on my face, her free hand on my shoulder. 'And now we have the royal stamp, too. We're connected to the Queen. What do you think of that, eh? We ought to get some sort of badge, don't you think? A brooch, maybe, an M inside a circle, that everyone would know stands for "Friends of Queen Mary"! I wrote and suggested it.' She grins at me, tongue in cheek, as if we share some secret mischief; and I do, vividly, recall that night in her dressing room when she wrapped me in her magician's cloak, ensnared me in her trickery, and made of me, briefly, a different Mary. But even then . . . as I have come to know . . . it was Alf she wanted.

'I beg your pardon,' I say, 'but I don't follow—'

'Ah, didn't you read it in the paper? They're asking all of us Marys and Maries and Marions in the Empire to send a donation to the Queen for a Coronation gift. Because we have the same name as her. But I think we should get something out of it, too. I sent five shillings and a note telling them so.'

I remembered then. Alf had read the piece to me one morning at breakfast and offered to send a pound note to the fund on my behalf – a staunch royalist, my husband, though he preferred the late King Edward, avid patron of the music hall, to the new King George, who pursues birds of a different feather, carnage on the grouse moors his favourite pastime.

'You gave five shillings?' I say. 'To that cause! You are exceedingly extravagant – and misguided, I think.'

Alf draws up his shoulders. 'Have a care, Mary. We are in public now.'

'I didn't send the whole five bob on my own behalf,' she says. 'It's to be shared out so that other Marys – poor ones who can't afford it – can have brooches, too. I said that in my note.'

'Brooches? For poor women?'

Alf glowers at me, and some of the company nearest us have ceased their chatter to turn their heads and listen. For I have raised my voice. They are surprised, I aver, to discover that Mary the Mouse can do more than squeak, but outrage ... and champagne ... have made me bold.

'What will a poor woman do with a brooch? She can't feed it to her children, or cover their heads with it in foul weather. She can sell it for gin, I suppose! But she won't have the chance, for there'll be no gifts from the Queen, I assure you. The Queen is the King's consort, and he has no regard for the poor. How can she be different? Wives are ruled by their husbands, Miss Prince, and must defer to them in all things, play the flunky's role, adopt the sycophant's pose, or else–'

'Mary! Enough, I say.'

A hush falls on the room, and a stillness, all the company frozen in their various attitudes, as if we were a tableau at Madame Tussaud's ... and, indeed, Alf's voice, harsh as a blow, has fractured my brain and rendered me inert, senseless. I lean back against the wall, a tipped-over waxwork doll, champagne spilling from the glass I cannot properly hold.

Alf takes it from me. 'You've had enough of this,' he says, his voice altered, dissembling indulgence. 'It's not tea, Mary.'

Mari Prince is staring at me. 'Not for food or shelter,' she says softly. 'Just for a little pleasure, Mary. No one's too poor to want that once in a while, are they?'

'Mary's had all the pleasure she's getting this evening,' Alf says. 'From the champagne, any road.'

A chorus girl titters and ends the paralysis that has seized them all. They resume their talk, their banter, with greater gusto than before.

'Alf, Mari, time to cut the cake!' A blonde with a harlot's painted face and a boy's straight body stands beside the tiered and iced concoction, the banquet's centrepiece, a knife poised in her right hand, her blue eyes glittering at me like shards of glass. Atop the cake, miniatures of the King and Queen mince and simper under a hoop of pink iced roses.

'The first slice for Mari,' Alf says. 'After all, she's a princess.' His hand on her elbow again, he turns her about and leads her to the table, there to hold a plate for her. All the revellers crowded about them and shut them from my sight.

I slipped from the room and went home in a taxi hailed by the janitor. Huddled in the back seat, I travelled through festive London, the lights and decorations mocking me, a reviled and rejected thing, a despised outcast of my husband's Empire where he had already crowned his queen. And I thought: Yes, Miss Prince, henceforth we are indeed connected, singled out, members of an exclusive sisterhood, you and I – and we wear the badge, the M within the circle, until I find the means, devise the method, to sunder the noose you strangle me with and free myself of you.

'Mother . . .'

But, hush. Footsteps on the path, the front door creaks . . . he is home. I must be quick now, for he will take one glass of brandy and come up. 'Your devoted Mary,' I pen hastily, fold the sheets into an envelope, seal the flap, unlock the drawer of my desk. The letter joins its kin. Over two and a half hundred of them now, one for every week since . . . since she stopped answering. I lock the drawer, hide the key, fly to the bed, snuff the candle, pull the covers up. I lie close to the edge and breathe deeply, evenly, as if I am indifferent, untroubled, asleep.

3

Mari: Friday Night

Mari reaches her tram stop with a few minutes to spare. At five to eleven on a Friday night, Leicester Square is bustling, the restaurants doing a roaring trade in after-the-show suppers.

In the Square, hundreds of false suns beam benevolently on the pleasure-seekers who mill about her as she stands – austere, guarded, her holdall bag hiding her chest, a plain brown scarf camouflaging her hair – at the end of a line of half a dozen people who, for whatever sad or bulky reasons, are homewardbound too early, like her.

But this new marvel, electric lighting, affords Mari small comfort. She knows a woman can't count on well-lit streets and crowds to keep her from harm. Only a few months back, she was standing at this very tram stop one night, minding her own business and waiting for the 11:02, when a dreadful thing happened. She still gets goose pimples and heart tremors recalling it.

Next to her in line that night stood a tall, well-built man in a tweed overcoat and yellow wool scarf. He had a bowler on his head and a parcel under his arm. A nice, respectable family man, Mari had guessed, taking a present home to his wife. She'd nodded to him, and they'd exchanged a few remarks on the weather and the lateness of the tram. More travellers had joined them and shared their conversation, a friendly group bonded together against the London Tram Company and the unkindness of January.

When three men came reeling out of a pub across the Square, knocking into people on the pavement and shouting obscenities, the man in the bowler said to Mari, 'Look at that. Frittering away their pay packets and causing a public nuisance, and they have wives waiting at home, I don't doubt.'

Mari had warmed to him, for his comment on the waiting

wives made him seem like a champion of women, and she had wanted to move closer to his tweed-clad shoulder. 'It's a scandal,' she said, though she knew well enough what drove men to beer. Her father had passed all his leisure time in a pub.

Then one of the drunks had left his companions and come staggering across the road to the tram stop. With his hands on his hips, he stopped in front of Mari.

'Sylvia,' he said.

The people in the queue had all stared at her, their faces altering, their mouths buttoning up. Mari had tightened her shoulders and raised her eyes high above the drunk's head. (He was a good six inches shorter than she.) 'My name's not Sylvia,' she told the man in the bowler. 'He's so stewed he can't see straight. He's taken me for someone else.'

'Sylvia, come over 'ere,' the drunk said. 'Why'd you run off like that, eh?'

Mari's cheeks burned, but she knew from experience that it's never wise to antagonize a man in his cups. 'Look,' she said reasonably, 'I'm not Sylvia. Why don't you go on home. Maybe she's there waiting for you.'

'Don't give me lip.' He tottered closer, his right hand formed into a fist. 'Don't tell me who you are and who you ain't. You trying to be funny with me?' And he fell against her, grabbing her shoulders to prevent himself from landing on the curb. 'Come on, Sylvie,' he whined as Mari struggled to free herself, pushing his beery mouth up to hers. 'You and me have to go home and make up.'

'Get off me,' Mari cried, more angry than frightened then. 'I don't know you from Santa Claus.'

But he had fastened his arms around her waist and, moving backwards along the pavement, dragged her out of the queue, handling her as easily as if she were a plaster-of-Paris mannequin, for he was a beefy man despite his short stature.

Mari can see it still, and feel it too – her body clamped against the drunk's, her senses nauseated by the stink of him, her cheeks hot with shame, her heart beating hard with rising panic as he pulled her along, both of them stumbling like people learning a new dance step. And all the time she had expected her former companion, the man in the bowler, to intervene, to tell the drunk to hop it before he kicked him in the rear, to take her arm and say, 'I trust you're not injured?' and lead her back to her place in the queue.

'But he never did,' Mari murmurs. 'He didn't do a bleeding thing except to pretend to be struck blind.'

No one had come to her aid, though she had shouted 'Help!' loud enough as she careened down Coventry Street in that mad, clumsy two-step. People had swerved to avoid them, some had laughed and some had yelled, but most, like the man in the bowler, had turned the other way. 'And 'course, there's never a bobby around when you want one.'

Finally, both of them panting, both shouting, she 'Help!' and he 'Sylvia!', he shoved her into a shop doorway and began to fumble at her clothes. She had slapped his face, he had punched her in the eye. Then he tried to kiss her and lift her skirt. Mari dragged it back down and tried to get her knee up, but he had wedged her legs between the wall and his own burly shanks. And so they had struggled until suddenly he fell to the ground, knocked out cold, not by her but by the alcohol.

Mari swallows hard and looks about her, ready to run for it if any drunk appears in the vicinity of the tram stop. But tonight, the only male who approaches the straggly queue is a paperboy bearing a sack of *Echo*es.

'Last edition,' he cries. 'Read all about the match at Twickenham tomorrer. England tipped to win. Paper, guv'nor? We'll beat the Welsh team hollow, forecast says. Paper, lady?'

Mari shakes her head. The tram arrives and she takes a front seat, placing her holdall beside her.

As the tram rumbles through the West End, past the illuminated fronts of theatres and restaurants, Mari watches the people coming and going. On the pavements, young dandies loiter, keeping an eye out for a showgirl or loose woman. When she was twenty-one and London brand-new, these swells had dazzled her more than any other sight the city could offer. She had not dreamed of such clothes, such charm, such generosity as these youths displayed. Compared with Lancashire lads, they seemed like princes. She had not given a thought then to their lack of sturdier qualities. Why should she? Fidelity did not interest her. She thrived on variety. Not until she was well past thirty did she look around for less sugary, more substantial fare. It was at this point that she met Antonio and fell in love for the first time.

She can't settle now for less than she had with him. Since he left, she has devoted herself to her act. Only – too late, if she's to credit what Alf said tonight, for what's the use of perfecting techniques if the Palladium goes dark and she has no stage to perform on? 'It's the picture palaces,' Alf said, but Mari can't condemn them, for it was at a picture palace that she met Antonio, at a matinée of *The Wrong Bride*.

It was the heatwave summer of King George's coronation. She'd gone to the Bioscope for the matinée. Engrossed in the film, craning her head forward to read the dialogue when it flickered on to the brownish screen, she'd barely noticed him come in. As he took a seat at the end of her row, four empty seats between them, she'd noted, without interest, that he was short, stocky, foreign-looking. Francis X. Bushman was on the screen, his eyes smouldering, his lips and shoulders working as he cast ravishing glances at the plump, reclining heroine, and Mari paid her neighbour no further heed.

But soon it became impossible to ignore him. At first she was aware only that he was fidgety. He jerked his head to right and left, plunged his hands into his pockets and out again. Distracted and annoyed, Mari had turned to give him a look, but his head had jerked away from her at that moment so he didn't see. She gave a little snort and turned back to the screen.

Just in time to catch the hero's words: 'You are very attractive, but I am promised to another!'

At this unexpected twist in the plot, Mari gasped and moved to the edge of her seat.

He feels something for her, she thought, but if he's promised to another . . . She squeezed the knuckles of her left hand in her right palm.

Just as the hero's crucial decision flickered on to the screen, her neighbour pounded the floor with the heel of his boot. Startled, Mari had snapped her head round, and missed Francis X. Bushman's answer.

Instead, she got the full gaze of the foreigner's black eyes. They were fine eyes, large, almond-shaped, fringed with long curling lashes. The lashes gave a touch of tenderness to a face otherwise notable for its strong, hard contours.

She turned her face back to the screen but now, instead of Francis X. Bushman she saw up there an image of her neighbour. He was handsome, no denying it. Long curly black hair – longer than any Englishman would wear it – and a thick black moustache shaped rather like Lloyd George's, whose picture Mari often saw in the newspapers, and whom she considered a very manly man. She moved her head slightly sideways to take a sly look at him. But caution was needless. He was engrossed in some object he had brought out of his pocket and now held on the flat of his left hand. Mari leaned closer and squinted. She saw that what he held was a stiletto. He had released its thin cruel blade.

Mari drew an audible breath.

The stranger's head jerked towards her. He slid the knife back into his pocket. For a moment they stared at each other. Then, moving so fast she almost screamed, he sprang into the seat next to her.

'Miss,' he whispered (but pronounced it 'mees'), 'you see nothing, you understand?'

He pressed so close his shoulder nudged hers, and she smelled the sticky-sweet scent of hair oil, and another aroma she couldn't place, strong and pungent. Mari bit her lip and stared into his eyes, only inches from her own.

The Bioscope was quite empty that afternoon because of the blistering June weather. She was sure he was a raving lunatic who'd taken advantage of the dark deserted theatre to rape and stab her. But then, all of a sudden, he slipped his arm around her and nuzzled her neck, and her heart beat to a different tune. And when their mouths met, he might have had his way with her, then and there, so deeply did the kiss affect her.

A lady behind her raised her voice to protest. 'Call the manager, Albert! They should stay at home if they want to do that.'

Mari and her new friend rose of one accord, went hand-in-hand out into the dusty sunshine, and boarded an omnibus for Holland Park. An hour later, in her big unmade bed, the liaison was consummated, to their mutual pleasure.

Mari had expected Antonio to leave soon after, but he seemed in no hurry. He lay on her pillows, one arm behind his dark head, smoking a cigarette and humming in a deep, thrilling baritone, a tune she didn't recognize.

'Would you like a cup of tea?' she said.

Antonio burst out laughing. 'You English!'

Mari tilted her chin. 'What's so funny? I'm only trying to be hospitable.'

'You are hospitable, *carissima*.' He cupped and kissed her breast.

'So what's the joke then?'

He waved his cigarette. 'The English amuse me. They are so . . .' he searched for a word and came up with one she'd never heard '. . . phlegmatic! For everything, they offer a cup of tea. Two lumps of sugar, a dash of milk, and the troubles of the world wash away, no?'

'Well, I wasn't offering my tea to the whole world,' Mari said tartly. 'But if you don't want a cuppa, it's no odds to me.' She had swung out of bed.

Antonio came up behind her as she stood in her petticoat, offended, looking out of the window. He lifted her hair and slid his tongue over her neck. 'Come, don't pout,' he said. 'Get dressed. We shall go out now. Our new love must be celebrated with wine – not tea!'

When he said 'love', Mari forgave him.

The tram arrives at her stop and Mari gets off. She's glad that none of the male passengers get off with her. They look harmless enough – a couple of young fellers in paint-splashed overalls, and an old bloke asleep in the back . . . still, you never know. A few yards from the stop, she turns out of Holland Park Avenue into Hanswell Terrace, a street lined with Victorian villas, semi-detached, each in its own tiny square of garden. Lights still burn in many of the houses, but all the curtains are drawn and not a soul in the street. She reminds herself, as she does every night, that the murderer has never come this way. But he might. He must be a feller who savours risks. It must be a game to him.

Mari shivers, and coughs to clear a constriction in her throat. She quickens her pace, too. Hanswell Terrace is a long, dimly-lit road – only four gas lamps the whole length of it – and the house where she boards nearly at the end.

Tomorrow is the day of the Rugby Union Final at Twickenham. Mari dreads this day every year. Thousands of supporters from all over the country pour into the city to watch their teams fight it out – it's England versus Wales this year – and afterwards, all of them, winners and losers, stay on to paint the town red. Many of these fans, half-canned and riotous, find their way to the Palladium, to whistle, cat-call, and shout obscene remarks from the gallery. Alf Ramsey never turns them away. They're good for business. Nell, in the box office, has been told to charge double to any bloke wearing a rugby scarf and a rosette. After the show they congregate at the stage door, grabbing and snatching at the girls as they come out, brawling among themselves, scaring off the regulars who have a sense of decorum and real money in their pockets. In Leicester Square they'll be roving in packs, like wild dogs, and a woman on her own will be easy prey.

Maybe, just for tomorrow, I ought to break my resolution and go with some feller, Mari thinks as she nears the third lamppost – halfway home now – but her stomach balks at the idea. She can't get it out of her head that the murderer might be one of those who frequent the Palladium.

As she steps into the fuzzy aureole of light cast by the street lamp, she sees someone approaching from the other end of the terrace. A man, tall and dressed in dark clothes. (Camouflage?) Mari leans on the lamppost, for the tightness has returned to her throat and makes her breathless.

What to do?

Open the nearest garden gate, run up the path, and bang on the front door. A light shines through the damask curtains of a downstairs room in the house directly across from her. She can knock there. She won't be disturbing anyone's sleep.

But he could be just a passer-by . . . and then, how foolish she'd look.

Better to be a fool than a dead woman. Besides, how many passers-by are there in Hanwell Terrace at nearly midnight?

Mari doesn't move. Thoughts run pell-mell through her mind, but her feet are cemented to the pavement, like the iron base of the lamppost, her eyes fixed on the approaching figure.

He comes into the light, and her breath returns with a splutter. She knows him!

'''Evening, Miss Prince.' Constable Dawes touches his helmet and smiles at her.

''Evening,' Mari wheezes.

'All right, are you?' The young policeman is looking at her with concern, and Mari realizes she must present a sight, slumped against the lamppost, gasping for breath. Most likely, her face has gone white, like death warmed up.

She straightens herself and forces a smile. 'Just a bit puffed,' she says. 'It's a fair walk from the tram stop, and I'm not as young as I was.'

'Get on, you don't look a day over twenty-one. Plenty of women'd change places with you tomorrow, given half a chance.'

He has a nice face, Mari has often thought so, warm brown eyes (not as dark as Antonio's, but then he's not Italian) flecked with gold, and a ready smile. Golden-brown sideburns show beneath his helmet, and he wears a moustache, thinner than Antonio's, lighter in colour like his eyes, and waxed at the tips. Is he married? 'Course he is!

'You must be in fine condition too,' he's saying, 'all the exercise you get nightly.' Mari is about to take umbrage at this, but he adds, 'Prancing about that stage at the Palladium.'

'Well,' she says, 'I am in fair shape, I suppose, for my age.'

'Still, you seem a bit under the weather tonight, if you don't mind me saying. Shall I walk with you to your door?'

'Oh, I don't want to put you out . . .'

'My pleasure.' He offers his arm and Mari takes it.

As they go on down the street, she says, 'Has any new evidence come in on these murders?'

'Not a shred, 'cept what was picked up at the crime scenes – kid gloves, a silk scarf, a gold cuff link. You read about all that in the paper, I expect? Planted those himself, they think up at the Yard.'

'Why'd he do that?' Mari has her own theories, but she wants to know what the law thinks.

'Well, it could be a sort of signature, see. It's a gruesome thought, but it might be his way of setting his seal on the murders – that and the . . . other thing . . . letting us know it's the same bloke getting away with it all. In his twisted mind, it's probably a matter of pride that he can do it again and again, and get away every time.'

'Like a game,' Mari says.

'Another train of thought is that those items are not evidence but decoys. Some think he's not a nob at all, but some ordinary feller confusing the case with false clues.'

Mari shakes her head. 'There's a hole in that one,' she says. 'Any ordinary feller'd soon be out of pocket buying gold cuff links and whatnot just to throw away. He's a nob all right, mark my words.'

They have reached her gate. She withdraws her arm and says, 'Thanks for your company.'

'Thank you for the treat,' Constable Dawes says. 'I hope I'll have the honour another time. Perhaps when I'm off duty?'

'Well . . .' Mari says. Antonio! her heart protests. 'Goodnight, Officer.'

''Night, Miss Prince. Sweet dreams.'

Going up the path, Mari glimpses Mrs Perkins, her landlady, in dressing gown and curlers, peering through a gap in the curtains.

She fits her key into the lock, sighs deeply, and murmurs, 'Home, safe.'

Inside, Mari locks and bolts the door and leans on it for a moment to savour the pleasure of security. Down the hall, Mrs Perkins's door opens and she puts out her head.

'Coming in for a cuppa, dearie?'

'Not tonight, thanks. I'm dead beat.'

'Just a quick one. I've put the kettle on.'

Mari would rather drink her stout than Mrs Perkins's Indian tea, but she says, 'All right then, I'll just come in for a minute.'

In her landlady's parlour, crammed with photos of her dead husbands and departed daughters, Mari puts her bag down and sits at the table.

'Any trouble tonight?' Mrs Perkins calls from the kitchen.

'No, all quiet. Far as I know. I hope the papers don't tell us different tomorrow.' Mari looks around at the sepia-tinted faces, not a smile on any of them, and thinks, I hope I don't end up this way, with my memories staring me out.

Mrs Perkins comes in with the tea tray. 'I daresay tomorrow night will be rowdy enough. Be a circus in the West End with all them geezers come for the game. Just the time he'd choose to strike again, I shouldn't wonder.' She puts the tray on the table and places a cup and saucer in front of Mari. 'I wouldn't have your job for all the world, dearie. Still off sugar?'

'Yes, I got to watch my figure.'

Mrs Perkins clicks her tongue. 'I don't know what for. Plenty'll watch it for you.' She pours tea into the thin china cups and hands the milk jug to Mari. 'That's why you have to be extra careful, a young woman like you, with that head of hair and fine figure. You're just the type that attracts him. All been good-looking, haven't they, them poor girls.'

Milk flows over the edge of Mari's cup, fills the saucer, and runs on to the red damask tablecloth. She watches, wide-eyed, as the liquid seeps into the cloth, turning it a deeper shade of red. 'What a horrible sight,' she says.

'No bother.' The landlady takes Mari's saucer and pours the contents into the empty milk jug. 'Shall I give you a fresh cup?'

Mari shakes her head. 'You know that's what I've been thinking. With my red hair and my big t— chest, I'm a walking target, aren't I?'

'Pity Antonio took off. You'd have been safe with him. You ought to find yourself another beau, Mari.'

'I bet he loves red hair,' Mari says.

'Why so?'

'Reminds him of blood, doesn't it?' She laughs a little at her macabre joke and Mrs Perkins joins in. Their laughter, Mari notices, is a bit thin and high-pitched.

'I'm glad none of my daughters is here. Thank the good Lord they all moved away to places like Plymouth and Aldershot. It's left a hole where my heart should be, but I'd rather see them safe. I had a letter from my Elsie this morning. The baby's doing well now. Had her worried for a bit . . .'

Mrs Perkins is right, too, about tomorrow. It would be a good night for him. The police will all be occupied keeping the rugby fans in order, breaking up fights . . .

'Croup, he had. A very nasty bout, and you do worry with the first one. But like I said, he's right as rain now.'

What'll I do? How shall I protect myself?

'A lot of those Welshmen and Northerners will be taken to the cleaners tomorrow night, I don't doubt. Won't be weighed down by their wallets when they run for the last train, will they?'

The solution comes to her in a flash, simple yet ingenious – foolproof: I'll go home with one of them Welsh fellers. Choose one that's never been in London before. I'll know he's not the murderer.

Mari blows out her cheeks. 'How old is Elsie's baby now?' she asks Mrs Perkins. 'I suppose teething will be next on the list.'

4

Mary: Saturday Morning

Dawn is the colour of my father's face when he lay dying. I sat by his bed and kept the death watch, three days and three nights until, on the fourth morning, he expired. I would not permit my mother to relieve me. 'This is my office,' I told her. 'I want to shut his eyes at the end, the last of many, more arduous tasks I have performed for him.'

She understood and went about her business, which was to sort and sift through the household goods, rid herself of his trappings and possessions.

He could not speak, he could not move. He could only stare at me with his fire-and-brimstone eyes. I saw the flame of rage leap in his pupils. He knew I had come not to mourn but to gloat, and he would have struck me senseless, as on other occasions, had he the power.

But the power was mine.

I did not revile or taunt him with my tongue, as I might have, fearlessly. I simply sat and smiled, sewed a little, sang softly when joy lifted my heart.

We had lived in London only two years when my mother sent for me. She wrote: 'He has suffered a stroke, Mary. The doctors believe he won't pull through. It is your duty to be here.'

I enjoyed the journey back to my mother, to my home, to my dying father. As London passed out of view and we rolled into the countryside, my heart took flight and I sang a little, a song I'd heard Mari Prince deliver on one of those few occasions Alf had taken me to the Palladium. It was the song I sang at my father's deathbed:

> Only a bird in a gilded cage, love . . .

She sang it with deep emotion, as if she really knew how it feels to be a prisoner. That is part of her artifice, her talent, to assume other forms: to pretend, convincingly, to be what she is not. She has a wide repertoire, I grant her that. But that night, she moved me. Her face, lit by that abundant halo, seemed ethereal, unearthly. Her pure soprano soared through the house, as if she were one who had learned to make a hymn of suffering.

Afterwards, when the lights changed, and she whipped off her white dress to reveal her more lurid conjurer's costume, I was not dismayed. It seemed to me legitimate that one who could penetrate the dark reaches of pain and transcend them in song, should also have access to other mysteries – communication with the supernatural, the ability to harness occult powers beyond the ken of lesser beings such as I.

I knew, of course, that her magic was all sleight-of-hand, trickery, illusion, *trompe l'oeil*: I was a grown woman, not a gullible child at a birthday party. Yet, for those few evenings when I sat in the stalls and watched billowy chiffon rainbows rise from her upturned hat and float out across the auditorium, my capacity for wonder was engaged, my own devils exorcised.

I insisted, the first time, that Alf take me backstage to meet her. In her dressing room, she sat at her mirror goddess-like, surrounded by cloudy phials, tinted bottles, quaintly-shaped vessels. A brass candelabra cast a pool of light about the table and her person; and all about the room, on screens and trestles, hung the accoutrements of her act.

When she rose to greet me, this illusion of a high priestess evaporated. Her handclasp was warm and human, her North Country accent unmelodious, elemental as clay. Beneath the make-up, I saw that her beauty was not exotic, excepting, always, her magnificent hair, unmatched, I affirm, except in the realm of deities.

I was not disappointed to find her made flesh and blood. Rather, I felt embraced by her vitality. She led me about the small dressing room, showing me her costumes, explaining the contents and uses of bottles, revealing, ingenuously, the secrets of her art.

At one point, she swung her velvet cloak over my shoulders, turned me about in front of the mirror, and said, 'See, Mrs Ramsey, it's not so hard to be a magician. If I put a bit of paint on your face and arranged your hair and showed you a few tricks . . . Mr Ramsey, what do you think? She has the colouring, such dark hair, such white skin, a figure I'd swap mine for any day . . .'

Alf stood in the doorway, looking bemused, discomforted. I cared nothing for him. She had made me extraordinary, awakened a sense of possibilities, powers, in the body I had thought inferior, unworthy of essay or adulation. In her magician's cloak, I made a leap and imagined myself a different woman – one capable of passion, desire . . .

So, she had wizardry in her after all.

But going home in the hackney, Alf said, 'I hope you won't make too much of Miss Prince, Mary.'

'Why not? I like her,' I said. 'I mean to write and invite her to visit me.'

'I'm afraid I shall have to forbid you this one thing, Mary. Surely, you can make more congenial friends amongst our neighbours?'

Perhaps, even then, he had picked her out for himself.

My father died, my mother sent me back to London; my husband bade me find my own pursuits and not trouble him again soon to take me to the Palladium. I did not write to Mari Prince. Because of things I had observed and deduced and dreamed, I grew to suspect and, therefore, to hate her. This is the substance of the fifteen years since I first wore the gold band on my finger, the iron bands on my heart and brain.

Only this last year, a purpose has entered my otherwise barren existence. A murderer walks abroad in London, and the entire populace holds this killer in awe and terror – emotions akin, surely, to esteem. In my breast, only gratitude stirs. With the murders, an idea came to birth.

As I read the newspapers, overhear gossip in shop and street, I am amazed that one and all, the law and the citizenry, never doubt the murderer to be one of the male sex. They assume a woman incapable of the audacity, the courage, the arrogance required to kill. Yet, did not Judith cut off the head of Holofernes? How many victims did Lucrezia number on her delicate, beringed, poisoner's fingers? And I . . . I sped my father's demise, ignoring his plea when he turned his eyes on the water glass, tipping his medicine into the chamber-pot, hastening the collapse of his heart with songs and smiles.

My plans are laid. I have discovered where she lives, what time she returns each night, and that she is always unaccompanied. In this grey and sickly dawn, I have fixed the date. Therefore, I call you up now, my devils, summon you to my aid. This midnight, I strike back at my tormentor.

5

Percy, Dai, Ivor: Saturday Morning

All decked out in green and white streamers, the South Wales to Paddington Rugby Special stands at platform two in Cardiff station, smoke billowing from her engine. A bed-sheet banner strung along the side of the first coach proclaims '*Cymru Am Byth*' in painted black letters. On the second coach, a banner asks 'Who Beat The English?' A third and final banner responds hopefully, 'Good Old *Sospan Fach*.' The train's compartments and corridors are jam-packed with supporters, all bearing their team's colours, green and white, on scarves and rosettes. One man has pinned a giant leek, the miners' emblem of Wales, to his lapel. He has stuck his head out of a corridor window and is twirling a wooden rattle to catch the stationmaster's attention.

'Ten past seven, Cliff,' he shouts, pointing at the station clock. 'We was due out at seven sharp.'

The stationmaster folds his hands across his stomach. 'I'm aware, boyo, I'm aware. But the Avon Fach charabanc haven't come in yet. You wouldn't want any of your butties left behind today, would you?' He smiles, and nods his head slowly like royalty. 'A historic occasion, a great day for the Welsh. I only wish I was going with you. It breaks my heart to stay home.'

A young porter comes running up the steps to the platform. 'Avon Fach bus just come in, Mr Morgan,' he calls, and a cheer goes up.

The men from Avon Fach sweep up the steps and pelt across the platform to the open doors of the train.

'Thanks for holding on, Cliff,' a thickset man in a black three-piece suit calls. 'You're a damn good butty. The old charabanc broke a wheel outside Abercynon, or we'd have been here a half hour back.'

'That's all right, Dai. I wouldn't let the train move an inch without you.' The stationmaster looks approvingly at the black suit, which sets Dai Bando apart from the other supporters, who wear sports jackets, second-best trousers, flat caps, and raincoats.

A cut above the rest of them, Cliff Morgan thinks. Shame to see a man like him on his own. Why haven't he found a good woman, I wonder?

'We made it then, Dai.' Ivor Parry, Avon Fach's lay preacher, comes up the steps. 'Looks like standing room only though. I don't know how my stomach will hold up to that.' He turns to the stationmaster. 'Overloaded, in't you? Could be dangerous, that.'

'Not overloaded at all, Ivor. Just looks that way 'cause they're all at the windows. Plenty of seats inside. Besides, the good Lord have given His blessing to this endeavour. No harm can come to you today.'

'I don't know as the Lord gets mixed up in rugby,' Ivor says. 'Shall we get on then, Dai?'

Dai Bando is looking down the steps to the station corridor. 'Where's Percy though?' he says.

'Percy?' Ivor jerks back his head and blinks, as if an insect had flown into his eye. 'I dunno. Must be on the train. I thought I was last. Thought I'd have to stop to be sick. Can't find those settlers Bethan gave me. She always gives me Rennies when I travel.' He taps the pockets of his raincoat and pulls out a packet, but it's a crushed pack of Woodbines not the stomach pills. He puts a cigarette in his mouth.

'Here, what are we waiting for now?' the man with the leek calls. 'You two Avon Fach fellers going or coming? Make your bloody minds up.'

The men at the windows begin to chant:

> 'Why are we waiting?
> Why are we waiting?
> Why? Why? Why?'

'I'll go on and get seats,' Ivor says and darts for the train.

'Lost something have you, Dai?' the stationmaster says.

'My young butty,' Dai says. 'I'm taking him up for the game. First time for him.'

'Was he on the bus?'

"'Course he was on the bus. But he was having a bit of bother getting his suitcase out of the rack, so I came on to ask you to wait.'

'Suitcase? How long's he going for?'

'Just the day, same as the rest of us, but he's getting married in the morning. He've got his wedding togs in the case.'

'Dai, I got two seats in a compartment with some Ponty fellers,' Ivor shouts from a window.

Dai turns his back on the train. Hands on his hips, he looks down the stairs. 'I won't go on without Percy, Cliff. He've been looking forward to this for months. It's his last trip as a single feller.'

His chin cupped in his hand, Cliff Morgan studies Dai Bando's back. The sight of that back, solid and tense, stirs old memories. He remembers the miners' strike and the demonstration two years back, in the summer of 1911. All the valley turned out to watch the men march into Avon Fach, and there was Dai in the front line, leading the procession. When they got to the Town Hall where the deputation was waiting, some of the men faltered, especially when they saw the soldiers lining the road. But Dai had stepped forward and spoken for them all. He as good as called the Avon Fach Council traitors and told the London MP what terms the men would settle for. Cliff had been standing on a beer crate outside Bevan's Brewery and seen it all. There's a bloody hero come among us, he'd thought. Wales has another Llewelyn.

No good luck had come of it though. The miners hadn't got the minimum wage until 1912, a whole year later, and two months after that strike of 1911 the colliery roof had caved in, bringing death and injury.

Cliff looks at Dai's crooked right leg, and at the trilby perched like a knight's helmet on top of his wild gypsy hair. He sees a darn in Dai's collar, where his black hair curls up, and shakes his head. That man hasn't got his deserts. 'Pen,' he says to the porter. 'I'm holding that train till Dai's butty gets here.'

'He's come,' Dai says. 'Here's Percy. Hey up, boyo!' he calls down the steps. 'You got the whole train waiting for you, like the flaming Prince of Wales. I hope you don't do this tomorrow. Ellen might not wait. Fickle, women are. Not like a butty.'

A tall thin young man with corn-coloured hair comes on to the platform. He wears a dark green suit and carries a blue suitcase. 'There was a bit of a muddle about my case,' he says. 'A Porthcawl lady had one nearly identical and the conductor gave me hers by mistake. I was half-way across the terminus when they called me back. Lucky she noticed, in't it?'

'It is that,' Dai says. 'You'd look a bit strange in a dress, Perce.'

Percy laughs nervously and blushes like a girl.

Dai lifts his trilby to Cliff Morgan. 'Thanks a lot, boyo,' he says and limps rapidly toward the train, Percy at his heels, his suitcase banging against Dai's bad leg.

The porter follows. With a sigh, he slams the door behind them.

The stationmaster raises his whistle to his lips and blows. The Red Dragon shudders, and the engine driver waves his spotted handkerchief, and amid cheers and the click-clack of rattles the train pulls slowly out of Cardiff station.

'Good luck!' Cliff Morgan calls. 'Mind you bring the trophy home safe and sound.'

'Think we'll win?' the porter asks as the train gathers speed.

'How can we lose, Pen? Got the best side, haven't we? A lot of old scores will be settled today. Damn, I wish I was going!'

'I wouldn't go,' the porter says. 'Not if you paid me. There's a chap up in London doing people in for fun. Fancy a cup of tea, Mr Morgan? The Rhondda's not due for a bit.'

'Aye, brew it up then,' the stationmaster says, his eyes on the distant trail of smoke. 'All the best, men. I hope you give the bloody English what for.'

In the train corridor, Percy Fly sets down his suitcase and takes a little leatherbound book from his inside pocket. He turns away from the compartment where Dai and Ivor sit among the Pontypridd supporters and pretends to look out of the window. Holding the book close to his chest so he can slip it out of sight if anyone comes by, he squints at the open page:

> A Prince I was, blue-eyed and fair of face,
> Of temper amorous, as the first of May.

As he reads, Percy's lips shape the words. Opposite the poem, behind a piece of tissue paper, is a black-and-white illustration of the amorous prince. Percy studies it and nods his head. Thin. All them princes were on the thin side. Like me. Looks about my height too. A six-footer, I bet. Longer hair though. I couldn't go around Avon Fach with hair like that. People would call me a mug. No point now, anyway. My fate is stamped. Who would have credited it, that a little bit of a thing like Ellen, in her airy-fairy dresses, her hair like a baby chick's, could bear down on a man with such crushing weight!

Dai had introduced them. Going down in the cage at the mine shaft one morning, Percy had said casually, 'We got some new members in our chapel, then.'

Dai was fixing a new battery in the lamp on his helmet and just said, 'Oh aye?'

'That blonde girl and her mother. They started coming a couple of Sundays back. Didn't I see you talking to them after service? Her mother wears them dresses with big flowers on them—'

Dai clicked the lamp into place and put his helmet on. He looked up at Percy. 'Daisy Allgood and Ellen. Just moved here from Pontypridd. Yes, Ellen's the girl for you, Perce. Stick with me next Sunday and I'll introduce you.'

'I don't want to rush into anything,' Percy said.

'Don't be daft,' Dai said. 'It's time you had a girl to court. We'll take a walk in the park after chapel, the four of us.'

So, Dai had rushed Percy from mere fancy into irrevocable action. Left to himself, Percy would never have moved so fast. He would have dreamed and debated, dilly-dallied, wondering, Shall I? Shan't I? Without Dai's intervention, he might still be stealing looks at Ellen over his hymn book instead of getting married to her tomorrow morning. He doesn't blame Dai though: I was keen, and when he said he'd get me off with her, I never contradicted him. And it was me who said the word 'marriage' all on my own. Dai wasn't there when I got down on my knees and proposed. Ah, but the circumstances that led up to that proposal have left a bitter taste in my mouth, like a 'flu powder when it don't all go down. Ellen's a fairy, all right. She beguiled me. Like that woman in 'La Belle Dame Sans Merci', except I'm pale and wan because I'm trapped, not because she ditched me.

Cripes! Percy thinks. I'm twenty years old, not even earning a decent wage yet, and I'll have a wife tomorrow, a baby in six months, and I got to live in her Mam's house and see those dresses every day, that give me a headache, and sleep in that room with the jungle-print wallpaper . . .

The town of Newport and its ruined castle speed past the window, the train crosses the border, and the fields and copses of England appear. '"A Prince I was,"' Percy says, and the grazing cows transform before his eyes into a noble company of knights and ladies riding down to Newport as they once rode to Camelot. At the head of the procession, mounted on a high-stepping white horse with a gold bridle and embroidered saddlecloth, is one who looks a lot like Percy, except his hair is long and flowing, and he wears a tunic not a suit. Behind him, her arms clasped around his waist, sits a woman in a drifting gown of green silk. She is not small and frail like Ellen. She's almost as tall as Percy himself, with generous hips and breasts and masses of hair tumbling over her shoulders in wild curls. She's only half human, and half symbol. She's everything I'll never have now, Percy thinks.

Oh, Ellen, you led me on, you know you did. All those evenings when your Mam was off to her ladies' club and you and me on the couch in the front room.

'I'll just turn the lamp off,' you said, 'because it hurts my eyes.'

And then you reached over and put your hand on my knee and said, 'Oh, Percy . . . you can kiss me if you like.'

That's how it started. I never would have had the nerve to start anything myself.

And after a week or two of kissing, one night you said, 'Percy, put your hand inside my dress.'

Remembering, Percy shudders, the way he did when his palm first closed over Ellen's small breast.

'Lift my skirt, Percy,' you said. 'You can touch me there, too.'

Oh, and when I had my hands on you like that, and you kissing and clinging and saying, 'Percy, Percy,' I lost my head, Ellen!

When you pulled your dress down all of a sudden and said, 'I can't go no further, Percy,' it was more than I could bear.

'Please, Ellen, please, love . . .' I said.

'All right,' you said, 'but if anything happens, promise you'll take care of me.'

That's when I got down on my knees and said, 'Will you do me the honour of becoming my future wife?'

You got me on false pretences, a drunken man, all inflamed and out of his senses. I can't forgive you for that. But I'll do the right thing, the gentlemanly act.

Percy becomes aware that Dai Bando is calling him. He slides the little book of poems into his pocket and turns to Dai.

'I said you can sit on my lap, Perce.'

The other men in the compartment snigger.

'I'd look a fool,' Percy says.

'What about your injury, Dai,' Ivor says. 'You got to think of that.'

'My injury is on my calf. It hasn't stopped me using my knees,' Dai says, 'nor anything else higher up.' He smiles at Ivor.

Ivor laughs briefly and says 'You're a card,' but Percy notices that he looks away quickly. Of course, being a lay preacher, he wouldn't care for jokes like that.

'Take my seat for a bit,' Dai says, 'if you won't have my lap. You been on your feet a good hour.'

'I'd rather stand,' Percy says, but Dai heaves himself up, straightening his right leg slowly, carefully, his hand on his calf. 'Go on', he says, stepping into the corridor. 'My leg pains if I sit too long, so you'll be doing me a favour. Got to put more Wintergreen on it anyway.' He limps away towards the toilets and Percy takes the corner seat.

The Pontypridd men nod at Percy and say, 'How do?'

'How do,' Percy says and looks down at his hands. He wishes Dai hadn't gone off and left him with this compartment full of strangers. He's always tongue-tied with people he doesn't know. Well, he knows Ivor, of course, but he's not a butty. Percy just goes to hear him preach on Sundays with his mother, a big chapel woman, and to watch Ivor's wife as she sings with the choir.

An image of Bethan Parry rising from the choir to sing solo comes before Percy, like the picture of Venus emerging from the waves, only not naked, of course. Always dressed very proper. He tries, not for the first time, to imagine Bethan without her clothes, wrapped only in her dark hair, reclining on a satiny bed. He feels himself stir and looks anxiously at Ivor.

'This lad's getting married tomorrow,' Ivor says.

'Oh aye?' The men look at him with interest.

Percy feels the colour leap into his cheeks. *Daro!* Now they'll start asking him questions.

'Congratulations. Who is the lucky lady?'

'Little girl's name is Ellen Allgood,' Ivor says. 'Pretty as an angel and got the temperament of one, too. Percy's the lucky one, not her.'

'Allgood? Now that name rings a bell. Half a mo'. Any relation to Daisy Allgood, used to be a barmaid at the Three Feathers in Ponty?'

'That'll be her Mam, I expect,' Ivor says. 'They do come from Ponty, I know.'

'Go on! Fancy! Used to know Daisy well at one time. Life and soul of the Feathers, she was. So he's marrying Daisy's girl.' The Ponty man smiles at his mates.

'What time's the wedding?' another man asks.

'Ten o'clock,' Ivor says. 'We're catching the last train back tonight.'

'Taking a bit of a chance, in't you? Train won't get in to Cardiff before six, even if it's on schedule.'

'We got it all planned. Percy'll get a good night's sleep, have a wash and brush up and change in the men's room at the station, and we'll catch the half-past seven to Avon Fach. Be there by nine, tidy.'

Go on, tell them the whole agenda, Percy thinks.

'And Daisy's girl don't mind him going off to London the day before? A lot of women would object. Must be broad-minded like her Mam.'

'Percy's never been to the Final. Dai persuaded Mrs Allgood and Ellen to let him go.'

He makes me sound like a big soft baby, Percy thinks. Still, he's not far wrong. Ellen's Mam does boss me about. I'll have to put a stop to that after we're married. I'll ask Dai how to go about it.

'*Looks* like he'd have a way with women, that chap. Got a glint in his eye, haven't he? Married man?'

'Bachelor.' Ivor's voice is snappy suddenly. He drags hard on his Woodbine (burning his fingers, Percy notices) before throwing it down and crushing it under his polished brown boot.

'That's no good, smart feller like him.'

'Do you have to keep your wives locked up?'

'You Ponty chaps have bad minds,' Ivor says. 'That sort of thing don't go on in Avon Fach.'

'As the hoor said to the first-timer!'

'Pardon?' Ivor says.

'"It don't go on, ducks," she said, "it goes up."'

The Ponty men roar. Percy blushes. Ivor lights another Woodbine.

Dai appears in the doorway.

Percy sighs. 'Where've you *been*?' he says.

'Just putting on my ointment and visiting down the corridor, Perce. Leave you too long, did I?'

'Here, Dai, your butty's trying to tell us Avon Fach don't have no sinners. Is that right?'

Dai looks down at Ivor. Watching their faces, Percy can't fathom the look that passes between the two older men. Anyone who didn't know them would think they were enemies, the way their faces go hard and tight. But they're friends. They've worked the same shift at Avon Fach colliery for years.

'Ivor here is a lay preacher, see,' Dai says, 'so he's got to think the best of everybody. I'm one Avon Fach sinner though. I can't speak for others.' He gives the men a broad smile, showing all his white teeth. 'And I hope I'll be sinning in London tonight.'

'Oh, know some places up there?'

'Depends on what you're looking for. Feller down the corridor recommends the Palladium in Leicester Square. Says it's a real good show – lot of half-naked chorus girls, and you can get off with them easy, he says. Be a crush, mind. First come, first served, so you better not stay in the pubs too long.'

'Not much time for getting off. Last train goes at half-twelve. Couldn't do much more than buy a woman a drink or two in that time – and be a waste of money, wouldn't it?'

Dai strokes his right sideburn and looks past the men to the window, his head on one side. 'What I have in mind is something more long-term.'

'What do you mean, Dai?' Ivor says. 'You got to be on that train tonight. You're Percy's best man.'

'I was thinking I might set myself up for future occasions. Come to some arrangement with an obliging woman, willing to show me the sights and give me a night's lodging. I fancy a weekend in London now and again. I'd make it worth her while, of course.'

'It's all right for some,' a Ponty man says. 'You're not married, I hear?'

'That's right. I'm a free agent.'

Envy floods Percy's heart, but Dai, he notices, doesn't sound glad at all.

'Good luck to you,' another Ponty fan says, 'but it wouldn't be my cup of tea, even if I could have it. They got expensive tastes, I bet, London women.'

'Oh, that don't worry me. I got money and no one to spend it on. Be my pleasure to treat a woman if she liked me.'

'You should settle down,' Ivor says, 'if that's how you feel.'

'No one in Avon Fach I fancy.' Percy watches Dai shift his eyes from the window to Ivor's face. He turns his head slowly, as if it's a great weight. 'No one who's available.'

'Always young widows where there's a pit,' a Ponty man says. 'Perhaps you're too picky.'

'Maybe I am.' Dai is still looking at Ivor. 'Ivor here has the best-looking woman in Avon Fach – in South Wales, I'd wager. Once you've seen Bethan Parry, she puts you off others.'

All the men look at Ivor.

'I do have a beautiful wife,' Ivor tells them. 'Married for twelve years. We have two boys, and Bethan dotes on them.'

'She's a good mother. No sacrifice she wouldn't make for the kids, right, Ivor?'

'Just as good a wife,' Ivor says. 'I won't be looking for women in London.'

'Mrs Parry's a first-class singer, too,' Percy says. 'Out of this world.'

'There you are, boys.' Ivor beams around the compartment. 'You can see I'm in clover.'

'Percy,' Dai says, 'let's have a spell in the corridor.'

The train rolls through fields, neat as patchwork, squares of brown, yellow, and various shades of green. Now and then a farmhouse pops up, or a clump of trees.

'There's flat England is,' Percy says. 'Don't it have mountains like Wales?'

'It do, farther north,' Dai says. 'Grand peaks up there.'

'You been around the country a lot, Dai?'

'Not so much, and not in the way I'd like. I worked in different coal mines, that's all.'

'Still, you've seen more than me. And now I'll never have the chance.'

'Getting the jitters, son? Common thing, I'm told, for a young feller to have last-minute doubts before he takes the plunge.'

'The plunge,' Percy says. 'That's a good word for it. I do feel like I'm diving in – over my head, to tell the truth.'

'Ellen's a nice girl. Make a good wife, I reckon.' Dai speaks slowly, as if he's thinking it over, as if the decision hasn't been taken, as if it still matters whether Ellen's nice or awful. 'So what's the trouble? Better get it off your chest.'

'Well, see . . .' Percy stares out of the window, one hand on his heart. He can feel the rectangular shape of the poetry book. 'I always hoped there'd be more . . . more excitement in life . . . don't laugh . . . more romance.'

'I'm not laughing. Don't you feel any excitement with Ellen then?'

'I don't know how to say this, but Ellen isn't my ideal woman. Not any more. She don't like any of the things I like, though she did at first.'

'What things are those?'

'Oh . . . reading. I used to read to her a lot and she said she enjoyed it. Now she'd rather I rubbed her feet or massaged her back than open a book.'

'Well, she do put in a lot of hours at the biscuit counter.'

This is what Ellen's mother says. 'And she's expecting, too, Percy. You have to cosset her a bit.' He wonders if he should tell Dai about the baby. So far, only Mrs Allgood and his own mother know. He decides not to.

'And reading in't everything, I don't suppose. You can still read by yourself when you get the urge. Don't need a partner for that. Anything else?'

'She used to . . . let me kiss her and that . . . you know. But recently, she seems to have gone off it.'

'That's a bit more serious than the reading. Have you asked her why, Percy?'

'She says it's my fault, that I don't treat her like I used to when we were courting.'

'Is she right?'

Percy shrugs. 'I don't think she likes loving. I just don't think she do. She only did it to lead me on and make me want to marry her.'

Dai clicks his tongue. 'Now don't start thinking those thoughts. That's hard on Ellen and a bad way to begin married life. Better think how you can persuade her back to the way she was.'

'How do I do that, Dai?'

'You have to be patient and court her a bit with soft words and fond looks, coax her with sugar like you would a wild pony, till she's eating out of your hand—' Dai breaks off with a laugh, a harsh, mirthless sound that startles Percy. 'Bloody hell, hark at me! Talking through my flaming hat! Patience, *daro*! Some of them want you to squander your life playing patience, with no guarantee. Just because they came to you once — and quick enough, too — they expect you to live on hope and memory. They think a man is made of wood or steel—'

Percy stares at Dai. He has clenched his fists against the windowpane, and Percy has the feeling he'd like to shove them right through the glass. Why has he got so worked up about him and Ellen?

'Maybe I've made it out worse than it is,' he says, to calm Dai down. 'I don't think Ellen's that bad. She wouldn't have said yes if she wanted me to hang about for her.'

'So will you call it off?' Dai says. 'Or go through with it?'

'I can't call it off, Dai! I wouldn't have the nerve. It's all set. My Mam knocked our two downstairs rooms into one and papered the walls for the reception. The cake's come, three-tier, from Howfield's. A lot of people are invited' — and Ellen's expecting — 'no, I can't call it off.'

'Right-oh,' Dai says. 'I respect you for sticking to your word.' He reaches up and pats Percy's shoulder. 'Don't worry, butty, it's the jitters, that's all. Besides, there in't no ideal woman.' He links Percy's arm. 'Look at that hill rising up. In't it soft and pretty? Like a woman's behind.'

'I'm looking forward to London,' Percy says. 'Are we going to that show, Dai — at the Palladium?'

'If you like. It's your choice tonight, Percy.'

'You'd think them women, them chorus girls, would be scared to go with strangers. With the murders and all, I mean.'

'Five women he's knocked off,' Dai says. 'I don't know how a feller can hurt a woman. Kill a man now, that's different.' Dai glances over his shoulder to the compartment. Ivor is leading the Pontypridd men in hymn-singing. 'I could never harm a woman, could you, Percy?'

'I could never commit murder,' Percy says. 'It isn't in me. That little hill *is* pretty, Dai.'

6

Mari: Saturday Morning

In the lounge at the Regent Palace Hotel, Mari sits in an alcove behind a giant potted fern. It's Friday night and the lounge is heaving. She can't see her beau, who has gone up to the bar to order drinks. It seems ages since he went, and she's beginning to wonder if he's changed his mind and ditched her.

She feels uneasy on other counts too. For some reason, she's wearing her stage costume, not her street clothes, and she fears the men in the room will spot her black sequined stockings and cleavage, take her for a whore, and descend upon her in a pack, their mouths frothing, their eyes reddened with lust. She does have on her magician's cloak, but each time she tries to wrap it around her, it falls back, slipping through her fingers like glycerine, and her semi-nakedness is revealed again. Crouching behind the fern, peering through its fronds for her escort, she's realized, too, that she's the only woman in the lounge. This is odd, for the Regent Palace is a respectable hotel where a gentleman may take his wife or lady friend for a drink before dinner without fearing that she will encounter offensive sights and sounds.

Is this the Regent Palace?

Mari looks about to see if she recognizes the fixtures. The wallpaper is patterned with bunches of purple grapes and ivy wreaths. A teardrop chandelier hangs from the moulded leaf cluster in the centre of the ceiling, like a great glittering flower bursting into bloom. Yes, this is what the Regent Palace looks like . . . yet her anxiety is not dispelled. Rather, it mounts and burns in her chest, for she senses something askew in the familiar scene, though she can't put her finger on what it might be. As she casts about carefully for clues, it dawns on her, too, that she can't recall who brought her here. Her escort's face and demeanour, the circumstances of their meeting, are a mystery. Indeed, does she *have* an escort, or did some malevolent force whisk her out of the night and set her down here, in harm's way, behind a flimsy, ferny camouflage, in a place that is and is not the Regent Palace?

Mari rises. Drawing her cloak about her, praying for a new power – the gift of invisibility – she steps out from the cover of the potted fern and makes her way across the room to the door.

''Scuse me,' she says to the men who jostle and leer at her. 'Let me pass, please.'

The men close ranks and reach out to grab her. Somehow, she evades them, slipping around and between their thrusting bodies and snatching hands, as if she were no more substantial than a shadow, as if her magician's cloak really had bequeathed her a supernatural agility.

She arrives at the door, but where the hotel foyer should be, a long, seemingly endless corridor stretches. She's on one of the upper floors where the guest bedrooms are situated (where she's often been an overnight, though never a paying, guest), and she must find her way down to the street. She looks behind her. Her assailants have vanished, the lounge, too; only a blank white wall meets her gaze. No jeopardy there – but no exit either.

Mari starts down the corridor. All the doors on either side stand wide open. There are people in the rooms, but they are not behaving like ordinary guests. No one is undressing for bed, or unpacking a suitcase, or taking a nightcap and a cigar, or quieting fretful children.

Instead, bizarre and terrifying sights present themselves, each one more horrid than the last, as if she cranked the handle of one of those picture machines young men flock to at the seaside to view 'What the Butler Saw' or 'The Adventures of Annabelle'. Except that what Mari sees would never be offered for public consumption.

The rooms are like torture chambers, devoid of the usual bedroom furniture and fitted instead with weird and cruel contraptions to which naked men and women are chained or strapped in every conceivable posture, and in inconceivable ones too, even to a contortionist. Other men and women are doing dreadful things to the prisoners with whips and surgical instruments, with their bare hands and knees and feet, and with huge phalluses fastened to their stomachs; all of them, the attackers, naked too. Blood flows freely but no sounds emerge from these rooms. The violence proceeds unaccompanied by screams, groans, or pleas for mercy, as though the victims concurred with their assailants and even took pleasure in their own pain. Only the sound of someone crying softly intrudes upon the silence, and this comes not from within any of the rooms but from somewhere just above Mari's head, though when she looks up she sees only the white ceiling, blank as the walls.

Mari wakes and reaches across the bed for the comfort of warm flesh. Her fingers meet only the wrinkled sheet, and she moans softly, turns on her back, and wraps her arms around herself instead.

She opens her eyes and, lying alone as the dawn turns from silver to dove grey, she slips back through the years, to the time when she shared a bed, no larger than this one, with three younger sisters. On Saturday nights her mother, too, slid into this bed, whispering, 'Shove over, I can't bear to be by myself, thinking on what your father's about. I keep a good home on next to nothing, and I've never denied him a man's needs, yet he must gallivant in the pub and the town, playing the stallion with Sally Linford and her ilk. I can't fathom him, Mari, can you?'

Mari would press her mother's hands and whisper, 'Hush, you'll wake the little ones,' for though she felt her mother's ache, she could never shape her tongue to say a bad word about her father. He was fond of women and gin, she knew, but all the laughter and gaiety in the house sprang from him. When he came home from the mill in the evenings, Mari and her sisters would run into the street to meet him, for he always had something to give them, a few sweets from the corner shop, a reed pipe he had whittled as he walked, a funny story, a kiss and a swing in the air.

Their mother read the Bible to them and heard their prayers. Their father showed them card tricks and taught them the words of popular songs. Mari, his favourite, was quickest to learn. From him she got her first coaching in magic, her delight in singing, and her taste for dark-haired men with a glint in their eyes and a tendency to disappear.

Once in a while, her father disappeared . . . well, not quite: he never vanished without trace like Antonio, here one minute, gone the next. Rather, he played truant, went absent without leave, but they always knew where to find him should a crisis occur – a death in the family, say, or a visit from the rent collector. Sally Linford kept her door on the latch for Mari's father and, sometimes, when he walked in he forgot to walk out again. Still, he came home eventually, of his own accord. In the end, it was Mari's mother who departed for good.

'I've had it up to here,' she told Mari, who was fourteen then. 'I can't stand no more of his shiftless ways. My sister Maggie has offered to take us in. You and me can work in her boarding-house and put some money by, and the sea air will do the little ones the world of good. Maybe Lily's chest will get better in Yarmouth.'

'What about my dad?' Mari said.

'Don't worry about him. His fancy woman will see to his requirements. Bring my wedding trunk down here, Mari. I want to pack the best china.'

Mari said, without even thinking on it, 'I'll stay and keep Dad company.'

It snowed the day they all trooped to the station. Seven-year-old Lily, light as a doll in Mari's arms, coughed against her shoulder and bloodied the handkerchief Mari gave her. Ten-year-old Bessie sobbed, and four-year-old Millicent whined, 'Stop pulling me, Mama!' Mari's father hauled the trunk in a neighbour's wheelbarrow and pleaded with her mother.

'Don't take the children away from me, Jess. It'll fair break my heart to part from my family.'

'You never was a family man, William,' her mother said. 'You lived like a single feller, and that's the cause of all this trouble.'

'Give me another chance then. I'll mend my ways.'

But her mother was a rock. 'I'm spent out of chances. I got to earn some for myself now.'

'I'll send money, Jess.'

'You should do that. It's your duty to the girls.'

'And soon you'll meet some clean-living Yarmouth feller, I daresay? You're still a good-looking woman. Your red hair–'

'Happen I will,' Mari's mother said.

Strange how things turn out, never as you expect. Of her parents, Mari would have bet on her father as the one most likely to overcome hardship and live to a ripe old age. He could laugh off trouble and find quick remedies for the dumps . . . his fiddle, the pub, Sally. But now William is six feet under and it's her mother up in Yarmouth who thrives, with a new home, a new husband, and a nest-egg. Mari has never visited her mother, but they write from time to time. So she knows of Bessie and Millicent's marriages and of Lily's death. Mari's letters back are brief and infrequent. She can't, after all, write what she believes: 'I'll never visit you for you broke Daddy's heart and I can't forgive that.'

The doctor had diagnosed excessive drinking as the cause of William's decline. Ernie Frith, the publican, said, 'More likely the mill. I seen many go from there at a young age.' William himself held his broken heart responsible for his broken health. 'That and my guilt,' he told Mari as he lay in bed, sinking. 'It's like a great weight on my chest.' Then he had raised his eyes to the ceiling and said, 'See that lump in the plaster up there? I been lying here thinking . . . we all got one of those over our heads. It's like an abscess or a wen, only you can't see it. And know what it's full of, darlin'?'

'What, Daddy?' Mari said, making no sense of his words but wanting to humour him.

'Our deeds, good and bad, what we've done since we reached the age of knowledge. When it's packed so tight it can't hold no more it bursts open and whatever's in it comes pouring down, covering us in joy or sorrow. My lump busted the day your mother left, and it filled all my blood with poison.'

'Hush, Daddy,' Mari said. 'You were good to all of us. You did your best.'

'I didn't treat her proper. I allowed my passions to rule me. It was all because of my wanderings, y'see. She'd have put up with the rest, but there's no room for wandering in marriage.' He'd taken her hand then. 'When you find a decent feller, Mari, be good to him. Don't play about like your daddy did and don't ever go with a married man, for if you do, you might bring a family to ruin.' His fingers tightened over hers. 'What'll you do when I'm gone? Will you go to your mother in Yarmouth?'

'I don't know,' Mari said. 'I can't think on that now.'

'I been a careless man, I fear. I'm leaving you nothing but the clothes you stand up in—'

'Good times, Daddy,' Mari said, her throat thickening, 'I got plenty of those to remember.'

His face had brightened then. 'Aye, there's wealth in memories, right enough. Sally will remember me, too. Will you speak a kind word when you bump into her, Mari? You won't turn your head the other way, will you?'

'I never have turned from her. I won't start now.'

They were quiet for a bit, then her father said, 'Will you do something else for me, darlin'?'

'Whatever you wish.'

'I should like a little drink. Be a good lass, run down to the Bird in Hand and get me a bottle. Would you do that for your daddy? And ask Sally to come up and share it. We'll have a little party, the three of us, to see me off. I'll play the fiddle and you'll sing and Sally'll dance. She always could step lively to my tunes.'

'It's on the house,' Ernie Frith said. 'I'm right fond of you and your dad, as you well know. What'll you do now?' Before she could answer, the publican, a widower, rushed on. 'There's a home for you here.'

'Thank you,' Mari said. 'I'm grateful for the offer. But I've always been straight with you about my feelings, and they haven't changed, Ernie.'

'Not that,' he said. 'Not if you don't wish it. I know I'm older than your father and you still a maid. Only . . . I shouldn't like to see you in want, Mari.'

'I shan't want,' she said. 'I've made up my mind about my future. I'm going to London.'

'London! What for?'

'I've a thought to try my luck on the stage.'

'Well . . .' Ernie rubbed his bald head. 'Where did this idea come from?'

'From my father, when we were talking just now.'

'Your dad's notion, is it?'

'Not in so many words, but Daddy passed his talents on to me, I think. Didn't I always bring the house down here at the Bird when I did my Marie Lloyd act and my conjuring tricks?'

'You're a star at the Bird in Hand, love. London may be different.'

'Oh, not so different,' Mari said, tucking the gin bottle under her apron. 'People like a bit of magic everywhere. I shall do some good in the world.'

'Well . . . remember there's a home here . . .'

Ernie's broad, worried face fades away. His offer – a home, marriage, children – vanishes with him. She's had many offers since, but never one like his. Not even from Antonio, though he loved her well.

Mari sighs and lifts her hands from her waist to cover her breasts. All the nerves in her body rally to arms and she is speared on the sharp blade of lust.

Doris's refrain starts up in her head, a song sung out of key: 'How can you do without, Mari? No wonder you're edgy.'

Alf Ramsey's tenor joins Doris's contralto: 'We ought to get together, you and me. We're partners in need.'

Then, Antonio's vibrant, thrilling baritone: 'I will tell you no lies, *carissima*. Too much joy to remember, one day will make our hearts grieve.'

'Learn proper English,' Alf used to tell him, 'and I'll raise you up with the great stars of music hall.'

'Italian is the language of the opera,' Antonio replied with dignity.

'I like opera, too, Toni,' Alf soft-soaped, 'and I don't deny a rousing aria goes down well with the audience on a Saturday night, but in this business, you've got to have variety. The crowd we get here aren't highbrow. They like to hear the popular songs. Now if you'd let Mari coach you–'

Antonio had laid his hand on the manager's shoulder. 'Alf, Alf, it is not my aspiration,' he said, 'to be a star of the music hall. I enjoy to sing at the Palladium and be with my Mari, but I have fish to fry, as you say . . . elsewhere. One day, when the time is fruit, I will be gone, poof–' and he had snapped his fingers – 'like the rabbit disappears into Mari's hat. Don't lay plans for me, Alf. They will all go up in smoke . . . a lot of smoke,' he had added darkly.

Mari had secured Antonio a spot at the Palladium, whisking him down to audition after listening to him sing as he boiled a pot of spaghetti or bathed behind her Japanese screen, and having discovered that he was currently employed hauling goods at a warehouse. Alf had tears in his eyes after hearing Antonio's repertoire. 'I'll set you on the road to fame, lad,' he had said, pumping Antonio's right hand and clapping him on the shoulder. And to Mari later, 'He's my gain and my loss both, love. He'll make money for me, I don't doubt, but look at the cost. I shall have to give you up to him, shan't I?'

Mari said, 'You can't give up what you never had, Alf. Besides, like you say, he'll make your fortune. There's nowt of sorrow in that.' Happy, hopeful, like all new lovers, she hadn't dreamed then that it was not fame but infamy her beloved sought.

Mari pulls herself up in bed, in defiance of the pain that would drag her down into the mire of useless memories. Her sudden movement activates a more recent injury, and she slides her hands round to massage her spine. Her backache had grown worse since that argy-bargy with the drunk in Leicester Square.

What time is it anyway? She squints at the clock on the mantelpiece. Ten past seven. Soon the paperboy will be coming down the road, and she will know if the Gardener struck again last night. She gets out of bed. If the news is bad she will bear it better washed, dressed, and fed.

In one corner of her room stands her Japanese screen, decorated with large exotic birds. The barrow-boy who sold her the screen in Petticoat Lane told her they were birds of paradise. When she lights her lamp at night, the colours in their long trailing tail-feathers shine like jewels. By lamplight, the screen becomes transparent, so that the birds seem alive, poised for flight.

Mari, shivering in her thin shell-pink nightie, lights the gas fire. Stepping behind the screen, she strips off her nightie and pours water from a rose-patterned jug into a matching ewer. With soap and flannel, she washes all over, then dries herself on a towel still damp from previous bathing. She has forgotten to take her towels and sheets to the Chinese laundry again. They lie crumpled and soiled in a wicker basket, the wet towels giving off a smell of mildew that overpowers the lavender cologne she splashes on her body.

This lapse of memory distresses her, for it shows how much she came to rely on Antonio, who took care of household chores, who cooked, cleaned, and kept the room immaculate, saying, 'You are *artiste*, Mari. That is your calling. I will be housekeeper so your mind is free to create.'

He had believed in her all right, Antonio. Wherever he is, she knows he looks in the newspapers and at show bills and theatre hoardings for her name. She studies the papers, too, fearfully, dreading to discover the headlines that scream his obituary. For she came at last to understand, to confess to her cringing heart, that his 'vocation' was one fraught with peril, a task so dangerous it might well cost him his life. A report of Antonio's violent death is the one thing she dreads reading more than news of a fresh murder.

Mari comes out from behind the screen and collects her washed and dried underwear off the silver candlesticks on either side of the mantelpiece, a pair of frilly knickers hooked over one, a lacy camisole dangling by one strap from another. A gift from Antonio, the candlesticks graced the table when she and her lover dined tête-à-tête on amorous evenings at home. Since his departure, she has never used them to give light, thinking it sacrilege to place them in proximity to a plate of sausage-and-mash or mutton stew when they have presided over veal parmigiana and chicken cacciatore. Besides, her spirit would surely break under a weight of mirth – votive candles lit for a solitary woman and a makeshift dinner! So, she has found another use for them.

Once, overcome by wine, laughter and passion, Antonio, undressing her, flung her camisole over one candlestick, flipped her knickers over another. 'There they fly,' he cried, dancing her to bed. 'The flags of sweet surrender!' Now Mari dries her underwear on the candles. Putting the candlesticks to use in this manner helps her get it all in perspective. It's the romantic traditions her lover introduced that she must dispense with, not the witty ones.

Besides, as she plucks her knickers off the left candle, she can almost believe that Antonio lies in the bed behind her, watching, about to compliment her 'proud buttocks', her 'legs of a goddess', or her 'hair to rival the rising sun'. Ah, how extraordinary, how superlative, she had felt, a queen among women, seeing herself through the eyes of Antonio!

Enough. On that road misery lurks. In her underwear, Mari crosses to the oak wardrobe to find a dress for the day. When her hand is on the brass knob, cut to resemble a multi-petalled, full-blown flower, the paperboy's cries rend the silence in the street beneath her window.

'*Echo!* First edition *Echo!* Londoners braced for assault. Read all about it!'

Assault? Is that a new alias for murder? Mari's fingers turn cold, inert as the brass flower she clutches, the chill spreading up her arm and into her body so that she stands immobile, stiff as a statue . . . or a corpse.

She hears the front door whine as Mrs Perkins goes out to question the newsboy before handing over a penny. She believes in getting value for her money.

'What you got today then, Freddy? If it's another miners' strike, or the old Kaiser again, I don't want to know.' She drops her voice. 'Has there been another murder?'

'No, Mrs Perkins, it's all about the Final this morning.' His voice is quick, lively, like his black eyes, like his fingers when they reach for money. He's not yet twelve years old, but he's a fellow who loves his work. Even when she doesn't want a newspaper, Mari gives him a penny for his gap-toothed smile and his gumption.

'Our team will wallop the Welsh geezers, me dad says. Paper says so too. Me and Dad are going out to Twickenham this afternoon. We got tickets for the stands—'

'All right, all right, I never asked for your life story. Sure there hasn't been another murder? 'Bout time for another by my reckoning.'

'There won't be any more murders,' Freddy says, 'and I know why.' He lowers his voice so Mari, straining, can't hear; but whatever he says is clearly outrageous, for Mrs Perkins hoots.

'Your dad's off his rocker, Freddy, if that's his notion. You better tell him to watch his step, too, slandering the Royal Family. He could be clapped in irons for treason.'

'Dad don't hold with royalty.'

'Well, I do,' Mrs Perkins says, 'and I'll thank you to bear that in mind when you speak to me of His Majesty's relatives. The near ones, anyway. I don't have such a high opinion of the German lot.'

'Do you want a paper, Mrs Perkins? It's a souvenir edition. Very valuable in years to come.'

'No, I don't want a paper, not if it don't have decent news in it. Off you go now. I can't stand here gossiping with nippers.'

The landlady clatters up the steps and slams the front door. Freddy's voice rises again, shouting, '*Echo!*' and fades away as he moves farther down the street.

Slowly the stiffness ebbs out of Mari's limbs and she becomes a live person again, capable of thought and action. Her first thought is: I do need a holiday. Doris was right about that. I been living in terror of my life since . . . since October when he done the first one in and I had that bout of croup straight after . . . and now it's nearly April. How have I carried on so long without losing my marbles? Coming home from the Palladium every night on my own . . .

Alf Ramsey says his wife's hardly stepped outside the door since the murders began. ''Course, she's a frail one, wouldn't say boo to a goose . . . it was the champagne made her so cheeky that night she told me off. Alf should never have brought her to London. You can see it's foreign as Africa to her. She never went out much before the murders, I'll be bound. Used to come to the Palladium though . . . and I believe she took a fancy to my company, that night in my dressing room. . . .

Mari shrugs. No point thinking of Mary Ramsey, whom she hasn't seen for two years.

What shall I do today then?

She tips her head back to contemplate the ceiling. Blue lines zigzagging across the white plaster remind her, suddenly, of waves. Yes, why not go to the sea, to Brighton.

I will! Mari opens her wardrobe with a flourish. And I'll wear that powder-blue costume I haven't put on since last spring.

7

Mary: Saturday Morning

Down in the street, the little girls have come out to play. Under the elm trees, they are a flock of spring birds in their bright jumpers and smocks, raucous birds, arguing who will turn the skipping-rope, who was first in line. The oldest girl, already putting her hair up, her breasts and hips disrupting the straight lines of her mustard-coloured smock, struts into the fray and scatters the squabblers, each to her place, two to hold the rope, the rest to form a queue behind her.

She braces herself, taps her foot, nods her head in time with the beat of the rope, leaps in.

They have a new rhyme these days.

'He came out again last night,' the girl sings.

'Who did? Who did?'

'The Gardener, that's who!' She twists her body violently, as if gripped by a manic hand. Her rich brown hair flies free of its moorings. A butterfly hairslide clatters into the road.

'Carved another woman up!' She slides her hand across her neck. Her eyes roll and her tongue lolls out.

A little ringleted girl at the end of the queue covers her eyes and cries, 'Sadie, don't!'

'Better watch out.' The older girl waves a menacing finger. 'He'll get you too.'

'How do you know?' her companions shout. 'Who told you so?'

> 'Better watch out. Don't go about.
> He's creeping in the night.
> The Gardener with his . . . pruning knife!'

She raises her right arm, plunges her fist against her breast, then laughs and leaps out of the rope, her face rosy as an apple, her hair tumbling about her shoulders. One striped stocking has come loose from its garter and hangs down over her buttoned boot. As another girl takes her place in the rope, she runs to the back of the line, jabs a hairpin into the ribs of the little ringleted girl, who screams, 'Sadie, don't! I'll tell Mama,' and the chant resumes: 'He came out again last night!'

The rhyme appals the parents of these children, but my sensibilities are not offended by the game. I understand well the rituals for ridding the heart of its terror and cleansing the soul of its hereditary taint. Highflown words, you demur, Mother. My Mary invests too much significance in childish play. Like hermits everywhere, she begins to see angels and devils emerge from the common sod to wage great battles, and fancies herself infallible interpreter of universal rights and wrongs. Next she will receive visitations and spout in tongues.

Wait. Let me present my own case before you judge me grown eccentric, boastful. You know, Mother, none better, that through all my childhood and the delicate, perilous years of youth, I was subject to the whims and decrees of an autocrat. I lived constantly in the shadow of a self-appointed god, more terrible, more exacting, more vengeful than the One on high. In truth, though he professed to raise me to love and fear my Maker, and though I pretended faith and devotion, I was never God's handmaiden but his only. When I sat with him in his study, my sombre and oppressive schoolroom, reading aloud from the Bible or copying passages, his dark presence got between me and the Scriptures so that I could not hear the word of God above the sound of my father's breathing, heavy with disapprobation. How sonorously he would inhale if I stumbled over a difficult word; his sighs when I blotted my copybook were thunderous, the boom of the sea in an underground cavern. His snort of contempt was leonine, his hisses venomous, his grunt when, rarely, my efforts satisfied, a rumble from the depths of a volcano. I lived under his breath, quailed under his black eyes, cowered when his hands reached for me. For you know, Mother, he reached only in anger, to pull my hair or my nose if my blunders irritated him; to grasp my shoulders and shake me insensible or, with one blow, strike me to the ground, if the error were grievous in his view and his fury aroused.

One morning in midwinter, a robin hopped on to a branch

outside the study window. He was a fine dandyish fellow in his scarlet waistcoat, and he had just come from a feast, set out by you on the back porch. He puffed out his little chest, chirped, and ruffled his feathers as if to say, 'Aren't I grand? Come, admire me!'

I laughed aloud.

My father lifted his head from his sermon notes. 'What noise did I just hear, Mary?'

'You heard me laugh, Father.'

'Ah, I thought so. Pray tell me what, in your reading, is a source of mirth?' He folded his hands, leaned towards me, his face a parody of geniality, attentiveness, one black eyebrow comically raised as if, upon hearing the joke, he too might laugh. 'Is it in the Book of Job that you find merriment? Do the Ten Commandments amuse you? Or perchance you are entertained by the doings in Sodom? Come, child, speak. Enlighten me.'

'It was not the Bible made me laugh, Father. There is a bird in the tree outside the window.'

He turned his head. Under his lowering gaze, the robin promptly flew away. He brought his eyes to bear on me again, to bore into me like shards of ebony, to sear me like live coals.

'A bird made you laugh.'

I bit my lip . . . so violently, Mother, I tasted blood on the tip of my tongue.

'So you are bird-watching this morning?'

'I happened to glance up–'

'You happened to glance up.' It was another trick of his, to repeat my excuses, my reasons. On his tongue, my words sounded ludicrous, the pratings of an idiot. 'Am I to conclude then that God's holy word does not engage you? That, so easily distracted, you must find your lessons tedious?'

I made no answer. Impossible to give him the truth, and a denial would merely feed the fire rising in his blood. He wanted an apology, and that I would not offer. Unlike you, Mother, I always withheld a part of myself from him. Obedience and service I would give, yes, to ensure my survival, but I never stooped to servility, I think. I never fell to my knees, as I have seen you do, except when he knocked me to them. I never laid my pride upon his altar, never offered up my soul as sacrifice.

Perhaps that is why he tolerated you, could even on occasion permit you some small indulgence – a brief smile, a few pennies from his pocket, permission to visit a friend in the town. Me, he hated and despised, knowing that I would never be wholly his possession.

I do not blame you, Mother. I propose, merely, that I devised different means for coping with oppression and formed myself into a woman unlike you in my dealings with him. Our tastes and pleasures coincide marvellously, and harmony reigns in my heart and senses in your dear company, yet there is a part of me that cries out 'I will not!' in response to those dark demands; or 'I will!' in defiance of those brutal prohibitions that rendered you abject, prostrate before the sword and the sickle of his rapacious will.

You complied, placated, pleased. I mutinied!

His words, his actions, his looks, spawned revulsion in my breast; loathing germinated the seeds of resistance, expediency nurtured them, and desolation brought forth the dark, secret flower of revenge.

I had means, Mother. A recourse and a refuge were at hand that winter morning when, thrice, he slapped my face for the sin of laughter and led me out of the house, without even a shawl for protection, and commanded me to walk in the garden an hour to freeze the devil that roiled within.

'Contemplate this barren scene,' he said as we stood, side by side, in the porch, his arm about my shoulders, his fingers digging into the grey serge of my sleeve to discover and punish the flesh. 'Contemplate and compare it with the landscape of your heart where goodness cannot flourish while you are in Satan's grip. Your mind is fallow, Mary, your body infertile, your soul impotent, your entire being a wasteland like unto this wintry garden until you prostrate yourself at the feet of Jehovah. You must submit in order to be raised up, humble yourself so that you may receive mercy. Wipe the dust from His feet and He will lift you on to His bosom . . .'

On and on he ranted, confusing himself and his Lord in his vaunting demands, while I shivered with cold and writhed in pain. Ah, Mother, oft when I disrobed at night, took off my plain grey dress, removed the modest white tucker and prim lace collar, the bruises and contusions I beheld befuddled my mind, belied my certainty, and, verily, I thought it was a whore's body I viewed in the mirror, not a virgin's.

At last the flow of recriminations ceased. He thrust me down the steps and stood above me, a figure clad all in black, save for the virtuous white collar of his calling; assuming the gigantic proportions, the monstrous rage, of the God he impersonated. He lifted his arm and pointed his finger the way I must go, down the garden path, away from the house, banished for an hour from one of God's sacred spots, the rectory, and from the presence of His holy minister, my father. Did he think, truly, in his arrogance, in his long-practised self-deception, that I suffered under this decree? The frosty air seared my limbs, but my heart – my heart rejoiced at the prospect of an hour's freedom.

I glimpsed your face, Mother, at the kitchen window, white as his dog-collar, though with a vastly different import. You suffered to see me chastised and abused. Your fingers wove together in shapes of pain, and you pressed your hands against your lips to keep from calling out. I was better served, you believed, by your private alliance than by an open display of your partisanship. My arbitress, you would waylay him as he returned to his study and plead for my reprieve or, at least, a lightening of the sentence. Sometimes, your gentle interventions succeeded; and sometimes, he spread the mantle of his rage to gather you, too, into its folds. Like God and the prophets, he was unpredictable, capricious.

In your eyes I saw bewilderment. Again I had disregarded your counsel to dissemble affection and respect, and, instead, perversely it seemed to you, revealed my repugnance. When he bid me to the judgment seat, you would have me crawl, weeping and penitent; or, another ploy you advocated, go with prancing feet and a yielding smile, so as to disarm his anger.

'Behave like a winsome child,' you whispered, '*his* child, and you will please him.'

'Dear Father,' I should have cajoled, as I crossed the vast space between my cold corner and his armchair next the fire, 'the robin is God's creature, too, and I laughed for joy.'

'How so, Mary?' he might have answered, his mood tempered by my pious words and meek tone. 'Tell me, how does God make us joyful?'

I could then have assumed a girlish gait and demeanour, imitated your soft blush and fluttering hands, wooed him as you do, and so dissipated his ill-humour that when I reached his black throne he would be disposed to listen to my entreaty.

I would next say, 'I laughed, Father, to think what a various world my Redeemer has created, teeming with divers species – and gazing upon the robin, I thought, too, my Father in Heaven loves and protects even this small insignificant bird. How great, then, His love for me, fashioned in His image and possessing an immortal soul.' Then I might lift my head, peep at him under trembling lashes and say, 'Is not this knowledge ample cause for happiness?'

'Out of the mouths of babes and sucklings . . .' or some other platitude would have been his response had I done all this, and he would have patted my head, perhaps, or drawn me into his arms.

God forbid! I would sooner cut out my tongue, maim my body, walk through fire, than play this role. I could more easily bear the torturer's rack or the inquisitor's thumbscrews than his caress. Let him heap pain and scorn on me, whip me, box my ears, pull out my hair in handfuls, I would bear it all, so long as he never subjected me to the ultimate horror of his embrace.

I turned from your grey eyes, the colour of neutrality, watching through the window, and began to walk down the avenue between the dead rose bushes . . . my path of thorns. I heard him slam the front door and knew that you would hurry to meet him in the passage and make your plea on my behalf. Most likely, he would indicate that words would not suffice and draw you into his study. There you would be forced to perform those abominations he inflicted upon you often . . . you, the surrogate sinner, a Magdalen by proxy.

Knowing myself unobserved, I broke into a run, swerved from the path and raced across the iron-hard ground to the copse. Here, rotted vines clung to the bare alders and interlaced the spaces between like a giant spiderweb. Behind this drapery stood the old summerhouse. In former times, when the rectory was inhabited by less gloomy occupants, it may have served as a playroom for merry children, a trysting-place for sweethearts. During the years that we were tenants (fourteen they numbered by the time I speak of, for you and Father had taken up residence in the year of my birth), the summerhouse, neglected, had fallen into decay.

You never sat out there, Mother, in the pleasant sunshine, while you waited for me. Yet, when I envision *myself* with child – and, I confess, such visions still occur, though I am past childbearing – I see myself reclining on a white wicker sofa in the summerhouse; the alders heavy with foliage and dappled with sunlight, a natural canopy for my daybed; and the air all around me filled with birdsong, redolent of honeysuckle.

Each of us lives a secret life that intercepts and tempers reality. In the life of my fancy, I am at home again, with Father gone, and you and I released at last from tyranny, the summerhouse restored, half a dozen children playing and prattling about our skirts, and Alf . . .

Ah, here the tenuous dream-life rips apart and sticks to my fingers like gossamer threads when I would repair it. Even in fancy, Alf will not fit into the tapestry I weave.

I came then, Mother, to the door of the summerhouse, my own and only private place, lifted the latch and entered. Inside, the house forms a perfect circle, and so I fancied it a magic ring such as I have read the faeries make. Crossing the threshold, I passed from our world into theirs. The faeries, old hidden storybooks informed me, are lawless creatures, ruled only by instinct and desire. They make no distinction between right and wrong, possess no concept of error or repentance. In their world, spells and charms hold sway, not decrees and commandments. Malice and trickery they do know, not because they are vengeful like us, but because, immune to mortal suffering, their mirth springs from tormenting befuddled humans. Thus, their laughter is never adulterated by shame or guilt. Why should they mourn that we mortals persist in self-flagellation and other foolishness?

In the summerhouse, where only a circular covering of meshed wire separated me from the copse, and where great gaps in the domed roof bid the sky enter, I became a changeling, a sorceress, and reduced my omnipotent father to a buffoon.

The summerhouse was not empty. Other families had left belongings deemed too old and moth-eaten to take with them when they moved, a sagging chintz sofa, its faded cushions piled with dead leaves, a cane chair missing one leg, a box of broken toys, a weatherbeaten chest filled with discarded clothes, stacks of mildewed books and yellowed newspapers, and an eyeless rocking-horse that creaked in the wind as if ridden by the ghost of some long-departed child . . .

And something else, too, inhabited the summerhouse. A thing I had fashioned and kept there, and which I visited whenever Father, or my own compulsion, drove me from the rectory. It hung from a cord I had fastened to a hook in the roof, and it turned and twisted in the same wind that rode the rocking-horse, for all the world like a body dancing on a gibbet. For that is what it was, Mother – a life-sized effigy assembled from pillowcases and a bolster I had smuggled out of the house, stuffed with rags and straw, and dressed in Father's wedding suit stolen from the attic.

The head I constructed from papier mâché, using wads of the old newspapers that lay in the summerhouse, mixing flour and water in a bucket I borrowed from the kitchen, moulding my creation into a replica – a cartoon – of his stern and arrogant features. Ah, I enjoyed that part, Mother! I prodded and squeezed my sculpture, gouged out his deep-set eyes, dragged my nail across his heavy brow to replicate the frown lines there, pulled on his nose until it hooked like an eagle's beak, pinched his full lips and clamped them shut, tweaked his ears and, finally, placed both my hands about his neck and strangled him to death.

Burnt matches served to colour his black eyes and brows, blood drawn from my own finger reddened his mouth, and for hair and whiskers I gave him the remnants of a charred mop I discovered in the summerhouse and set fire to myself, stamping on the blaze when I judged the hue and texture correct.

What a clown he looked when I was done! Yet, the resemblance was close, and my heart exulted when I had tied the rope and suspended him from the hook. I congratulated myself on my invention, marvelled at my ingenuity, and felt, for the first time, the euphoria of malicious gaiety. I looked on my hanging man and gloated, Mother!

But this is not the end of it. I come now to the second part of my revenge. My foe was cornered and depended upon my mercy. Amen! I showed him no quarter. Does not the Old Testament say, 'An eye for an eye, a tooth for a tooth'? God Himself has granted us permission to flay our enemies and cast them down. I gave him tit for tat, cut a stout stick from the copse and belaboured him until he jigged indeed and his innards spilled out. And as I thrashed him, I cried, 'Hypocrite! Pharisee! Swindler! Whited Sepulchre! Judas! Father of Lies! Cockatrice!' and many more insults – or, rather, home truths – that flowed unceasingly from my tongue as if I were divinely inspired.

For a space, the beatings and the invectives appeased my appetite for revenge . . . for a space, but not for long. All too soon, a growing sense of unfulfilment replaced the satiety I had first experienced at the end of a strenuous bout with tongue and stick. As with all pleasures too frequently indulged, this one began to pall, even as my desire to mortify my persecutor increased. Necessity, too, forced a change of tactics. He was becoming so mangled, so lacerated from the floggings that I feared to obliterate him entirely and thus defeat my purpose. Punish him I must, but also, perforce, preserve him. It was with this dilemma in my mind that I entered the summerhouse on that morning with which my tale commenced.

There he hung, a ludicrous and sorry scarecrow with straw and rags dangling from the cavities in his arms, legs and chest. One leg was almost severed at the knee, one arm drooped for lack of padding as if withered by leprosy or some other wasting disease, a great gash across his waist promised soon to divide his torso, and his head sank upon his chest – his hair manged, his nose broken, his bulbous bottom lip swinging loose, attached only by a thread.

From the oak chest I took a musty blanket, wrapped myself in it for warmth, and sat among the crumbling leaves on the old sofa to contemplate my handiwork and fathom a new torture that would degrade but not destroy the puppet.

My mind wandered back along the way I had come, to the rectory, and to the two of you, and what you would now be about. As if I peeped through the study window, I saw you both, and the act that engaged you, as clearly as I had ever seen it in fact, kneeling to a keyhole or peering through a pane when you thought me out of the way, asleep in my bed or ejected from the house.

Again, I aver – I do not blame you, Mother. You were driven by desperation and diplomacy into schemes and machinations inimical to your nature. Demand, not desire, was your taskmaster. And yet . . . to concur in such lewdness, to gratify wishes so lascivious, to play the nymph to his satyr and demean yourself with a smile and feigned relish . . . I confess I wished you had chosen some other course, sought another means of intercession; or even, if all else failed, had resisted and borne the consequences as I did. Anything but that—

I never wanted you to do that, Mother!

Forgive me. My words suggest censure even as I vow sympathy. It is simply that the oft-repeated scene, imprinted on my heart, remains, years later, more vivid to me than the events of yesterday or the happenings of today. We never spoke of it. I never told you. Let me unburden now. Look through my eyes and see what I, your daughter, your dependant, your devotee, beheld:

He stood before you, his legs spread, his hands resting on his hips, a colossus of lust and scorn. You dropped to your knees in front of him and pressed your palms to his thighs, your face to the place between, and rubbed and kissed the coarse cloth there, lightly at first, then with increasing urgency until, when you lifted your head, your cheeks and lips blazed red from this rough contact. I felt your pain, Mother, remembering how the biting wind bruised and buffeted my face just so when I was put out of doors in harsh weather. He groaned when you paused in this activity, not for your suffering but for the deferment of his delight. He took your head in his hands and pressed it again to the place you had pleasured. Now, Mother, you moved your fingers and unbuttoned him and drew from its hiding-place the thing of horror, the swollen hungry thing that writhed in your hand and seemed to me to resemble one of those pale, deep-sea, carnivorous organisms composed of a single rigid stalk and a mobile, gaping mouth. This you drew to your own mouth and caressed in diverse ways, licking your tongue along its length, nibbling at it with your lips, pressing kisses upon it and, at last, allowing it to plunge deep until I thought you must surely swallow it. Instead, it brought forth a noxious liquid that spilled from your mouth and stained the bodice of your dress. He threw back his head and emitted howls, whinnies, yelps, the sounds of his bestial rapture. When, after some minutes, his composure returned, he raised you up. And then came the finale to this hideous circus. You stepped, willingly it seemed, into his arms and allowed him to press his mouth to yours in a long, intimate kiss while you patted, fondled, and at last returned to its cubby the thing that had so abased you, Mother.

I was seven when I first became an unwilling – but compelled! – voyeur of this atrocious burlesque. Another seven years passed until that dismal January day when I discovered the antidote to horror and initiated my own version of the charade with Father's witless twin in the summerhouse.

Huddled under the threadbare blanket, amid the decomposing leaves, I learned the significance of ritual. I had heard of the Black Mass, celebrated in dark woods in the deep of night by Satan's acolytes. To establish ascendancy over the Divine Enemy, they practicse contradiction and reversal, reciting the Lord's Prayer backwards, parodying Holy Communion with the real blood, the real flesh of newborns, and mocking the Virgin Birth with copulation between whores and rascals. To remedy the evil that blighted my life and drag the self-proclaimed god from his pedestal, I must do likewise.

I rose and crossed the circle, unbuttoned my manikin and repeated on him your ministrations, with this difference: when I lowered my head to that simulated place, it was not to nuzzle but to batter: when I opened my mouth, I spat where you had licked, bit where you nibbled, and when I had a piece of the cloth between my teeth, I tore until it ripped and I tasted dry straw and foul rags. And I laughed till the tears flowed.

When his voice rang stridently across the garden – before my hour was up, for you had softened him – I darted from the summerhouse, skirted the copse and returned, under cover of the privet hedge, to the front of the rectory, sauntering into view just as he called a second time.

'Why don't you come when I bid?' he said.

'I *am* come, Father,' I answered. 'Hastily.'

He grunted. 'Yours is a dawdling haste. Well, have you profited from your sojourn?'

'I have learned a great lesson.'

'See you remember it.'

He turned his back and strode indoors. I followed, smiling, the taste of his anguish still salting my tongue.

Yes, I know why the skipping girls jeer and scoff at the killer who menaces London. Ridicule assuages terror, defiance mends despair, and pretence is the only stronghold of the hapless. In my girlhood, the summerhouse was my sanctuary and my fortress, and if I had not there turned chaos into ritual, I surely would have murdered someone, Mother!

It passed ... or I passed beyond it. As these children must forsake the skipping-rope, I deserted my doll (though I never cut it down, and it outlived Father). I grew up. I grew less daring, more restrained. Alf appeared, and the wild witch-child was a guise I could no longer wear. It shrank like last year's frock when he cast a wishful eye on me; and I donned a new dress and said, 'Now I will be a woman.' And for a while, I lived within the gates of Paradise.

But that is another tale, and an old one. Father preached it often: 'Let your souls love God and ye shall live forever. Lust not after the flesh, for the flesh will die and rot in Hell.'

She who lusts must pay the price.

                Your loving Mary

8

Percy, Dai, Ivor: Saturday Afternoon

At five minutes to twelve, the Red Dragon, gasping and belching, grinds to a halt in Paddington Station, her banners grimy, streamers torn. She has striven valiantly against high odds – three hundred miles of uneven track, a faulty feeder, a crippling overload – to deliver the comrades to the front. Now her part in the war is over. Soon attendants will strip her of battle insignia, hose her down, and transform her into the sedate 3:15 to Swansea.

Out of her belly the Welshmen pour, like the Greeks from their wooden horse, or like their own reckless ancestors, leaping out of woods, armed with clubs and courage, to ambush the top-notch legions of Rome.

'Aw' right, 'ere they come,' a Cockney porter alerts the ticket collector. 'Stand yer ground and don't let any of 'em through wivout a ticket.'

'Gawd 'elp us,' the ticket collector cries as the horde bears down on him, 'are they 'uman?'

Dai Bando is one of the first off. Shoulders squared, legs apart, he plants himself in front of the door so that his compatriots, disembarking, must swerve to either side. Thus he keeps clear a little square of platform for Percy, when he comes, to alight with his suitcase.

Ivor Parry jumps down beside Dai. 'We made it in one piece then,' he says. 'I don't mind telling you I was afeared for my life on times.'

'Where's Percy, Ive?' Dai says.

'Coming, coming. I told him to let the crowd off first. Easier then with his suitcase.'

'We have a big responsibility to that lad today,' Dai says.

Ivor purses his lips and sucks on his cigarette. 'How's that then?'

'We got to see he has a good time, Ivor, from first minute to last. This is his big binge. We got to give him something to remember. But in addition . . . we have to take great care it don't break his heart. See the problem?'

Ivor's face assumes a reflective cast, as if he ponders the difficulty his mate suggests. His eyes, Dai observes, are the same leaden grey as his raincoat.

'I don't follow you, Dai,' Ivor says at last. 'What's his heart got to do with it?'

'If we show him too much, let him out on a rope too long, he may pine ever after in captivity.'

'Captivity!' Ivor jerks his head back and stares down his nose at Dai, an expression that often assails him during his Sunday evening sermons when, recounting certain unsavoury episodes from the Bible to warn his congregation against folly and vice, he is struck forcibly by the horrors of human depravity. 'What a word to use for the blessed state of holy matrimony.' His voice wheezes with shock and swallowed smoke. 'That's an insult to the Lord, Dai.'

'Why?' Dai says. '*He* didn't invent marriage. Adam and Eve were living tally, weren't they?'

'Never! That's blasphemy—'

''Course they were, Ive. God just put them in the garden and let them get on with it. Marriage in't natural and it in't holy—'

'I could debate this with you,' Ivor says, 'if I had my Bible handy. But it don't have nothing to do with Percy—'

'Yes, it do. He don't want to get married.'

'Get away!' Ivor jerks a second time. 'Did he tell you that?'

'Yes,' Dai says, 'I believe he did—'

'You believe he did! That means he didn't say it straight out . . . and if he didn't say it, you're only guessing, in't you? It's a grave error that, it's sinful pride, Dai, to think you can read another's mind.' Now it's Ivor's turn to smile. 'What isn't said can't be taken as intended.'

'Touché,' Dai says, and transforms his broken posture into a mocking bow.

'Here's Percy,' Ivor says, his voice flat, as if the single thrust has sapped all his energy. 'We can get going now, butty.'

'Dai?' Percy calls, and Dai straightens up, pulls himself

together, and springs, as ably as a man with two good legs, to help with the suitcase.

'Turn it sideways, Perce,' he says.

'Oh, aye!' Percy laughs and colours. 'There's daft I am.' He turns his case to a more manoeuvrable position and steps off the train. 'I don't know where my brains are. I'm thinking like a baby today.'

'Only natural,' Dai says. 'You got more on your mind than luggage.'

'My mind *is* my luggage just now, that's the trouble.' Percy speaks mournfully, and arches the long, wilting stalk of his body down toward Dai, six inches shorter, like an attenuated vine in search of a sturdy stake. His face is pale and delicate, more suited to a girl than a feller, Ivor has always thought. (In fact, until Percy began to court Ellen, he had had suspicions about the lad.) Ivor watches, his bottom lip curving in disapproval, as Percy's lily-like face descends towards Dai's, his limbs closing the gap decent men observe in their intercourse with each other.

He's got no backbone, Ivor thinks. Lord knows how he'll bear up under the saddle of a wife and children. I'd be sorry in my heart to see a daughter of mine tied to such a wit-wat.

Dai, too, is perturbed by Percy's oscillations. For a moment, he dreads his young butty will fall on his chest in a swoon. He gets ready to support him. But no, Percy's calamity is not physical. His mouth opens when he is close enough to kiss Dai, and he says, too low for Ivor to hear, 'I had a long struggle with myself on the train, and I've made up my mind what to do. Before I tell you, I got a confession.' He pauses and sucks in air. 'Ellen's in the family way.'

'Christ,' Dai says. 'That's burned your boats then, hasn't it, boyo?'

Percy's head moves up and down, as if pulled on a string. His blue eyes water. 'I only got one option left—'

'You got to go through with it—'

Percy's head swings in the other direction, from side to side. 'I'm stopping in London—'

'Here, steady on.' Dai reaches up to grasp Percy's shoulders. 'Half a mo now—'

'What's the confab about, fellers?' Ivor comes beside them,

curiosity winning over distaste. 'Not nice to leave me out, is it?'

'No confab,' Dai says. 'Percy's a bit knocked out by the trip, that's all. Not used to travelling, are you, Perce?'

'A cup of tea will set him right,' Ivor says. 'I could do with one myself. Wouldn't say no to a plate of fish and chips either. I have to get my food regular or my ulcer plays murder. Bethan made me promise I'd have two full meals—'

'Shut up a minute, Ive,' Dai says. He presses his hard calloused fingers into Percy's stooped shoulders, hoping to knead some sense into the boy. Stopping in London, indeed! It never occurred to Dai that Percy might bolt. He'll have to watch him like a hawk. 'We got two hours before the match, Perce,' he says. 'Let's find a café and get some grub down us. You're hungry, see, and it's making you light in the head.'

'Yes, I'm hungry.' Percy's tone makes Dai more uneasy. 'Very hungry. Ravenous. Famished—'

Dai fastens his hand on Percy's wrist. He'll have to wangle an opportunity to speak to him alone, get Ivor out of the way for a bit, give him the slip if needs be, for things have taken a serious turn. Stopping in London! It's the most dismaying statement he's heard since, a year ago, the woman he still adores said, 'I'm not coming here any more, Dai. I can't square it with my conscience.'

When they reach the barrier and hand over their tickets, the porter says, 'Taking your time, mates. Ain't you anxious to get out and see the capital city?'

'Cardiff's our capital,' Dai says. 'Is there a place not far where we can get a decent meal?'

'Turn left outside the gates, left again on Windsor Terrace, and you'll come to the Royal Café.'

'Royal prices, too, I bet.' Ivor sniffs.

The ticket collector is staring at Percy. 'Is this young bloke all right?' he asks Dai. 'Looks like he's had a nasty turn.'

'He's just come over a bit faint,' Dai says. 'We had a jerky ride up, and it was close in the carriages. Once we're out in the fresh air he'll be right as rain, won't you, Perce?'

The three Welshmen pass through the barrier.

'Hope we don't give you too much of a battering this afternoon,' the porter calls after them. 'Don't want to send you blokes home blushing.'

'No fear of that,' Dai calls back. 'We got a top-drawer team.'

'Top in Wales, maybe, but not in England, mate. It's like pitting the top corgi against the top greyhound, ain't it?' The ticket collector laughs.

The porter slaps him on the back. 'That's a good one, Eddie.'

'"Pride cometh before a fall,"' Ivor intones. And raising his voice, 'Just you wait. We'll be laughing ourselves silly next time you see us.' As they come out of the station into the street, he says to Dai, 'Think the selection committee made a mistake putting Royston Pugh in so soon after his knee injury? Got me worried, that. He could be our side's weak link.'

'It's all politics, Ive,' Dai says. 'Royston's uncle is a big man in the Rugby Union. It's always who you bloody know, not what you know, in Wales.'

'That's a fact. Change hands for a bit with that suitcase, will you, Perce? It's making my leg black and blue.'

'Look how they passed young Marsden Thomas over, and he's been playing like a champion all season. Brilliant game against Ireland a few weeks back. Only Clem Lewis did better in my opinion.'

'Well, Clem's in at least. We got to turn left here. Not many people about, are there?' Ivor says. 'More crowds in Ponty market on a Saturday morning. Young Marsden have had a good season, but you could argue lack of experience against him, I suppose. Never played on the All-Wales team, has he?'

'That's a roundabout argument, Ive. How's he to get experience if they don't give him the chance? Fair do's.'

As they reach the Royal Café, Percy speaks up. 'Life is always unfair to the young,' he says. 'When we're most ready we're most denied and hoodwinked. All things conspire to cramp and crush us.' He straightens his body suddenly and throws back his blond head. 'But we mustn't stand for it! We got to shout at the top of our lungs, "No!"'

The few people on the street turn to look at the trio. Ivor raises his eyebrows at Dai, his other features tautening in alarm. Percy, always a bit of a flag, seems to have flipped at last.

Dai, with a minute shake of his head, indicates to Ivor that Percy's lapse is passing not permanent, and hustles the young man into the café where they are immediately greeted by the mingled aromas of various fried fare and the pungent scent of Indian tea brewing.

When they have settled themselves at a window seat and given the waitress their orders ('And bring our teas straight away, love,' Ivor tells the girl. 'We're sinking for a cuppa') Dai and Ivor resume their discussion of the Welsh fifteen.

'Pity Trew's out,' Dai says. 'We could do with him today, but the doctor wouldn't pass him, would he? Passed Pugh, but not him . . . funny business, uh?'

'We got a warhorse in Hywel Humphrey, anyway,' Ivor says. 'No stopping him once he's got the ball.'

'Aye, well the English side know that, don't they? You can bet they've been briefed to keep him out of the game. Be on him like jackals this afternoon . . . but it's the bad man in that worries me most. Royston Pugh's not a team player, and that could prove to be a worse injury to our side than his gammy knee.'

Percy, tuning out this tedious talk (he's never been a rugby fanatic; that's not why he's in London today), stretches his long legs under the table, drapes one arm over the back of his chair, and turns his eyes to the window.

He has reached a crucial decision and must plan, now, a course of action. First, how to escape from Dai, who has gripped him tight, with hands and eyes, ever since he mistakenly confided in him on the platform at Paddington. Up to now, Dai has always given him unstinting sympathy and encouragement, and Percy has come to think of him as a mentor, indeed, as a replacement for his own father who died of silicosis when Percy was nine. He is surprised and hurt that Dai has switched loyalties and takes Ellen's part. Surely, he should see it would be a marriage based on exigency, a back-door alliance that springs, not from love, but from irony, because he, Percy, was awake before he was wise? What hope of happiness for him, Ellen, or the baby, tied by the frail cords of predicament? Believing that Ellen, kokum beyond her years, took advantage of his ignorance to put the mockers on him, he must feel bitter towards her, and resent, too, her instrument, the unborn child.

So I'll bring them both to sorrow, staying instead of going, Percy thinks. They'll do better without me. Once I get a job in London I can send money, and Ellen's young. She can move to another town, give out that she's a widow, and marry a man for love, a well-to-do chap possibly, for she's pretty enough and a smart dresser. Sometimes you have to cause a person temporary misery to secure her well-being in the long run.

Ellen can only see the here-and-now, her vision limited by the narrow valley she was born in and its shortsighted customs. But I have stood on the mountain top and my eyes have penetrated the magic mists of destiny. One day, Ellen will look back and say, 'Funny, all my good luck dates from the day I thought my heart would break.' And she'll thank me then, though I won't know it, for I'll be in some faraway clime, never again heard or seen in Avon Fach after I vanished at the Wales–England rugby game.

What about my Mam though? She might go to pieces, for I'm her favourite, and she pulled me through double-pneumonia and St Vitus's Dance, and she's a big chapel woman, too. And if there's no wedding, there'll be no reception, and she'll have gone to the expense of knocking two rooms into one and buying a three-tier cake for nothing . . .

. . . And what if Ellen *don't* recover and meet a good husband? What if she pines for me and goes out of her head and can't look after the child? If it's a boy, it might grow up to be a hooligan, and if it's a girl, she might become a loose woman, or one that hates men. Or Mrs Allgood might bring it up, and it'll be the spit of her, even down to those dresses with the big flowers.

No matter what, good or bad outcome, there'll be shame on Ellen tomorrow, jilted at the altar, and people will talk behind her back ever after . . .

'Percy, your sausages and chips have come.'

Percy turns from the window to look into the stern face of Dai Bando, his eyes black and unyielding as small-coal, his mouth a knife slash across his face, so tightly he tucks in his lips.

'You haven't touched your tea,' Ivor says. 'It'll be lukewarm by now.' He lays his half-smoked cigarette in the ashtray and takes up his knife and fork. 'Chips look a bit limp, but plenty of gravy on the pie. Pass the salt, Dai, please.'

'Eat, Percy,' Dai says.

Percy looks down at the two fat brown sausages, pink mincemeat showing through their blistered skin, beside them a mound of pale chips, piled one upon the other and splattered with sauce, shaken on by Ivor. The plate of food is a picture, an omen, a configuration of his future should he weaken and let myopic Propriety with its guttering candle be his guide, instead of enlisting under the high-flying banner and shining sword of Destiny.

He pushes the plate from him. 'I won't eat,' he says. 'I got no stomach for offal.'

9

Mari: Saturday Afternoon

As she strolls along the deserted promenade at Brighton, Mari, who prides herself as a connoisseur of colours (a skill indispensable to one who lives by magic), plays a naming game, picking out the many shades of grey that tint the afternoon.

Above her head a battleship sky glowers, darkening to gunmetal over the distant granite cliffs where seagulls wheel and a storm threatens. Below the olive-grey railings of the promenade, the damp sands have a pearly sheen; and beyond the beach, the wide calm expanse of sea is a variegated quilt, a patchwork of greys, bright as steel where a vacillating sun glints on its surface, leaden under the shadow of the cliffs, plumbago where it meets the smoky lilac horizon.

Fickle weather, can't make up its mind to rain or shine! Last Saturday, Worthing Pier was wrecked in a gale. 'I wouldn't go to the seaside if I was you,' Mrs Perkins said. 'You could be risking life or limb.'

Rubbish! It's in London, not in Brighton, that danger lurks.

Forget about London for now, Mari! That's why you're here. Look at the scenery . . . all these greys. What's the composition, eh? Mesh all these hues and tones, and what's the prevailing mood, would you say?

Well . . . grey is a neutral colour, it doesn't arouse passion, stir the emotions, give flight to fancy. I don't often use it on stage for those reasons, unless . . .

Except when I do my levitating-woman act. I always wear a pearl-grey robe for that, and swathe my hair in a matching chiffon turban to mute it, and Bert shines the mauve spotlight on me, all the rest of the stage in shadow. Puts the audience in a sad mood, brings a yearning on them. That's the effect I aim for, 'cause levitation is akin to raising spirits, and they all have ghosts they'd like to wake. So, when I float six feet up in the air, it's not me they're seeing but their own secret apparitions.

Is he dead then, do you think?

Ah, I don't know! Don't bring that up, not this afternoon, my holiday . . .

It's your greatest fear. May as well face it.

I'd rather fancy him in another woman's arms, mindless of me, casting me further from him with every warm word and deep embrace than to believe he's an ashy corpse. I'd rather he was a traitor than a dead man!

A traitor to king and country?

England wasn't his country. Nor Italy neither, to hear him talk. 'I am a sojourner, Mari,' he used to tell me – beautiful words he used, Antonio – 'I have no home but you.' He wasn't happy with the way the world is. He wanted to see the rich cast down, the poor raised up, and government done away with . . .

He was preaching anarchy only you were too besotted to know it!

I knew he was talking trouble and I said so. (I didn't dream he was an Anarchist until he told me!) 'You're courting trouble,' I said, 'with those thoughts.'

'Yes, trouble!' he cried, and he leaped up in bed, all excited, as if I'd said something lovely. 'Trouble is my mistress, the only rival of you. But don't be sad, *carissima*. I don't love her . . . only, she has bewitched me with a vision!'

Ah, he raved like a lunatic, and his words cut right through me (reminding me he'd had a knife in his hand when I first saw him) and I was wild with jealousy, as if there was really a woman come between us. But there, it makes no difference, does it, woman or thing? Whatever steals your man, the feelings are the same.

Mari stops walking and rests her arms on the rail, one hand under her chin. A breeze whips up from the beach to bell her skirt and tug at her chignon, prying the pinned hair loose and tossing it in ringlets about her face. She should have brought her coat. It's not cold exactly, but the powder-blue merino costume was fashioned for the milder days of spring. It does not resist the March wind, which whisks up under her petticoat and thrusts chilly fingers between the grenadier fastenings on her jacket.

She had thought to walk as far as the Palace Pier where, one summer evening, she and Antonio had sauntered arm-in-arm under the slender arches sparkling with fairy lights. Instead, since seeing the pier today will not warm her, she turns and scans the front for shelter. Not too far ahead, among the bay-windowed hotels, she spots the red awning of a restaurant, an 'Open' sign in the plate-glass window.

It's well past midday dinner-time, and Mari remembers she's had nothing, not even a cup of tea, since breakfast. Cheered to discover a hunger and thirst that can be gratified, she sets off briskly, humming to keep her renewed spirits buoyant, a song from Doris's repertoire:

> As I walk along the prom
> With an in-de-pen-dent air,
> You can hear the girls declare,
> That's the man who broke the bank
> At Monte Carlo!

The restaurant is empty. A waitress, some years older than Mari, moves languidly among the tables, flicking a feather duster over the white cloths.

'Not doing a roaring trade today, are you, love?' Mari says as she takes a seat.

'It's out of season.' The waitress crosses to the cutlery table, picks up a knife and fork and a linen napkin and brings them, slowly, to Mari. In her long black dress, her face whitely powdered, her movements listless, she wouldn't be out of place at a funeral. 'If you'd come last week, we wouldn't even have opened up yet. What'll you have? Most things are off.'

Mari scans the menu, which doesn't take a minute, so many items are scratched out. 'I'll take a poached egg on toast and a cup of tea, please.'

As she gives her order, the waitress looks at her curiously, her eyes travelling from Mari's bountiful hair down over the lines of the merino costume to her black leather boots. 'Visiting relatives in Brighton?'

'I'm visiting the sea.'

'Didn't choose a very good day for it.' She has dyed blonde hair, piled high on her head in elaborate curls. Her eyes are red-rimmed (a cold, or some private grief?), her lips chapped. Now

Mari is curious. Why does she take so much trouble with her hair and then disregard her face – no rouge, no lip salve, all that spectral powder!

'I don't mind the weather. It keeps the crowds away. I like Brighton when it's quiet.'

The waitress compresses her nostrils and gives a soft little snort. 'You wouldn't say that if you had to live here like I do. It's a dead hole from October to May. Hard to make ends meet, too, through the winter. Do you want your egg fried, scrambled or poached?'

'Poached, please,' Mari says again.

She watches the waitress shuffle across the dining room to the kitchen, her body moving stiffly beneath the long black skirt, as if she has no joints from the waist down. She can't be more than forty, but from the back she looks like a life-battered sixty, reminding Mari of the elderly women she sees on the streets of London, flower-sellers, pie vendors, hawkers of lace doilies and collars, hoarsely crying out their wares as they take the last reluctant steps on the long road of toil. At home, she has a drawer full of doilies and embroidered hankies she'll never use, and every evening in summer she arrives at the Palladium with a corsage of violets in her lapel.

'If you'd saved all of them sixpences,' Mrs Perkins said when she offered her the pick of the drawer, 'you'd have pound notes stacked in there instead of fripperies.'

'You have a good heart,' Antonio said, 'but a misguided one. The little gesture makes no great matter.'

'I know that,' she said, 'but what else can I do?'

'Be a fighter,' he said. 'Turn your soft heart to steel and join the rebels.'

'Do you mean them suffragettes? Chain myself to railings and get carted off in the Black Maria? I couldn't make myself such a spectacle!'

'Not the suffragettes. Brave ladies, but *British* to the stump. They still believe in government–'

'I should hope so! We wouldn't get far without it–'

'No vision,' he said, his face dark, unloving, 'you, the suffragettes, all the people of this country. You are stupid, Mari. Happy to dole out your hard-worked money to your government–'

'Hard-*earned*,' she had corrected him, and flounced out of the room, pained that he found fault with her. It hadn't been all honey living with Antonio.

The waitress comes from the kitchen, bearing a tray with Mari's food. Poor thing! What a life hers must be. Perhaps, too, she has ailing parents to support, or a shiftless husband, children to keep in shoes and stockings. At least Mari has only herself to worry about, and a job she loves.

Ah, but is it comfort to know you're alone in the world? And if Alf's on the mark, might she not be shortly out of work?

'How do you keep yourself in winter?' Mari asks as the waitress slides her plate in front of her. 'Must be hard when the restaurant's shut?'

'I do for the gentry. Cleaning, washing, and that. What line are you in?'

'Entertainment.'

'Oh yes?' The waitress compresses her nose.

'I do a magic act at the London Palladium.'

'Got to watch out for the men, I'm sure. It's not easy for a woman to be on the stage . . . if she's respectable, I mean. Gives a man ideas about her.' The waitress's eyes have fixed on the gilt buttons that fasten Mari's jacket snugly over her breasts. 'Do you have a lot of bother with men?'

'I manage to avoid it.' Mari sips her tea. It's scalding hot and burns her tongue. She puts the cup down and lifts a forkful of food.

'And now there's a murderer on the rampage.'

The fork halts at Mari's lips. Her mouth is open, but she can't take the food in.

'Be hard to avoid *him* if he had you marked, wouldn't it?'

Why has the waitress suddenly swerved to murder as a topic, uttering words that sound like prophecy? Is she the mouthpiece of some malevolent force, reminding Mari that she can't escape, that her days are numbered no matter which way she stumbles? She lowers the fork to the plate, her appetite flown.

'I'll have my bill.'

'You're not finished.'

'I'll have it all the same.'

'Fourpence for the egg on toast. Tuppence for the tea.'

Mari opens her purse. This is pay day so there's not much in there. She takes out a sixpence and places it on the table. Why tip the waitress for giving her bad news and ruining her meal? Then she thinks of the woman's hard life, sighs, and dips into her purse again. She has four shillings and three sixpences left for her fares and for dinner at Nan's Pantry tonight before the show. She puts another sixpence on top of the first one, deciding she'll do without dessert.

Outside the restaurant, Mari pauses to compose herself and plan her next move. Should she visit the Pavilion King Geoge IV built when he was Prince Regent? Might be something going on there, a band concert or an exhibition. But she has no heart for jaunting now. Another walk along the prom then, since it's on her way to the station and she needs some deep breaths of fresh sea air. As she passes the window of the restaurant, she sees the waitress sitting at the table she left, drinking her tea and eating her poached egg.

The long promenade stretches drearily into the distance, its only visitors the gulls who swagger on the paving-stones or squawk and tussle around the penny peep-show machines. Half a mile away the Palace Pier rises, a blind hump-back monster on spindly legs. At the end of the beach, the sea, turned cross, hurls debris.

'Ah, it's gloomy,' Mari says. 'I don't know why I came. I've not enjoyed myself.'

From the belly of the pier a figure emerges, tottering as it crosses the wooden planks to the prom. At first, Mari can't make out whether it's a man or a woman, for it is covered, neck to ankles, in a long shapeless overcoat, the collar turned up to hide half its face. The straggly white hair she can see is sexless.

But as she watches, approaching on slower feet, the figure pulls from a pocket a crushed bowler hat, punches a fist into the crown, puts it on its head, and assumes a gender. He turns down his collar and rubs his hands along the length of the coat, as if he hopes to smooth out its myriad stains and creases. Then he reaches behind one of the slot machines, produces a walking-stick topped by a fancy knob, and proceeds spryly towards Mari, whom he has spotted now, for he grins and touches the knob of his stick to the brim of his bowler hat, his shoulders squaring smartly.

When they are level, Mari sees that he is getting on, in his seventies probably, but with a good colour in his face, sharp blue eyes, and what look like all his own teeth. His large veined nose is red and shiny as a hawthorn at its bulbous tip (but that's not from fresh air, I'll be bound, she thinks). Still, tippler or no, he cuts a fine figure for a man his age and wearing slept-in clothes.

'Afternoon,' he greets Mari, and without more ado, 'Spare threepence for a cuppa, can you? I left me wallet at home.'

Mari opens her purse and hands him a sixpence. 'You can get something to eat for that, as well. They're open . . .' She points back towards the restaurant she has just left.

The tramp shakes his head. 'Too posh for a chap like me. I know a homely place up the town that'll do me proud for a tanner. Thank you kindly, miss. You'll be rewarded for your generosity.'

'That's what they all tell me! Don't squander the lot on booze, will you?' But of course he will. He didn't get that garnet nose bending over bowls of hot soup. She makes to pass on.

'From London?' the tramp says.

'That's right. How did you know?'

'London's the only place for a handsome girl like you . . . and them clothes was bought in Oxford Street, or I'm a tailor's dummy. Spent a lot of time in London in me youth. I was better set up then. A gent, you might say.'

'Really? Well, mind how you go. I have to be getting to the station–'

The old man turns about. 'I'll accompany you. They're doing out me room at the Grand so I've time to kill.'

'That's a smart walking-stick,' Mari says, to make conversation as they go along.

'A souvenir of me past life. I wouldn't pawn this stick if I was starving. Part of me get-up it was when I went out on the town on a Saturday night. Do you know the Palladium in Leicester Square by any chance?'

'I should say I do. I work there.'

He stops and looks up at her. 'Go on! Fancy that. I wish I had a tanner in me pocket for every show I seen at the Palladium. Singer are you?'

'I do a bit of singing, but magic's really my line–'

'A star at the Palladium! Here, let me shake your hand. What's your name, if I might ask?'

'Mari Prince,' Mari says, 'but onstage I go as The Infamous Princess Marie.'

The old man slaps his forehead. 'I knew it! I knew I'd have heard of you. Mari Prince. That's a famous name in music hall.'

'You must be thinking of Marie Lloyd—'

'Never, Marie Lloyd's past it now, I wouldn't mix her up with a young lady like yourself. Mari Prince is the name, right enough. I've heard you highly spoken of by them what goes up to the shows. You got a rare talent they say.'

'Well, you must come to the show on me if you're ever in London again.' She knows he's buttering her up, getting ready to ask for another hand-out most likely, but she can't take umbrage with one so down-and-out yet so zesty. She could never be as cheerful if she slept on the Palace Pier at night.

'Used to do a turn meself at the Palladium. Long before your time, mind. You won't have heard of me, but Harold Bains is the name. I'll show you a bit of me act, shall I?'

She'll never get to the station at this rate, but he is looking up at her with such a daft, happy smile she hasn't the heart to say no.

'Just you stay where you are and pretend you're in the stalls at the Palladium.' He trots several yards ahead, turns, and calls 'Ready?'

'Curtain!' Mari calls back.

And he comes strutting towards her, his coat flung open to show off an ancient three-piece suit, one hand on his hip, the other twirling his cane as he rasps the words of a song Mari knows well:

> I'm Henery the Eighth, I am!
> Henery the Eighth, I am! I am!
> I got married to the widow next door,
> She's been married seven times before—

When he reaches Mari he cries, 'Join in now! Let's hear it from you!' and they sing in unison as he marches up and down in front of her, turning his toes out, swinging his shoulders, bearing the stick in his fist like a sceptre, their voices rising merrily over the shrieks of the gulls and the pounding of the ocean:

> Ev'ry one was a Henery—
> She wouldn't have a Willie or a Sam.
> I'm her eighth old man named Henery,
> Henery the Eighth, I am!

'My socks, that brings back happy memories,' Harold says, slapping Mari on the shoulder. 'And you can belt out a song good as me. Bet you get encores up at the Palladium!'

'More for my magic than my singing—'

'I'll give you a sad 'un now, just to show you me range.'

'All right,' Mari says, 'but we better walk on. I can't miss my train.'

He offers his arm with a flourish, she takes it, and as they bowl along the street Harold gives a heart-felt, off-key rendering of 'The Miner's Dream of Home'. When he reaches the chorus he elbows her ribs and she joins him:

> I saw the old homestead, the faces I love—
> I saw England's valleys and dells;
> I listened with joy as I did when a boy,
> To the sound of the old village bells.

With tears in their eyes, they arrive at the station.

'No place like home,' Harold says. 'It's where the heart is, ain't it?'

'And only our hearts can go back.'

'You said a mouthful there. Here's where we part company, Miss Prince.'

'Pleased to have made your acquaintance,' Mari says. 'I enjoyed your act, Mr Bains. It gave me the perk I needed.'

The tramp sweeps off his bowler hat and lays it over his heart. 'Honoured, I'm sure.'

As she turns into the station, he says, as if he's just thought of it, 'Here, Miss Prince, couldn't manage another sixpence, could you? I'd like to stand a round at the Prince Albert tonight and drink yer health with me mates. It's been the day of me life, this has, a fallen star like me meeting one what's bright in the heavens.' He opens his palm and gives her a disarming, head-on-one-side grin. 'Got to look after each other in the profession, ain't we?'

Mari clicks her tongue. He's no more a veteran of music hall than she's a lord's daughter, but she has to admire his gall. She hands him a shilling. 'You deserve it for the show you put on,' she says. 'There's many half your age don't have your gumption. Good luck to you!'

'And to you, Madam.' He treats her to a bow as he slips the shilling into his pocket. 'You'll get it back, one way or another, mark my words. I'm something of a fortune teller. My old granny had gypsy blood in her veins. Cross me palm with silver and—'

Mari bursts out laughing and waves him off. 'No fear! All I got left is three and six. You're not doing me out of that, you old swindler.' She walks swiftly into the station.

'I'll come up and see you one of these days when I get me financial affairs in order,' Harold Bains calls after her. 'Treat you to a slap-up supper in the Strand.'

Mari raises her hand and wiggles her fingers. 'Toodle-oo!' she shouts, and sprints for her train as the guard blows his whistle.

The compartment she dives into is empty, as is most of the train . . . not many people travelling from Brighton to London at three o'clock on an overcast March afternoon. Mari sits in a corner by the window and puts her feet up on the seat opposite. As the streets of Brighton speed past, she smiles at her reflection in the darkening pane. He did her good, that old geezer. What a character! Half the fun of going out is the types she bumps into, and she does attract some rare ones, no mistake.

She takes off her hat and lays it down beside her, resting her head on the back of the upholstered seat. She looks around the carriage. The decor is red brocade, dusty, somewhat faded from the friction of many behinds; framed seascapes decorate the walls between the tops of the seats and the rope luggage racks. Gaslight casts a cosy glow over this interior, especially in contrast with the wintry sky and dark, flitting shapes outside the window.

Mari sighs.

Despite her aching calf muscles, she feels refreshed . . . content . . . and though it would be nice to have someone to chat with, someone with whom she'd shared the day, she tells herself, 'You can't have everything,' and begins to sing softly:

> Oh, Mr Porter, what shall I do!
> I wanted to go to Birmingham,
> But they've put me off at Crewe!

Perhaps tonight, after the show, she'll manage to persuade Doris to go home with her for a nosh and a natter. They'll share a meat pie and half a dozen bottles of stout – or something fancier, her treat – and she'll tell Doris about Harold Bains. If, later, when she's in her cups, her mood turns melancholy and she wants to reminisce about Antonio, Doris will hold her hand and give a sympathetic ear to her woes, and eventually Mari will drop off in the armchair – Doris must have the bed, of course – perchance to end a pleasant day with one of those happy dreams in which she is reunited with her lover . . . the love of her life . . . 'the next Caruso' . . . the gaslight brightens and he steps on to the stage, splendid in black bow tie and dinner-jacket, his hair brushed and brilliantined, his open hands and eloquent dark eyes uplifted as his heart-thrilling voice reverberates through the packed house and he sings 'O dolci mani' from *Tosca* ('For you, Mari. I sing for you–').

Mari's head bounces off her chest like an india-rubber ball as the train shudders to a halt. They have reached a station. The compartment door opens and a man enters. A quick glance before she turns her eyes modestly to the window shows her a top hat, a spruce moustache and goatee, a handsome theatre cloak, a silver-topped cane. A gentleman. But travelling by train, second class? Why isn't he in the front of the train, enjoying the comforts and services provided for first-class passengers?

Mari's heart speeds up as a likely answer occurs – he has come into this compartment because he saw her there. Should she feel flattered or frightened? Her heart doesn't know, it simply prepares for the unexpected, like a soldier leaping to attention. She lowers her feet from the opposite seat and plants them firmly on the ground, straightens her back, braces her shoulders, prepares for the fray if there's to be one.

Her companion thrusts one gloved hand into a breast pocket. Vigilant at the window, Mari tenses. He withdraws a silver cigarette case.

'Your permission to smoke, Ma'am?'

Mari turns and looks him in the face, a handsome face . . . if you like the type that seems moulded from marble, like the statues in Kew Gardens: high cheekbones, a Roman nose, hazel eyes; a haughty lift to the eyebrows repeated in the flare of his nostrils, the curl of his moustache, and the perfectly tapered V of his beard, the colour of an otter's pelt.

'Ma'am?'

'Yes?'

'May I smoke in your company?' Something in his tone, and in the tilt of his eyebrows, suggests there is a joke afoot, yet nothing humorous has been said.

'Please . . .' Mari says.

'Will you join me?' He proffers the case. Gold cuff links flash when he stretches out his arm, a signet ring glints on his finger.

Mari shakes her head.

'Ah, you don't. I beg your pardon. One never knows these days whether invitation or omission will give greater offence to the fair sex. So many ladies have taken to the habit.' He gives her a brief cool smile, then rolls up his eyes as if in despair at his failure to amuse.

Mari, who sees nothing funny in his remarks, can only stare.

That silk scarf . . . the gloves he has removed and placed across his knee . . . one of the murdered women was discovered with a scarf like that wrapped around her neck, another with just such a glove draped over her breast, steeped in the blood from the knife wounds.

Ah, stuff and nonsense! Expensive accessories are the mark of his station. Scotland Yard would have to round up all the rich men in London if kid gloves and a silk scarf make a man suspect. Her fellow-traveller is not the sort to commit murder. He's insolent, yes – she sees that in his gestures, hears it in his voice – but not violent or vicious. In fact, the well-bred profile he presents to her, his eyes turned now to the window, suggests one who sniffs at life and keeps a healthful distance from its more noxious odours. He'd never get his hands dirty . . .

Mari, immersed in a scrutiny of her carriage companion, becomes aware suddenly that she, too, is being inspected. Yet, he is not looking at her, is he? He faces the window–

The window! She raises her eyes. And meets his gaze in the glass turned mirror. For a moment, they stare at each other. Then–

'Caught!' he says, and turns his head to give her another arrogant smile. 'It appears, Ma'am, that we intrigue each other.'

Mari rubs one hand along the nap of her merino skirt; the other reaches out to touch her hat, to feel for the hat-pin stuck in its brim. Her fingers close on the pin's knob, an imitation pearl. She draws it out and shuts it in her palm.

'A mutual attraction, shall we say? Or is that too forward on my part?'

Well . . . she *was* studying him. What's a man supposed to think when a woman gives him the eye – or seems to?

'It's out of the common,' Mari says, 'a gentleman like yourself travelling second class.'

He takes a last draw on his cigarette and stubs it in the ashtray. Releasing smoke slowly from his barely opened lips, he contemplates Mari.

'It's none of my business though–'

'So I'm an anomaly, am I? A puzzle, eh? Well, so are you.' His mouth twitches up at one corner and he narrows his eyes, making his gaze more intense, more amused. 'It's not *common* to meet a female travelling alone in these uncertain times.'

'Uncertain?'

'You are surely aware, Ma'am, that a murderer is abroad?'

'In London,' Mari says. 'Not on the Brighton train.' Her fingers tighten around the hat-pin.

'True, but there's nothing to prevent him from changing his habits, is there?' He lifts one of his gloves from his knee and puts it on his left hand, smoothing the leather over his fingers. 'Who knows, he may want to add a little spice to what must by now have become rather mundane.' He puts on the other glove, as Mari watches, repelled and fascinated. So white . . . white as alabaster . . . and so pliant, like a second skin. 'Besides, our train terminates in the capital – his haunt – doesn't it? Are you not in the least perturbed, Ma'am?' He moves his gloved hands one over the other, stroking the kid. 'But perhaps friends are meeting you at Victoria?'

'I can look after myself,' Mari says.

'Ah, so you are a new woman, although you don't smoke to prove it. Tell me, do you think ladies should have the vote?'

Inside the gloves, he works his fingers, as if to make the fit more snug. Or as if to practise his grip! The space between his hands, between his gyrating knuckles, is the size of a woman's neck.

'I think we should be left alone–'

'Then you should have travelled in the "Ladies Only" compartment.'

Oh, she never thought of that!

'But perhaps neither of us are what we seem?' His smile indicates that he has made another joke, but Mari can't get the hang of his brand of repartee. Her brain is out-of-order, her heart working overtime: Escape! it cries with every beat.

Mari jams her hat on her head and gets to her feet. Her companion stands too – as a gentleman must when a lady takes her leave.

He bars her path to the door.

'Excuse me, please,' she says.

'But this is not a station–'

'Let me pass!'

'I had hoped to escort you–' He is a head taller than she. An imposing figure, with his hands on his hips, his cloak spread, blocking her view of the exit.

'Let me by, or–' She shows him the hat-pin.

His face alters, the smile giving way to a grimace. For an instant, she thinks he will strike her. But no – he sinks into his seat.

'The Lord preserve us,' he says, waving one white hand languidly toward the door, 'from the suffrage movement. There are no women any more, only harridans and harpies.'

Mari bolts. Down the corridor she plunges, past many swaying, empty compartments until she finds one occupied by a family – a bowler-hatted father bouncing two small boys in sailor suits on his knees, a mother rocking a wailing baby, a grim little girl, her hands tucked into a pink muff, her lips tucked between her teeth.

'Evening all.' Mari collapses into a seat.

'Evening,' the adults respond.

The twin boys ignore her. 'You're giving James more bumps

than me,' one of them whines, pulling at his father's sleeve.

The little girl puts out her tongue at Mari.

The baby wails on.

Mari closes her eyes and thinks that in life, unlike in music hall, you really have no way of telling which act will come next, nor when the final curtain will fall. In life, there's no programme, no Master of Ceremonies.

But she's not sure what use it is, to know this.

10

Mary: Saturday Afternoon

I must turn my narrative backwards, Mother, and tell you of events that occurred in early March, following the date of the last murder which the one whom they call The Gardener brought off on the final Saturday in February:

At the back of his wardrobe, Alf kept a suit he never wore after we came to London. 'Out of date,' he said when I asked him about it one morning at breakfast. 'Must be more than fifteen years old.'

'Yes, it's the one you wore in Yorkshire.'

He lowered his newspaper. 'My courting suit. Give me another cup if there's one in the pot, will you?'

'And you haven't worn it since. It seems a waste.'

He flipped open his cigar box and frowned at its contents, as if there were a choice to be made, though he only stocks one brand. Naturally, he was puzzled that I brought up the matter of the suit after so many years. He could not know the powerful reason that impelled me.

'It wouldn't fit me now I've put on a bit of weight, any road. Thin as a rake in my youth. A wonder them Yorkshire winds didn't bowl me off my feet!'

A memory rose from his words and hovered wraithlike over the empty silver epergne, a memory as tenuous as the smoke from the cigar he had just lit. Our eyes met briefly, accidentally, and I saw that it was a shared memory, but one that saddened him. Quickly we turned our gaze from each other, seeking safer, insentient objects.

'Slenderness became you as a young man,' I said, 'and you had a gladsome manner, different from what I was accustomed to. As if the world were an apple you tossed in your hand, like a young prince—'

'Here, steady on, Mary!' He stirred his tea, studying the silver apostle spoon in his hand, embarrassed . . . but not, I think, displeased.

'Oh, but it's true. You were gallant and gay then, Alf. You came into . . . our town' (I had almost said 'my heart') 'like a hero—'

'I came to visit my aunt.'

'—and conquered us all! How those Yorkshire lasses primped and preened for you. Why, you gathered hearts like mulberries!'

He sipped his tea, a crease forming over the bridge of his nose, between his heavy, drawn eyebrows. 'And so, Mary, you married me because others wanted to. That's a reason that brings no joy . . . as you've since learned.'

He startled me when he spoke thus. My fancy had flown into bygone days, the glowing days, when I was young and so ardently wooed by Alf, chosen by him from all my kind, as Esther was. His words hauled me back into the dim present as harshly as my father's hands when he shook me out of a daydream, and I felt like a bird maimed on the wing.

'We were speaking of your suit,' I said. 'If you have no use for it, may I dispose of it? I am preparing a bundle of clothes for Millie to carry to the Salvation Army.'

'Do as you like.' Alf rose, brushing crumbs from his plum-coloured waistcoat. 'I've no fondness for the suit any more.'

I followed him into the narrow hall, dark, barricaded with furniture, like all the rooms in our house. 'I suppose you'll be gone all day, Alf?'

'Till late tonight, Mary, as usual.' He took his astrakhan overcoat from its peg on the hallstand, donned his hat, checked himself in the gilt-edged mirror. He is still a handsome man, Mother. Beside him, in my white morning dress, my hair loose on my shoulders, I looked like the ghost of his past.

Alf selected an ormolu-knobbed cane from the antler tree. I handed him his gloves. When he opened the front door and I looked out on the bright winter day, my heart grew faint with longing. If only I were stepping out beside him, to go arm-in-arm down the street, children trotting in front, the neighbours watching us from their windows and remarking, 'There go the Ramseys. Come to the window, dear, and tell me . . . do you think Mrs Ramsey is expecting again?'

But that was foolish fancy. We have no common destination, Alf and I, no heirs to mingle our fortune. I shrank back into the dark passage.

'You look peaky, Mary,' he said. 'Wrap up warm and take a walk. You'll feel better for it.'

'I don't feel unwell, thank you, Alf.'

He studied my face for a long moment, as he is wont to do at our morning separations, loitering on the doorstep like a man who knows he has forgotten something but can't think what.

'You will be late,' I said, for I cannot bear to be scrutinized so. Under such eyes as he turned on me, I felt my face might crumple, my body too . . . and then I should be at his mercy.

'Goodbye then, Mary.'

'Goodbye, Alf.'

He had difficulty opening the gate for the latch had frozen during the night.

Years ago, on a romantic mission, he had leaped the rectory gate to show me his spryness and his ardour as I ran down the path to meet him. And I laughed and clapped my hands to think how he defied and mocked my father. But this morning he pushed and fumbled and, at last, kicked the gate open.

Once he was out in the street, frustration fell from his shoulders and he marched off jauntily enough, whistling 'My love is like a red, red rose', in anticipation, no doubt, of meeting his mistress.

An hour later, when Millie the housemaid arrived, I told her, 'I have an errand for you on your way home. A suit of Mr Ramsey's he no longer wears requires altering for a young relative. Deliver it to the tailor, will you? No need to mention this to Mr Ramsey—'

Millie laughed. 'I understand. My Dad's the same. Won't part with anything, even his patched trousers and worn-out shoes. Men! They don't have the care we do for clothes. Except my Robert. He *is* a smart dresser. I declare, I could never walk out with a man who was slovenly. Mr Ramsey dresses well, too, don't he? I'm sure he wouldn't be seen dead with a darn in his coat.'

As I climbed the stairs, I thought (as I often do) that Millie would be a hard wife to keep—unless she learned like her father to do without. The thought of her skimping and pinching oppressed me. How I should have spoiled her, were she my daughter—as she might have been, for she is barely eighteen years old.

But as I drew Alf's discarded suit from the wardrobe another image occupied my mind: 'Mr Ramsey wouldn't be seen dead with a darn in his coat.'

What misbegotten deed was I about? Murder is the most heinous of crimes – and to plot the murder of a spouse as well as his lover! Discovered, I would be abhorred, reviled, receive no quarter.

Yet, even as I struggled with compunction, I had stripped to my undergarments and was kneeling to pin up the hems on the trouser legs. I made tucks in the waist, tapered the side seams and shoulders of the jacket, drew from the wardrobe a clean white shirt and put it on. It swamped my meagre frame, but that was no matter, for this misfit the suit would cover. Clad in the pinned-up trousers and jacket, I presented myself to the mirrored door of Alf's wardrobe. A pallid epicene gazed out at me, a hermaphrodite with a man's body (albeit slender, effeminate) and a woman's long hair.

Yet – I will pad the shoulders, I thought, and hide my hair under a hat . . . purchase a cloak for extra bulk . . . and under the cover of night –

Yes, I would pass! Triumph vied with loathing for, undeniably, I had accomplished a masterstroke. In my man's suit, I could roam the city without fear of molestation or ridicule. I must avoid, of course, the well-lit places where people gathered for society – the restaurants, theatres, drinking-houses – but I felt no regret for that. Conviviality was not my object. I sought, as I have said, revenge without indictment, and my plan was ingenious yet simple.

Stealthily, one Saturday evening, I would trail Miss Prince on my insomniac's feet, silent as any night creature's, a knife and a pair of white kid gloves in my pocket. In some dark untravelled spot (and there are many in our London suburbs) I would catch her up, attack from behind. One swift stroke and the deed would be accomplished, before she could take alarm, resist, cry out.

When she had expired, I would have to rip her clothes, wound her further, to make the act authentic. I confess my woman's heart demurred, at first, at contemplating this additional violence, but during the week I waited for the tailor to do his work, I brought myself to accept the necessity.

Once I had laid evidence to incriminate the one already guilty of five murders, I would leave the indisputable clue – a white kid glove, carelessly cast upon her body. The other thing, the one I abhorred, I would not now, due to a recent fortunate aberration in his procedure, be forced to imitate. He had always set his signature, a blood-bedewed rose, on the right breast or inner thigh of his victims . . . always until the last. She was not thus mutilated, owing, a Scotland Yard detective told the newspapers, to the extraordinary resistance she had put up. Evidence discovered at the site of the murder suggested that she had wounded him and forced him to cut short his horrid work. Poor girl, how tenacious of life she must have been – a wonder to me, for her life seemed dreary enough: a shop assistant, her home and her future in the squalid East End, her fiancé a rough bargee. Be that as it may, Rose Doyle had done me a favour, had dispensed with that part of the deed I could not envision: myself kneeling over the lifeless but still fine body of Mari Prince.

With all speed then, after casting down the glove, I would quit the area, make my way home by cab, alighting in a street some distance from my own. Arriving before Alf (I can depend upon him to stay out late, dining and drinking with business cronies and patrons), I would clean the knife, hide the suit, go to bed and feign sleep. In the morning the newspapers would scream that the London Gardener had claimed another victim.

What a face Alf would show when he perused the front page at breakfast! And how I would lavish sympathy, pretend shock, offer more tea, 'Or a drop of something stronger, perhaps?' knowing that soon he would partake of a strong draught indeed. (Which lies even now in a vial in the locked drawer among your letters.)

When I tried on the altered suit a week later, it fitted to perfection. With my hair tucked into a hat of Alf's, I so closely resembled those effete young denizens of Leicester Square I hardly recognized myself! Surveying my twin in the mirror, I felt elated and vowed I would test the disguise that very night.

At eight, I dressed. For an hour I paced the empty house, practising the arrogant swagger of the young blade. Without skirts or modesty to hinder, I managed this new gait admirably. When the clock struck nine, I fastened on the cloak I had purchased and made my way to the High Street to hail a cab. Terror seized me when I had, perforce, to name my destination to the driver.

'Leicester Square,' I said, speaking from the back of my throat to make my voice gruff. This, too, I had practised.

'Right, guv.' The driver showed no suspicion in his tone nor in the brief glance he gave me.

In less than an hour I alighted outside the Palladium. What a brilliant frenzy assailed my unaccustomed eyes! I am sure I stood for many minutes squinting like an owl at the blazing electric lights and the human merry-go-round that whirled beneath them.

A little girl of twelve or so approached and peered up into my face. Fearing the urchin had penetrated my disguise, I drew back and glared at her, hoping to frighten her off. She merely dipped one gloved hand into the basket over her arm and drew out a posy of silk violets.

'Buy 'em for your lady. Only sixpence a bunch.'

The child was unkempt and uncared-for. Her gloves were more holes than stitches, her dress in tatters. For protection from the winter night, she wore a handed-down cape. Its hem dragged the pavement and impeded her steps, so that she stumbled about like a little inebriate. On her head she wore a woman's hat (plucked from a dustbin, no doubt), a battered straw on which the remnants of artificial flowers wilted.

I handed her a sixpence but shook my head to the proffered violets.

'God bless you, sir.' She hobbled off to importune others.

She had not gone very far before she herself was accosted. A roguish-looking fellow of thirty or upwards lounging in the doorway of an emporium had spotted her. He bent to whisper in her ear. The child hesitated. He patted his coat pocket and winked. She shrugged, an acquiescent gesture, and off they went, the man placing an arm about her shoulders to guide her through the crowds.

Rage and nausea overwhelmed me. Almost I forgot my mission and pursued the pair – to do what, I cannot tell, save that all my being rose up in protest and I would fain have been the protector of the hapless little flower-seller.

I took hold of myself. To confront the man would ensure exposure, for I could not hope to dissemble under the scrutiny of the curious crowd my intervention would surely draw. And what if the blackguard engaged me in fisticuffs!

I turned my head, forced my eyes to other sights, not without a large measure of self-castigation. So be it, I have my punishment. Indelibly, the picture of the ragged child in her ludicrous clothes, trotting off to engage in adult commerce, is imprinted on my memory, another memento in the dusty album I keep there.

Leicester Square was not lacking scenes to beguile and tempt the idle. As I waited at the mouth of the gaslit alley from which, at length, my quarry would issue forth, I watched the parade of fashion and folly with no small interest, for it was as novel to me as to any rustic. I gawped often, I daresay . . . at a resplendent jewel in a shell-like ear; an exquisite ivory griffin's head atop a polished cane; a finely-turned ankle in a satin dancing-slipper.

Outside the Palladium a Salvation Army band played, while their leader, a black-bearded evangelist, declaimed from a makeshift pulpit of wooden crates, pointing a finger at the whores, who smirked at him and twitched their uncorseted hips.

Should all this have shocked me? A modestly-raised woman, a minister's daughter, should I have felt abhorrence and left the scene for fear of taint? Whether the unaccustomed garb and my imposture altered my nature, I know not, but I felt none of the horror or dismay you might expect.

Rather, my spirits rose to a kind of euphoria, and I comprehended a freedom hitherto only guessed at as I stood in the midst of the fairground, untrammelled and untroubled by the usual obstacles of my sex. So potent was my delight that I entertained, for a moment, the idea of marching up to the stage door and inviting Miss Prince to accompany me to dinner! What a lark – to steal her from under Alf's nose!

Again, I took possession of my wayward impulse. As the chorus girls came through the stage door in a flurry of feathers, furs, and high-pitched laughter, I withdrew into the shadows to recollect my purpose and my true gender. At the door a band of males had assembled and each now attached himself to a girl, with less discrimination than promiscuous bees plundering blossoms. The girls linked arms with their just-now escorts and merged into the traffic in the Square, vanishing among the other ephemera there.

By dribs and drabs, more performers came out – comedians, singers, contortionists and their ilk, and the members of the orchestra, carrying their cased instruments. And then, for an interminable time, the door remained fast.

I feared I had missed her, that she had escaped me in the bevy of the chorus. But impossible! I had scrutinized each face as it passed. Besides, if memory served, Miss Prince was not one to be overlooked, even in that handsome, flamboyant troupe. What then? Had she been taken ill? Left the show in a sudden pique? Inside my man's attire, my limbs trembled in a most unmanly fashion as I absorbed disappointment.

Next moment though I understood the reason for her lateness. She was with my husband – with Alf – regaling him with her magic in the deserted theatre, performing at that very instant, while I stood without, the erotic tricks that had untethered his fancy.

A vision rose before my bemused eyes . . . Mari Prince divesting herself of her flowing cape and scant shimmering costume to emerge naked and grand, her breasts and hips formed on the scale of a marble Venus, but infused with the glow and tremor of living, ardent flesh . . .

Even as I battled with the jealous turmoil this image produced, the stage door opened and the hazy lineaments of my apparition solidified and settled into the real human form of Miss Prince herself.

Yes, she was come . . . but how different she was from what memory and imagination had made her. So great the discrepancy that at first I thought my eyes, longing for sight of her, deceived me with another illusion. The height and stature of the woman who now made her way hastily up the alley were true to my recollection – but what had become of her amazing hair, her great luminous eyes, her luscious red mouth, and, most of all, that magnificent bearing that cast her as a goddess among mortals?

As she approached me, I gathered the presence of mind to move, to cross the mouth of the alley as one simply passing, and then to infiltrate the heckling crowd of Palladium patrons the unlucky evangelist had now drawn. When she crossed the

Square, I followed, and when she joined the queue at a tram stop, I halted in front of a jeweller's window, pretending to examine the display. From here I could easily cover the short distance to the stop when I saw the tram approach.

By now I had understood the striking (and dismaying) alterations in her appearance since I last saw her. She had concealed her superb hair under a scarf of unprepossessing colour and design, a drab thing such as northern mill girls wear. Her face was scrubbed clean of make-up, and without eye shadow, rouge, lip tint, her features were pleasant but not remarkable. Gone, too, the queenly deportment and Amazonian grace I remembered. Her shoulders bent, her step hurried, Miss Prince resembled a woman who has received a blow of great force and who rushes to get out of the way of another.

I could not make out reasons for this change, but as I watched her, pity seeped in and weakened my resolve. Waiting with her, unbeknownst, for the tram to come, I remembered the last time I had seen her, how she had dazzled me as she sang, danced, and conjured; how later, in her dressing room, she had draped her magician's cloak about my shoulders, turned me to the mirror, and shown me a most flattering and thrilling image. I had desired then to retain her friendship, to foster the warm sisterly intimacy I experienced when her hands rested on my shoulders and she embraced me with a smile so glowing, I wanted ever to bask in its radiance.

The tram rumbled into sight, I moved into the queue, boarded, and took a seat several rows behind her. I sat with my legs carelessly sprawled, as a man would, but kept my head turned to the window so that none should examine my features. We left the stop and merged with the traffic, the cabs, the buses – and the new motor cars, so rare when I was last in the West End, now so omnipresent, like the electric lights illuminating restaurants and theatres and casting a futuristic brilliance over all.

When at last we had passed through many gaslit suburban streets, Miss Prince rose. I found myself rising behind her, casting off prudence, bent only on seeing her safely to her dwelling, an anonymous figure following at a distance, but her protector nonetheless.

Had she turned her head, she would have seen me. Luckily, all her attention seemed riveted on the deserted road before her, and she walked so swiftly that I, keeping close to the sides of buildings where I might duck into a doorway, had difficulty keeping her in view.

She turned off Holland Park Avenue into a side street. I increased my pace, all but running now. When I, too, rounded the corner into a street of semi-detached residences, another transformation astonished me. Magician that she is, she had acquired an escort, a constable of the Metropolitan Police.

Struggling with my hodgepodge emotions, I proceeded at a slower pace, keeping close to the evergreens that grew behind the low wall separating the gardens from the street. If Miss Prince and her policeman halted, I would slip through a gate or, if need be, hurl myself over the common wall into a shrubbery.

They did stop eventually. Fortune stood at my side and brought me at that very moment abreast a gate which swung open at my touch. Within, I found myself beside a tall yew tree. The winter moon, unimpeded by clouds, sent forth its torch and illuminated – to my great surprise – a path, a narrow sort of natural alley consisting of the wall and its decorative shrubs on one side, fir and yew trees on the other. Through this unexpected byway, I could pass along all the gardens until I came level with the place where Miss Prince and her companion lingered.

I set out, bent double so that the wall would give me cover. The journey, which could not have extended beyond a hundred yards, seemed interminable. Low hanging boughs grazed my face, thorny branches of holly and hawthorn scratched my hands, and my limbs ached their opposition to my unnatural posture. Once a cat skimmed, hissing, across my path, and once I almost collided with a dustbin. Yet, long and arduous as the passage was, I was not prepared for her voice when I heard it just beyond the wall –

'. . . not much these days. My tastes have changed.'

A deep, pleasant, though not refined, male voice replied, 'Have you considered the loss to your admirers? If you'll pardon me speaking frankly, a woman like yourself can't take into account only her own tastes – not when they lead her away from society. If you was plain and frumpish now, you could please yourself and no one the worse for it. But see here, a handsome woman must have a care for those she's drawn to her –'

Her laugh, robust and tuneful like her singing, interrupted his accolade. 'Constable Dawes, you flatter me!'

'Not a bit, I promise. I could name one right off who'd give his front teeth to walk out with you—'

Again she deterred him with laughter. 'He wouldn't make a very pretty companion then! I don't know as I'd like to go about with a toothless gentleman.'

She pushed open the gate and stepped into the garden where I cowered behind the bare branches of an azalea. If she looked down, saw me . . . She did not. 'Thank you for the pleasure of your company—'

'I wish you'd accept more of it.'

'— and goodnight.'

'Goodnight, Miss Prince. If I was a more forward man, I'd wish you to dream of me.'

'Oh, you wouldn't care to figure in *my* dreams, Constable!' She went up the path, fitted her key into the lock, and vanished inside the door.

The policeman sighed, said, 'Damnation!' in the tone of one who has suffered long, and then resumed his beat. I waited until the echo of his footsteps had died away then stood and stretched my painful joints. Meanwhile, a light had flickered into life in one of the upper windows. She had appeared briefly to draw the curtains — but not, I observed, all the way.

A larch tree grew in the garden, directly in front of her window, its topmost branches brushing the roof tiles. I looked up and down the street. It was after midnight and not a soul stirred abroad. I could climb the tree, of that I was sure, for the branches were broad and symmetrical, almost like the rungs of a ladder. It was less sure, but unlikely, that anyone would enter the street at that hour. Circumstances favoured me . . . but time was in opposition. At this moment, Alf would be taking his last glass of brandy, forking up the last morsel of dessert in whatever restaurant he frequented for his customary late dinner. Soon, fortified by liqueurs, sweetmeats, and *bonhomie*, he would step out into Leicester Square to hail a cab. I was closer to home than he, but I had at most fifteen minutes to spare if I were to arrive there first.

Well then . . . fifteen minutes must suffice, for I could not depart without a final glimpse of her. I wanted above all things to see her in the privacy of her own room, to see how she looked and behaved when she thought herself unobserved.

I laid my cloak on the ground and mounted the larch. What a bizarre sight I would have presented to any chance passer-by, a man in full dress-suit and top hat hauling himself up through the branches of a tree! A wind lifted my coat tails and flapped at my trouser legs, but I felt no chill, rather an increased buoyancy. Under my feet the boughs swayed, as if I clambered up the rigging of an old sailing-ship, a sailor about to descry the misty coastline of an exotic, long-searched-for country. The moon lit my way, her benign smile bathing each upward branch, and risk sharpened my exhilaration as I ascended, sure-footed as an aerialist, nimble as my girlish self scaling the rectory elms to hide from my father.

I gained the window, hooked my arms over a branch and leaned forward to peer through the chink in the red velveteen curtains. What wonders then astonished my eyes! On the windowledge within, from a large porcelain bowl patterned with roses and ringed with blond cherubs, an aspidistra sprouted, a jungle in miniature, its broad leaves dividing my view of the room into kaleidoscopic shapes. This room glowed with vibrant colours, red, blue, and gold predominating, as if I knelt before a hearth and gazed at the flame-pictures in a richly burning fire.

She sat within feet of me, at a sideways angle, dozing in a peacock-blue Turkish chair, her skirt and jacket removed and tossed on to the needlepoint rug. Clad only in a pale primrose petticoat, she was breathtaking, her fine shoulders and swelling breasts disclosed by the low-cut lacy bodice, the contours of her hips and Junoesque legs revealed beneath the thin clinging satin.

A gold-tasselled hanging lantern shed light on her hair, a massive halo, an embrasure of fiery curls. Her stockinged feet were propped on a mahogany centre table in front of a gas fire, its filaments pale reflections of her own living tresses. Three bottles of stout stood on the table beside a silver filigree frame, the picture it held turned away from me.

Behind her, a half-canopied brass bed stood against one carmine wall, its blue swagged draperies caught up at intervals by scarlet satin rosettes. The quilt was dusky rose, the plentiful pillows edged with lace and threaded with blue and red ribbons. It was a bed for a goddess to slumber and sport in, and it must have cost a pretty penny, the wages of months. A deep admiration overwhelmed me as I recognized and paid homage to her extravagant soul, her voluptuous imagination.

Near to where I crouched behind the aspidistra, a Japanese screen elegantly disguised what I knew to be a washing and dressing area. Flamingoes adorned the screen, and birds of paradise in full flight. A lamp, cleverly placed, shone from behind, obliterating the light-coloured background so that the birds seemed live inhabitants of her Arabian Nights room.

There was much else in the way of chinoiserie, needlepoint, ormolu, and bric-à-brac, but I was forced to halt my study well before I had seen all. For she stirred. Her eyes opened and she sat up, looked about, as if a footfall or voice had awakened her and she searched eagerly for its owner. Seeing no one, she sighed, opened a stout bottle, and took a long draught.

'Oh, I don't know!' she said aloud. 'Dreams and delusions! Waking or sleeping, he torments me.'

Her voice crackled with harsh emotion, jarring the sensuous opulence of her surroundings. She rubbed the back of her hand across her eyes and lifted the bottle again. Then, thrusting it between her knees, she leaned forward and plucked the framed photograph from the table. Holding it in both hands, close to her face, she addressed the image I could not see:

'Rascal! Look at the mischief you've made! I can't have you, and I don't want another, so what's to become of me? I gave you my heart and my body . . . but you, you'd rather be married to . . . to a chimera! You've taken a ghost, a maggot, to your chest, a vaporous thing with no flesh on its bones, and it will be the death of you, I know it will!'

She ended on a loud wail and proceeded to smother the maligned image with ardent kisses. Then she pressed the frame to her breasts, sank back in the Turkish chair and wept profusely.

As for me, I had grown so numb my hands could barely clutch the branch I clung to. The picture was of Alf, of course, and I the 'vaporous thing' she hated.

But she would learn differently. She would come to know that I was not to be so stamped upon by her scorn. 'It will be the death of you . . .' True words. The death of both. A pair of profligates, a whore-monger and his harlot: the world would be well rid of them.

By some means, I know not how, I descended the tree, made my way back to Holland Park Avenue, hailed a cab, and got myself home. In the dark house, I stumbled up the stairs, undressed, thrust my suit into my wardrobe, pulled on a nightgown and cast myself down between the covers of the icy bed.

I did not care about the cold. Her cruel words had already cast a bleaker winter over my soul than any I was likely to encounter without. Yet, in the midst of my dark woe, my resolve stiffened, my body an icicle, sharp, unyielding, a weapon ready to pierce its victims.

I stop this letter to rest. Writing wears me out and I must preserve my strength for tonight's grand finale. Oh, I evolved from my misery a better plan than the first, one more fitting for a she-devil incarnate. You shall hear of it anon, Mother. I go now to seek the eau-de-cologne bottle and the sleep of an hour.

11

Percy, Dai, Ivor: Saturday Afternoon

Twmas-John Bevan, the vital number eight player on the All-Wales team, crouches, alert and crafty as a fox at the chicken coop, at the back of the scrum. As the ball flies out, he catches it deftly between his feet, grips it tenaciously when the English backs jump him, and relinquishes it adroitly to Brynley Lewis who passes it, quick as a wink, to the fly half, Royston Pugh. Royston starts up the field towards the English line.

A roar goes up from the Welsh supporters, a cacophony of rattles, a field of waving flags, and the strains of '*Sospan Fach*'. The game is twenty-five minutes into the second half and the Welsh are losing. The supporters, who have suffered taunts, raspberries, and obscene remarks from the English fans, as well as the humiliation of seeing their side give away several penalties, unite now to urge Royston on to heroics.

'Go on, boyo!' Dai Bando yells as English players converge on Royston. 'Don't let the bastards stop you. Half a dozen of the sods in't worth the blood of one Welshman!'

'Language, Dai,' Ivor reprimands, but he too is excited, for it seems that Royston will score a much-needed try. Despite his hotly-debated leg injury and his uncle on the selection committee, he shows true valour, hurtling up the field, shrugging off opponents like horse-flies.

'That's the ticket!' Ivor shouts. 'Oh, lovely stuff. Can't hold him, can they, Dai?'

But now the English backs are massing, a wall of muscle, and there appears no way through for Royston. Groans shudder the Welsh ranks . . . but hold on . . . all is not lost. Here comes that good boyo, Hywel Humphrey, oldest member of the team, always reliable in a tight spot, loping up the field with great easy strides. Sly as a prowling lion, he knows the English attention is on

Royston, and he's found his own place. Free, ready, he stands, waiting to catch the ball and bear it on to victory.

'Pass! Pass the flaming ball!' Dai Bando cries. 'There's Hywel out on his own. Give it to him!'

Royston, however, holds on, the ball tucked under his arm like a huge *bara brith* he is determined not to share with anyone. The backs pounce, one of them grabs him around the neck it looks to Dai, Royston's knee buckles, he falls, the backs crashing on top of him, the rest of the field swooping toward the melee.

'Foul!' Dai bellows, and his countrymen take up the cry, 'Penalty! High tackle!'

On the field, the sport has changed suddenly to a wrestling match. Contorted limbs wave out of the body of the fracas, an effect like a gigantic spider in its death throes. The ref runs around this hybrid creature, blowing his whistle, pushing away the few players who have not yet tumbled in – and there is no sign of the ball or its erstwhile bearer.

'*Was* it a foul, Dai?' Ivor says.

''Course it bloody was, Ive. Flamer caught him in a stranglehold, didn't you see?'

'Serve him right if he's choked,' a man behind says, thrusting his head between Dai and Ivor. 'Blasted prima donna. Should've passed. He's not a team player, Royston Pugh.'

'None of them are team players today, if you ask me,' Ivor says gloomily, reaching behind his ear for a Woodbine nip. 'My youngsters could put up a better show than our Welsh fifteen.'

'Ref's separated them, anyway.'

'Now we'll see fair play,' Dai says. 'Foul!' he roars again as the players rise and resume their individual bodies.

The luckless Royston, still cradling the ball, is helped up by two team-mates. But once on his feet, he clearly can't stand. His leg gives up and down he goes again.

'Injury! Foul! Penalty to Wales!' Dai leads the chant.

The referee shakes his head, blows his whistle for a scrum, waves Royston off the field. Royston turns, as if to obey, then lunges at the back who, Dai would swear on the Bible, tackled him in a neck hold.

'Knock the bugger into the middle of next week!' Dai encourages. 'He deserves it.' His own fists are up.

Ivor places a restraining arm on his sleeve. 'You might be mistaken, Dai,' he says. 'I didn't see it.'

'Because you're bloody blind, that's why. You can't see what's going on under your nose half the time.'

Ivor drops his arm as if Dai's coat sleeve has sprouted fangs suddenly. 'What do you mean by that?' he says.

But Dai isn't listening. Like all the fans, he's vicariously engaged now in the pitched battle that has broken out on the field. Mud-daubed Welsh players are laying into the English with desperate violence, as if this were Llewelyn's last stand and the fate of their nation at stake. Hywel Humphrey, a bellowing colossus, the hair on his shins as thick as the shag on his head, delivers an uppercut that knocks the English captain off his pins. Other Englishmen are going down, too, falling like skittles before the fierce onslaught. In the stands, the Welsh supporters whoop their war chant: '*Cymru am byth! Sospan Fach!*!'

The English captain holds a cloth to his nose and exhorts the referee to end the game. The two teams, though parted, niggle each other with jibes and raised fingers. The ref banishes Hywel Humphrey and Royston Pugh to the sidelines and awards a penalty to the English. One of their forwards takes the kick and, egged on by his team and their fans, sends the ball soaring between the uprights. The referee blows a long blast and the game ends on a crescendo of noise from the cheering English and wailing Welsh.

'They played well,' Ivor says. 'You got to grant them that.'

'Who played well?'

'The English side, Dai. *Wara teg*, now. Let's be good sports after all, in't it?'

'Good sports!' Dai spits out the words. 'Take it from me, Ivor, a man don't get anywhere being a sport. I know. I been one for years.'

'Well . . .' Ivor says, '. . . we're talking about different things, I expect. But a man don't get far being a cheat, either.' With a surge of courage, he looks Dai in the eyes.

'Cheating is taking something underhand,' Dai says, in a voice Ivor is well tuned to, 'something that don't belong to you. I never took what wasn't freely given.'

Ivor can't hold Dai's black stare. He looks elsewhere, notices the absence of Percy, and says, 'Hullo, where's our boyo then?'

Dai, distracted, looks around too. 'I haven't seen him for a bit, come to think of it.'

'He went to buy a bottle of pop at half time, I recall,' Ivor says. 'He must never have come back after.'

'We better get down to the main gate and try to meet up with him.' Dai shoulders his way into the departing crowds, all his attention turned now to finding Percy. If he's bolted, it will be Dai's fault, and he curses himself for not keeping better watch.

'He's a funny bloke, in't he?' Ivor says, moving in Dai's wake. 'He don't like what normal men do.'

'How do you mean?' Dai says.

'He don't like rugby for one thing.'

''Course he do. Percy's got other things on his mind today, that's all.'

'And he don't really like coming down to the pub for a pint on a Friday night. You can see he's not easy there.'

'I never thought you'd hold it against a fella that he's not a boozer,' Dai says as the Welsh avalanche rushes down the steps, bearing them in its midst. 'You ought to be shouting halleluja. In't abstinence what you preach every Sunday in the pulpit?'

'Not abstinence, just moderation. I'm not a big drinking man myself, as you well know, but I do like a half of bitter and the company of my butties once a week. It's only natural.'

'Percy's all right. He's a bit of a dreamer, that's all.'

'There, you put your finger on it,' Ivor says as they reach the bottom of the steps and the flood of supporters breaks into tributaries, dispersing toward the various exits. 'His head is in the wind, and that won't do, Dai. It does harm to others.'

'Stop a minute,' Dai says, 'and let's see if we can spot him.'

When they pause, Ivor lifts his raincoat by its shoulders and shakes it over his body. '*Daro*, look at the creases in my mac. Bethan pressed it beautiful, too, this morning. She's a dab hand with the iron. You should see the job she's done on my suit for Percy's wedding. Perhaps I can leave my mac at home. Living nearly next door to the chapel, I can make a dash for it if it's drizzling.'

'You won't have time to go home,' Dai says.

'Oh, I got to, Dai. Bethan will be upset if I don't have a swill and a change and drink a cup of tea. It'll take ten minutes at the outside. Besides, she wants us to go into the chapel together, husband and wife. She said so.'

Dai digs his hands into his pockets and looks across the fast-emptying grounds. He sees quantities of litter blowing about, a confetti of pink, green and white tickets, discarded flags, lost rosettes, a brief swirl of aimless gaiety. The cleaners are already advancing with their brooms.

'He's not in here,' Ivor says. 'We better have a look outside.'

As they cross the grounds, Dai says, 'How does Perce do harm to others then?'

'What?' Ivor is trying to light a Woodbine, but the wind blows his matches out. 'Oh, because he's a dreamer, like you said, Dai.' He stops to cup his hand over a match.

'Nothing wrong with dreams. I've had some myself.'

'Dreams in't reality.' Ivor's cigarette-end glows at last.

'They're better.'

'Not if you try to twist and squeeze everything to fit them. A dreamer upsets people and causes havoc, walking around in a daze, seeing things that don't exist, and barging through things that do. No respect for the rights or privacy of others 'cause they're just figures in his dream.'

Ivor's vehemence, unusual out of the pulpit, surprises Dai. He's usually so wishy-washy in his opinions, his feelings so sluggish – anger, jealousy, or joy always demoted in him to mere irritability or mild pleasure. But he has no time to ponder his butty's sudden fervour, for now Ivor says, 'There he is!' and points to a bench just outside the gate, where Percy sits, one hand resting on his suitcase, the other grasping a book, his head back, his eyes closed.

'He's bloody sleeping!' Dai says.

'See, I told you. Can't bear to be parted from his dreams for long.'

They cross a patch of withered grass to Percy's bench. Dai shakes his shoulder until Percy opens his eyes.

'Oh,' he says, looking at Dai from far away. 'Is it time?'

Ivor has a point, fair play. Looking into Percy's eyes is like gazing at a summer sky, all wide blue reaches and plenty of yonder, but no centre to focus on.

'Time for what?' Dai says. 'The match finished fifteen minutes back.'

'You missed the whole second half,' Ivor says.

'Did I?' Percy sits up, remembers the book in his left hand, colours, and slips it into his inside pocket. 'I just sat down for a minute after drinking my pop and I must have dropped off. Who won?'

'They did,' Dai says. 'All the penalties our side gave away, you'd have thought it was bloody Christmas present time.'

'Oh well . . .' Percy squints about, as if he's not sure where he is. 'P'raps we'll win next year.'

'What shall we do now, Dai?' Ivor says. 'Go down the West End, is it?'

'What do you want to do, Percy? Do you want to see a bit of the sights first?'

'I've always fancied seeing Buckingham Palace,' Percy says, looking more alert.

'That's a bit out of our way, in't it?' Ivor looks at Dai. 'Take ages to get there and then back to Leicester Square, if we're going to that show you talked about, Dai. I hope we are. I'm looking forward to seeing the music hall.'

'We'll get a cab and go in style,' Dai says. 'First to the Palace and then to the Palladium.'

Ivor sucks air through his teeth. 'A cab will be very dear – double the normal price, I bet, for Welshmen.'

'I don't know as my funds will run to a cab–' Percy says.

'Our treat, Perce, me and Ivor's.' Dai ignores the pressure of Ivor's elbow. 'We want to make your dreams come true today, in't that right, Ivor?'

'We should settle a price before we get in,' Ivor says.

In the cab, while Dai and Ivor discuss the match, Percy looks out of the window and thinks of the poem he read before he fell asleep. It's one of the many he knows by heart:

> O what can ail thee, knight-at-arms,
>   Alone and palely loitering?
> The sedge has wither'd from the lake
>   And no birds sing.

Many summer Sunday afternoons, Percy has wandered the

hills above Avon Fach, in his best blue suit, a fine heather tweed, his washed hair golden as any princely crown. Eagerly, he has waded waist-deep among giant ferns in response to a flash from bright eyes watching him in their midst, or clambered down a slope to a reedy pool where a glimpse of something milky-white among the bulrushes suggested the body of a sleeping nymph.

But among the ferns only startled sheep scattered at his approach, and beside the pool, his water nymph turned into a white, sunlit stone. Still, he would ramble on, undeterred, in pursuit of lovely phantoms, until the chapel bells called him down to his mother's pew. Often he was late for service . . . before he saw Ellen, and her ethereal charms smote him. How was he to know that her butterfly dresses hid a carnal body and a plotting heart? Now he is pale and ailing for the wrong reasons and will never know the enchanted kiss.

Dai is tapping his knee. 'Look, Perce, that's the Houses of Parliament across the river. See Big Ben?'

'Oh, aye,' Percy says. 'Great.'

'That's where Lloyd George speaks on the rights of Welsh miners – when he's not too busy chasing women.'

'Don't say that, Dai,' Ivor says. 'He's a good man for the Welsh. He promised he wouldn't let the Chinese come in and take our jobs, didn't he? And he've kept his word.'

Dai makes a harsh noise in his throat, something between a laugh and a growl. 'It's not the Chinese we have to worry about. It's them blokes–' he jerks his thumb towards Parliament, 'in their pin-stripe suits, filing their nails all day and reading the racing results. They're the ones who'll take our jobs in the long run.'

'Oh never, an MP wouldn't give up a cushy job to go down the pit.'

'They don't want to do our jobs, Ivor, they want to do us out of them. It's a different thing altogether. See, they got us doing shifts round the clock, and if that keeps up, what's bound to happen?'

'A lot of men do get silicosis–'

'In the long term, the coal seams will be all worked out, decades before they should be, the mines will close, there'll be massive unemployment . . .' Dai sighs. 'I told you all this before. You ought to come to Union meetings, Ivor, instead of Band of Hope and prayer meetings.'

Ivor shakes his head vigorously. 'No, Dai. If there's trouble looming like you say, I'll put my faith in the Lord.'

'And Lloyd George. They're two of a kind, both great speech-makers.'

Ivor opens his mouth to answer, but before he can speak the cab comes to a sudden shattering halt and he is thrown out of his seat right into Percy's lap.

Ivor gets off him, saying, 'Sorry, boyo. Hope I didn't do you an injury?'

Dai, who got out of the cab as soon as it stopped, is talking to the driver, being told by him what none of them need explained, for they can see that a large crowd spilling into the road up ahead forced the cab to a standstill.

'Maybe the King is coming out,' the driver says. 'That's Buckingham Palace over those railings.'

'The Palace!' Percy says. 'I thought it was a barracks.'

'Not up to much, is it?' Ivor agrees. 'Avon Fach Town Hall is fancier – not so huge, of course.'

Dai comes to the window. 'Shall we see what all the rumpus is about?'

Percy and Ivor get out at once. They would both love to see the King.

His gold crown . . . his ermine robe . . . his orb and sceptre, Percy thinks. He had wanted to visit the Tower to see the jewels, and the rooms haunted by the ghosts of ill-starred noblemen and cast-off queens, but it had seemed too much to ask of Dai and Ivor. Seeing real, living royalty will be even better. And perhaps His Majesty will wave to him.

'Wait for us, please,' Dai tells the cab driver.

Ivor, already imagining Bethan's face when he tells her, 'I saw him, love, close as you're standing to me now,' doesn't argue about the mounting cost. It will be worth every penny to see her eyes brighten and her cheeks flush. 'Oh, never, Ivor! Fancy that!' she will say. He hasn't had news of great import to give her since the day he asked her to marry him.

Home from service in London, four months pregnant, deserted by her city lover and shamed in the town, Bethan had cried, laughed and glowed all at the same time when Ivor popped the question.

'No other man in Avon Fach would do this,' she had said, 'though a lot of them tried for me hard enough at one time.'

'Well, they all want brains except me,' Ivor had answered.

Since then, though they have an ideal marriage, he has never been able to elicit another show of vivid feeling from her. It's all pastels now . . . and darker shades, too, recently, for she has become prone to spells of silence and moping over the past year.

Ivor is thinking about this, about the unsettling and mystifying change in Bethan, as (having stopped to light a Woodbine) he walks some distance behind Dai and Percy towards the crowd gathered around the Palace railings. What does it take to please a woman? No . . . he draws deep on the Woodbine . . . that in't the question. Bethan is pleased all right. She has her own home in a nice street, sons, a good husband, a solo in the choir, respectability again. He knows she appreciates all that by the way she takes care of him. And often, when she's quiet and he asks what she's thinking, she says, 'Just counting my blessings, love.'

How do you lift a woman to joy . . . *that's* the question . . . and if he knew the answer, he'd carry it out to the letter, regardless of toil or toll. Everyone in Avon Fach thinks him fortunate now to have a wife like Bethan. And he is, he adores her, but he carries a secret burden too – the burden of a lover whose torch lights no fires.

Dai and Percy have reached the edge of the crowd. Ivor looks at his butties' backs, observing again Percy's frailness: a long-stemmed plant bearing a gilded lily, pretty but useless, any little squall would topple him. And Dai, a different sort of man, nothing flowery about him, more like a mountain pony, solid in build and reckless in nature. Like the fox, too . . . sly and secretive when he wants to be. That comes from living on his own, no company except the little whippet bitch he keeps to hunt rabbits.

'He should get married,' Ivor said to Bethan recently. 'Plenty of tidy, single women in Avon Fach. Who can we get him off with?'

But Bethan said, 'A man has to make his own choice.'

'He haven't though, and he won't without a push, far as I can see.'

'You can't see everything,' she said.

A sharp, familiar pain lunges in Ivor's stomach. As he comes up beside Dai and Percy he reaches into his mac pocket for his tin of Rennies. 'What's up then? Can you see, Percy?'

Percy shakes his head. Even with his lengthy advantage, he can't see over the forest of bowlers and the women's monumental hats. 'It's not the King though. They're jeering in the front. Must be some drunk or loony acting the goat.'

A large woman, taller than Percy, planted in front of him, turns round. 'It's one of those suffragettes,' she says, 'making a fool of herself and shaming our sex.'

'Pardon?' Percy is transfixed by the woman's appearance. She is draped in dead creatures – a prostrate blackbird on the brim of her hat, a double sealskin scarf wrapped around her throat, the twin seals' heads criss-crossed on her bosom.

'She's chained herself to the railings.' The woman's dark eyes are as vitrified as the eyes that stare at Percy from her chest and her hat. ''Course, she could have done worse. They're not opposed to throwing stones or bombs or setting fires to draw attention to themselves.'

'Police will be here in a minute to cart her off,' the woman's companion, a mustachioed man in a grey fedora, says.

'What she doing it for?' Percy asks.

The woman looks down her nose at Percy. 'Don't you read the papers? They want the vote. Can you imagine? Fine state we'd be in with that lot voting. May as well put the Anarchists in Parliament.' She turns her back again.

'I didn't know women did things like that,' Percy whispers to Ivor. 'Bombing and stuff. Violence. Do you believe her, Ivor?'

'This is London, Percy,' Ivor says. 'I'd believe anything. Where's Dai? We may as well get back to the cab. I got no interest in seeing a chained woman.'

Dai has pushed his way to the front of the crowd. The suffragette is sitting on the pavement, her legs drawn up under her skirt, her head turned away, a wing of chestnut hair hiding her face. Her raised right wrist is fastened to one of the Palace railings by a padlock and chain.

Dai is surprised. He has never seen a suffragette before, but he has read about them in the newspapers. The pictures accompanying stories in the *South Wales Echo* and the *Western Mail* showed wild fist-waving women fighting policemen, kicking and punching, so he had expected this one to be big and fierce, a spitting swearing virago.

Instead, she is small and slight, and she sits on the pavement as demurely as if she were taking tea in someone's parlour. And she is neatly, quietly dressed, a black plush cape embroidered with soutache modestly covering her to the waist, a flounced grey kersey skirt reaching to her ankle-boots, on her head a straw turban trimmed with a single black rosette. Dressed thus, she could attend Avon Fach Baptist chapel, and even the carping old fogies would approve of her.

Yet, the men around Dai are laughing and making ribald remarks, as if she were a fan dancer putting on a show for them.

'Believe women should have the vote, do you, ducks? How about free love, do you believe in that, too?'

''Course she does. They all do.'

'Some of 'em couldn't get it any other way.'

'We ought to test her convictions. See if she practises what she preaches.'

Dai balls his fists. Any man who steps forward will get a sock in the jaw. He'll take them all on, if pushed; it won't be the first time he's fought against the odds.

But now a large black van draws up to the kerb, scattering the crowd. Several policemen with truncheons jump out. While constables disperse the onlookers, a sergeant goes up to the woman and taps her shoulder.

''Ere, Miss, you can't do this, you know. I'll have to book you for disturbing the peace.'

The woman lifts her head. Dai, who has stood his ground, sees that she is young and very pretty, fair-skinned and fine-boned. But it's her eyes that strike him. Dark brown, potent, startling, impossible to turn away from, they are the eyes of a person who won't give in at any price, not even at the cost of life and limb.

Dai has the eerie feeling that he knows her from somewhere. It's impossible, yet the feeling mounts to conviction. Without knowing that he would, he finds himself speaking. 'She's only standing up for her rights,' he says. 'It's them fellers who were breaking the peace. Why don't you arrest them?'

The sergeant looks at Dai. 'Are you with this young woman?'

'No,' Dai says, 'but—'

'Then I'll ask you to move on, please, and not obstruct the law.'

A constable comes with a jemmy and goes to work on the chain.

Dai, his fists still rolled, moves in. 'What did you do it for?' he asks the woman. 'In't there another way?'

She looks up. Slowly, she smiles. 'They didn't listen when we asked nicely,' she says, her voice light, girlish. She can't be more than twenty. 'In this country, if you want the government to listen, you have to kick and scream and make yourself a public enemy.'

Dai nods. 'Aye, I know what you mean. I been feeling a bit that way myself, lately.'

'Are you a supporter?'

'No . . . I don't know. I never thought much about it, to tell you the truth.'

'You're a working man, aren't you?'

'I'm a coal miner from South Wales.'

'You have a good face . . .' She winces as the chain twists, but her eyes never waver from Dai's. She is looking at him as if the recognition he felt earlier is mutual, and a great current wells up inside him, acute and pressing as sexual desire, though it is not . . .

'You are a supporter, if you think about it.'

The sergeant steps up beside them. 'We're taking her in now,' he tells Dai as the constable helps her up. 'You'd better be moving on.'

'Wait a bit,' Dai says, but the woman shakes her head. 'It's all right. I know what to do. Speak up for us in future, won't you?' She looks very frail and defenceless between the two policemen.

'Good luck to you – and to your cause!' he shouts after her.

'Goodbye,' she answers and gives him a wonderful, promising smile over her shoulder, as if they are to meet again in different, more auspicious circumstances. Dai knows they won't, but the smile boosts his heart nevertheless. 'We could have had something, me and her,' is what he thinks, and he's amazed and grateful to know that another woman, not the one he's hankered for so long and uselessly, can still lift him like this.

Ivor and Percy come up beside Dai.

'Do that woman know you, Dai?' Ivor says.

'Don't be bloody daft, Ive. I've never seen her before in my life.'

The three men turn to walk back to the cab. They have only gone a few steps when, behind them, a woman screams.

Dai spins round, in time to see the suffragette, broken free of her escort, run into the road, straight into the path of an oncoming omnibus. The bus swerves, but not fast enough to avoid her.

'Christ,' Dai says, as the crowd regroups in front of him. 'Jesus effing Christ.' He clenches his right hand and presses it against his mouth.

'*Daro*,' Ivor says, 'what did she do that for?'

'She was trying to run away,' Percy says. 'In't that right, Dai? She never done it on purpose, did she?'

Dai, squeezing his knuckles against his teeth, tastes blood.

'Loony,' Ivor says. 'Only a half-tapped person would carry on like that.'

'I could have stopped her,' Dai says, 'but I didn't know . . . I never dreamed . . .'

He stands with his arms hanging loose, a queer vacant expression on his face that troubles Ivor.

'I should have known . . . I saw her eyes.'

'Here, Dai, you're talking daft. The shock's been too much for you. You need a pint and something to eat. Let's get back to the cab and drive to Leicester Square.'

Dai starts to walk, by sheer luck it seems to Ivor, in the right direction.

'I wish we'd never come to Buckingham Palace,' Percy says. 'It wasn't worth seeing anyway. And look, Ivor, the flag's on the half. King George in't even at home.'

In the dark carriage, rattling towards the West End, they don't speak again. It's as if a fourth person, a stranger, rides along with them, making them tongue-tied, too shy to converse in front of one who might laugh at their Welsh accents and mock their muddled attempts to make sense of the scene they have just witnessed.

'It's a lesson,' Percy thinks, '. . . but like algebra . . . I never could get the hang of those equations.'

'"Now is my soul troubled,"' Ivor recites silently, '"and what shall I say? Father, save me from this hour."'

In Dai's head, a single word repeats itself like the monotonous pounding of a hammer: '*Jawl . . . jawl . . .*'

12
Mari: Saturday Evening

As she waits for the kettle to boil, Mari tidies up her room, stuffing stray underwear into drawers, dusting surfaces and knick-knacks with a pocket-handkerchief. It's the first bit of cleaning she's done in a long while, and it's in honour of tonight's guest. Out of consideration for him, too, she removes Antonio's photograph from the mahogany centre table and lays it in the drawer where she keeps her other mementoes.

In bygone days, she sang as she prepared for a visitor, waltzing from one piece of furniture to the next, waving a feather duster like a magic wand, endowing cut glass with the glitter of diamonds and turning gilt into gold. When the cleaning was done, she'd find herself tipsy almost with the anticipation of the night to come.

This evening her heart hangs heavy in its cocoon of sticky, tangled nostalgia, and in six o'clock twilight everything looks shabby, tawdry, too long neglected to respond to her belated lick-and-promise.

The kettle whistles. She pours tea into the pot, covers it with a tea-cosy, and refills the kettle with tepid water from the washing urn. The aspidistra, a survivor against odds, reprimands her silently as she waters it, drooping its head and displaying the brown spots on its leaves.

'I know, I know,' Mari says. 'You'd rather have him tend to your wants. Well, he's not available, so you'll have to make the best of what's going, won't you?'

For Antonio, the aspidistra had grown like a forest, sprouting new leaves every day, as a woman in love and beloved continually sprouts new charms. 'It is my singing,' he said. 'She thrives, Signorina Aspidistra, on love for me!' Laughing, he had kissed Mari's neck. When she turned to embrace him, he whispered in her ear, 'It also help, *cara mia*, that I keep the window clean!'

Mari blows out her cheeks, and exhales the air on a 'Poof!' Then she flicks her finger under an aspidistra leaf. 'Chin up, dearie! Can't let bygones ruin your nowadays. Here, I'll give you a song!' Planting her hands on her hips and shaking back her hair, Mari belts out a music-hall hit:

> Let him go, let him tarry,
> Let him sink or let him swim.
> He doesn't care for me, and I don't care for him.
> He can go and find another
> Which I hope he will enjoy
> For I'm going to marry a far nicer boy!

She flops into the Turkish chair to drink her tea, her eyes on the aspidistra, sternly, as if it were a sulky child who refused to buck up. The windowpane behind the plant is indeed grimy. Suddenly Mari shivers, so violently that tea slops into her saucer and dribbles on to her lap. For a moment, she thought a face watched her through the glass; but it's only a trick of leaf-shadow and gaslight, a composition of aspidistra limbs and the spaces between that suggest, vaguely, a pair of dark staring eyes and an open mouth.

Hisht! She's still a bag of nerves from this afternoon's commotion on the train. That won't do. Ruin her plans for tonight. She puts down her cup and saucer and crosses to the bed to rest for half an hour. Her own passion . . . it has hibernated overlong, though not without those flutterings and fitful bursts of wakefulness that let her know it is merely asleep and not dead. Under amorous hands and a desirous gaze, surely it will rouse itself and leap from its wintry habitat to gambol again in the fields of spring. Well . . . she's ready to try. Should the climate bring chills instead of warmth, disappointment won't do her in.

Unhappy choice of idiom!

Now her mind is off course again, venturing into dark byways and devious alleys where terror stalks, decked out like a gentleman, in a silk scarf and gloves of white kid.

Oh, turn away, turn back while there's time. Pick up your skirts and skedaddle from this place!

Don't, Mari . . . don't turn down this crooked street, lit only by flickering gaslight, no end in view, only a sinister bend curving like devious intent, a tunnel spurned even by tuppenny whores in these hazardous times.

And now the shadows thrown on the walls by the unsteady gaslight assume female contours, as you knew they would. The first apparition steps forward as you pass, to give you her name and her brief history, which you already know by heart:

'I am Becky Simm, twenty-two last birthday. I was in service in St John's Wood. The master of the house had an eye for me, but I held him off. A girl can't squander her main commodity. "Make me housekeeper," I said, "and then we'll see."

'I always had Sundays off to see my family, on account of the master wanting to get in my favour, and I slept at home on Saturday nights . . .' She breaks off, her blonde head drooping, her hand coming up to cover her heart. 'It's a Saturday night last October I'm going to tell you about.

'I was crossing Piccadilly. He came up behind me and twisted my arm behind my back. I thought at first it was my master, taken leave of his senses as he often swore he would if I didn't cease my cruel treatment. But it wasn't the master . . . it was him . . . I was his first victim. Look here, proof of what I say . . .'

Blood spills through her fingers, through the torn cloth she clutches. Her face and throat are all bruised and lacerated. She raises her grey melton skirt and points to the ragged long-stemmed rose on her right thigh. 'See, there it is . . . the mark of his esteem . . . the lover's gift. I'll have no lover now. I'm not fit to be seen, though I was looked at above my share once. Mistress and the housekeeper are glad to be rid of me, I daresay, but I know my master mourns for Becky . . . for what might have been . . .'

She retreats into the shadows as another shape flits out – a fey, light-footed creature, more air than substance she must have seemed even in life. She is not above seventeen, and she wears the dark blue skirt and cloak of an orphanage child, her brown hair bound into a single thick plait that reaches her waist.

'Sarah Collins, a waif of the streets,' she says, 'until the good doctor found me and took me in. Some say orphanage life is harsh, but I don't complain of it. If you obey the rules, they treat you decent enough . . . and I got an education. I'd have become a teacher on my eighteenth birthday and earned a wage. That's better by a long chalk than picking pockets or selling yourself for a living, the only professions open to an abandoned girl.

'One Saturday night I slipped out to meet a young fellow, a carpenter's apprentice. We'd exchanged words and looks on the sly, when he came to the Home to do repairs. And I'd been reprimanded by Matron, too, for lingering in rooms where he was at work. Oh, her tongue could make you smart sometimes, worse than the switch!

'I knew she was right. I came from a bad lot, and I should be humble, industrious and circumspect, as befits one lifted up out of vice. But soft words are ever more persuasive than harsh reproof, and a girl in love can't be stayed by consequences!

'It was seven o'clock when I left the Home, a dreary damp November night with a mist coming down. The street I lived on was half a mile from Piccadilly, where I'd agreed to meet Tom under the statue of Eros. I knew a short cut, a lane that ran behind a row of shops, much used by the inhabitants of the area, and I had traversed it countless times myself. It was deserted that night, but familiarity precluded fear. Besides, I lived in a safe, respectable part of London, not the brawling, brutal East End.

'I knew, of course, that a woman had been murdered near Piccadilly a month back, but I felt no anxiety on that score either. The very next day, the papers had announced the arrest of a prime suspect, the murdered woman's employer. Letters had been discovered in her room at the house where she was parlourmaid, written in his hand, and very incriminating, for they confessed love and jealousy and begged her favours. Furthermore, the housekeeper came forward as a witness, saying she'd overheard her master tell the maid, "You shall have whatever you ask for, so long as you don't ask my restraint." So, everyone believed the murder a crime of passion, and though I followed the newspaper accounts with much curiosity, to tell the truth they had no more effect on me than the romance novels I secretly squandered my pennies on.

'I walked down the lane rapidly, but eagerness propelled my feet, not terror. A figure stood at the other end . . . or, rather, lounged there, his back against a lamppost, his face turned toward busy Shaftesbury Avenue, where I would soon emerge, just steps from Eros and my sweetheart.

'As I drew nearer, I saw this loiterer was a gentleman, at least in the cut of his clothes and in his carriage. Pride flowed through the ample folds of his beaver cloak, which hung from shoulders moulded broad and straight by a life of plenty. Under his top hat, the tilt of his head showed the arrogance of one who has never met with denial.

'At once I guessed his purpose in lingering there at the entrance to the lane. A girl who has lived on the streets is well acquainted with the tastes of certain gentlemen, whose perfumed lives often drive them to seek a saltier, more pungent air. Yet, I did not fear. If he sought female company, London abounded with all varieties, and no pleasure-seeker need trouble an honest girl as she passed by.

'Closer yet I drew, close enough to hear him humming a tune. It was "Henery the Eighth", and I wondered if he were a lover of the music hall, one of those who would solicit delight at the stage door of the Palladium later on.

'I could see the electric lights of Shaftesbury Avenue in front of me now, and the people passing to and fro, and my heart outsped my feet, flying forward to the young man with the errant lock of hair on his forehead and the roguish smile that tempted me to imagine all sorts of playful mischief.

'At this moment, the gentleman turned his head, and the gaslight gave me a clear view of his face. My feet stopped, time ceased, the bright image of my lover fled away. A horrid visage loomed above me . . . black eyes, a black beard, his lips drawn back over sharp, white teeth . . .

'Like a wolf, he sprang, and his arms enclosed me. I screamed. He stifled my cries against his chest. I struggled, but to no avail. He ripped my clothes, thrust me against the wall, and with gloved hands squeezed and pinched my flesh – as if I were not human but some lesser species he might explore and torment without compunction, as I have seen the orphanage boys tear the wings from butterflies or pierce worms with sharpened sticks. But this torture gave him less pleasure, I believe, than those urchins derived from vexing insects, for the noises he made (he never spoke) were sounds of rage. Soon he unwound his silk scarf and twisted it around my throat.

'Pity the poor orphan girl!

'Pity the maid who sped toward her first embrace and met, instead, a devouring beast!

'Matron will say, "Blood must out, and what's bred in the bone . . ." and will believe I gained the wages of disobedience.

'Tom will find another lively, blushing girl and forget me with a kiss.

'I am buried in a pauper's grave, though my life expired in silk . . . and see, I wear his rose upon my breast . . .'

The child slides away into the gloom that must always have hovered, it seems to Mari, at the edges of the new life she wove for herself, flimsy as an embroidered handkerchief.

And fain would Mari turn away now, out of this alley constructed of newspaper stories and her own imagined histories, a mixture of facts and feelings, fashioned from her need to know the murdered women, not merely as victims, but as people who lived and hoped, as she does.

Another phantom materializes. With vaporous hands and incredible will, she urges Mari forward, whispering, 'I'm Fanny McAllister, done away with on Boxing Day . . . Come from the pub rolling drunk, Your Honour, I admit it . . . but I plead against the harshness of the sentence. I had two fatherless babes at home. Only myself, Your Honour, standing between them and the workhouse, where they are now, and will grow up to be like their mother, taking any man who offers them a glass of gin and the comfort of an hour's loving.

'And here's Rowena Long, another like me . . . "scum" they call us . . . who ran from a brawl with her sozzled lover out into the January snow and the arms of a far worse man. You needn't stop with us, Mari, or shed any tears. The gin, or the morphine, or an old crone's knitting-needle would have got us sooner or later if the Gardener hadn't. But here's Rosie coming. Tarry for her sake. She's different from us, a cut above. She stood up to him, Rosie did. Gave him a taste of his own medicine.'

Mari has come almost to the place where the lane curves out of sight. Around its bend the last woman in this parade of unfortunates appears and drifts towards her, hands stretched out, as if she imagines, even now, someone might save her.

'No one came,' she tells Mari in a soft Irish brogue, 'and sure I didn't let him take me quiet. I screamed and cried out "Murder" until he got his hand over my mouth and shut me up.'

She shakes her head, a lovely tinted flower on a slender stalk. Rose Doyle's hair is red-gold, and she wears it in clustered curls beneath a sailor hat of cream-coloured taffeta, trimmed with muslin carnations and shaded foliage, a stylish jaunty hat such as Mari herself prefers. In her green eyes a glimmer yet remains of the fighting spirit the newspapers commended so highly, for Rose had so fiercely battled with her attacker that drops of dried blood had been discovered along part of the escape route he must have taken; and, at the mouth of the alley where her body lay, a silver hat-pin topped by a tiny jet bird in full flight.

'I stuck himself many times before he finally stuck me. But what use is a pin against a knife? The last time, I plunged it so deep into his hand, he couldn't draw it out, and he bellowed like a bull, but it only made him drive the knife deeper into my heart. See, though . . . not a mark on me saving my death wound. He had to do me in quick. Couldn't cut me up as he did the ones before me.' She lifts her head proudly. 'No rose for Rosie!'

'You did a brave thing,' Mari says. 'The papers called you a heroine. They say it's because of you he's held off so long. First of April soon and no woman murdered in March.'

'Nursing his wounds,' Rose says. 'But a rabid dog must have blood. He'll strike again. Better watch out for yourself. Beware of men, Mari.' She melts away, only the echo of her warning sighing along the lane where Mari now, with laborious steps, trudges back into the light and comfort of her room. . .

It's time to dress. The gilt clock on the mantelpiece has already chimed half-past six. If she's to have her usual Saturday evening dinner at Nan's Pantry, she must leave in half an hour.

Usually, Mari can be ready in ten minutes, but this Saturday she takes time to make up her face. She'll have to wash it again at the theatre in order to put on her more striking and colourful stage make-up, but no matter, tinted cheeks and lips help the mood she is trying to induce, the happy temper of a woman who shares a mutual attraction with the opposite sex. 'Beware of men, Mari.' Ah well . . . Rose is biased now, of course.

Mari's outfit is already selected and hangs on the wardrobe door. The ivory satin blouse has a high-standing collar and is stitched with embroidered flowers, daring lace panels over her snugly ensconced breasts. Her costume is royal-blue serge, a long fitted jacket and a deeply-flounced skirt, a pattern of black velvet-strap diamonds and loops circling the hem. To complete her re-emergence as a fascinator, she dons a spectacular hat, a mushroom-brimmed straw, drooping gracefully, coquettishly, on the right side, trimmed with a large Alsatian bow of stitched black satin, caught in front with a rhinestone clip. On the hat's left side, a bouquet of pink roses draped in black Chantilly lace lies in the hollow of the upswept brim. Despite the weight of hat and hair, Mari holds her head regally as she turns about in the mirror. Satisfied . . . thrilled, in fact, that she can still look so fetching . . . she picks up her handbag and costume and leaves to take a tram to the West End.

13

Percy, Dai, Ivor . . . and Mari: Saturday Evening

Dai, Percy, and Ivor are seated in a Leicester Square restaurant adjacent to the Palladium, ordering dinner before going on to the show. At least, Ivor has engaged the waitress in a discussion concerning the varieties and vagaries of the fare. Percy has protested that his stomach is too jumpy to digest food, and Dai, silent and sullen, replies to all Ivor's kindly suggestions and requests for a consensus, 'I don't care. Whatever you fancy.'

'Shall I come back when you've made up your mind?' The waitress addresses Ivor, curtly.

'Well, it's a toss-up between the beef and the lamb,' Ivor says. 'What's your preference, Dai?'

Dai is drawing invisible lines on the tablecloth with his index finger. No, they're capital T's, Percy realizes, one line down, one line across. Dai has chosen a seat that presents his back to the crowded restaurant, his face to the wall, where there is only a hanging plant and a framed watercolour of Westminster Abbey to look at. Not like Dai . . . he usually wants to see all that's going on. He hasn't even glanced at the waitress. If he was himself, he'd have put her in her place long ago. But he hasn't been himself since . . . Percy pulls down his mouth and shudders, as if racked by a sudden intestinal pain.

'I don't care,' Dai says. 'It's up to you. I'll have a pint though.'
'We only serve wine here. The Sawdust Ox down the road–'
'Bring me a pint of that then.'
'Do you mean a carafe, sir?'
'Aye,' Dai says, dragging his finger across the cloth. 'If it's a lot.'

'We may as well settle for the chicken,' Ivor says. 'Can't go wrong with white meat. Mashed potatoes won't be lumpy, will they, love? I'll have cabbage as my choice of greens. Dai?'

137

'Aye, aye,' Dai says.

Percy waits until the waitress's pencil stops moving across her pad. Then he says, 'I'd rather have cottage pie if it's all the same to you. With peas.'

When the waitress has whisked away to another table, Ivor says, 'Not a bad-looking girl.'

'Dry as a chip,' Percy says. 'I like jolly girls who can crack a joke without cracking their faces.'

Ivor is surprised. He has never heard Percy express this preference before. He's a bit perturbed, too, for the description certainly doesn't fit Percy's betrothed – his wife by this time tomorrow.

'Well,' he says, 'Ellen's on the serious side.'

'I'm aware.' Percy is looking away over Ivor's right shoulder, watching patrons come and go through the plate-glass door, 'Nan's Pantry' inscribed on the glass in gilt letters, elegantly looped and sinuously curved. A long window, stretching the length of the restaurant's frontage, reflects the diners, their outlines haloed in the glow of the ornate low-hanging chandeliers. People in the street outside cross this phantom scene, their solid shapes passing through the spectral window images, as if Percy were imprisoned in a dream, watching reality.

'And you're a quiet bloke yourself,' Ivor insists. 'You don't care to lark about and act the goat, so I don't think a live wire would have suited you, Percy.'

It's pointless trying to explain to Ivor, yet Percy feels bound to make a statement. 'I've come to realize,' he says, 'that there's a lot to life a serious feller can miss. Being serious is like standing behind a big wall, or . . . on the wrong side of a window.'

Ivor's face assumes its pinched expression. He's concentrating, but he doesn't get it. 'How do you mean, Perce?'

'To live a proper life . . . to gather all its riches . . . you got to be willing to embark on the adventure. It's like a trading ship, see . . .'

'Half a mo', Percy.' Ivor's face shows bewilderment. 'What's like a trading ship? You've lost me now.'

'Life,' Percy says. 'Life as it is known on the high seas.'

Ivor shakes his head. 'I don't know how you went from talking about women to talking about ships.'

'Women? What was I saying about women?'

'Well, see how you get off track, Percy. You said you like one that can crack a joke. And I said a serious chap like yourself—'

'Oh,' Percy says. 'Oh, yes. Well, it's not just women, it's all of us. If you can't laugh, you can't take risks, and if you don't take risks, you might as well be dead. That's the point I'm hammering.'

Ivor sits back in his chair, his Woodbine dangling from his lips, and stares at Percy as if he is a carnival sideshow. 'That's loony talk,' he says.

The waitress appears and places a cut-glass vase on their table. Percy *thinks* it's a vase at first, then sees it is full to the brim with wine.

'*Diws annywl*,' Ivor says, 'that's enough booze for a rugby fifteen.'

'A carafe like he ordered.' The waitress flicks her head at Dai.

She's treating us like dirt because we're up from Wales, Percy thinks. I'm not clubbing in for a tip.

'You're not used to wine, Dai,' Ivor says. 'Won't make you drunk, will it?'

'I hope so,' Dai says.

'I'll help you drink it, Dai, if you don't mind.' Percy fills Dai's glass. 'I could do with a drop of cheer.'

Ivor covers his glass with his palm. 'Not for me, thanks. A hot cup of tea with my afters, I'm looking forward to.'

'How about you, love?' Percy raises the carafe as if to toast the waitress. 'Might put a smile on your face.' He doesn't know where his daring comes from, but it seems a good thing, this first step on the gangplank of the brave ship.

The girl cocks her nose up and closes her eyes momentarily. When she opens them, they are fixed on the teardrop chandelier above Percy's head. 'Cottage pie is not *à la carte* tonight, Chef says.'

Damn, who does she think she is! Just because she works in a fancy restaurant and knows a bit of French, she's acting like Lady Muck. Percy is sick to the heart of snubby women who make every word they speak sound like a rebuff or an accusation. He can hear Ellen saying, in the waitress's tone, 'Sex is not *à la carte* tonight, Percy.'

Percy fills his glass and takes a sip. 'Not bad. I've had better.' He looks up at the waitress. 'I suppose I'll have to have the lamb then. I hope it's more tender than you.'

The waitress sticks out her lower lip, but she darts away without comment, save the crackle of her starched pinafore.

'What's come over you?' Ivor says. 'I never heard you giving lip before. Why've you got it in for that little girl?'

'Can't you see the way she's treating us? Acting like she fell out of the top drawer and we ought to get down on our knees and thank her for it.'

Ivor shakes his head. 'You're talking riddles tonight, boyo.'

'Life's a riddle,' Percy says, 'but I think I'm getting to the answer at last.' He takes a long drink of wine, then another. 'I think so.'

'What is the answer then?' Dai speaks in a hollow tone, as if his voice were the echo in the Cwm Ammon caves back home. 'If you got it, you'd be doing me a favour to share it.'

'All right are you then, Dai?' Ivor leans across the table to study Dai's face. 'I thought you'd gone into a bit of a soc.'

'*You* know the answer already.' Percy refills Dai's glass, which he has emptied in two swallows.

'Do I, Percy? It don't feel like I do.'

'I been living in a dream,' Percy says. 'Not acting, not doing, but letting others do to me. I been like . . . like that wine vase there . . . an empty thing for others to pour into.'

'*Daro!*' Ivor says, lighting a Woodbine. 'There's daft you're talking, Percy. I'd lay off that wine if I was you.'

'You're not like that, Dai. Nobody can pour into you because you're full to the brim with your own self–'

'Chesty,' Dai says. 'Domineering. I know I am.'

'No, I didn't meant it like that–'

'I meant it, Percy.'

'Well, a man's got to have a bit of bravado, Dai. That's what I'm saying. You got to laugh in people's faces when they throw clodges at you. Laugh at your mistakes, too. Laugh at danger and run into it full pelt–'

'Hold on, hold on,' Ivor says. 'I don't like the way you're drifting, Percy, drink or no. I think you're going radically wrong here. Laughing and racing into danger in't no way to live. Look at that girl we saw a few hours back. Look what happened to her. She acted like you're saying, didn't she, and it put the mockers on her. Her Mam and Dad in't laughing tonight, I guarantee.'

To his surprise, Ivor finds Dai and Percy staring at him, their faces rigid with shock, like Lot's wife turned to a pillar of salt.

'Why are you two looking daggers at me? I'm only saying the truth. Reckless behaviour don't pay. "Blessed are the meek," the Bible says, "for they shall inherit the earth."'

'They'll inherit the bloody leftovers,' Dai says. 'Give me a fag, Ivor, please.'

'You don't smoke, Dai. You gave up two years back on doctor's orders, remember? That nasty bout with your chest—'

'Ivor, will you give me a fag, or shall I go out and buy a packet?'

'No, no, help yourself.' Ivor pushes the Woodbines towards Dai. 'I wasn't being stingy, just thinking of your health.'

Dai draws a cigarette from the packet and taps the end on the tablecloth. 'Percy,' he says, 'what's put all this in your head?'

'It was seeing that woman, Dai. What she did . . .'

Dai lights the Woodbine and takes a long drag. He blows out the smoke in a slow stream, his head tilted towards the ceiling. 'Changed my mind about women,' he says. 'I'll tell you that much. I never knew women had the gumption. Forty years old and I never saw it in one of them till today.'

'I don't think Welsh women have it,' Percy says. 'Except my Mam, maybe. Though she's not a suffragette.'

Welsh women have more sense, Ivor is thinking. Pity Welshmen can't appreciate it. 'As a jewel of gold in a pig's snout, so is a fair woman without discretion' sums up what *he* thinks of suffragettes.

'She laughed, Percy, when I had a few words with her. Knowing what she was going to do, she still laughed.'

'There's fine,' Percy says. 'You'll always remember that, Dai, like a gift.'

'Like a love affair,' Dai says, blowing tangled curls of smoke. 'I feel like I was the man she loved at the last. And *deuce*, I loved her back with my whole heart!'

'Glorious,' Percy says. 'I believe I'd give *my* life for something like that.'

To Ivor's relief, the waitress arrives with their dinners. 'Thank you, love,' he says. 'Will you bring us three cups of tea, please? One medium, two very strong.'

'I'm hungry,' Dai says, taking up his knife and fork, 'after all.'

''Course you are,' Ivor says. 'Nothing in your stomach but air and wine since twelve o'clock. Chicken looks good, all breast meat. Decent helpings of veg, too.'

'Good as Bethan's cooking, eh, Ivor?'

'Well . . . I wouldn't go that far.'

Percy plays with his fork and gazes into the smoke wreaths that still waft over their table. Through this hazy curtain, he sees the restaurant door open.

Mari, in all her finery, sweeps in and stands poised, looking about for an empty table.

The fork drops from Percy's hand. His dinner forgotten, he feasts his eyes on her as she turns her queenly head about. Her face . . . her sunset burst of hair . . . her deportment . . . her dress, the colour of the sky on a summer night . . . all is as he imagined it. Beyond what he has imagined, for his dreams grow wan and sickly compared to this vivid creature, this Queen of Sheba, this Morgan Le Fay, this Titania, borne to him on the London night from who knows where? Oh, the tricks Fate pulls from its sleeve! Here she is, in a place and time he'd never have expected her, catching him all unprepared, his loins ungirded, his wits unsharp, his brain befuddled with wine.

What to do then? Act, he must act now.

Percy rises.

Dai looks up. 'Where you off, Perce?'

'The lav,' Percy says. 'I'm coming, love.' Under his breath he murmurs, 'I'm on my way.'

Does Mari see the slender golden-haired youth intrepidly bearing down on her, his blue eyes ablaze with the zeal of his mission?

Well, yes . . . but not in any way to speak of. She notices, amid the bustle of the restaurant, a young feller who seems a bit the worse for drink, getting in the way of the waitresses and stumbling over chairlegs, and thinks, 'If they can't hold it, they shouldn't take it.' She observes, too, the green satin rosette pinned to his lapel and thinks, 'Oh, a Welsh supporter . . . no wonder.' And she'd thought of going with one tonight!

Forgot, didn't she, what boozers they are? But now she sees a couple leaving a table near the window, and speeds towards it, moments before Percy reaches the spot where she just stood.

Percy watches Mari cross to the vacant table. Other men raise their heads to watch her, too, a trail of admiration spreading in her wake as she sails by as grandly as a flagship in full regalia. She seats herself with the dignity of a duchess, her head held high under her splendid hat, her legs crossed, the royal-blue skirt flowing in waves over her limbs, a tantalizing glimpse of ankle beneath the hem. Percy can only stand and stare, a mariner adrift already, only moments after casting off from shore.

Mari glances over the menu. She doesn't have much money tonight, most of it gone into Harold Bains's pocket (or out of it by now), so she scans the cheaper items and says, 'Sausage and chips, please, and a cup of tea and a glass of wine while I'm waiting.'

When the waitress moves off and Mari looks about the restaurant, she notices again the fair young Welshman. He hovers near the door, his eyes fixed on her, his face all flushed, his body quivering.

Mari's heart begins to pump. She had thought him drunk when she first saw him. Now, his face so feverish, his eyes so intent, it's more likely he's a madman.

Sweet Jesus, she does get them! All the lunatics and lackwits in London run sniffing at her heels, as if she had some special scent . . .

Is he really dangerous? Should she call for the manager? No, she can't do that. He hasn't done anything yet except stand there. No law against standing, or against staring either (though there should be). She'll just turn her head away, ignore him, and hope he moves on.

Mari looks out of the window into the Square, concentrates on a chemist's shop opposite where brightly-lit billboards advertise Vin Vitae for Weak Women, Crinshaw's Brain and Liver Tablets, Dr Higginbotham's Cure for Drunkenness and Opium Addiction. In front of these signs and their larger-than-life illustrations of unfortunate sufferers – a wraithlike female, a sprawling man tipping a bottle to his mouth – swims the demented face of the Welsh youth.

He reminds her of someone . . . of Antonio. *Antonio?* Bloody hell, she must be going mad herself. And yet . . . putting aside the obvious differences . . . something in that look, in the nervy way he holds himself . . .

The waitress places a cup of tea and a glass of wine in front of her.

'Ta,' Mari says, and glances anxiously towards the door.

He's gone!

Mari blows out a breath.

She looks around the tables. There he is, sitting with two other fellers, still staring at her. But she feels easier now. Seeing him with companions, eating dinner like everyone else, takes the edge off the fear she felt when he seemed by himself, a man come in off the streets to do mischief, a lone wolf searching for prey.

Ah, that's it! That's where she sees a likeness. Antonio, in the Bioscope, a stiletto in his hand, and she thinking he was about to murder her. All on edge he was, just like this bloke. Mari realizes she is returning the young man's stare and quickly looks away.

'Have you heard of Malatesta?' Antonio asked her once, a question to foil a question.

'Just tell me where you go,' Mari had pleaded, 'and who you meet.'

She'd grown suspicious of the evenings, two every week, Tuesdays and Fridays regular, that he spent away from her, 'to be with old friends from Italy'.

'No, I've never heard of him,' she said. 'Is he one of the pals you go off to see?'

Antonio had snorted. 'Ravachol? You have heard of Ravachol?'

'No!'

'Lucheni? Acciarito? Bresci?'

'No, no, bloody no!' They were shouting at each other by this time. 'They're all Italians, I suppose. They all have funny names, anyway. And funny goings-on too, I'll bet, or you wouldn't be so clemmed up about it. Why won't you tell me, Antonio—'

'They were all Anarchists, *carissima*,' he said, quiet suddenly, 'and they are all dead. I can meet them now only in spirit.'

'Anarchists go around throwing bombs and murdering people,' she said, '. . . and getting themselves hung . . . or blown up, like in Sidney Street. You're not one of them, Antonio. Tell me you're not.'

'Ah, Mari,' he said. 'You are like all the English workers, an ignorant serf–'

'And what are you?' Mari said. 'The next bomb-slinger? The next head for the hangman's noose? What's the use of that?'

Tears creep into Mari's eyes now, remembering. She blinks them away, sets down her cup, and looks out of the window. She'd thought she could change his mind, keep him from risk by lavishing love. If she'd known the outcome she'd have joined him, tossed the bomb he handed her and gone to her death crying, '*Vive la Révolution! Vive l'Anarchie!*' – the slogans he had taunted her with.

But no . . . she could never have killed, not even for Antonio. He was wrong, her best-beloved. You can't build dreams or self-respect on charnel heaps.

Her sausages and chips arrive.

She eats, but the food on her plate might as well be of papier mâché for all the pleasure she gets from it. After a few bites, she can't stop herself from turning again to the young man who brought all this on, the blue-eyed highly-strung Welshman in whose starved looks and jittery body she recognizes a kinship with her once-and-nevermore lover – the suffering posture of the devout assassin.

Mari and Percy stare at each other. This time Mari does not flinch, knowing that whoever that lad might knock off, it won't be her. On the contrary, he fancies her, with all the instant and unbounded passion that seized Antonio in the dark cinema, compelling him to put away, for a while at least, his knife, and choose, over the Anarchist's bloody deed, her embrace.

There's no denying it, the old excitement is welling up in her again as she links eyes with her partner-in-wishes, her thoughts hotfooting it to closer, more intimate carryings-on in the seclusion of her room, which she pictures now in all its ravishing lusty charm, swept clean of nostalgia at last by the promise of a here-and-ready lover. After all, it's fated. She *did* decide last night on a Welshman.

Well, how to bring it off?

If she crooked her little finger, he'd leap tables to come to her, but she'd rather have a quiet word than a public scene, and besides there are his companions to think of, to get out of the way. Both have their backs to Mari, so they are unaware of the turmoil whipping up between her and their mate.

She's famished suddenly, and the food seems so flavourful after all. She hardly notices that the chips have grown limp, the sausages slippery with congealed fat.

When her plate is empty, still hungry, she hails the waitress. 'Another cup of tea, please, and a slice of Manchester tart.'

While she waits for her dessert, she flirts with Percy, treating him to her extensive repertoire of smiles and glances, vastly amused to see how he strives to juggle his attention between chattering with his mates and making love to her behind their backs.

Her tart and tea are brought, she consumes them, and makes up her mind. Enough dallying. Time to act, or she'll be late for the Palladium. Mari puts a sixpence beside her cup, picks up her bill, and rises. Throwing Percy a significant look, she crosses the restaurant to the counter where Nan herself sits, dressed in black satin, her hair a formidable concoction of indigo curls, sequins, lace, and paper flowers, like a wedding-cake in the wrong colour. Her fingers nimbly press buttons to whisk up price cards in the window of her till. She gives Mari a smile as lavish and false as the rouge on her cheeks and says, as she rings up the bill, 'Everything in order, was it?'

'Lovely, thanks. Couldn't have been better.' Mari addresses these words to Percy who, in response to her bidding, has come to her side. She must tilt her head back to gaze into his face, and she likes this novelty of looking up at a man, the feeling of littleness and fragility not often permitted to a woman of her size.

'Three-and-six, please,' Nan says.

Mari's head swings round, her face altering rapidly as she stares into the till window. 'Can't be!'

Nan's face changes too, her mouth tightening as she rattles off the items on Mari's bill: 'Sausages and chips, two shillings, glass of wine, sixpence, two teas, threepence each, Manchester tart, sixpence.'

'Oh, blast it!' Mari opens her purse, but she already knows she's eightpence short. Made witless by Percy, she forgot she wasn't supposed to have wine or dessert. She picks out the coins and holds them in her open palm for Nan's inspection. 'Two and tenpence is all I have, unless I take back the tip, and I won't do that, 'cause I know how hard waitresses work, so be a sport and let me have the sweet on tick till tomorrow, will you, dear?'

Nan, her mouth a thread of scarlet, shakes her head.

'What can I do? You can see I haven't got the right money.'

Nan looks over her shoulder and says to the man operating the tea urn, 'Step into the street, Joe, and find a constable.'

Mari throws up her hands. 'Ah, come off it! I'm a regular customer–'

Suddenly, four bright shillings rattle on to the counter top. Just above her hat, Mari hears for the first time the voice of her wooer. 'I'd be happy to pay for this lady, and I'd thank you, Missus, to keep civil. If you ask me, there's too much rudeness *à la carte* in this establishment.'

'Likewise,' Mari snaps at Nan. 'And keep the change since you're so hard up.'

She spins on her heel to Percy. 'I thank you for coming to my aid like a gentleman.'

Percy's head reels with pleasure. 'I'd come anywhere, any time, for you.'

'Right-oh,' Mari says, 'come to the stage door of the Palladium at half-past ten and I'll pay your money back.'

'The Palladium?' Percy's eyes open wide as this trick of Fate presents itself, a coincidence some would say, but he knows better . . . the cards are falling into place.

'I do a magic act there,' Mari explains. 'Mari Prince is my name, but onstage I'm The Infamous Princess Marie.'

Percy nods his head. 'A magician. It all fits. You couldn't be anything else, nothing ordinary would suit.'

Mari savours the compliment and flatters him in return with a faint blush and a downward fall of her eyelashes. 'Will you come then?'

'I'll be there,' Percy says. 'You can count on it. But not for my money. It's the reward of your company I'm after. I'm Percy . . . Percy Fly.'

Mari gives him one last long look, a pledge of full recompense, and as Percy stands amazed, spellbound, glides out of the restaurant to vanish into the blue-black night where electric lights wink and flicker like will-o'-the-wisps and smoky apparitions dance above the chestnut-vendor's brazier.

14

Mary: Saturday Evening

How the day has lingered, tiresome, stubborn, a busybody who sat in the parlour still when I woke from my brief but crowded hour of sleep.

The hall clock was just chiming five. I rose from the couch and crossed to the window to search, as eagerly as a lover, for the approach of night. Out in the street the children played and neighbours gossiped over garden fences. Tuesday will be the first of April, and the days begin to draw out. Countless spring and summer evenings I have stood behind windows watching other lives, listening to the laughter and shouts of children, the voices of men and women. No matter. It is almost over now, and I shall not be here to see buds turn into leaves. Soon I will sell this house of pain, pack my belongings, leave the city of heartbreak, and be off home to northern air and northern space.

Yet . . . daylight mocks my ambition, a duenna at my heels as I go out of the parlour, whispering, 'Mary, you shall not.' And, also, I had a dream that did not augur well. . . .

I go into the kitchen for a glass of water.

I dreamed . . . what did I dream? Standing in the kitchen, holding a green majolica dish in the shape of a spread leaf, I try to recall. Usually my dreams are so vivid that, waking, I remember them more clearly than events of the previous day. And I know from feelings that linger, from the way my heart beats, from my taut nerves, that this afternoon's dream was as powerful and affecting as its predecessors. Why then can I recall only pieces, a view of the whole tapestry eluding me, as if I peeped through a keyhole or a curtain chink?

Ah, there were obstacles in the dream, too, and these I do remember. First, the front wall of a great house, moss-covered stone, turrets, gargoyles over the door and winged creatures in the roof niches: a mansion, the dwelling of some aristocrat. In my dream, I entered the house. I saw and did things there . . . but in memory I cannot enter, the great oak door and all the windows remaining fast.

A cat appears on the terrace, a magnificent creature, a full-blooded Persian, preening itself and showing off. I stoop to stroke its fur – and draw back my hand in revulsion. Blisters as big as carbuncles, and pus-filled, disfigure its body, a horrible, stinking mange teeming with maggots. I aim a kick at the creature with the toe of my boot and it slithers away, hissing, into a rhododendron bush.

But this is not in sequence! It is not accurate! It was something I saw *inside* the house that first beguiled me and then brought repugnance . . . but what, what? I can't remember!

A fence, too, covered in vines, I dreamed, and behind it the splash of water and the sound of voices. A river, I thought, and bathers, and would climb the fence – but someone stood behind me and pulled me back – and then other events occurred between this person and myself, a thing done that I did not want but could not prevent . . . And there the links snap and I hold a broken chain in my hands.

I look down and it is not the majolica dish but the carving-knife I grasp. Yesterday I sharpened it on the grindstone, such a fine edge on the blade that when I draw it lightly across my index finger, blood wells out.

Daylight at my elbow tut-tuts and says, 'You'll never pull it off, Mary. You are no Anarchist, no revolutionary. No Queen Boadicea, you. Why, you'd never have given Alf that thrust and you know it well. It's not like pouring an old man's medicine into the chamber-pot, is it? Murder – real, violent, bloody murder – takes guts you haven't got. So there it is.'

It sounds like my father's voice, forever harping that I must not, I am not able, I am not permitted.

'I can! I will!' I cry. 'I must!' Insults and obscenities fly to my tongue, the demons lashing out, and I shout at the top of my voice as I whirl around the kitchen, lunging with the knife.

My fracas with the phantom draws me into the passage, for he recedes before my onslaught, this shadow of my father, ever dodging and evading the death-blow I would deliver.

The mocking smile, the scornful eyebrows, the arrogant tilt of his great bushy head madden me. I want him resurrected, like Lazarus, so that I may kill him again and again – a continuous, eternal act.

I enter the quiet dining room and see that he has vanished, flown up the chimney or melted through the picture window. He has retreated to his after-world, where he walks, I daresay, with others of his kind, vicious prophets and misogynist saints, Isaiah, Jeremiah, Paul, Augustine. With massive pride, he tells them, 'I have a daughter and I scourge her, sirs,' the worthies all nodding their hoary approval.

'Woman is born in sin, and in the stinking pit of sin she will wallow like the sow until man raises her up. You men are the guardians of women's souls. Forget it at your peril. Be wary, ever, in the company of woman, lest by her wiles she drag you down into the mire with her. . . .' This from the pulpit.

And in his study, the two of us alone in that room of stern, unyielding shapes, the ponderous desk, the forbidding tomes, 'Mary, Mary, you are a hopeless, helpless case. You have neither the wit nor the willingness to learn. Bend over my knee. I will beat you into shape or beat you to pulp, for I can brook no in-between.'

I dreamed . . . I dreamed . . . I remember not!

Across the room, I meet my own face in the sideboard mirror, an elf face, pale as mist. Behind my hair, all tousled and damp from exertion, my eyes glitter like some malevolent sprite's, a creature risen from the miasma of a swamp to befoul the pleasant upper air with her poisonous breath.

What have I to do with Mari Prince! It is like the story of the frog and the princess. Carelessly, she tossed a brightly-coloured ball, I caught it where I stood knee-deep in quicksand and tossed it back. For that I expected rich rewards, outrageous favours, believing she had given me special, not accidental, notice.

Does one whose eyes turn briefly on your face, who plays with you the game of a moment, owe you, therefore, a lifelong obligation? Or does obligation lie with the one noticed, a debt of gratitude for that fleeting but ecstatic instant when the ball lay in the palm of your hand . . . for that joyous second when you raised your arm and put the ball in flight again?

So I thought with daylight hovering at my shoulder as I

crossed the room to meet myself in the mirror beneath the grinning, carved wolf's-head. I laid down the knife and pressed my palms to the wooden grape clusters.

'Come to your senses,' I commanded my image. 'It is *his* head you want on a platter, not hers, not Alf's. And you can never have it. In life or in death, he thwarts and spurns your endeavours.'

Daylight scoffs at and discredits all night affairs. Yet, no matter how long she seems to tarry, her watchful eyes must close at last. Like a worn-out nurse, she nods off; and then night, and we the outcasts, its offspring, come into our own again. And so as I stood before the mirror, night's harbinger, evening in its grey cloak, came at length to whisper in my ear, 'Soon, Mary, soon.'

I picked up the knife, left the dining room and came upstairs to write, Mother, this last letter to you. Next time we speak it will be face-to-face, my hand in yours, my head resting on your shoulder. But first I must do the deed . . . and before that, tell you all that has transpired these past weeks and how my plan has shaped itself and why I cannot, now, renege on my promise to Miss Prince.

After that first time, I paid further visits to her abode, always by night, always uninvited, but not unrewarded. On the contrary, my pleasure heightened and my sangfroid increased with each occasion that I sallied forth as a gentleman. On my second visit, I went straight to her street off Holland Park Avenue at a time of night when I knew she would be occupied at the Palladium, for my purpose was to find an entry to her house. After hearing her revile me as she made love to Alf's photograph, I had resolved that it would be more fitting, more satisfactory, to make her reacquaintance. I could no longer settle for revenge as an anonymous assailant. She must know that *I* was the avenger . . . the victor . . . cower and weep before me ere I dealt the blow, and be fully cognizant of her weakness and my power. I wanted her in awe of me, subjugated. Nothing less would suffice.

Thus, I must gain access to her room, hide there until she fell asleep, tiptoe to her bed, knock her into a deeper slumber, bind her hands and feet, and when she woke . . . Well, I have dwelt long and delightfully upon the exchanges that would occur between us then. I will not tell you this part yet. Kept secrets bloom like hothouse flowers; spoken, they shrivel, plucked from their rarefied air by the inclemencies of language. When it is over and I am sated, you shall perhaps be my confidante, Mother.

I arrived in that genteel, law-abiding street at ten o'clock and found, as I had expected, no one abroad.

A light shone from the front parlour where, I supposed, her landlady sat up; the rest of the house was dark. Boldly I pushed open the front gate, strode to the door and tried the knob. The door was locked, but I had anticipated this and suffered no disappointment.

I walked round the house and tried the back door. That, too, was fast, similarly the windows on either side. Who in London, even in the fortress of the suburbs, neglects to lock up at night when a murderer stalks?

There were no other means of reaching the upper windows, no tree here, no shed that might house a ladder. And so I knew I would have to climb the larch again.

I rejoiced in this knowledge! It was what I had hoped for, to be forced into that fearful and exhilarating ascent, to have it ordained by fate.

To the front of the house I ran, looked up and down the road, saw it deserted, mounted the larch and sped up through its branches like a monkey. Her window was dark tonight and I could see nothing save the leaves of the aspidistra spread against the pane. I pressed my fingers against the cracked and blistered wood that edged the glass and pushed. A creak, a shudder, and the window rose, as I had known it would.

I pushed the window wide and climbed in, squeezing past the aspidistra. I could see nothing at first save the dark blocks of furniture, but as my eyes grew accustomed to the gloom, and aided by moonlight, I gradually made out the lavishly bedecked bed, the wardrobe and dressing table, all at one end of the spacious room. Standing in her room, touching her life at its core, I felt the old awe and wonder possess me, and I hungered to know more of her, to see all that was dear and private so that I should touch her heartbeat, connect with her thoughts, and hear, I hoped, the fluttering of her soul.

I removed my shoes and padded about the room, running my hands over everything, satin, wood, brass, and ormolu. I opened her wardrobe and gently rifled her clothes to feel their texture and contours. Then I pulled out the dressing-table drawers and fingered the lace and silk of her under-garments. One drawer was full to the brim with lace handkerchiefs, more than I had ever seen or she could ever use. So I took one as a souvenir and slipped it into my breast pocket.

It was time to depart. I had settled that my hiding-place would be beneath the bed itself, for I had lifted the red satin coverlet and discovered ample space. How I longed to lie for just a minute on that bed which promised such luxurious repose, but this I forbade myself, for fear a rumple in the coverlet, a misplaced pillow, might alert her.

One thing remained, and though I had put it off as the only possession of hers I had no wish to touch, yet I must now, if only to regain my strength of purpose. I took up the photograph in its silver frame. The dark face was hard to make out by moonlight, a man with a moustache and sideburns, like thousands of others, but I did not need to see the likeness. Bitter bile rising in my throat assured me it was Alf, and I was resolute again.

I climbed through the window, a more delicate feat than entering, but one I accomplished with the agility of an acrobat.

As I strode along the pavement, a figure rounded the bend and marched towards me. My heart lurched, my feet faltered and stumbled. It was the policeman whom I had seen with Miss Prince, her protector and would-be suitor.

I took hold of myself. He was simply walking his beat, and I had as much right in the street as he. I was simply an honest gentleman, minding my business, and so he would perceive me.

As we drew level, I nodded and touched the brim of my hat. I dared not risk speech or look him in the face. He stopped, but I hurried on, my heart bumping now against my chest, an alarm pounding in my head.

Mother, I have passed the hours, and the hall clock has struck nine. I must leave you and dress for my engagement.

15

Saturday Night at the Palladium

Norman Fairchild, the Palladium's resident comedian, reaches the end of the raucous and risqué routine that keeps the audience in stitches every Saturday night.

In his box above the stage, the Master of Ceremonies rises, suave in his dark suit and white carnation. 'Thank you, Norman,' he says, twirling his moustache and twitching his eyebrows, 'for advice on how to have a jolly good time at the seaside. Perhaps I'll leave the missus at home this year. She's been showing me the wrong sights, I believe.'

The men in the audience clap and hoot. The Master of Ceremonies raps for order with his gavel, and when quiet is restored, says in a different voice, more weighty and portentous, 'Mesdames, Messieurs, our next act features an *extra*-ordinary lady, a star with a galaxy of talents, the toast of Europe and the darling of America. She sings like a nightingale, dances like a prima ballerina, looks like an angel and, if that's not enough, she's a magician unequalled in the Western hemisphere, a conjurer par excellence, a female Houdini, an English Circe –'

Cries of appreciation interrupt him. He lifts his hand. 'Yes, you know who I mean – the delightful, the magnificent, the mystifying – ladies, gentlemen, guests from Wales – The Infamous Princess Marie!'

He sits down amid thunderous applause. As the houselights dim and assume a weird greenish cast, the violins in the orchestra pit begin an eerie, high-pitched tune and the curtains swing back to reveal a backdrop of oriental domes and minarets beneath a sky thick with glittering sequined stars.

Sitting between Dai and Ivor in the front row of the gallery, Percy holds his breath. Now is the moment he has yearned for all his wistful life. He feels as if a great, illustrious hand had reached out of the sky to point a finger at his breast, a sonorous, disembodied voice intoning, 'You, Percy Fly, are one of the chosen. You shall be numbered among that small exalted band for whom a wish comes true.'

Percy folds his arms on the gallery rail, rests his chin on his hands, and gives himself up to Mari, dressed in shimmering aquamarine pantaloons and a black satin tunic hung with pearls, as she glides from the wings to centre stage.

She stands still and silent until the applause dies, and when the house is so quiet the whisper of a lady's gown might be heard, she raises her right arm, the bracelets on her wrists clinking merrily, and flicks her hand, as if to toss a gift out into the audience.

At this sign, the orchestra strikes up an energetic tune. Mari believes in quick changes of pace, a layering of moods which she throws out fast and thick, wrapping her patrons in a rainbow of emotions. When the music reaches the right bar, she places her hands on her hips, and belts out her theme song, her body swaying in time to the lively beat:

> From old Baghdad to London town,
> I am a lady of renown!
> Kings have had me out to tea,
> Sultans sold harems for me.
> Royal hands have made a pass,
> And royal hearts I've broke – alas!
> All around the world you'll see
> Gentlemen who pine for me,
> 'Cause I'm the Infamous Princess Marie,
> That's me! That's me!

To punctuate the last line she high-kicks twice, first with the left leg, then with the right, the gauzy pantaloons billowing over her strong supple limbs as the male patrons shout, clap, and stamp their admiration. Mari smiles and bows her head. Her pleasure is genuine. She wrote the words of the song herself.

Now the lights dim, and for a few seconds the house is plunged into the deep black hush of midnight, only the winking stars on the backdrop visible. Percy breathes hard, out of puff already with the exertion of keeping up with Mari's switches.

Slowly a soft pale light creeps across the stage. When it

discovers and embraces Mari, Percy gasps. In those blacked-out moments she has changed completely. Gone the exotic costume and oriental finery. Now she is clad in a dress woven of English blossoms – paper roses, lilies, and yellow daisies fashioned by Mari's own hand and stitched to white cotton by the Palladium seamstresses to create a gown that seems, under artificial light, a great bouquet of real flowers. On her head, a similarly bedecked hat adorns her vibrant hair, and on one arm she bears a wicker basket filled with violets.

Many (like Antonio) might think this extravagant costume inappropriate to the song she is about to sing. If so, her sweet ethereal soprano will soon disarm these cynics, convincing the doubters that her outfit is symbolic, not literal. Mari sings:

> Underneath the gaslight's glitter,
>   Stands a little fragile girl,
> Heedless of the night winds bitter,
>   As they round about her whirl.

Here the light flickers; an unseen stagehand applies himself to the bellows, and a draught lifts the hem of Mari's gown and flutters all the paper petals:

> There are many sad and weary,
>   In this pleasant world of ours,
> Crying ev'ry night so dreary,
>   Won't you buy my pretty flow'rs?

Applause erupts again when Mari reaches the final verse, handkerchiefs appear as soft-hearted ladies dab their eyelids . . . and again the lights expire.

Percy's eyes, too, are wet; his heart brims and then overflows, like a goblet tipped up, a potent brew flowing through his veins. He feels himself engulfed by sorrow and desire, and shudders with delight.

The lights come up. Once more the stage is suffused in a watery, greenish glow, an under-sea glimmer in which the Eastern backdrop seems insubstantial, shifting, like a reflection. Mari has donned her long black magician's cloak and holds a top hat in one hand, a black wand in the other. She has come to the conjuring part of her act and, like a true enchantress, she has again altered her appearance. Tall and stately in the flowing cloak, she is an other-worldly being now, a queen of nether realms and invisible hosts, her hair an elfish oriflamme, her face spectral, her violet-shadowed eyes mysterious as rune-stones.

She places the hat upside down on a small table covered with a scarlet velveteen cloth deeply fringed and tasselled, taps the brim with her wand and holds out her left hand. Out of the hat and into her poised fingers a strip of amber chiffon springs, followed by other diaphanous bits of colour, blue, mauve, silver-grey, indigo, beryl, magenta – a fountain of chiffon, airy and graceful, rises from the hat and drifts through Mari's fingers to float out high over the heads of the audience, an iridescent arch, a multi-coloured corona, a faery phenomenon such as our world (Percy thinks) could never produce.

As he joins in the collective sigh sweeping through the audience, Mari opens her hand and the yards of chiffon glide back to the stage, back to Mari's charmed fingers and, piece by piece, the aureole sinks into the hat like the rays of another planet's variegated sun sinking below the horizon. When the last shard of colour has vanished, applause rings out.

'What a spectacle,' Percy murmurs. 'What a masterpiece!'

'*Daro!* how'd she do that?' Ivor whispers.

Dai clears his throat. 'Strings,' he says. 'Just strings, Ive.' Then he adds, 'She's a fine-looking woman though. You nearly want her to take you in.'

Tonight Mari gives the house the best of her superlative repertoire. Her new lover is out in the audience and awareness of him makes her generous and showy. She levitates, mind-reads, chops herself in half, and vanishes behind a curtain to reappear from the wings, scantily dressed in rhinestones, feathers, and fishnet to offer, for the first time, a brand-new marvel – daring, dazzling, death-defying (if anything goes amiss she will end up with concussion at least).

Again she taps the brim of the top hat. A live bird, a snowy pigeon, hops on to her finger and climbs her outstretched arm to perch on her shoulder. Another tap, another bird, and so on, until a dozen pigeons are perched on each of Mari's arms and she seems to have sprouted wings.

'Oooh . . . ahhh . . .' the audience murmurs.

A mauve spotlight transforms Mari into an ancient mythic goddess, half woman, half swan, as she stands motionless and eerie before the mesmerized house. A haunting tune starts up from the orchestra and before the spellbound, terrified eyes of the audience, she begins to ascend, a female Gabriel, towards the proscenium.

Her head vanishes, then her body, for a split second her legs hover, a spasm passes through them making her knees jerk, then they too rise, a little unsteadily but nevertheless miraculously, out of sight. She has disappeared, the stage is bare. The lights come on. The audience is in shock, only a cough or a nervous titter breaking the silence here and there. Then the tension explodes in a resounding volley of applause. The front row is up, the second, the third. Soon the entire house is on its feet, whistling, calling 'Bravo! Encore!' and crying Mari's name, 'Princess Marie! Princess Marie!'

But Mari can't come back to take a bow. Two stagehands are detaching her from all the wires, some of them entangled now in her hair and her costume.

'The leg ones don't work proper, Danny,' she tells one of the hands. 'I thought I'd come a cropper when half of me was stuck. I could have landed on my behind, you know.'

'I had a bit of a turn myself, Miss Prince, when you wouldn't budge. Afraid you'd drop back down, wasn't I?'

'Flat on my arse. That would have been a grand finale.' She laughs, then slaps the other stagehand on the wrist. 'Here, don't get personal, Tom! I'll do that one myself, thank you.'

'Fantastic, Mari love!' Doris whisks by, leading the chorus girls. She pinches Mari's cheek. 'A proper genius, you are. My heart was in my mouth.'

The girls, in cheeky caps, brass-buttoned tunics, and black tights, blow Mari kisses, flick up their thumbs, or tip her a wink, a word of praise.

Alf Ramsey appears in their wake.

'You brought the house down, Mari.'

'And myself very nearly.' Freed from the wires she flexes her shoulders and tosses her hair. 'It came off all right, though.'

The way he's looking at her makes the colour rise in her cheeks and she turns away. 'We'll have to do something about those leg wires, Danny.'

'I'll work on 'em, Miss Prince. We need to double 'em up, maybe.' The stagehands depart with handfuls of Mari's wires.

'How about you and me doubling up after the show?' Alf says softly just beside her right ear, so close Mari can feel his breath on her cheek.

'Oh Alf, don't start. Can't you get that off your mind for once?'

'You, Mari, not *that*. *You're* on my mind . . . every minute.'

Mari turns her back on him and concentrates on Doris, leading the chorus in a soft-shoe shuffle to the tune of 'Oh, Mr Porter'. As they slide across the stage in weaving lines, the girls croon, 'Whooo, whooo, shhh, shhh,' and a shiver runs up Mari's spine, their imitation of train noises is so erotic.

Doris, in silver tights and a purple tunic, strikes a pose centre stage, wide-legged and wide-eyed, her hands folded on the knob of her cane, her chin and her breasts tilted. Her voice is a mixture of girlish innocence and brazen innuendo as she sings:

> Oh, Mr Porter, what shall I do?
> I wanted to go to Birmingham
> But they've put me off at Crewe!
> Oh, Mr Porter, help me if you can!
> Oh, Mr Porter, what a silly girl I am!

Alf's hand grasps Mari's bare shoulder. His palm is warm and capacious; his fingers pressing her skin cause a rash of goose pimples, as naughty visions frolic like the chorus line in front of her eyes.

'How's your wife, Alf?' she says.

'As refusing as ever.' His tingly, tenacious fingers press harder. 'A thorn in my side Mary is, as her father warned me.'

Mari pulls away and turns to face him. 'Roses have thorns,' she says.

'Mary's not a rose, take my word for it.' He shakes his head slowly, definitely. 'No flower, my Mary. Just a prickly Lancashire briar through and through.'

For a moment Mari stares into his grey eyes, into the hunger she would (no point denying it) like to feed, to feast on indeed, for he's a man whose body proportions suggest a banquet of lusts, a cornucopia of sexual delights for the woman he invites to dine at his table.

'You're a married man, Alf,' she says, 'I've no appetite for that,' and walks away from him to her dressing room.

Mari is brushing her hair in front of the mirror when Rudolph, the janitor, appears in the doorway of her dressing room. 'It's nearly your curtain call, Miss Prince. Mr Ramsey sent me to fetch you.'

Mari fastens on her magician's cloak and goes with Rudolph down the corridor to the wings.

'That was a true sensation you put on tonight,' Rudolph says as he hobbles beside her. 'Ain't seen the like since Queen Victoria's Jubilee parade. You ought to be performing before royalty, like you say in your song. I don't know why you ain't as famous as Vesta Tilly or Marie Lloyd, you got more parts than them. You deserve to rise in the world–'

Mari pats the old man's shoulder. 'I do, Rudolph, I do. Every Saturday night I rise six feet in the air, and tonight I rose twenty at least!'

Alf, standing in the wings, lifts a finger to his lips and tells them, 'Shh!'

The Master of Ceremonies is requesting, 'A big hand for a fellow who could make even the old Kaiser crack his face. If there's a war with Germany, ladies and gents, we'll send him over as our victory weapon. A dose of British humour will knock those Huns on their *derrières*! Here he is, Mr Mirth himself, Norman Fairchild!'

Norman roller-skates on to the stage, tooting his fake cigar and waving a little Union Jack as the audience cheers in patriotic unison.

This time last year Antonio would have been standing beside Mari waiting to take his call after Norman. As she stands in the wings, she feels his presence, as if she were really a sorceress able to conjure up spirits; but tonight his aura is dimmed, another shape interfering with his image, as when someone steps in front of a lamp and diffuses its glow. This someone is a tall blond youth, his eyes as blue and promising as a Bank Holiday sky, and full of midsummer ardour.

'You have got a lot of gall, Mari,' Doris says, leaning in the doorway watching Mari dress. 'You could have broke your neck.'

Mari, fastening up her jacket, gives Doris a brilliant smile. 'I wasn't thinking about my neck. I got other parts of me on my mind tonight.'

'Ah!' Doris lifts one eyebrow and taps her cane on the toe of her patent shoe. 'I knew it! She's not getting all done up like the cat's pyjamas for nothing, I said to myself. You got something better than a bottle of stout lined up tonight, haven't you?'

'My heart is on the mend, I believe,' Mari says, fastening up her hair in the mirror. In the glass she's a brilliant sight, for she has kept her stage make-up, the silver-green and violet eyeshadows, the rouge and lip tint, sensing that her new beau has a taste for the mysterious, the exotic.

'Who's the lucky feller? Here . . .' Doris lowers her voice '. . . you haven't given in to Alf at last, have you?'

Mari laughs. 'No fear! I may be tricky but I'm no thief, Dor. This one's brand-new, I believe . . . never been with a woman by the look of him.'

Doris opens her eyes wide. 'Sounds like you're robbing the cradle.'

'He's not that young . . . just not experienced.'

'Sure he's not queer, are you?'

'Not if I can read a look, and I think I can by now.'

'Well . . .' Doris looks at Mari head to foot. 'You do look smashing, love. I hope it goes great for you, I do really.' Her pale forehead creases. 'You're a bit green yourself, if you don't mind me saying so, when it comes to men. Remember you landed on your arse last time. Sure you've made the right choice, are you?'

Mari, affronted, lifts her head high and laughs, huh-huh, down her nose. 'What a joke! I been with enough fellers, I should think, to know what's what. You're insulting me, Doris.'

'I don't mean to, love, honest. It's just that . . . Antonio . . . he nearly cracked you up–'

'This feller's not a bit like Antonio. He's not an eagle, he's a canary.' Mari smiles and her eyes go soft. 'A fluffy yellow canary in the palm of my hand.'

'I don't like the sound of that either,' Doris says. 'A man's got to have some backbone or he'll bend this way and that–'

'Oh, shut up, Dor!' Mari jabs the last hairpin into her French roll and puts on her hat. 'You've been telling me for a year I should find a new beau. I thought you'd be happy for me, but you're going on like Grandma Grunt!'

'Sorry, love. I am happy. I hope you'll have the time of your life.' She opens her arms and when Mari steps into them hugs her hard. 'There, I'll ruin your get-up. Go on then. Don't hang about when you got a fine feller waiting.'

Mari hurries down the corridor toward Alf Ramsey's office. The manager stands in the doorway, a stack of envelopes in his hand. Silently, he hands Mari one that bears her name.

'Thank you,' Mari says and slips her wages into her bag. Then, as he turns his face from her, his clamped mouth refusing even a 'goodnight', 'Don't be like that with me, Alf. It's not fair. If you were a free man–'

'I'm as free as any man without bonds,' he says. 'As free as a ship without a rudder, Mari, as a tree without roots, free as a hurricane dashing itself out on a hard rock . . .'

Mari stares at him. Has he been drinking? Or is he beginning to crack under all the pressures?

She touches his arm. 'Here, Alf . . .'

His eyes when he turns them on her are full of misery.

'You're all decked out,' Alf murmurs. 'Who's your new suitor? He'll never suit you as I would have–'

Mari turns on her heel. There's nothing to do about such a look, nothing to say in answer to such a tone, except 'Goodnight, Alf.'

She pushes open the stage door . . . and walks straight into an ambush. A whoop goes up from the two dozen or so men waiting there. 'It's her! It's the Princess!' someone cries, and the men whoop again.

'I'd like a private show, Princess Marie.' A man steps forward and offers his arm. 'I bet you have more tricks up your sleeve, don't you?'

'I'm done conjuring for tonight,' Mari says.

'Allow me the chance to persuade you different over dinner at the Alhambra.'

'Or the Ritz.' A second man taps her sleeve. 'Nothing too fine for a princess. I'd be honoured–'

'No, thanks,' Mari says, looking about, 'I'm already engaged.' Where is he, drat him? Did he get cold feet?

There he is, leaning on the lamppost, at the edge of the crowd, his eyes prayerful but his body immobile; he makes no move to claim her, though he must see he's in jeopardy of losing her in the lists to others more combative than he.

'Hullo,' Mari calls and waves to him.

His body jerks violently and he leaps away from the lamppost like a soldier coming to attention. 'How do,' he says, and goes beetroot when all the men turn to look at him. He's shy of course! Shy and worshipful. She'll have to go to him because he hasn't the nerve to come to her, not for fear of his rivals . . . it's herself he's afraid of!

Well, that makes a nice change.

'Excuse me,' Mari says and marches down the path that opens as the men step back and clear her way.

'You didn't forget then,' she says when she reaches Percy.

From a long way off, Percy looks down at her (he must be six-foot-four at least, Mari thinks), and his face is an angel's floating in the air above her head. She'd like to reach up and pull it closer . . . but not yet.

'I'd have to lose my memory to forget you,' he says.

The chorus is coming out now, all perfume and giggles and colourful draperies, and behind Mari the bidding for favours resumes.

'Where do you want to go then?' she says.

'Wherever you take me. To the end of the world if that's what you fancy.'

'Well . . .' she says, '. . . we don't need to tire ourselves out with that sort of journey. I don't live too far. Would you like to come and have a bit of supper at home with me?'

'Of all things,' Percy says, 'I should like that.'

He bends his long body towards her and when she takes his arm quivers like a stalk of golden-rod when a bird alights on it. Indeed, as they go arm-in-arm down the alley towards the lights of Leicester Square, Mari feels as if she's been handed a delicate plant without proper instructions for its care.

'Why've you got a suitcase, Percy?'

'I brought it on the chance you'd invite me to stay.'

'Go on! You didn't even know you were going to meet me. What's in it, really?'
'Just a change of clothes, Mari. Nothing important.'

Mari and Percy: Saturday Night

'So what did you think of my act, Percy?' Mari says as they swing arm in arm down her road. 'You haven't mentioned that yet. Did you like it?'

Above their heads the sky is so heavy with stars, Mari is sure it would topple were it not for the moon catching it up in her long slender fingers like the folds of a damask skirt.

'What did I think of it?' Percy bends his shoulders to bring his face close to hers. Mari, gazing up at him, catches her breath. He might be the moon's own consort, his hair so silvery, his eyes all a-glimmer. 'It's just another part of the whole blooming marvel, Mari, that you turn out to be a lady of renown. When I first set eyes on you in that restaurant I knew you were the one I'd been hunting for all my livelong days. Up hill and down dale, I searched for you, Mari, and just when I was on the verge of giving up, you appeared, out of nowhere like, in all your blazing beauty. Well! After that nothing could surprise me, not even your fame, or your genius, or the way they idolize you at the Palladium. Thrill me, yes, it did do that, but surprise me, no. Your act was superlative, Mari, just like yourself.'

They arrive at her front gate, Mari pushes it open and says, dropping her voice, 'You have to hush up for a bit now.'

He has talked non-stop all the way from Leicester Square, but it's not from boredom that she quiets him. How could she be bored when she herself has been the sole topic of his outpourings? Her hair, her eyes, her voice, her walk, Percy has praised them all; and in those areas where his tongue modestly refrained from comment, his gaze carried on the accolade.

'It's my landlady,' she whispers as she unlocks the front door and ushers Percy inside. 'She don't object to me having a gentleman up, but she'll want to chat if she hears us.'

Percy presses his finger to his lips and, as Mari softly closes the door, looks up the narrow staircase that winds out of sight to the place where a crown of bliss awaits him at the mountain's peak.

'It gets dark further up,' Mari says in his ear as she mounts the stairs first, 'so you'd better hold my hand, love.'

Eagerly, Percy gives her his hand. 'Be thou my guide and lead me on, like a comet in the night sky. I'd follow you—'

'Keep your voice down! And don't drop that suitcase, mind!'

'I got it safe, Mari.'

As they go up, a tinkling sound accompanies Mari – 'like faery bells,' Percy thinks, charmed. 'Drat!' she says. 'It's the bottles in my bag.' She shifts her carrier to her other hand, away from the wall. 'Put your hand on my waist, Percy, instead.'

Percy complies, and is pierced with delight when his palm slips into that inward curve between her chest and her hip, those parts of her that are very much on his mind.

'I wish you'd let me pay for the wine,' he says.

'Silly, you can't pay for everything. You treated us to supper. I got to chip in, too.'

'Your treat is your company, worth a fortune.' Now that he is a couple of steps below her as they ascend, Percy's head is level with Mari's, and he can enjoy the wavy pleasure of brushing his lips against her hair as he whispers, 'No way I can match that gift.'

They come to the second flight where the light in the hallway does not reach, and total darkness engulfs them. Blinded, Percy grips Mari's waist tighter.

'Flipping heck, it's black as the pit. Blacker, 'cause we got lanterns down there.'

'Are you an employee of the dark gentleman, Percy?' Mari giggles, an eerie sound that thrills Percy's nerves.

'Who's he?' he says. 'I'm employed by the Senghenydd Colliery, Mari.'

'Oh, you're a miner, are you? That's a relief. For a minute I thought Old Nick was your boss. He's a pit owner, isn't he?' She is giggling still, and Percy joins her, enthralled by her disembodied trills and amazing wit.

'I'd be a devil if I worked for him.'

'You'd be wicked, wouldn't you?'

'Infamous . . . like you, Mari.'

'That's just my stage name.'

'Still, no smoke without fire, is there?'

'You are a wag, Percy. You can carry a joke, I see. A man after my own heart, I must say, for I do love a laugh.'

Percy, dizzy with joy to discover himself capable of amusing his lady, emits a loud guffaw. 'You never spoke a truer word. I'm after your heart all right!' And he bounds up the three steps that separate them, meaning, in a fit of sudden daring, to kneel at her feet.

But Mari has stopped and turned to face him, for they have reached her door, and so Percy collides with her full force and almost knocks her flat. His arms rushing round her prevent the fall as he clasps her body against his own in an embrace more intimate and more violent than he intended.

'Oh, Mari . . .' Percy says. 'Oh, *Iesu Mawr!*'

'Here, wait a bit. Steady on, lad.' Mari pulls away.

Percy releases her at once. 'Excuse me,' he says, sinking against the wall. 'I wouldn't offend you for a king's ransom.'

'I'm not offended.' Mari reaches her key towards the lock. 'Just a bit shaken up that's all—' The key slips from her hand and clatters on to the oilcloth.

Percy bends to retrieve it, saying, 'Allow me, Mari,' and when he straightens up, the key in his hand, 'I'm shaken up, too, and feeling like I was drunk. But I'll tell you here and now, before we set foot inside your door, my intentions are as honourable as King Arthur's or any of his knights' . . . to me you are a *real* princess and I'll respect you accordingly.' He declaims loudly, passion thrusting caution aside, and goes down on one knee for the second time in his life, pressing her hand to his lips. 'Forever and beyond, Mari, into eternity—'

'Percy, Percy,' Mari pleads, 'get up. You're running away with my sense and I can't think straight—'

'Don't think, Mari.' Percy, rising, holds her hand still. 'Thinking has nothing to do with the heart. Not even distant relations, are they, thinking and feeling? The heart—'

'What was that?' Mari speaks in a different voice suddenly, abrupt and fearful, a tone not at all in keeping with the scene Percy is immersed in, and it jolts him out of his mood.

'What was what?'

'I heard something ... a noise ... a sort of thud inside my room. Didn't you hear it, Percy?'

'No,' Percy says, a bit testy. 'I can only hear the thud of my heart, Mari.'

'Well ... open the door then. I'm cold, and our supper must be, too.'

Mari knows she has spoiled something for Percy, but she can't help it. Now that she's felt his body, heart to heart, and thigh to thigh, what until moments past was an engrossing and thrilling pastime has become suddenly a terribly dangerous occupation.

'Open the door, Percy,' she repeats, and it sounds as if she's saying 'Buzz off!'

Unlocked, the door swings open and a chill wind blows out of the dark room, making them both shiver. Mari is surprised. Her room is never draughty; on the contrary, the gas fire, always on when she's home, makes it permanently stuffy in winter, a temperature she likes for its woollen-blanket embrace, its fur-coat hug, so she never opens the window from November until well into April.

But the window is open. She sees that as soon as she steps inside, fishing in her bag for matches, telling Percy, 'Hold on till I light—'

'What's up, Mari?' Percy comes beside her and puts his hand on her shoulder. 'Have you seen a ghost?'

'My window's open, Percy.'

'No wonder it's like the North Pole in here. You shouldn't leave the window open in winter. You might catch something. I'll close it, shall I?' He crosses the room and pulls the window down. 'There, that's better. It's warmed up already.'

'Yes,' Mari says. 'That's funny.'

'Shall we have a light on, now?'

'I didn't open that window.'

'Eh? Who did then? Your landlady?'

'She never comes in my room unless I ask her. Somebody else did it.' She strikes a match and lights the wick in the hanging lamp.

Darkness transforms instantly into glowing colours and familiar luxuries ... there is her bed draped in lace and satin, its scarlet and blue hangings rich and glistening in the golden light, her Turkish chair (she rests her hands on its velvety back), and her Japanese screen, the glorious birds poised for flight . . . and there is Percy, her golden lad, looking around, taking it all in, trying to speak and finding no adequate words, but never mind, his speechlessness is eloquent and gladdens her.

He is awed, entranced, astonished, as she meant him to be; and watching him turn his head this way and that is like sitting in the audience at the Palladium and watching her own illusions, as a part of Mari always does each time she performs – which is why she's so good, like a good lover, a good parent, or a good general . . . and almost she forgets the matter of the open window.

But not quite.

'Percy,' she says, 'just look around, will you, and see if . . . if there's anything amiss. I'd be grateful to you if you'd just peep in the wardrobe and under the bed–'

''Course I will.'

Mari watches while he looks. 'There's nobody in here, is there, Percy?'

'Nobody but us two, Mari . . . darling.' Percy savours the word, a daring endearment that rolls off his tongue so easily, so silkily, leaving a taste in his mouth more delectable, more tantalizing, than any food or beverage he has relished. Then he sees Mari's face, her posture, the way her hands work on the chair back, and realizes she is still agitated.

'Here, Mari, are you sure – positive – you didn't open that window yourself?'

Mari lifts one hand, presses her fingers to her forehead. 'I might have. I did do a bit of cleaning earlier. And I did wipe the windowpanes and dust the aspidistra–'

'There you are then! Mystery solved. You opened the window so you could reach out and wipe the other side, see.'

It must be so, for if not, how can she become herself again, get on with her night, this gift of a night which has brought her Percy? 'Yes, I must have. My memory isn't so good any more – you must think I'm a proper fool, Percy, to get so jittery, but with these murders and all–'

In one stride Percy is beside her. He places one hand over hers. 'Don't you worry any more. I can see how it is, Mari, for a woman living on her own with that madman on the prowl–'

'Oh, yes, Percy!' Mari says. 'It's terrible really.'

'But see, I'm with you now, and you needn't be afeared, for I wouldn't let him or any feller harm a hair on your head. Do you believe that . . . darling?'

'Yes, Percy.'

He dips his other hand into the bag she has laid on the chair and shows her the newspaper package. 'Look, here's our supper, safe through it all. Let's eat it, shall we? You're hungry, aren't you?'

'I'm starving,' Mari says.

She has laid the table for two and placed in the centre Antonio's twin silver candlesticks. She lights the candles now, as Percy unwraps their supper. As he places a pie, a rissole and a Cornish pasty on each of their plates, Mari turns down the wick in the hanging lamp, unpins her hat, and returns to the table with the wine bottle and a corkscrew.

'I hope you'll like this wine,' she says as she pulls out the cork. 'It was the favourite of a friend of mine who knew what was what.' Mari lifts her glass. 'Here's to your health.'

Percy lifts his own and says, '"Drink to me only with thine eyes, And I will pledge with mine."'

Mari feels herself blush, though it's not embarrassment that flushes her cheeks, but more like the feeling of sitting close to a roaring fire on a winter's night. 'Is that poetry, Percy?'

'It was written by a feller named Ben Jonson, nigh on three hundred years ago.'

'Fancy.' Mari takes up her fork. 'You read a lot of it, do you?'

'Some people think a man's a fool if he likes poetry.'

'Oh, no, that's not right. I think it shows . . . breeding in a man, I do really. I mean, you have to have taste, don't you, and . . . and brains . . . to take pleasure in words, and the sounds and the pictures they make. You have to have imagination, Percy, and that's something I value myself.'

'Perhaps,' Percy says, 'you'll let me read you a bit of poetry while you're finishing your supper. Would you like that, Mari?'

'I should love it,' she says. 'And pour us more wine, too, won't you?'

Percy refills their glasses and lifts his own. 'To your magic.'

'And to yours,' Mari says, and Percy's blood somersaults.

He draws the little leatherbound book from his pocket and flips through the pages while Mari keeps her eyes on his face, finding the food on her plate by touch.

'Here's one I think you'll like. It's one of *my* favourites, any rate.'

He bends his head over the book and Mari gazes at the play of candlelight on his hair of rumpled silk:

> I whispered, 'I am too young.'
> And then, 'I am old enough',
> Wherefore I threw a penny
> To find out if I might love.

Percy pauses and looks up at Mari.

'Yes,' she says softly, 'that's how it is, just like throwing a penny . . . just luck.'

> 'Go and love, go and love, young man,
> If the lady be young and fair.'
> Ah, penny, brown penny, brown penny,
> I am looped in the loops of her hair.

Percy looks up again. 'It reminds me of you, Mari . . . "the loops of her hair."'

'It's lovely, Percy. Read another.'

'Here's one by William Shakespeare.'

> No longer mourn for me when I am dead
> Than you shall hear the surly, sullen bell
> Give warning to the world that I am fled
> From this vile world, with vilest worms to dwell.

Images rise from the page and Percy sees himself laid upon a bier among fresh flowers, his hands crossed, a wreath of lilies twined around his head; Mari, ravishing in black silk, leans over him to kiss his cold lips and wet his closed lids with her tears. He sees the slow stately procession to the cemetery, Mari borne along on Dai Bando's arm . . . he hears her breath catch on a sob.

> Nay, if you read this line, remember not
> The hand that writ it; for I love you so.

Another sob punctuates the pause he makes for effect. Something in the sound, a certain harshness, clues Percy in that it's not of his own invention, and he looks up.

Mari is staring at him with glittering eyes (a naiad's eyes, Percy thinks), but then a tear rolls out and he realizes why he has picked a watery image – there's a river trembling between her eyelids, threatening to flood.

'Here, Mari.' Percy rises.

Mari shakes her head, bites her lip, and clasps her hands, but the effusion can't be dammed by any effort of will, and the tears pour out.

Percy leaps around the table to kneel beside her and closes her hands between his own, wrapping his fingers around hers like a bandage to poultice her woe.

'What is it, Mari, darling?' he asks softly. 'Did the poem upset you so much? Shall I read you a happy one instead?'

Mari shakes her bent head. In a voice broken with sobs she says, 'I don't want to hear any more poems just now, Percy. Poetry is too . . . too . . . it reminds me too much of old things I'd rather forget.'

'There, there, then,' Percy chafes her hands, 'we shan't have any more reading tonight.' He produces a large white handkerchief from his breast pocket, neatly ironed and folded that morning by his Mam, a curly-tailed P embroidered in one corner in blue thread ('To match your eyes,' his Mam, who dotes on him, said). Glancing at the embroidered letter as he dabs the handkerchief to Mari's cheeks, Percy feels a twinge. His mother would be shocked if she could see him now . . . and tomorrow, when he doesn't turn up at the chapel . . .

Percy tosses the thought away, a small crumpled package of obligation he will deal with later, not now . . . not with Mari so stricken, and so lovely, more fetching than ever in her grief, sorrow adorning her shoulders like a mantilla, her bowed head heavy with swathes and curlicues intricate as filigree, but the colour of autumn leaves. And her response to poetry astounds him, matching his own . . . nay, surpassing it: he has found indeed a soul mate before whom all impediments must fall.

There's something about a weeping woman, Percy thinks, brings out the best and finest in a fellow – *noblesse oblige*.

Percy's tender ministrations with the handkerchief soothe

Mari's jarred heart and quiet the discord incited in every nerve by the cruel poem, which sounded to her like Antonio's voice, the very words he would speak (words only a man, with a hard side to him, could speak) if he could see her now, half in love and on the verge of betrayal.

For when he vanished that night down by the docks, minutes before three policemen and a mackintoshed detective appeared at her side, wasn't the night filled with signs, omens, of some dreadful fate stalking Antonio? A dense fog, stifling as a shroud, had wrapped itself about them as they walked, Mari whispering, 'Why have we come here, Antonio?' and receiving as answer only the mournful hoot of a ship's siren, owl-like, a messenger of mishaps about to occur.

Hadn't she known then, before he disentangled their embrace and slipped away as his enemies materialized out of the peasouper, hadn't she sensed *then* that doom walked abroad and that Antonio was its victim?

Ah, he's dead, Mari, for sure, and you're not a jilted woman, you're a widow. Have the decency to behave so.

'Oh, oh,' Mari moans, beyond tears now, and lifts her head to show Percy her drowned eyes.

'Mari!' Percy draws her into his arms, draws her up out of the chair so that he can enfold her, clasp her, and caress all the grief out of her with his massaging hands and his petting lips.

'Come on, Mari, love,' he coaxes, his mouth against her cheek, the tip of his tongue tasting and relishing the salty wounds tears have left on her skin. 'Give over, do. It's not worth breaking your heart over, a poem isn't. You and me are alive, in't we, and in the pink, too . . .' He licks her earlobe, and proof of what he says leaps up in Mari – a bright, sharp flame from the burning embers in the deep reaches of her body, a fire down there rekindling now as Percy's mouth slides ticklishly along her jawbone to her chin, and up to her own mouth.

Mari parts her lips, and his kiss, her first since that foggy night a year ago, fans the fire into full blaze. It consumes her ghost, or rather sends it flying off like smoke to take refuge in a more distant place, in some far-flung part of Mari's self where the inferno of Percy's kiss cannot singe it.

Percy and Mari kiss, and kiss, and kiss.

And when they must pause to draw breath, cheek to cheek, Percy reaches behind her and begins to pull the pins from her hair. Silently, the hairpins fall on to the Brussels carpet and Mari's locks come pouring down over Percy's trembling fingers; her shoulders tremble, too, as he removes the tortoiseshell comb, the last fastening, and delves into her tresses with eager hands, whispering like a miser glorying in his gold, 'What opulence, what riches, what wealth untold.'

And now his right hand moves down over the embroidered blouse, slowly, as if he savours the feel of every stitched flower and leaf, his fingers tracing their shapes, until he reaches her breast and a different shape, Mari's erect nipple rising from the centre of a lace daisy to greet Percy's honing thumb and index finger.

'Mari,' Percy murmurs, 'would you do something for me?'

'Yes,' Mari whispers, believing she knows what delicious request is coming and loving Percy more for remembering – at this far-gone point – good manners.

'Will you show me a bit of your act?'

Mari stiffens and pulls away. Percy must stretch his arm to keep in touch with her, she withdraws so far.

'What do you mean, Percy?'

'It's all so . . . so mysterious and magical, Mari–'

'My *act*?'

'Yes . . . no . . . what's going on between us. I never felt like this before. I want to . . . to keep a hold on it, Mari . . . ah, I can't explain . . . the wine, the poetry, your crying, me kissing you! I'm all wound up in it, and I want . . . do it for me, Mari!'

Looking into his blue eyes, darkened now to a colour near indigo, Mari softens, seeing how a performance of hers offered to Percy, an intimate audience of one, in the privacy of her room where every bit of drapery, every tassel, rosette and ornament collaborates in the exotic proceedings afoot . . . well, she's never done this before, but yes, she sees how it might enhance and intensify what is yet to come.

'All right,' she says, 'you shall have your wish. Sit there,' pointing to her bed, 'and make yourself comfy. Take off your shoes and your jacket, cross your legs and pretend you're a sultan and – I shan't be long, Percy!'

She snatches up her costume bag and flits out of sight behind the Japanese screen where Percy can see her silhouette through the coloured wings of the birds of paradise. She unbuttons, unhooks, unzips, steps out of her clothes, seeming also to shed and emerge from the vivid plumage of the painted birds, like the princess in the fairytale who could change at will from woman to swan and back again.

Her naked body dazzles Percy's eyes, fevers his brow, and sets up a grand commotion in his loins, a mighty warrior rising there, stalwart and doughty, and for two pins he'd leap across the room, knock down the screen, and ravish her on the spot. He can see himself doing this, as many a lusty knight has done before him, but with all the activity going on in other parts, his feet seem paralysed, and he can only watch his phantom rush forth to do the deed for which he has every inclination but none of the necessary motion.

All motion belongs to Mari. As she stretches, bends and dips, tossing her red hair, rival of the jewelled hues on the screen, she seems herself to possess wings ... to be acquiring those appendages right before Percy's eyes, for a billowing substance has risen all around her, as if she were wrapping herself in feathers, clouds, or some such airborne stuff. He screws up his eyes but can't make out the source of the transformation.

'Ready or not, Percy, here I come!'

She steps out.

'*Daro!*' Percy exclaims. Her appearance makes him believe that he has been transported indeed, to an Arabian tent, a Persian palace, or to some immortal realm where Mari reigns, Queen of Spirits.

From her shoulders to her feet, she is clad in a rainbow of shimmering chiffon scarves, brass bangles on her bare arms and bare ankles, a brass circlet around her forehead, holding back her massy hair. She lifts on to her toes. From behind the screen a scratching noise, then music, soft and swishing, like a wind soughing through the oasis at night, reedy pipes, tinkly tambourines, a low-pulsing drum like a heart-beat or the hooves of distant horses. An exotic aroma accompanies the music, jasmine-scented incense wafting to Percy's nose from the area of the screen, which might now be the entrance to a treasure cave or a caliph's harem.

'Hail to the nabob,' Mari murmurs as she pirouettes in front of Percy, the scarves flying, fluttering, falling. Bangles clink as she sways her limbs, her hair tumbling forward, backwards, as she arabesques, rotates, undulates about the room. The music quickens, she changes her pace, prances back and forth in front of Percy's mesmerized eyes, like an exuberant sylph skipping through fields of lapis lazuli. She lifts one leg, points her toe, the multicoloured scarves parting to reveal her calf, her knee, her thigh.

'*Dee!*' Percy says. '*Daro, daro!*'

Mari stops suddenly, her arms stretched above her head, a temple statue, and gazes at Percy with strange luminous eyes, the eyes of a sphinx. Her fingers make little snapping noises on the air, her toes twitch, her body shivers. And now Percy witnesses a feat as magnificent and impossible as he's ever likely to see again if he lives to be a hundred.

One by one, the chiffon scarves drift from her limbs, petals blown from a flower, and flutter to her feet, baring her bit by bit, her polished shoulders, her swelling breasts, her raspberry nipples. More scarves fly away, as if transported by invisible sprites (he really can't see how she's pulling it off, this incredible trick), and her stomach emerges, her hips, her thighs, the red hair between, an abundance of moired silk. The last wisps of chiffon drift down and she stands before him, a voluptuous icon sculpted from precious ores by an artist in conflict, torn between the divine and the erotic.

'It's your move, Percy,' Mari says softly as the music scratches to a halt.

Percy gasps. 'For me, Mari? All mine?'

'As much as you want, lad. A feast if you wish it.'

Percy springs to his feet, pulling at his tie, tearing at his shirt buttons. Ripping off his clothes, he advances on Mari, who finishes the undressing when his hands are too occupied fondling her breasts.

'Oh, Mari, Mari,' Percy says, 'you've shown me such magic tonight as my wildest dreams never gave shape to.'

'Percy, I got more to show you. You haven't seen the half of it yet.' With her free hand pressed against his chest, she guides her imbibing lover back towards the bed.

Percy tumbles, toppling Mari too. Their limbs connect and, all a-tangle, they roll about the oceanic bed, cavorting like merfolk on a tidal wave.

'Oh, you sylph, you fairy, you nymph,' Percy gasps as various delightful parts of Mari bump against him and her hair washes over him like silky sargassum.

'My own true love,' Mari breathes. 'At last I've found you.'

It is twelve o'clock, the witching hour, when wishes ride abroad on snow-white steeds, and Fantasy reigns supreme. When, for a moment, you can have your cake and eat it, too.

17
Mary: Saturday Night

In the hall, the grandfather clock makes a doleful noise, the steady beat of a ruler rapping on a small offending hand. 'One, two, three . . . a dozen of the best you shall have for this error, Mary.'

It is midnight, the most dreadful hour. Black bats mass at the window. Tiny malicious eyes penetrate the thick damask curtain, wings beat upon the pane, talons scrape at the glass.

'Let us in, Mary. We are your sisters. Let us in!'

On the roof, cats prowl and screech; mice scutter behind the wainscot, and out in the garden, beneath the monkey-puzzle tree, a mad dog bays at the moon. The night is raucous, yet my neighbours sleep sound, every house dark, only I – wandering, listening, insomniac, ailing, assaulted.

I have taken off my motley, my domino, my carnival clothes, and put on a white flannel nightdress. Ah, but I wear a heavier garment, too; invisible but stifling, the cloak of failure covers me from head to foot, shame dragging in deep cumbersome folds, disappointment a cowl for my bowed head.

'And what is it ails you, Mary? Pray, tell us, what is the nature of your malady?'

They look up at me from the sofas and the deep tufted chairs. Our parlour was intended for large gatherings, for entertaining the many – oh, many – acquaintances we should have made, had I not become a recluse, a madwoman, a millstone around Alf's neck.

'Hysteria of the womb,' a matron whispers behind her fan. 'She's barren, poor creature.'

'Why, that's not the story I heard,' another murmurs, ostrich feathers nodding in her hat. 'The marriage was never . . . She refused her obligations I'm told.'

The throng rustles and hisses as I pace among them, wringing my hands.

'They say he has a mistress.'

'Can you blame him? A man can't deny his nature.'

I spread my hands and cry 'Begone!' and they vanish, evaporate into the antimacassars, sink into the Turkey carpet, fade into the stencilled wallpaper.

One figure only remains, leaning on the marble mantelpiece. 'You couldn't be a daughter, Mary. How did you hope to be a wife?'

I turn my back on him, cross to the window, gather damask folds into my fists.

'A girl learns from her father how to behave in the world, but you would never heed me, never do as I bid. England was built by men, Mary, our great empire forged from manly steel, and God, our Father, rules over all. Woman must know her place in the hierarchy or she will be thrust from the gates to live with the devils, outcasts, and whores.'

'I am not a whore,' I say.

'Your thoughts are as scarlet as Babylon, as lascivious as Sodom.'

I shake my head, clutch at damask roses, tell myself he is nothing, only the raving, babbling image of my madness, my own self-mockery dressed in beard and surplice. I turn to face him, lifting my chin, assuming the old insolent posture.

'You know about whores, Father,' I say. 'None more learned, more erudite than you in all the complexities of sin and degradation. It was your life study, was it not, human debasement? And you did practise what you preached, I grant you that.'

His face alters, the arrogant smile giving way to rage, his black eyebrows lowering, his nostrils contracting, his bared teeth and black eyes flashing, the face of thunder and lightning.

And I am afraid again, all the childhood terror welling up even though I know he is a thing fashioned from shadow and memory.

'Your speech is discourteous, Mary,' he says. 'Your manner is unfitting. Apologize.'

'I will not,' I say, 'for I am not sorry.'

'I see I must force contrition. It was ever the case.' He rises up from his leaning posture on the mantelpiece. An ebony pillar with a griffin's head set atop, a stone monster, yet empowered to speak and move as if he were human, he strides towards me, my vampirish father who had drunk my blood and gorged on my heart all the years of my life. A satyr's grin twists his mouth as he reaches for me, and I have no weapon in my hands, no means of defence. I sink into the folds of the damask curtain. His nails graze my face and I scream.

'Mother! Mother!' I cry, and my voice, hysterical, terrorized, evokes a deep-buried memory which even now, recounting this to you, I cannot wholly recover. But it seemed to me, Mother, that I had cried out your name in just that desperate manner once before . . . and the rest escapes me.

Tonight the parlour door did open, and for a moment I thought to see you enter, transported by I know not what supernatural means, to redress your old omission, to save me this time.

It was not you. Alf came in, all agape and flustered. 'Mary, Mary, what is this? What's about?' and other bewildered words he uttered as he rushed across the room, passing through the towering, menacing shade of my sire, and caught me in his arms and lifted me up and carried me to a sofa.

He laid me in his lap and stroked my hair, and I wept against his breast, and it was the first time in many years we had been so; not since we were first wed, not since the night he ravished me, have I permitted those caresses he gave me a few hours past, my arms entwined about his neck and myself given up to the support of his body, a poor shipwrecked creature dashed upon a rock.

And strange to tell, as the hysteria passed and he comforted away my fear, a new sensation . . . or, I surmise, an old one, long dismissed . . . began to seep into my limbs, to soothe my heart, a feeling such as once was elicited by the prospect of a pleasant, protracted sleep in the crook of his arm.

I lifted my wet face, thrust back the bedraggled strands of hair, said, 'Kiss me.'

What weight, what portent, often hangs upon a moment! We say this, do that, take one option over another, acting not on consideration but rather, caught in the flux of things, on whim or humour; and the future is set in motion, an express train, an incoming tide, a ticking clock – swift or slow, it is always implacable, and we cannot turn back, recover the moment, make a second, better choice.

Alf hesitated.

Not, I think, from reluctance or revulsion. His face showed, merely, surprise. I might have placed my hands on his careworn cheeks and my mouth on his, or I might have waited, simply. I did neither. In that moment while he demurred, a vision of his mistress passed between us. I saw Mari Prince in his eyes, not my own reflection, as if we two stood before a mirror, her blazing image eclipsing mine.

I leapt from his lap, paced the room to the mantelpiece and leaned there. 'You are home early,' I said, distance restoring the indifferent demeanour I have learned in the school of affliction, where expediency is first on the curriculum.

Alf stares at me. At last, he speaks. 'Is that all, Mary?'

'All? What more should there be?'

'I confess, I do not understand you. I find you in a frenzy, you scream and weep, and then embrace me as if . . . as if . . . and now you stand as far from me as you can manage and yet remain in the room, and tell me, coolly, that I have come early. What if I had not come? What then, eh?'

What then, indeed! I dare not speculate, for he had me, truly, my father – his quarry again, shrinking, powerless . . .

'You know I am subject to these rare fits,' I say, 'a product of mild hysteria, Alf, to which I have ever been subject. But they pass . . . they pass.'

He shakes his head, straightens his askew cravat, runs his hand over his hair. The fire is dying out, only the flickering embers persist. 'I should like a drink,' he says, 'my usual sleeping-draught,' and makes to rise.

And I leave him to his comfort and his misery, to think about his mistress who, perhaps he knows as well as I, cuckolded him tonight. I climb the dark stairs, more perilous by far than the larch tree I ascended earlier, for Defeat awaits me at the top. A merciless, cackling crone, my childhood nurse, the chaperone of my youth and now the keeper of my house, she will take my hand in her skeleton grip and lead me back into emptiness, back into the sombre nursery where all the toys are broken beyond repair and a child forever weeps.

I will lie abed and think on my humiliation. She brought home a swain who cried out his devotion to her beyond the door of the room where I lay, entombed, beneath her couch of sinful pleasure. I, who had thought, myself, to lie fleetingly with her (her last and most resolute companion, ravenous, famished for the deed that would unite and sever us for aye). I must perforce take flight – bolt from that place where I had thought to triumph, hurl myself through the window, scuttle down the tree, and speed along the street where, only an hour before, I had trod the pavement with a sure stride.

He saw me again, the policeman. We passed with a nod, and from him, a 'Good-night.' No matter. He thinks me an inhabitant of the area . . . I do not care what he thinks, for he, and all who walk God's earth, are powerless to thwart my endeavour.

There, I have written, Mother, and I am calmer now, my resolve strengthened again; nay, rendered staunch, invincible by what I have endured. For now the cloak of my vengeance spreads to enfold Alf, whom she has also wronged and made a plaything of. Unwittingly, she has linked me again to my husband, and, albeit unbeknownst to him, I unite with him again in a shared sorrow and a common goal, to free us both from the grip of the harlot.

That man she brought home will not last, will not persevere beyond candlelight, I know. I heard it in his voice: such impassioned words on so slight acquaintance, such hyperbole, bespeak instability, an inconstant love like the momentary flicker of a match, sudden, bright, but a spark merely. She may burn her fingers on him, but he will never warm her heart.

Tomorrow then.

Or, rather, tonight, for already another daylight, another opportunity approaches, wanting only the passing of the hours, which I have learned to wait out.

She deserves her penalty, does she not? She is a feckless, fawning creature who has shied from the hard road of honour to become a mendicant, cringing beside the highway, begging alms of men.

As you did, Mother. As you did.

18
Dai and Ivor: Sunday Morning

'I don't know, Ive, I don't know . . . I don't know what to say . . .'

His head tipped back, Dai Bando contemplates the ceiling of the all-night buffet at Paddington Station. Three beer mugs sit on the table in front of him, two empty, one half full. Next to this mug Dai's trilby rests, and he drums his fingers on its crown, a monotonous tune to accompany his refrain. 'I'm at a loss for words . . . just don't know what to say.'

'Not much *to* say, is there?' Ivor lifts his teacup, frowns at the chip in its rim, and takes a swallow. '*Daro*, there's a cheek to call this tea and charge so dear for it. Tastes like a miner's bathwater. I'll be glad to have a proper cup at home.'

'He might be lying in some alley with his throat cut for all we know.'

Ivor sighs. Dai has listed a score of times all the nasty events that might have befallen Percy, and he's getting sick of hearing them. 'I doubt that seriously. Probably on his way here in a taxi this very minute. Just got lost when he was parted from us in the crush outside the Palladium, that's all.'

'That was three hours back. It don't take three hours to get from Leicester Square to Paddington.' Dai shudders and lowers his eyes. 'There's a lot of violence in London. A murderer loose, too.'

'Aye, well, he's only out to kill women so Percy's safe there.' Ivor lights a Woodbine. 'See, the way it is, Dai, he probably couldn't find a taxi for a bit, all them people trying to get one, and Percy not a chap to push. I expect he waited for the crowd to thin out and that took time—'

'It don't explain three hours, say what you like.' Dai lifts his mug, then sets it down again. 'You know what's got me flummoxed? The way he disappeared. One minute he was by my side and I was saying, "Stick close now, Perce, so we don't get split up"–'

'That was when we was coming out of the show. I was right behind you. I heard you say it.'

'Next minute we did get parted–'

'All them people pushing and shoving. No manners up here, is there?'

'But how it happened, Ivor, that's what's so bloody strange. Percy wasn't *shoved* away from me. He did it himself, barging into the crowd like he'd suddenly lost his box, like it was a race he had to win. I shouted, "Steady on, Perce! Wait a bit!" but he didn't take a blind bit of notice. I thought he was feeling sick and had to get out in the air, but when we got to the pavement there was no sign of him, was there? If that magician woman had tapped him with her wand he couldn't have vanished quicker.'

Ivor takes a long drag on his Woodbine and squints at Dai behind the smoke. 'You didn't tell me this part before. Puts a different slant on things, don't it? Where was he off to then, do you think?'

Dai picks up his mug, drinks, and wipes his mouth with the back of his hand. 'I haven't wanted to say this, even to myself, but no use hiding facts. He bolted, Ivor.'

Ivor's neck jerks, his head snapping up like a yo-yo. 'Bolted? Run away, do you mean? Done a bunk? Percy? What for?'

'Because he don't want to get married tomorrow.'

'Never!' Another spasm seizes Ivor's neck. Information he can't believe always has this physical effect, shocking his muscles first, as if to warn his brain of a stunning message coming up. When Bethan said, 'Of course I'll marry you,' he'd gone into such contortions her face had blanched and she had asked, very frightened, 'Is it epilepsy, Ivor?'

He can see her now in that green dress, and the russet cloak she wore to hide the swelling of her stomach, standing on a ferny mountainside up near the ruins of Morlais Abbey where they'd gone for a stroll one Sunday evening. He had trotted all the way from chapel to Bethan's house in Tydfil Terrace because the Lord had answered his prayers and given him the courage to ask her.

'It's the truth,' Dai says. 'He told me on the train coming up. He've changed his mind about Ellen. Are you listening to me, Ivor?'

'I am, Dai. I just can't credit it. You think he's gone for good then?'

'That's my fear. My *hope* is he'll come to his senses before the train leaves.'

'Do he know what time it goes out?'

'I told him the milk train, twenty to five, and I made him write it down on a slip of paper in case we was parted.'

'Well, we got a good two hours yet–'

'You're not catching on, Ivor. All the time in the world's no use if he's not coming, is it?' Dai drains his glass and gets up. 'I'm having the same again. How about you?'

'I'll have a stout, please. This tea is poison. What'll we do, Dai?'

'When I know that, Ive, I'll tell you.'

Ivor watches Dai cross the buffet to the counter.

Bethan once said, back in the days when she would talk about Dai, before she turned against him, 'He's got the devil's eyes, that one. I bet he knows every trick in the book,' not speaking as if she condemned this, but with laughter in her voice. 'Watch how many converts he makes in this town. Welshwomen do fall for evangelists and rogues and Dai Bando's a bit of both.' So Ivor had understood that Dai's wicked eyes, always a bit unnerving to him, would find favour with women – for Bethan had said so, and she was wise in ways that Ivor was not, and he always deferred to her knowledge, humbly and with gratitude.

Why has she set herself against Dai though? When he first arrived in Avon Fach, five years back, she took him under her wing, asking him often to Sunday dinner, sending the boys to his house on weeknights with special dishes she'd cooked, saying, 'A man on his own after all. There must be a lot he's without.' Doing all that a lay preacher's wife should, but not just out of charity to a stranger; delighting in his company, too, Ivor saw, in the jokes and stories he told at table, always humorous but never off colour; blushing, saying softly, 'Ah, get on with you' to his compliments, her speech quick and her step light when he was in the house.

And Ivor happy to see her girlish again, glad for any pleasure and admiration she received, her entitlements after all.

Then, suddenly, for no reason anyone could put a finger on, in September when the leaves were changing and children putting on their woollen hats and scarves again to trot off to school, Bethan and Dai had fallen out.

'No point in discussing it, Ivor,' Bethan had said with a tight mouth. 'He's not the man we thought he was, that's all.'

'Leave it there, Ivor,' Dai said, when Ivor took him aside at the colliery. 'Me and your wife don't see eye to eye is the gist of the matter.'

Then an unbudging silence from both parties.

Grim events followed the break-up rapidly, like dangerous, uprooted objects hurtling in the wake of a storm. Dai dropped out of the choir, Bethan soon after, and then tragedy had struck Avon Fach. In October the colliery roof caved in, killing fifteen men, injuring many others. Dai with a ravaged leg was hospitalized for months; Bethan sank into a cheerless mood, as if she wore a mourning veil; and Dai, when he came back from the colliers' sanitorium in Aberystwyth, had lost his banter and kept to himself, a dark-browed hermit with a limp.

Two years have passed since then. Things are not so bad now, on the mend, Ivor trusts – Bethan in the choir again, Dai lifting a pint at the Prince Llewelyn on a Friday night, Bethan smiling oftener, Dai from time to time cracking them up in the pub in his old jaunty manner.

But something else has merged with and altered the shape of his sorrow . . . something he senses but can't fathom in Bethan's moods, in Dai's hints, in the dark eyes of his oldest son (so like Bethan and naturally nothing like him) when the boy lifts his head from his homework to say, 'Dad, can you help me with these sums?'

'Why don't you kiss me, Ivor?' Bethan, pregnant, had said that long-ago summer evening on Morlais Mountain, when he asked her to marry him.

He had taken her into his arms for the first time, and with all that he was feeling, with all the love he had kept for her, holding off from all others, never faithless even with a look or a word, the kiss should have moved the mountain.

It did not.

Oh, it was sweet and tender enough, a balm to his love-sickness, a mingling of myrrh and frankincense, a coming home to Gilead . . . and yet, with all of that, something missing, something truant where the core should have been . . . and not only he but Bethan felt it. As she drew away from him she said, 'You can still change your mind. I won't hold you to words spoken unknowing.'

'Oh, love! Oh, love!' Ivor had cried, and drawn her back swiftly, hungrily, into the shelter of his arms. As they went together down the mountainside towards the lights of Avon Fach, he had kept her close, her soft wing of hair against his cheek, his left hand resting where the curve of her belly began, and thought, 'It'll come, it'll come. It's bound to when God Himself has joined me to her.'

A good and loving wife, her virtues and comforts not to be counted; but like a sequestered mountain lake, in sunshine or in shadow, quiet and cool, placid water where he swims without risk, yearning for the dam to break, for the rapids, the rip-tide, the whirlpool. He knows these forces are within her, their oldest son proof of it, but he cannot find their source. When he loves her with his body, only ripples stir that lovely, tranquil surface.

Dai is coming with their drinks.

'That woman says there's an all-night waiting room with easy chairs down the station a bit. Maybe we should go there after we drink up and get a bit of kip. Be fresh for the morning.'

'For the wedding you mean? You do think Percy'll come then?'

'I told you I'm hoping, Ivor. I wouldn't like to think he's the sort who'd leave us all in the lurch. Change my opinion of him drastically, that would.'

'Still, it may be for the best. To call it off. If Percy's unwilling, I mean.' Ivor draws a Woodbine from the packet he has laid on the table and tamps down the end.

'That little girl's in love with him.'

'Well, that's it. He's not in love with her, you as good as said. What's the use if it's only one?'

'I never thought to hear *you* say such a thing, boyo!' Dai's black eyebrows lift. 'Sounds like you're condoning Percy running off. And you a lay preacher, and a married man yourself. Never thought I'd have to tell you about obligations.'

'Obligations don't make people happy,' Ivor says, and takes a long drink of stout, for his mouth is parched.

Dai is looking hard at him. His curly hair falling in his eyes, he looks a bit like a bandit. 'When did you find that out?'

Ivor lights his cigarette. 'Obligations are like flagstones. You set one down, you have to lay another . . . and another.' Ivor stops, for he really doesn't know what he's talking about, or why this idea has come to him, a man who takes pleasure in performing his duties. He wishes Bethan were here to help him. 'If Percy don't turn up at the chapel tomorrow, I believe Bethan would say it's for the best. Once she knows the circumstances.'

'Why would she say that?' Dai has stopped looking at him. His arms folded, he gazes into his beer, already half gone, the empty part of the glass flecked with foam like the tiny lamb-clouds of summer.

'She's got sense,' Ivor says, unable to put into words what he knows and feels about his wife. Despite the awkward, blood-letting separations, the gloomy hours when she retreats into a dark wood where he can't follow her, he has this comfort: he knows the stand she takes in the world, for it is his stand also, the stand of two decent Christian people. How sweet it is, in the end, this like-mindedness, the yea of marriage where two minds are in accord. Makes up for a lot that does, and he shouldn't forget it when he's wishing on moonshine. 'I know Bethan,' he says.

Dai lifts a grim face. 'And she knows you, don't she? Is that a reward or a penalty of being married?'

'You think too hard of marriage, Dai. It wouldn't kill you to try it. Might change your mind for the better.'

'Maybe I should stand in for Percy tomorrow?'

'Well, a man could do a lot worse than Ellen, a lovely, clean-living girl. He's lucky to have her.'

'So you say, Ive. One feller's luck is another feller's hard lines, seems like. No, I wouldn't have Ellen, even if she'd have me, and I wasn't old enough to be her father. She's too much of a Welshwoman.'

'What do you mean by that, Dai? I happen to have a high opinion of Welshwomen.'

'Too narrow, Ivor, like the valleys they live their whole life in, too domineering like the mountains they never look up at. Wives and mothers from the day they're born. They don't know there's anything else to be. I'd suffocate with a Welshwoman.'

'Well!' Ivor says. 'There's harsh words, indeed. And you a Welshman too, fancy!'

'I'll tell you what though. I been living in error until today. Until today I thought all women were the same. There's naive, there's bloody *dwp* I've been!' His shoulders hunched, Dai thrusts himself forward, speaking into Ivor's face, his own face all fired up with *hwyl*, the way he gets at the Prince Llewelyn when the talk is fair wages for miners, when he says, 'We have to come out, boyos, march and picket, and bloody riot, too, if it's called for. Now who's with me? Who's a true Welshman here?' (Holding a higher opinion, apparently, of the men than of the women.) Knocking back his chair as he rises, his right fist clenched above his head, the ruddiness of Welsh beer and of Welsh fervour in his cheeks. 'Are we English peons or are we our own masters? Who'll keep the red flag flying over South Wales collieries?' *Daro*, he ought to have been a politician or a preacher, happier then maybe.

'Today,' Dai says, 'I saw a woman of a different stamp. A woman with the guts and the sight I thought only men had, a woman in shining armour like Joan of Arc, like our own Boadicea, and Nest, and Heledd, and Tydfil – a breed that's died out in Wales, the face of a bloody angel but a will of iron. There's bloody wonderful! Privileged I was to see that and have my eyes opened!'

Oh *daro*, he's going to harp on that suffragette again. There's definitely a screw loose if he can admire a woman that did herself in. Madness recognizing madness, it is, birds of a feather . . . dear, dear, that pit accident damaged more than his leg it's obvious, never been right in the head since and getting worse it seems.

'Dai,' Ivor says, 'think what you're saying now. She killed herself, that woman did. Is that what you wanted, eh?'

Dai slumps in his chair. 'No, I didn't. I'll regret till the day they carry me off I didn't save her.'

No, this is not the way to go either. Mustn't let him fall into pining, into that daft idea that he's to blame.

'So what are you looking for in a woman?' Ivor says, hoping to lead him from the particular to the general.

'She should stand up for what she believes.'

'Welshwomen do that, Dai, fair play. They've always stood behind us when we've come out, you can't say different.'

Dai's fist comes down on the table. 'I'm not talking about bloody politics. I'm not talking about *support*!' The word comes out with a hissing sound, as if he spits on it.

'I'm sorry,' Ivor says, huffy. 'I thought you was. What are you talking about then?'

Dai runs his finger around the brim of his black trilby. 'Take a woman,' he says, watching his finger, 'who does something she don't believe in and follows it to the letter, because people . . . her Mam and Dad, Mrs Jones down the street, the preacher, her Auntie Gladys . . . tell her it's the right thing. So she does this for years until one day, all of a sudden, up pops something she do believe in, with all her heart. What does she do then, Ivor . . . this woman?'

Ivor shakes his head, reaches for a Woodbine, changes his mind and dips into his pocket instead for a Rennies. His stomach is playing up. He flicks open the round tin Bethan handed him as he was leaving and looks at the white pills, each one a little token of her abiding concern. 'I don't know,' he says, and hears his voice as heavy as stone. Painful, these flashes, like a knife stabbing into your vitals. He swallows a pill, washes it down with stout, decides that he does want to know.

'What *do* she do?' He raises his head to look Dai in the eye.

'Nothing,' Dai says. 'Don't look so ragged, Ivor *bach*. She don't do a damn thing different than you'd expect, I promise you. Just keeps following the straight road if she's a Welshwoman.'

Ivor shuts the lid of the Rennies and puts the tin back in his pocket.

Dai pulls his silver watch from his waistcoat. 'Three o'clock. Drink up, Ive, and we'll go to the waiting room and rest for a bit.'

'I still don't know what you're looking for,' Ivor says. 'In a woman I mean.' He's not sure why he keeps on the subject when Dai's obviously willing to drop it. Something contrary in him wants to hear his butty say, this-and-this, so he can answer, not-so, and tell himself that Dai, after all, doesn't know much about . . .

'A woman who can have a good laugh.' Dai downs the remains

of his pint. 'Laugh in the face of the devil, and of the righteous, too, even if it damns her to Hell.' He stands up. 'Ready, Ivor?'

Ivor rises. Those Rennies work fast. The pain has subsided already. 'You're right there, then,' he says. 'You'll never find a Welshwoman who'll do that.'

As they pass the buffet counter the waitress says, 'Good-night, gents.'

Dai stops. 'If a tall young man with a suitcase comes in here, do us a favour, will you, love? Direct him to the waiting room. I'll be much obliged.'

'Anything for you, dearie.' She parts her red lips and winks one blue eyelid. 'Wish I could do more.'

'So do I,' Dai says, 'but I'm a bit pushed for time. Hope to see you next year.' He lifts his trilby which he has jammed on top of his curly hair.

As they come out on to the platform, he nudges Ivor's arm and grins up at him. 'See, she was ready to fall all over me. Can't be such a bad chap, can I?'

'She don't know you, Dai,' Ivor kids.

'How can she? How can anybody? I keep surprising myself!'

Now this is more like it, Ivor thinks as they walk down the chilly deserted station to the lighted sign that says 'Waiting Room'; Dai cheered up again, his stomach settled down, and nearly time for the Red Dragon to come and carry them home. 'We'll keep a welcome in the hillsides, We'll keep a welcome in the vales,' the men had sung on the way up, homesick as soon as they crossed the border, like true Welshmen. Going home again now . . . If only Percy comes, everything will be right as rain.

'Send that lad instructions, Lord,' Ivor prays silently. He has decided after all that marriage is the best thing for Percy. Marriage abides. Continues the race. 'Multiply and replenish the earth,' the Bible instructs. No point ending up like Dai, two flags in the wind and no safe harbour in a squall.

19
Mari and Percy: Sunday Morning

Her spread hair flickers in the guttering candlelight like shot silk, a red-gold effulgence like the sun on a beauteous evening, lambent as fire, the tresses of a Circe, a Diana, a Rhiannon. In contrast, her naked body is white as marble, as lambswool, as eggshell, as ivory, her contours so perfect they might be carved, chiselled, yet soft, pliant under desiring hands, her stomach a pillow of swansdown. Delicate tints highlight her snowy expanses, touches from the brush of a watercolourist, a nestling of marigold petals in the valley between her thighs, rosebuds tipping her breasts, her closed eyelids the blue of hyacinths.

So Percy fancies, coming back into the room after a trip to the toilet and seeing Mari again with the eye of a lover already besotted by the manifold pleasures of that body he gazes on. Imperfections are invisible to him.

As he tiptoes to the bed, Mari opens her eyes.

'Not sleeping, love? I thought you were.' Percy prepares to stretch out beside her and gather her charms again.

'Just closed my eyes to think better.' Mari sits up, plumping a pillow behind her. 'We should have a talk, Percy.'

'Oh,' Percy says, glancing slyly, regretfully, at the taut and quickened bowstring between his legs. 'Oh, all right then. What do you want to chat about, darling?'

'We've had a nice time, haven't we?'

'A glorious time, passing all description,' Percy corrects her. 'But why do you say "had", lovely, as if it's over and done with? We've just come into our kingdom, Mari.'

'Does that mean you want to go on then?'

Percy takes her in his arms. 'How can you ask? I shouldn't have thought my wanting's in doubt.' He presses his groin against her thigh in case she's failed to notice the enormity of his passion.

'I'm not doubting *this* feller!' Mari says, fitting him snugly into a cylinder made of her two hands. 'To put it plain, Percy, do you want to stay with me for more than this one night? And if so . . . can you give me an estimate, just a rough one, of how long?'

'Forever!' Percy says at once. 'I told you that hours ago, and I'm not a man to change my mind in these matters. What's made you wonder, sweeting? I hope I haven't said anything to wound –'

'No, no, you've done everything right. Past experience is working on me, I suppose. I had a bad experience not so long ago and I shouldn't like it repeated.'

'Did some man let you down? What a scamp! A fool, too. Well, his loss is my gain.'

'He wasn't a scamp or a fool, Percy. He was a good man and I loved him true.'

Percy feels the bodkin of jealousy stab between his ribs. 'He didn't deserve you all the same, did he? Must have been something wrong with his brain, and his eyesight, too.'

'He was an Anarchist,' Mari says softly, her voice muffled against his chest.

'Come again?' Percy can't believe his ears. He hopes she said 'pianist', or 'architect', or 'acrobat', or 'anti-kiss' – anything but the word he thinks he heard.

Mari lifts her head. 'An-ar-chist. Don't you know what that is, Percy?'

'Aye, I know. I've read about them in the papers. Fellers who go around throwing bombs at people and trying to kill off royalty. Here, you're not serious, are you? You're pulling my leg.'

'I lived with him for nearly a year.'

'Lived with him? In this room? Slept with him, too, in this bed? Are you one of them yourself then?'

'No, I can't stand killing. I didn't know for a long time.'

'Well . . .' (It's not her fault then, she was duped. Could happen to anyone.) 'So did you show him the door when you found out? Is that how you parted?'

'I lost him. One night down by the docks. He slipped away 'cause the police were after him. They took me in for questioning.'

'Did they put you in the lock-up?'

'They let me go after a bit. Sent a policeman round later though, and he took off all Antonio's things. Wouldn't even let me keep his shaving-brush as a memento. Evidence, it was all evidence. His initials were engraved in gold on the handle of the brush, part of a set his mother gave him, and I should have liked to have kept it—'

'Hold on, hold on,' Percy says. 'Let me get this straight now. Antonio his name was? Foreign then?'

'Italian. He came from Naples and he could sing opera songs—'

'Italian,' Percy says. 'There's an Italian family keeps a café in Avon Fach, name of Bracchi. They're not Anarchists, though. Well, you must have been glad to see the back of that bloke after all the trouble he caused you!'

'He didn't cause me any trouble. He just broke my heart when he left.'

During this conversation Percy and Mari have moved apart.

'Sounds like you don't regret any of it, Mari, except that it ended.'

'That's right, Percy. Of course, now that I've met you—'

'And would you have stayed with him then, knowing what you knew?'

'I told you I loved him.'

'Love don't excuse everything!'

'Why are you getting all hot and bothered? It's finished—'

'I'm not hot and bothered.' Percy rolls his left hand into a fist and hammers it on his right. 'I'm just trying to understand this, *daro*!'

'What's hard to understand?'

'How could you be in love with a killer after you knew he was one?'

'Don't call him a killer.'

'You called him one yourself. You said he was an Anarchist.'

'It's not the same.'

'Bloody hell, it's as different as white and brown sugar!'

'I don't know why you're so angry.' Mari's eyes fill up. 'Has this changed your feelings for me?'

'No,' Percy says, the sight of her sorrow softening the hard lump that has formed in his heart, melting it a little, as rain liquefies ice. 'No, love, it's not that. It'll just take a bit for me to get used to this – this—'

'Would you like a cup of tea?'

'Thanks. I am a bit dry in the mouth.'

Mari gets up. She takes her dressing gown from the peg behind the door, puts it on, and ties the belt. It's a man's dressing gown, brown and beige check, a bit baggy and worn; but comfortable in the chilly room where the gas fire has long since gone out.

Percy lies back on the pillows and watches her as she moves about, filling the kettle, lighting the gas ring and the fire, measuring tea leaves into an ornate silver teapot grand enough for a Buckingham Palace garden party, but much too big and showy for just the two of them.

In fact, everything in this room is too big for it – the Turkish chair, the massive centre table, the larger-than-life birds on the Japanese screen, and this gigantic bed he lies in. Hardly space to move really ('No room to swing a cat,' his mother would say). And all those knick-knacks crammed on every surface, dust-collectors (Mrs Fly again), not to mention the big plant (ugly, aspidistras are) that must shut out most of the daylight. She's living in a museum, in the back room of a furniture shop, in delusions of grandeur.

'Sugar and milk?' Mari looks over her shoulder and the sweet smile on her face makes Percy ashamed of his thoughts. He tries a new fantasy: she's aristocracy fallen on hard times, a member of the landed gentry whose father gambled away their land, an heiress without a fortune, a Russian princess dethroned, living among salvaged heirlooms, memories of the grand life.

No, it won't work. In that bulky, frayed dressing gown she looks what she is, a woman tired out from a long day and a long night. Handsome, of course, no denying. But putting on a bit of weight around the middle, and with dark circles under her fine eyes. A woman who has had, by her own admission, a remarkable lover before him, a grand passion, a throbbing affair of the heart ... who did with that lover in bed everything she has done with Percy, even those things he thought they'd newly discovered together since he'd never done them with Ellen. She is not, after all, his pristine faerie lady, his ideal woman ... Well, *daro*, how could she be! She's no spring chicken, as he can now clearly see.

'How old are you, Mari?' Percy says.

'I'll be thirty-six next birthday,' she says with her back to him. 'In August if you want it exact. Are you asking for any particular reason?' There's a sharpness in her voice he hasn't heard before. Reminds him a bit of Ellen.

Ellen . . . tomorrow, no, later on today, *jawch*, she'll be walking down the aisle on Dai's arm, Mr Type the organist playing the Bridal March, Reverend Morris from over Aberdare way, a big man in the valley, come specially to marry them; Mrs Fly in a fancy hat (Percy was with her when she bought it in the Co-op) occupying a front pew, Ellen's Mam in one of her flower-show dresses, Bethan Parry up in the choir, ready to sing the solo she has practised for weeks (Ellen's request, *'Calon Lan'*). And the guests all a-flutter because the protocol's wrong, the bride coming in before the groom, causing a stir, an ill wind rising, a whispering and a fidgeting, and Ivor slinking out to look up and down Hebron Street, but Percy not coming.

Oh there's daft! There'll be no such high drama, for Dai will put a stop to the proceedings, rushing to Ellen's house straight from the train to break the news to her while Ivor stands sentinel at the chapel gate and turns the guests away, 'Sorry, there have been a slight hitch. Percy never came back from London. We have got Scotland Yard looking for him.'

Would they do that, Scotland Yard, put him on their wanted list? He'd be a fugitive then, like this Antonio chap, have to grow a beard and dye his hair . . .

The kettle hisses and belches steam. Mari, who still keeps her back to him, rock-silent, pours boiling water into the teapot.

Will Ellen collapse when Dai tells her? Will she have hysterics, pull her bouquet to bits and slash her wedding-dress with the kitchen knife? No, she's not the violent sort. Fragile, Ellen. She may not bear up under the shock. He sees her lying pastry-pale in her bed, like the Lady of Shalott in her boat, withering away, dying of a broken heart. She's not robust like Mari, not hardened in the ways of the world, delicate and shy as the first snowdrop, and with child, too (oh, *Iesu Mawr!*), it could do her in, this lot.

Mari brings their cups of tea on a tray. She places the tray on the sheet and sits down carefully, facing Percy.

'You didn't answer my question,' she says.

'Pardon?' Percy forces himself to look at her.

'Never mind. How old are *you*, Percy?'

'Twenty last October.'

'I suppose you're noticing the difference, are you?'

'Pardon?' he says again, foolishly.

'Now the magic's all gone.'

He can't hold her look that lies on him so heavy, like a millstone, eyes like terracotta, jagged with pain. Oh, what trouble he's got himself into!

Mari looks up, shaking her hair back, and – it must be a trick of the light, which the hanging lamp sheds full on her face – she is breathtaking again, a stained-glass figure suffused in the lamp's glow. The dressing-gown tie has come loose and reveals her golden breasts – 'apples of the sun,' Percy thinks – and the gilded column of her neck. Her hands clasped, her eyes uplifted, she might be an ancient Celtic queen about to be martyred for her faith.

Hold on, hold your horses, Percy counsels himself, but to no avail. His hands reach out to enfold hers and he hears himself say, 'I don't know what got into me, darling, to upset you so. My heart bleeds to think I gave you pain.'

Slowly Mari lowers her eyes to his face. Her gaze is still far away though, an ebbing ocean that leaves Percy beached.

'Here,' he says, 'don't go off me now because we had a lovers' tiff. I'm that sorry, I'd do anything to make up with you.' He chafes her hands as if to infuse warmth into her. 'Say you forgive me, or I'll be miserable as sin.'

'You're a strange one,' Mari says. 'You change and change about so fast, like a false spring.'

'I'm not false, Mari. I was just . . . jealous, see, to think of you loving another feller so deep before me.'

'And him an Anarchist, too.'

He doesn't like her tone, which matches her eyes and bodes ill for him. Yet, the more aloof she is, the more vigorous Percy's ardour grows.

'I don't care. I don't care about what you done, or what he done, or anything before you and me. Come to bed now, lovely, and I'll show you my real feelings.'

'Better drink your tea while it's hot.'

'Will you come back to bed if I do?'

Mari shrugs and picks up her cup.

'Look,' Percy says, desperate, 'I can prove I love you by telling you what I've give up – willingly – to stay with you here in London.'

Mari raises her eyebrows, the gilded rim of the cup resting against her bottom lip.

'You're not the only one who has had a past love.'

She sips her tea. 'Are you giving up another woman for me, Percy? Is that what you're hinting?'

Percy's head hovers between a nod and a shake. He has spoken without thinking, desire overruling sense, as it has before in other dodgy situations, and never for the best. (Desire made Ellen pregnant; sense would have kept her a virgin and him free.)

'I *have* left someone for you, Mari.'

Mari rattles her cup on to the saucer. She's surprised, as he meant her to be, and her eyes are lively again, all attentive glitter. She has not thought him a man of the world, a man with an adventurous past like ... what's his name ... Antonio the Anarchist.

Now that she has an inkling of it, a whiff of a different Percy, her eyes are kindling with love again. Look how she thrusts her body towards him (the dressing gown slipping off her shoulders), her lips parted, her hands wide open, connected only at her thumb tips, as if she reaches for something – for him, surely, for his manliness, which she must see has swelled into a handful indeed.

'Tell me,' she says, her voice low and throbbing. 'Tell it all, Percy!'

What passion he's stirred, his turn to enchant now, to put on the magician's cloak, wave a wand and conjure up a frenzy. What an inflamer, what a firebrand is jealousy! And what an alluring story he has up his sleeve, with years of avid reading to draw on.

'A young girl, fresh and fair as May, fell mad in love with me a year ago,' he begins. 'It was love at first sight for us both, to tell the truth, like Tristan and Iseult after they drank the potion. And nothing to be done but we must consummate our love at the earliest moment, which soon came, and ever since, Ellen – that's her name – has cleaved to me, rejecting all others, though many have tried their suit. As I said, as if she'd drunk a love potion, she has eyes for none but me.'

'And you feel the same?'

'I did until I saw you, Mari. You broke the spell, and now Ellen must pine like Elaine for Launcelot, for I have found in you my Guinevere, my fate, my future.'

'Which she . . . Ellen . . . doesn't know yet?'

'She will tomorrow. Today, I mean.'

'Who will tell her, Percy?'

'My butties, Dai Bando and Ivor Parry, when they get back on the train.'

'But they don't know about you and me.'

Percy flicks his right shoulder. 'They'll know I've stayed in London. That's enough.'

Mari is silent, but her eyes speak, and though he can't make out a distinct message, he sees it's the language of passion.

'So now you know what I've given up for you, Mari.'

'Nothing,' she says at last. 'You haven't given up a brass farthing. What you've done is robbery.'

This response jolts Percy like a fist in the stomach, it's so different from what he expected. Winded by shock, he can't speak. When he opens his mouth to try, only a gasp comes forth.

'Robbery twice over, her and me both.' Mari stands up, rises to her full height, a caryatid with a fierce aspect. Too late, Percy realizes the passion in her eyes was rage. Now she lets him have it:

'You've stolen precious possessions, dearer by far than gold or sovereigns – trust, faith, happiness, honour . . . yes, and love . . . that's what you've thieved, not from one woman neither, but from two. And you hardly old enough to wear long trousers! Shame on you, Percy Fly, you're a fly one, sure – a fly-by-night, a fly in the ointment, a gadfly, a bluebottle–'

She pauses for breath, and Percy manages to say, 'No need for name-calling. You don't have to insult me–'

But then she's off again, prancing in front of the bed like a harpy. 'Insult you! You deserve to be horse-whipped! Oh, I feel sorry for that girl, and sorry for myself, you . . . you flyspeck!'

'If that's how it is,' Percy says, angry himself now, 'I needn't stay another minute. The train haven't gone yet.'

He gets up, crosses to the Turkish chair where his clothes are strewn, and begins to dress. Before he's got beyond pulling up his long-johns, though, a change comes over Mari. She collapses on to the bed, knocking the tray to the floor, spilling what's left of their tea on to the carpet, and proceeds to sob with abandon.

At first Percy takes no notice, but the sounds she makes are so wrenching, so bitter, he can't finish dressing. His heart, which isn't in on this leaving idea anyway, turns to her. He follows it and puts his arms around Mari . . . cautiously, for he's not sure she won't punch him in the eye after all she's said. But Mari throws herself upon him and continues to break her heart against his vest.

In all of this, the dressing gown has fallen to her waist, and Percy is once again holding her nakedness. Astonished pleasure, renewed lust, chase away prudence. He moves his left hand from her shoulder to her breast. Mari gives a little shiver, a little gasp, a momentary hiatus in the sobbing. Encouraged, Percy attempts a bolder caress. Her nipple buds under his palm. He continues. Soon there's more sighing than crying. Valiantly, he slides his hand down to her thigh and lowers his mouth to her breast. Mari's legs part. Her head droops on his shoulder.

'Ah, Percy, look what you've gone and done,' she says. 'You've made me fall for you.'

'I've fallen, too, Mari. It can't be helped. Love can't be halted or denied. You see that, don't you? I'd be no good to Ellen, loving you, would I now?'

As soon as he says this, Percy knows he's erred. At the sound of Ellen's name, Mari stiffens, and before he's finished speaking, she has drawn away, got on her feet again and pulled up the dressing gown. He thinks he's in for another tirade, but she only says, 'You must tell her yourself, Percy.'

'How can I do that?' Percy says. 'When I'm up here and she's in South Wales?'

'You must go back and tell her. It's the proper thing. If she knows, she'll get over it in time. Especially as she's so young and so courted as you've said. But if you vanish, she'll fret all her life. Nothing's worse than disappearing on a person, leaving them never to know what befell. It's a hole in the heart, that is, a bullet that can't be pried out.'

'If I go, can I come back and stay with you after?'

'Yes,' Mari says. 'If you do it all above board, then yes.'

'When do you want me to go?'

'Now. You said the train hasn't gone yet.'

'I can't go now, not in the middle of the night. It don't make sense. I'll go tomorrow, I promise, just one more day, that's soon enough—'

'Tomorrow's just putting it off.' Mari moves to the Turkish chair and begins to scoop up Percy's clothes, tossing his shirt and trousers on to his lap. 'I'll come to Paddington to see you off.' His tie lands on top of his trousers. 'We'll catch a taxi and be there in no time.' She picks up his jacket and gives it a shake, upside down. A Twickenham ticket stub falls out, a spare hankie, a scrap of paper, his wallet – and a little box of dark blue velvet. Mari stares at the box. Then she bends and picks it up.

'What's this, Percy?'

'Nothing. I don't know. A present I bought for my Mam.'

Oh *Duw*, *Duw*, she's flicking the catch.

'A wedding ring,' she says. 'You bought a wedding ring for your mother?'

Better think fast, boyo. 'Yes, she lost hers. Dropped it in the fire. I thought she'd like to have another.'

'From London?'

'That's right.'

'That's wrong. It says inside the lid here, "Highwell Hopkins, Jewellers and Fancy Goods, Avon Fâch".'

'Hywel,' Percy says, his voice a croak. 'Hywel, not High-well.'

'Liar!' Mari snaps the box shut and aims. It strikes Percy on the nose, then drops into his lap with the rest of his possessions. 'It's for her, isn't it? You were going to marry that girl. When? Tell me when, Percy, and don't lie, for if you do, I'll knock your teeth down your throat.' She has balled up her fists and seems likely to do it.

'Today,' Percy says. 'Eleven o'clock this morning in Avon Fâch Baptist Chapel. That's why I was catching the milk train, because it gets me back to Cardiff in time for the connection, one hour up to Avon Fâch by bus. Cutting it a bit fine, but I got my wedding outfit in that suitcase—'

'Milk train!' Mari cries. 'Milk train! You milked me, all right, Percy Fly!'

'I'm sorry I didn't tell you. I'm glad it's all out so we can start clean.' He lays his clothes on the bed, gets up, and puts his shirt on. 'I *will* go down today and tell Ellen. I can see it's the gentlemanly thing, though I was going to leave it to Dai.' He finishes buttoning his shirt and gets into his trousers. 'Dai have been a close friend of the family for a long time, so I thought he'd break it gently, and he would have.' Percy knots his tie. 'Still, be that as it may, I'm going, for if I do, it'll be better between us when I come back again.'

Mari holds out his jacket on one finger.

'Thank you. I hope you see I'm on the right road now?'

'I'll be ready in two ticks.' She goes behind the screen and Percy hears the sound of her dressing, but this time he can see nothing for she has not put on the light. He sits on the bed, his arms dangling between his knees, and tries to rally his spirits which have decamped and gone absent without leave.

Mari reappears, in two ticks as she promised. She slings her bag over her shoulder. 'What time does this train go?'

'I wrote it down.' Percy feels in his pockets, but the piece of paper Dai wrote on, a corner torn off the *South Wales Echo*, isn't there. 'Ten to five. I remember.'

Mari looks at the clock on the mantelpiece. 'It's twenty past four already. Lucky for you we're close. We can do it in less than twenty minutes if we find a taxi quick.'

Percy picks up his suitcase.

'Don't forget that.' Mari points to the box on the bed.

'No point taking it now,' Percy says. 'I won't be needing it, will I?'

Mari snatches up the box and drops it into his pocket. 'You have to have a ring to get wed.'

'I'm coming back to you, Mari. We've settled it.'

'No, you're not.' She opens the door. 'I don't go with married men.'

'I'm not married.'

'You will be before this day is out.'

'Mari, you're talking like a loony.'

Mari snorts. 'Get a move on, or I'll magic you down the stairs.' She shoves Percy out of the door and slams it after them.

20

Sunday: Everyone

The milk train stands at Reading station, its final stop before Paddington. When the last churn is lifted off, one of the porters steps into the stationmaster's office to tell the driver, who sits there by the fire, drinking tea from a blue-rimmed enamel mug and discussing the latest news from Germany.

'Right-oh, son, I'm on my way,' the driver says, and to the stationmaster, 'Mark my words, Reggie, he don't have good intentions, the Kaiser.' He pulls on his hand-warmers. 'Promise of neutrality my foot! I hope Mr Asquith and Lloyd George don't fall for his ploys.'

'Now, Selwyn,' the stationmaster says, 'he's the old Queen's grandson, bear in mind. We're sort of related, us and the Germans.'

'What's that got to do with it?' The driver opens the door wide. A cold wind enters, lifting the time-tables on the walls, shuffling desk papers. 'Relatives are the worst ones, sometimes. I got relatives I wouldn't trust with my back turned.'

'Get on with you,' the stationmaster says as they walk out on to the platform. 'You Welsh are a pugnacious lot, Selwyn. Always looking for a fight.'

The driver jams on his cap. 'Scoff if you will, but there's an ill wind blowing across the Channel, and bad things happening all over. We lost the Final at Twickenham yesterday, too.'

'Ah well, you may have better luck next year.' The stationmaster is English, but from Cornwall, so he feels some kinship with the defeated Welsh. 'Meantime, the world will go round.'

'Aye,' the driver says, 'and so will a drunken man, Reggie.' He raises his hand. '*Bore da*. See you now jest then, on my way back. Brew up the tea about half-past five.' He hurries across the platform in a squall of blown newspapers and empty cigarette packets.

The stationmaster lifts his lantern and blows his whistle, and the train grinds out of the station into the quiet starlit countryside, a wailing Welsh monster, fire roaring in its mouth as of old, but with no chieftain on its back and no warriors in its belly, only a load of milk churns for the Londoners.

Dai and Ivor stand at the gates of platform three, first in a long line of beery-eyed Welshmen waiting to board the train and fall comatose on the upholstered seats.

'Plenty stayed up,' Ivor says, 'and made a night of it, too, by the looks of them. *Dee*, look at that feller's black eyes, Dai, swollen bigger than my prize tomatoes. And look at that one with a sleeve ripped out of his coat! We have given ourselves a bad name in London, I fear.'

'A lot gone back earlier though,' Dai says, scanning the queue. 'Percy would have had room to stretch out and sleep proper. A good five hours he could have had.'

'I wonder if we should have informed the police?'

'What for?'

'You did say he might be murdered.'

'Wishful thinking, Ive. Sitting in one of those all-night places in Leicester Square, he is, or gone home with some woman, I shouldn't wonder. Easy enough to pick up company, as you saw yourself.'

'They were all whores.' Ivor makes a face. '*Ach y fi*, I don't think Percy'd take up with one of them. His Mam raised him too clean.'

'He's done a dirty enough trick now though, hasn't he?' Dai makes a noise in his throat as if there is phlegm there. 'Damn his eyes!'

Mari taps the cab driver on the shoulder. 'Can you step on it, please? We have to be at Paddington by ten to five.'

'Can't go no faster, ma'am, sorry.'

'But there's no traffic!' she wails.

'Ain't that, just they haven't invented the motor car yet that'll top thirty.'

Mari swears under her breath.

'We'll make it,' Percy says, 'worse luck. We still got quarter of an hour to spare.'

'If you get us there in ten minutes,' Mari tells the driver, 'it'll be worth your while, I promise.' To Percy she says nothing. Sitting up very stiff and straight, eyes front, she is formidable and forbidding, a profile on a coin, lovely but immovable, rock-ribbed, a metallic sheen to her upswept hair, her nose and chin obdurate as bronze.

I've had it, Percy thinks, cooked my goose proper . . . and yet . . . and yet . . . isn't there a tiny, minuscule twitch in her cheek, a glimmer at the corner of her eye? If he says the right word, does the right thing . . . is there still a chance?

Well, what *is* going on in Mari's hidden self, the self beneath the white face, the rigid limbs, the stylish hat?

Oh, what a commotion there! What a civil war! For the heart has risen up in mutiny against the will, wishfulness laying siege to principle, a battering-ram at the gates, and hunger-weakened troops within. If they don't reach Paddington in ten minutes, the citadel may fall yet.

'How much longer?'

'Round the next corner, lady!'

'Hip, hip, hooray!'

'Oh, heck, already?'

'No sign of him, Dai.' Ivor has his head out of the compartment window. 'Platform's clear now and a porter's closing the barrier. Our hopes are dashed, I fear.'

Dai, slumped in a corner, lifts with both hands his bad leg and rests his foot on the opposite seat. ('Keep it elevated, Dai,' Dr Pritchard advised, 'much as you can, see. Hard for a working man, I know, but do your best, boyo.') On that seat, Percy's slender form would now be laid out in sleep, if Percy were here. Dai would like to lay him out, all right, give him what for, knock him into the middle of next week. He raises his eyes to the station clock where the big hand trembles before making its momentous move, one minute off the big black number eight.

'What's up now?' Dai asks, afraid himself to look. If only Ivor were to shout, 'Here he comes! He's knocked the barrier down! He's running like old boots! He's jumped into the last compartment. Percy's made it, *wara teg*!' Even at the eleventh hour, Dai would forgive his young mate, embrace him and cover him with glad words, 'Here you are then, *bachgen bach*, good boyo, bloody champion you are.'

'Stationmaster's getting ready to blow his whistle,' Ivor says.

The hand of the clock jerks to the eight, the whistle screeches, the train shudders, objects outside the window – the porters' carts, the milk churns, the benches – jolt into life and move up the platform, out of sight. From a compartment farther down the corridor, someone who fancies himself as a soloist begins a rendition of '*Cwm Rhondda*,' his tenor voice competing with the rumbling baritone of the milk train.

Ivor shuts the window and sits down. 'We're in for it now, Dai. Never thought I wouldn't be looking forward to going home, did you?'

'Damn his eyes,' Dai says. 'And damn his bloody wit-wat heart.'

Mari has the door open before the taxi stops. She stumbles on to the pavement in front of the station entrance, trips on the hem of her skirt and almost comes a cropper but rights herself, turns and reaches into the cab, grabbing the handle of Percy's suitcase in one hand, his coat sleeve in the other.

Percy scrambles from the cab and stands shivering on the pavement while Mari has a hasty exchange with the driver.

'Wait for me here, please. I'll be going back.'

'That's all right, miss,' the driver says, 'but what about my fare from Holland Park?'

'No time now. I'll pay you for both ways when I get back. Come on, Percy, show a leg!'

'Half a mo–' the driver objects, but she's already dashing under the great iron arch with Percy on her heels. The driver sighs, climbs out of his cab, and hot-foots it after them, though he has chilblains on his feet. He's heard it before, that 'I'll be back' line. They never are, of course.

'Which platform, Percy?' Mari pants.

'Three, I believe.'

The station clock points to four forty-five. They have made it with five minutes to spare, but there's no train standing at the platform, and no passengers, only a porter leaning on a barrier smoking a cigarette.

'Where's the train then?' Mari addresses him in an accusatory manner.

He gives her a cold stare. 'The Taunton train isn't due till six o'clock, madam.'

Mari turns to Percy. 'Is Taunton one of your stops?'

Percy shakes his head. 'I want the milk train, the one that goes to Cardiff,' he tells the porter.

The porter smirks. 'You're a bit late for that one. Went out at twenty to five. On the dot, as always.'

He turns to walk away, but Mari reaches over the barrier and grips his sleeve. 'Just a minute, mister. You must be wrong on that. Didn't you say it goes out at *ten* to five, Percy?'

Percy nods but looks unsure.

'You telling me my job, miss?' The porter pulls his sleeve from Mari's clutching fingers. 'The Cardiff train went out ten minutes ago. I'd advise you to look at a timetable for verification. You'd have done well to do that in the first place.'

'What time's the next train to Cardiff?' Percy whispers, fearing the answer, which, if the wrong one, could hurtle his timidly ascending heart down into his boots again.

'Only one train going to Cardiff today, and it's on its way to Reading as we speak.' The porter pulls his cap at Mari, a gesture more like a jeer than a salute, turns his back on them and strides off down the platform toward an empty milk trolley where some of his mates are sharing a can of tea.

'What'll we do now?' Mari's voice is mournful, her question addressed to the air above her head.

'I don't know, love.' Percy tries to sound sorry, too, but it's hard when his heart is dancing a jig and a brass band going oompah, oompah-pah-pah in his brain.

'You can go tomorrow,' the cab driver says.

'Aye, that's a good idea.' Percy smiles at him.

And now, encouraged by the triumph within, he risks an arm around Mari's shoulders. 'Let's go home, darling. It was meant to be,' he whispers in her ear. 'There's more powerful forces at work here than just us two.'

He kisses her cheek.

'Tomorrow is another day,' the cab driver says.

But it's not . . . not for everybody. For some it has to be this day or never again, and Percy's bride-that-was-to-be down in Avon Fach is one of these. It's for her, of course, that Mari's feet drag – for Welsh Ellen who passes sentence on her for assault and battery.

Just inside the arch there's a timetable board attached to the wall. Mari stops to read it, hoping against hope that the porter may have misled them. He did seem the spiteful sort.

Percy sighs. 'No use doing that, love. And in't you glad anyway–'

'Shut up!' Mari says. Her finger has found Sunday and there it is in black and white, the 4:40 to Cardiff. But wait . . . wait . . . calling at . . . She reads the names of the stations, a number of them between Paddington and Reading, a few minutes' stop at each, ten whole minutes at Slough, and at Reading–

Mari whoops. 'Half an hour! A whole thirty minutes. Plus all the other stops and the travelling time between. Upwards of an hour, easy. Here,' she turns to the driver, 'how long will it take you to get to Reading, eh?'

'About an hour, but I don't–'

Mari links his arm, links Percy on her other side, and propels them through the arch to the waiting taxi. 'You have to take him,' she's telling the driver. 'It's a matter of principle. He's getting married at eleven o'clock this morning.' She releases them both and opens the back door of the taxi. 'Get in, Percy, quick. You haven't a minute to lose.'

'Mari–'

'It's outside my area, miss–'

'Double fare! How much?'

'Counting the trip here–' He calculates and tells her.

'I don't have that,' Percy says.

The fee is almost as much as she has in her purse, her entire pay packet bar a few shillings. Mari opens her bag and counts the money into the driver's palm. It's a fair price really when the alternative is a life of guilt. 'Now, skedaddle,' she says and the driver jumps into his seat.

Mari and Percy look at each other, face-to-face for the last time. Percy doesn't know what to say.

'Go on, hurry,' Mari says. 'This is not an outing, lad.' Her voice is light, but her face quivers when she tries to smile.

And suddenly the right words come to Percy. 'This is noble, Mari,' he says. 'This is a deed befitting a princess.'

'Well ... see you treat that girl of yours as if you've kept company with royalty, Percy Fly.'

'A kiss—'

She gives it, and a shove, too. Percy's long body folds into the taxi.

'I'll never forget you, Mari.'

'You'd better, for I shall forget you!'

'It was nice—'

'Passing all description.' She laughs. 'What fancy words you know, Percy!' And slams the door in his face. 'Don't hold your horses,' she tells the driver. 'I paid through the nose for this.'

The taxi draws away from the curb. Percy waves through the back window and blows many kisses.

Mari keeps her right arm up, her palm flat, fingers straight, until the taxi disappears. Then her arm falls to her side, like a wooden post knocked down in a gale. The morning, however, though cold, is neither windy nor bitter. After all, it's almost spring. She turns into the station where she noticed a buffet open. She's in need of a cup of tea, and besides she doesn't fancy the long walk home on her own, not till it's properly light. She has to take into account again that there's a man in London whose chief pastime is murder. She must be on her guard, take all possible precautions, to avoid becoming a victim.

Mari quickens her step toward the lighted buffet. Unbidden, unwelcome, Percy's image keeps pace at her side. Almost she can feel the weight of his arm on her shoulders. Well, at least she knows how he went and what will become of him. At least, this time, she had a say in the matter. And she did the right thing ... that should be a comfort. A bell jangles above her head as she pushes open the buffet door and a waitress steps from behind a hissing tea urn, her sleepy, kohl-rimmed eyes opening wide at the sight of Mari, all dressed up and unaccompanied at five to five in the morning.

'A cup of tea and a bun, please,' Mari says.

The waitress carries out her order with her mouth and eyes dipped. She doesn't like tarts coming in.

Sixty-seven minutes later, as Mari is trudging toward Holland Park Avenue under a drizzling sky, Percy arrives at Reading station.

'Thanks a lot,' he says to the driver as he jumps from the cab. 'You've done your bit to make a lot of people happy today.' He doesn't add that he is not one of that joyful number.

'Don't forget your suitcase, mate.'

'Oh, aye.' Percy grabs the case and sprints into the station, feeling in his pockets for his return ticket.

'Good luck!' the driver shouts after him. 'You'll need a ton of it, getting spliced.'

'The Cardiff train?' Percy asks a porter.

'Platform two,' the porter says. 'Just going out.'

Percy whizzes on, holding his ticket aloft in his left hand, though there is no one to accost him at the rapidly approaching barrier, and no one on platform two, just the train, chugging into motion.

Briefly, the thought flits through Percy's mind that he could miss it easy, just by slowing down a bit. In fact, he could miss it even running at his present speed. But to what end? Mari wouldn't like it if her grand gesture were muddled up by him. No welcome back from her. Percy's as sure of that as he's ever been of anything. Better to aim for a welcome home then.

He makes a supreme effort, racing as he never knew he could. He leaps and lands on the steps at the end of the train, pulls the door shut in the nick of time to prevent a nasty fall, stumbles into the corridor and collapses against the rocking glass partition of the last carriage, gasping for breath, his cheeks puffing in and out like a hard-to-inflate party balloon.

Percy scrutinizes the faces in each compartment, for a great longing has risen in him to see Dai again, though Dai will be put out and berate him, and he'll have to face Ivor, too, worse luck, with his nosy questions and disapproving *daro-daro*s.

And here they are, with a compartment to themselves, Ivor dozing in one corner, Dai with his leg up but awake, his face turned to the window, his profile reminding Percy of Mari in the taxi, no resemblance in the features, but the same flinty look.

He slides open the glass door and says, 'Hullo again!'

Dai's head turns, Ivor wakes. They stare at him in shock, as if he's an apparition, or a person out of the far-back past whose face they can't put a name to.

'I missed the train at Paddington,' Percy says, 'so I came on to Reading by taxi.'

'*Daro!*' Ivor says at last.

And Dai's iron face relents. His white teeth appear, his dark eyes crinkling. He heaves his leg off the seat and stands up. '*Bachgen bach,*' he says, and opens his arms. 'My best butty. Come to Dai, lovely boy.'

Percy folds himself into Dai's embrace.

'You've made my heart glad, Percy.'

Dee, this is nice indeed!

'Where've you been then?' Ivor says. 'How did you manage to miss the train? Must have cost a bit, coming all that way in a taxi. Did you have enough money on you?'

Dai draws Percy into a seat, the two of them sitting opposite Ivor, Dai linking Percy's arm and looking at him with an eat-you-up expression.

'What did you do all them hours you was separated from us?' Ivor says. His body jerks suddenly. 'You was never with a woman, was you, Percy?'

'Ivor,' Dai says, 'I bet Percy'd like a cup of tea. We could all do with one. Buffet must be open, and you got two good legs to my one.'

Ivor looks at Percy.

'I wouldn't say no,' Percy says. 'I fancy a piece of toast, too, if it's no trouble.'

Ivor rises. 'Don't tell what happened till I'm back then. I don't want to miss anything.'

When he has left the compartment, Dai says, 'Had some adventures have you, boyo?'

'Oh, Dai, you wouldn't believe . . .' And out it all comes, the saga of Mari and Percy. Talking fast and fluent as Welshmen can when the *hwyl* fires them, he gives Dai the whole story from the first setting of eyes on each other, 'instant love, it was,' to the last heart-rending goodbye waved from the window of a speeding taxi.

Dai listens intently, which gratifies Percy, for it shows his story is worth hearing, and Percy himself, in the telling, relives the wonder of it. Fancy, he's thinking as he speaks, here I am, Percy Fly, telling about my love affair with The Infamous Princess Marie, a star of the London Palladium! Who, among his acquaintance, could cap such a tale! Not Dai, for all his doings with life and women, and if not Dai, who has been all over the country and lived as a free man, then no one else in Avon Fach, nor in the whole of South Wales, probably. And it occurs to Percy that he's a fortunate man, a privileged one, for no matter how dull his life may be from now on, he has what many lack (even Dai, he suspects) – a marvel to keep in his heart, to cherish and embellish and gloat over when days are dark.

Regretfully, he realizes that he can't tell anyone but Dai for the time being, but that's a small sacrifice. Already his vision flies forward into a distant time when, a long-married man with grown children (Ellen passed on, perhaps), he can tell his tale to all and sundry at the Prince Llewelyn and sun himself in his butties' admiration and envy. Ah, it's not as bad as he dreaded, leaving Mari. There are compensations for the pain of parting, a pain that has diminished already, so much of it poured out with his story.

The story is told now, and Dai is not saying anything.

'I hope you don't condemn me?' Percy says, a small doubt discolouring his pleasure like a bruise on a peach.

Dai lifts his eyebrows. 'What for?'

'For going with another woman when I'm about to be married.'

Dai says, 'Huh!' and flicks his head in accompaniment to the short, hard sound. 'I'd be a fine one to condemn that, Percy. I haven't let marriage stand in my way, neither.' Then he puts his hand on Percy's knee and smiles. 'A young feller should sow a few wild oats. Too many straight furrows to plough, in't there? In a better frame of mind now then, are you?'

'Oh, I am,' Percy says. 'I'm ready to marry Ellen.'

'There's glad I am you came back, Percy, for Ellen's sake and your Mam's and all of us, not to mention the little 'un on the way. A lot of heartbreak in Avon Fach if you'd stayed in London.'

'I did the right thing.' But saying this, Percy feels a tweak of conscience. 'Well, to be honest . . . as I told you . . . Mari made me come once she found the ring.'

'That was decent of her.'

'She's a fine woman.'

'So how do you think she's feeling about it all, Percy?'

Surprise puckers Percy's face. 'I don't know.' He thinks for a moment, calling up Mari's image, as she looked at the last, which hasn't figured in his story as told to Dai, the final scene focused only on himself, waving from the taxi. 'She misses me, I expect,' he says, 'for her feelings were true, I'm certain of that.' For a moment, thinking of Mari down in the dumps casts a shadow over Percy, but it passes and his sky brightens again. 'She'll be all right. She laughed and made a joke right at the end. Made fun of something I'd said earlier . . . in a nice way, I mean . . . and laughed. And then she told me to forget her because she'd forget me.'

Dai nods his head, as if he'd been there and seen all this; as if he, too, had met Mari.

'Very fine,' he says. 'Better than most could do.'

'A noble act. On top of everything else, I got to be grateful to her for showing me how to be noble.' Percy sees himself standing beside Ellen in a few hours' time, answering Reverend Morris's question with the two brief but momentous words, 'I do,' Ellen and the whole congregation – except Dai – never dreaming how far he has travelled, what renunciation he has made, to utter them.

Ivor appears in the doorway with three mugs of tea and a plate of buttered toast on a tin tray. Percy has never been so delighted to see him.

'It was right at the other end of the train, the buffet,' Ivor says, 'and so much shaking, I've slopped the tea. Toast is a bit soggy, I'm afraid. You can take the crockery back, Percy.'

'I will,' Percy says. 'I'll be glad to do that, Ivor.'

Ivor sets the tray on the seat and they each take a cup and a slice of damp toast.

'Never mind,' Ivor says, 'saves us dipping it in the tea.' He lifts his cup to Percy. 'Here's to you. Be toasting you in champagne later, won't we?'

'Ellen's mam have ordered a whole case of it. Got it cheap, too, from the pub where she used to be barmaid.'

Ivor bites into his toast and sips his tea. 'Ah, this is more like it. I can taste Wales in this brew already. Come on, then, Percy, tell us all that happened to you.'

'Oh, nothing to tell. I just got myself lost for a bit.' Percy glances slyly at Dai, hoping for a wink.

But Dai's head is turned to the window and he seems engrossed in the scenery, though there's nothing much to look at, only a lot of flat fields with cows in them.

When Alf dismissed me and I came upstairs, I thought I would write to you, Mother. I laid paper and pen in front of me on the desk and reached for matches to light the candle. But my hand was stayed by a shaft of moonlight.

The moon is the goddess of subterfuge and trickery, and as I gazed, enthralled, at her handiwork, her transformation of my own ordinary flesh into a thing of wonder, she slipped, slyly, a vagabond thought into my head: what is the feeling of falling in love?

Love began with a flutter, light as a moth's wing brushing my cheek as I perused a book by lamplight. I thought it a momentary distraction; a handsome young man, a stranger, leaning in the doorway of his aunt's cottage, enjoying the summer afternoon, he had nothing to do with me beyond the tremor I felt at the sight of him, a shift in the breeze which soon would blow in another direction.

He wore no hat to hamper the profusion of his brown hair but, as we passed by, he doffed an imaginary one, bowed from the waist, and said, 'A fair day,' smiling full into my face, as if it were I he meant to compliment and not the weather.

We nodded, and you gave him a little sideways smile to show polite disdain. I, I think, merely stared.

He came to church that Sunday evening, hatless still, careless of the old men's muttering, the young ladies' whispers. Oblivious to censure or favour, he looked about until he saw me, then chose a pew where he had me in his sight. And his eyes never strayed from my face. When I looked up from my hymn book or from prayer, his gaze was upon me, not smiling then but sober, as befits a man at worship . . . but it was I who entranced him, not the word of God. I knew he was no regular churchgoer. He had come to see me again.

On the way out he contrived to stand close to me in the crowd, opened my hand and slipped me a note, shutting my palm over the folded paper, and inside his own for a moment, whispering, 'Mary, comply, I beseech you.'

So our meetings began. In the woods and on the moors, ours an open-air passion, wild and boundless as nature. And I believe that had we lain together on a grassy bank, or on a mantle of bluebells beneath the rowan trees, and had he then persisted, I might have vanquished terror and concurred. For all things that summer persisted – thrusting, blossoming, buzzing, warbling, mating, nesting, and I, too, in the midst of it all, felt creation's urge, the stumble of the blood like a foal finding its legs, a fledgling its wings.

All newborn creatures dither on untested limbs, in need of a gentle push, a loving nudge . . . but we humans lack the unerring instinct of other species. We can neither scent nor sense the ripeness of the moment, relying as we do on the false indicators of speech, deportment, etiquette. Alf took me at my word, desisted, and the moments rushed away, bearing us along on their current, to a place, a time, where determination not instinct held sway, and desire became exigency. In the country I might have been seduced; in London I was coerced.

You think I say this with rancour and hatred – Mary with the same old story to tell, hers a tedious, repetitive tale, a lament the only music she has learned.

Nay, not so!

The wind has shifted, I know not how, and some softer climate emerges to replenish the shoots of memory I thought despoiled by the long winter of neglect. Now they grow luxuriant, as grass and wild flowers and sturdy seeds will spring at last to cover ground laid waste by sword and fire. It is Nature's way, to restore what she is robbed of and we, her offspring, resist and thwart her laws at our peril. Opposed, she is likely to run amok . . .

As you did, Mother, when I thwarted your will and murdered

Father, and his aberration that you nursed . . . ah, wait, this is not the memory I meant to evoke . . . this is not the path I would retrace . . . no honeysuckle or wild rose here, only the burdock, the nettle, the deadly nightshade, weeds that sting, strangle, poison . . .

Take care, Mary! Memory is a maze of devious paths. Halt now, while you are yet safe, while the way ahead lies clear. See how the moon lights the road you must choose, there at the tips of your fingers where they scratch upon the glass. Yes, see, the moon's fingers knit with yours, as a mother takes her faltering child by the hand. Do you falter?

You are a lily-livered thing, a creeping worm, a hopping toad! Spineless, brainless, heartless creature!

There is one who rises against you, who means to step on you and snuff you out if you permit it.

I would discover the way that leads back to where Alf and I began.

But *she* obliterates it!

What shall I do then, Father?

Rid yourself of her, what else?

I must disguise myself again—

As a man. Men rule the earth. Have I not told you that?

Mother . . . ?

Do as your father bids, dear.

Listen to me, child. I know what's best. On your knees now and say the words I have taught you. Say them! Come, do not force me to chastise—

Thy will be done!

21

Percy, Dai, Ivor: Sunday Morning

In the Gentlemen's Waiting Room at Cardiff station Percy Fly dons his wedding clothes. The black worsted suit is brand-new. Roberts the tailor sewed the last stitches and gave Percy a final fitting Tuesday night just past. Percy can't see how the suit looks now for there is only a half mirror above the fireplace in the waiting room, but buttoning the braces he feels how well the trousers fit, neither too loose nor too tight at the waist, and a nice weighty feel to the legs.

Ivor is holding out the jacket now, saying, 'Lovely cut. Knows his business, Roberts, don't he?'

Dai helps Percy fasten the mother-of-pearl cuff links Percy has borrowed from his brother, Royston, and reaches up to straighten the black bow tie.

Percy steps into the jacket and turns so his butties can see him frontways. 'How do I look then?' he says and feels the blush rising in his cheeks. In this wedding suit he feels more naked, somehow, despite the heavy cloth, than he did a few hours ago when Mari stripped his clothes off.

'Bloody smashing,' Dai says, 'don't he, Ive?'

'A real toff,' Ivor says. 'One of the crack-crack you are today, Percy.'

Percy can see by their faces they mean it. He turns to the mirror over the fireplace. 'My hair . . . sticking up a bit, in't it?'

Dai crosses to the *bosh* in the corner, runs water over his hands, and comes back, shaking drops off his fingers. '*Twti* down a minute, Perce.'

Percy bends his knees and Dai smoothes his damp hands over his hair, like a caress . . . like a blessing.

Ivor, squinting, says, 'Over to the left, Dai. It's a bit skew-whiff by his ear.'

There's nice it is, to be well in with your butties, to be the focus of their goodwill, and so much more of this to come today, love and generous feelings pouring like champagne from his relatives, his friends and neighbours, the people he's known all his life. Right this minute, every one of them up in Avon Fach is thinking of him and wishing him luck . . . and Ellen, too, of course. His Mam, having a cup of tea before getting dressed, is thinking, 'I hope that girl and her mother appreciate him and treat him as he deserves.' She's never said a word against Ellen and her mother, but he knows she wishes he'd waited a bit, gone around more and found out what's what before tying himself down. She thinks the world of him, his Mam, the apple of her eye, he is . . . and to think he nearly broke her heart.

'Have a look now, Percy. Is that better?'

Percy rises to look in the mirror again. Now that his hair is in place, a gratifying sight awaits him in the splotchy, fly-specked glass. Sleeked down, his wavy hair has the gleam and softness of silk, falling in delicate ripples about his clean-shaven face. (Dai brought his own razor in case Percy forgot, which he did.) Above the black bow tie and well-cut shoulders of his jacket, his long, narrow face looks distinguished, a sensitive, poetic thinness to his nostrils and lips, the face of a young aristocrat, the faint line of hairs he has left over his top lip (because a moustache will suit him as a married man) a sprinkling of gold dust, his eyes, thanks to five hours of baby-sound sleep, an August-morning blue. 'A prince I was, blue-eyed and fair of face . . .' *Daro*, he will cut a fine figure today, no two opinions about that!

'All set, Perce?' Dai says. 'The Avon Fach bus will be in by now.'

'Ready to go,' Percy says. Lifting his chin, squaring his shoulders, he adopts a posture befitting a high-minded act, and walks between his two butties to the door of the waiting room, towards his appointment with the rest of his life; towards his bride, his Mam, and all those people by whom he is doing the right thing.

They arrive in Hebron Street with ten minutes to spare. Old Mr Howells, a deacon, stands at the chapel gate looking up and down. 'For me,' Percy thinks. 'They must have got worried by now.' He imagines himself not there; Mr Howells's face if he hadn't turned up, the faces of his brothers, Royston, Marsden, and Ieuan, all in black suits and bow ties. Those faces which now light up with relief would have dropped a mile seeing only air between Ivor and Dai. Percy is glad to feel himself present, solid in his heavy worsted suit. Mr Howells waves with both arms, his wrinkled face, so sombre when he carries round the collection plate, cracking into a smile as he lifts his eyes to the overcast sky and says, '*Diolch yn fawr!*'

'*Daro*, you fellers have taken your time,' Royston says when they reach the gates. 'We was afeared Ellen'd be here before you. Mam's having forty fits, Percy, thinking you won't make it.'

'Hard job persuading her to stay in her pew,' Marsden says. 'She wanted to go down to the bus depot to look for you.'

'Daisy Allgood's calling you rotten,' Ieuan says.

'*Jawl*, this is a nice warm welcome for the groom,' Dai says.

Percy's brothers look at Dai and their faces alter, disapproval changing to ruefulness so fast, Percy has to smile. It's like their faces were made of dough and Dai kneading them into shape. Percy is not overly fond of his brothers who, being so much older than he, have always bossed him about. But they respect Dai, as all the men in Avon Fach do, though they're not thrilled to bits that he's Percy's best butty.

'Just anxious we were, see, Dai,' Marsden says. 'You can understand that. Never mind though, since all's well. Poor show our boys put up at Twickenham yesterday, I hear.'

Ivor, who has been twitching and shifting beside Percy, says, 'Look, I've got to go and get Bethan and the boys now. She must be wondering–' He puts one foot forward in the direction of his house, four doors up from the chapel, but Mr Howells lays a hand on his arm.

'Bethan's gone in already, Ivor *bach*. She said to say she couldn't wait no more because it would look bad, see, if she was to take her seat in the choir late. Mrs Fly have got your boys with her.'

'Oh *daro*,' Ivor says, his face falling. 'Upset, was she?'

'Everybody's upset,' Ieuan says, and then quickly, glancing at Dai, 'but they'll be happy now. Better go in then, is it, and let Percy show his face?'

As they walk up the chapel path, Marsden says, 'Pity about Royston Pugh dropping that try. Was it bad luck or fumbling on his part, Dai?'

'His knee gave up on him,' Dai says, 'but selfishness helped. He don't like to play with the team, as you know.'

'Letting a good name down,' Royston jokes as they enter the chapel foyer.

Crowded by his brothers and assailed by the sonorous music, Percy is suddenly attacked by claustrophobia. His eyes turn to the path beyond the chapel's main door, to the gate and to Hebron Street which turns into Cross Street, which runs into High Street, at the end of which stands the bus depot. He is not actually thinking of running away, but buses and trains rumble through his head, louder and more portentously than Mr Johns's music, accompanied by phrases repeating themselves like a nonsense verse, 'Selfishness helped . . . play with the team . . .'

'Better step on it,' Royston says. 'The bridesmaids have come.'

And so Percy discovers himself walking down the aisle beside Dai towards Reverend Morris. When they reach the minister, the organist strikes up the bridal march, so that Percy knows that Ellen, too, has arrived. The wedding will start on time after all.

'Courage, brother,' he hears Dai say, an undertone in his voice, a bit of humour behind the sobriety. Well, that's Dai – perking him up – but easy for him, really, standing on the safe side of the altar after all.

Rustle, swish, crackle, a soft indrawn breath, and she's beside him, the heady scent of mingled flowers, a vision of falling snow out of the corner of his eye as a bridesmaid settles her long veil. 'Percy,' she whispers.

Percy turns his head. And, *daro*, there's pretty she is! Is it the figured satin dress, the little coronet of seed pearls on her forehead, the gauzy veil, or is she always this lovely and he forgot? Well, her expression is certainly different than it has been of late . . . shy, smiling, the fragile-flower look of their early courting days.

'Hullo, love,' he says, and tries to show her by his voice and his face that he would gather her into his arms if he could and protect her now from everything she nearly had to go through. Ah Ellen, well may you wear that tremulous look. It was more touch-and-go, this meeting of ours, than you'll ever know.

'Brethren, sisters,' Mr Morris intones, and Dai nudges Percy to face front, 'we are gathered here to witness a happy and blessed event . . .'

Percy tries to concentrate on the service, on Ellen pressing so close, tries to keep one true statement fixed in his mind . . . 'I'm getting married' . . . but other words, and their images, flit into his head like a flight of moths: 'I'll go into the wildwood no more . . . selfishness helped . . . team player . . . Do you like my magic then?'

Dai nudges him, Ellen fluttering on the other side.

'Say, "I do," son,' Mr Morris prompts.

'I do,' Percy echoes.

'Do you, Ellen Dilys, take this man . . .'

'I do,' Ellen says, with only the pause of a heart beat.

'Those whom God has joined together, let no man put asunder.' Mr Morris drops his grandiose tone and slips into his ordinary voice, a bit tired-sounding, to say, 'You may kiss the bride.'

Again Percy turns to Ellen. Under the misty veil her eyes are wet; shining like stars, Percy thinks, and all this cloudy stuff around her, my sky bride, nothing of earth in her . . . which is what I wanted once, but I've learned since there's got to be some ballast somewhere.

She helps his fumbling fingers lift her veil efficiently enough, however.

The service over, the music resumes and now, as Percy and Ellen turn to face their audience, as the congregation rises, a voice soars above their heads, angelic, ethereal, notes as pure as water cascading into a hidden pool where naiads romp, naked, unseen.

Percy looks up to the balcony where Bethan Parry has risen from the midst of the choir to stand alone. Dressed in an ice-blue costume, her hair upswept under a blue boater, she reminds Percy of a figurehead on a ship's prow, of a wave-drenched goddess, so easy to imagine in that form-fitting costume . . . ah, don't imagine . . . listen and let her voice clothe you in goodness, boyo, for she's singing of marital bliss, not the other sort. And now all the faces are upturned to her as she unites the congregation with her song.

. . . All faces except Dai's. His head down, his eyes are fixed on his boots, a frown on his face as if Mrs Parry were singing out of tune. What's wrong with him? He should be in his oils now that he's won the match.

Ah – it's all a mystery! Percy turns his eyes to Ellen. She gazes at him, all soft love, and he would like to eat her up. Maybe he shouldn't have these thoughts in chapel, but they're a man's thoughts, after all, and focused now on his lawful wedded wife. Off to Swansea they are, after the reception. That's good. A week to themselves before he moves into Daisy's house. A lot can happen in a week. Look how much happened in a night!

The song ends, drifting away on a low thrilling note that cuts through Percy's breast. Then the organ resumes, and he and Ellen are going arm-in-arm down the aisle, and people are patting them, leaning out of pews to smile in their faces, children looking up at Ellen in awe. Here's his Mam, no tears in her eyes, she's not that sort, but her big, wide-boned face gleaming with love and pride.

Even on this day she's dressed in the deep mourning she's worn ever since his Dad died of the dust sixteen years back. Not putting a damper on the proceedings though, not at all, but seeming to verify the rightness Percy feels, her black hat as dignified as a scholar's mortarboard, her eyes glinting owlish behind the black half veil, her broad lips tucked in tight as they always are when strong emotions vie for first place over prudence. As he passes her, he brushes shy fingers across her hands, gripping a hymn book, and murmurs, 'How be, Mam?'

'My good boy,' she mouths.

Then they are outside, he and Ellen, and she says, 'Let's run, Percy,' and hand in hand they dash down the path to the waiting car, but not fast enough to escape a shower of confetti and congratulations hurled at them by pursuing well-wishers. 'Help me with my dress,' says Ellen, breathless. 'Quick!'

Her high-strung state, half fear, half elation, quickens the moment, the getaway, with a sense of high adventure; and Percy, exhilarated, remembers other times, far back, when she sounded that way. 'You can touch me there. . . .'

He gathers her dress in his hands, slippery satin bunched in his fingers like seaweed, or wet smooth skin, as if he has captured a mermaid. Her gauzy veil blows across his face, and the scent of flowers, as she balloons into the back of the car, he stumbling after her, banging his head on the roof in his haste.

'Oh, Percy, did you hurt yourself?'

'No, love, just a tap.' In fact, his head is reeling a bit, but he doesn't mind, likes it. It goes along with the unreal feelings of moonlight, deep water, and mer-things.

She slips her hand into his.

'I can't get close to you in that dress.'

Islwyn James starts the car. 'Miner's Hall the reception is?'

'Aye, that's right, thank you.'

'Do you like it, Percy?' Ellen whispers.

'Not getting close to you?'

They laugh into each other's faces, the first shared joke of their married life, there's nice. 'My dress, I meant!'

'It's beautiful, fit for a queen . . . which you are, to me.' Then he leans closer and murmurs, 'But not a patch on how you'll look later, love, when we're by ourselves at last.'

Ellen sighs and presses herself against him. 'I was afraid you wouldn't come back from London,' she says in a timid little voice.

Percy, trying to kiss her cheek, gets her veil in his mouth. It's scratchier than he would have guessed, and when he pulls it away, it grazes his bottom lip. A tiny drop of blood staining the white gauze perturbs him for a moment, but it's hardly noticeable, will probably wash out. He folds the stain out of sight and says, before kissing Ellen, 'Now there's a daft notion. Nothing, not even a catastrophe, could've kept me from you.'

Dai Bando, one of the last to leave the chapel, loiters in a narrow foyer near the bowl of yellow daisies. The members of the choir are coming down the stairs, Bethan in the midst of them, Mr Jenkins the choirmaster with her, saying, 'Lovely, them high notes, Bethan, perfect pitch. I think we did right to have that final practice last night, whole choir, though I didn't like bringing everybody out on a Saturday, and I understood the objections . . .' Mr Jenkins, frail as a lamb with his white woolly hair, looks up into Bethan's face, adoring her, as they all do, all the lonely bachelors of Avon Fach Baptist; and Dai, watching, waits for her to say the proper, the comforting thing.

'You were right, Iory, and we all know it today. Shameful, the fuss we make about extra practices. I don't know why you put up with us.' Her voice has the soft Welsh lilt, but she speaks as she sings, never slurring her words in the South Wales manner. Her smile is balm to solitary hearts.

Dai's own heart turns over. He's seen her often, from a distance, since they fell out, but it's long since he heard her voice. She sees him and stops on the bottom step, her smile vanishing, another look coming over her face, one he can't fathom, a mixture, he supposes, of many things. He wonders how his own face looks, if his feelings are showing there, and he rolls his hands into fists behind his back, as if by hiding one part of himself he can hide another.

The choir members hurry out of the chapel, hoping to see the bride and groom before they leave in the hired car. Soon Dai and Bethan are alone.

She speaks first. Still standing on the bottom stair, one foot in a high-heel, blue court shoe thrust over the edge, she says, 'I knew I'd be seeing you today.'

Is she telling him she's barricaded her heart against the meeting, or that she's glad to come, innocently, by this chance? No way of knowing from her voice, and she's got control of her face, too. Always could get a grip on herself fast.

('I won't be coming here any more, Dai. I've made up my mind. I can't square it with my conscience.' And she just risen from his arms, sitting on the side of his bed putting on her stockings, where moments before she had trembled and spoken very different words.)

'Hullo, love,' he says. 'I hope I haven't made it awkward for you. I'd have stayed away rather than do that.' A lie, but never mind. All's fair . . .

'Don't be foolish,' she says. 'You're Percy's best man. You've more right here than I do.'

'I don't think of rights where you're concerned.'

He sees how her hand grips the bannister. 'The reception—'

225

'Don't worry. I'm going up home now.'

'Oh, you mustn't do that. They'll be expecting you. It would look funny—'

He seizes his moment, though it's a risky one. 'I'm going home in the hopes of a visit from you. While they're all busy at the Miners' Hall, you could slip out easy—'

'Hush, Dai!' Distress on her face now, real enough. He can still move her then.

She crosses the foyer to the chapel door. For a second she's close enough for him to grasp her arm. But he keeps his hands behind his back.

On the threshold she says, 'I haven't changed my mind.' But as she steps out of the door she turns suddenly: a look over her shoulder, as if he has spoken her name, and her eyes – the unshielded wish he sees there momentarily – flash hope into his heart. Then she's gone.

Outside he hears Ivor's voice. 'Here you are, love. You just missed Percy and Ellen going off. Everybody's saying there's lovely you sang.'

Dai goes back into the empty chapel and sits in a back pew to wait until all the guests have cleared off to the Miners' Hall. No one will wonder about him until he doesn't show up there.

To pass the time, he flips through the pages of a hymnal, reading snatches of hymns here and there:

> Rock of ages, cleft for me,
> Let me hide myself in thee...

> We plough the fields and scatter
> The good seed on the land...

> Onward Christian soldiers,
> Marching as to war,
> Wtih the cross of Jesus
> Going on before...

Is this where she finds her strength, her sustenance, in the stirring words she sings, empty vessels in themselves, he knows beyond doubt, but filled up with feeling when she pours her voice into them? Must be . . . it's not in Ivor's bed, any rate. Damn her! Pride is her sin. Which goeth before a fall. Please let her fall again, Lord. And I know it's all right to mouth such a prayer, for You aren't there to be shocked by it, to hurl me into Hell. Where I'd be at home anyway, wouldn't I? He stretches his bad leg out of the pew, heaves himself up. . . .

Dynevor Cottage stands on a hillside overlooking Avon Fach but hidden from its eyes by a copse of myrtle trees. It's an isolated spot, a one-up-and-one-down drover's cottage, uninhabited for years, the roof caving in, until Dai took it for two shillings a week after Ivor introduced him to his wife one Saturday in the High Street. She'll never come to me if I live in the town, he'd thought, and moved out of his digs and into the cottage the next week.

To get home, he must walk in the opposite direction from the wedding party and climb the Big Tip, a steep paved hill, a precarious terrace of miners' houses on either side, their doors and window trims painted in bright clashing colours, red, yellow, green, blue; a little, well-kept, poorly attended Catholic church at the top where Dai leans on the railing for a breather. On the church's narrow front lawn a statue of the Virgin Mary, blue-eyed and blue-cloaked, reaches out her plaster arms to the passer-by, the wayfarer, the lost son. She is the woman Dai wants at this moment, the woman he wishes Bethan to become for him, her arms an opening to her body and her heart, a benign forgiving smile on her face. He has often toyed with the temptation to go to Mass, but held off because he has heard that Catholics have all sorts of rituals the uninitiated can't learn, and he doesn't want to make a fool of himself in religion as well as in love. He was raised a Baptist; better to stick with what he knows, even if his role is the backslider's ignominious one.

The lane he turns into divides the miners' garden allotments from the hill, in a hollow of which his house stands.

After moving into the cottage, he whitewashed the walls inside and out, repaired the roof, painted the door a fresh, light green (the colour that seemed suited to her) and planted flowers in the front garden, all in preparation for the day when she would come, as he had known she would from the first, when she stood beside

Ivor in the High Street, a reserved young matron offering him a cool hand, her eyes, black like his, skittish when he tried to hold her gaze.

He pushes open the gate, walks up the path past the stalks of last year's flowers, unlocks the door and steps into the single room that is kitchen and parlour both. It's a silent house he enters, for he left his little whippet bitch with a butty while he went to London. He misses keenly her eager bark and wagging tail, her paws on his knees when she leaps to greet him. A good companion, never moody or refusing . . .

In the downstairs room everything is tidy, spotless, for Dai is a methodical housekeeper, never leaving unwashed dishes or unraked ashes when he goes out. A clean, comfortable house is a nice thing to come back to, like the arms of a welcoming woman.

A cast-iron fireplace with a hob and oven for cooking, an airing cupboard on one side, the door to the upstairs room on the other, takes up one wall. On the speckled marble mantelpiece above the grate two china King Charles spaniels sit, one at each end, and in the centre, a statue of a shepherd boy, his hand on the neck of a large black-and-white collie.

Dai likes big dogs, would like to keep one, but it wouldn't be right to coop a large animal up in an empty house all day just for his own pleasure – a bit like the situation he's in with Bethan. Except, he had the privilege of choice, which an animal would not. Or did he? It's a mystery to him, why he chose a married woman, a chapel woman, the wife of a lay preacher . . . Did *he* make that misguided choice or did her coltish black eyes, so out of keeping with the rest of her demeanour, choose for him?

A large picture window set in the wall opposite the door gives a view of the apple tree in the back garden and through its branches a spread of distant mountains, the Aberdare range, an ever-changing view in sun and mist and storm – like a vast canvas, so satisfying, so engaging, that he feels no need to hang pictures; so the whitewashed walls are bare, a dark walnut dresser holding white china crockery on its shelves against the wall opposite the fireplace, next to it the *bosh*, above it a square mirror in a black varnished frame embossed with leaves and fruit clusters. Under the window, his scrub-top table is covered with a brightly checked oilcloth, beside it an inlaid walnut chair and footstool, padded and tufted, a deep rich amber like autumn leaves, or like the light over the Aberdare mountains on a summer evening. A red, amber, and green needlepoint rug covers the polished wood floor. A sparsely furnished room, suited to a man whose life has not yet settled, it is still cheerful, warming, for Dai takes pride and pleasure in his furnishings.

He strikes a match, lights the fire laid yesterday morning, puts on the blower to draw it, and sets a kettle on the hob. Then he opens the door next to the fireplace and climbs the narrow stairs to his bedroom, almost filled by the big brass bed he has owned since a year after leaving Port Talbot, the year he discovered he had a way with women, that he would always find loving company without the complications of rings and promises. He changes out of his black suit into a pair of grey trousers and puts on a grey cardigan over his white shirt, leaving on his tie, neatly refastening the knot. (A smart dresser herself, she appreciates neatness in a man.) Then he goes downstairs, his tin of Wintergreen in his hand.

Waiting for the fire to blaze and the kettle to boil, Dai props his foot on the stool, rolls up his right trouser leg and massages his permanently bruised, twisted calf with Wintergreen. The unguent penetrates his skin, a burning sensation like whisky rushing through his limbs, the antiseptic scent restorative, cleansing as the first breath of fresh air at the pithead after a long shift underground. It clears his head and soothes his nerves, jarred by the encounter with Bethan, and by the trip to London, hard on his leg all that traipsing about, and hard on his feelings, seeing that woman . . .

He rests his head on the quilted chair-back, closes his eyes, and sees her again, the woman he might have saved with the right word, the timely action . . . but now it's Bethan's face that looks up at him, *her* wrists in chains, her life in danger, and the flames that engulf him spring neither from the Wintergreen nor the crackling coals in the fireplace, but from his own zealous passion to save and protect his beloved, stubborn as steel, obdurate as stone though she is. It's a fervour akin to religious fanaticism, but without the balm of righteousness, and corrupt, of course – he knows that – infused as it is by lust. She'll never leave Ivor, and it's past time for his leaving Avon Fach. He's never stayed in one place so long before. London, he should try . . . the women there . . . a different breed, as he told Ivor . . . surely one among them with a fervour to match his. Ah, but can he go where Bethan is not? And fair do's, what use would he be to a woman, a man whose heart is in worse shape than his gammy leg?

A rapping at the front door pulls him upright, pulls him out of his brooding. He rolls down his trouser leg, heaves himself up, wincing when he puts weight on his right foot. Without giving him time to answer, the knocking continues through the heart-stopping moments when he hesitates beside his chair, prepares himself to cross the room, open the door, and find her on his step. Her, or another – one of his butties come to fetch him to the reception, perhaps. Better prepare for that disappointment.

It's a long journey, the half-dozen steps, as hazardous a path as he's ever travelled; he can hardly make it really, aching like an old man in his leg, and like a very young one, too, with a green and headlong heart. His hand on the doorknob shakes, he can hardly grip it, a two-faced hope dividing him, he wants it to be her and he doesn't. For to have it all start up again, that maybe – maybe not, I can – I can't business . . . he'll never know where he stands, coming or going . . .

He opens the door.

'Dai,' she says, breathless, her face flushed, her hair in disarray under the ice-blue hat. 'I shouldn't have come–'

'No, *cariad*, you shouldn't have,' he says and fastens his arms around her, drawing her into the furnace where the blaze, surely, is hot enough to bend steel, to melt stone.

22

Mari: Sunday Night

In her dressing room at the Palladium, Mari sits in front of her mirror removing false glitter from her eyes. With wads of cotton wool dipped in cold cream she is wiping her face clean of makeup. As each wad becomes saturated with colours, emerald, silver, violet, tawny-beige, she tosses it on to the tabletop and picks another out of the jar beside her. So far she has used six without much result, for she's inept tonight, unable to make her usual swift, expert strokes. In fact, she's made a mess. Eye shadow streaks her cheekbones and lipstick smudges her chin, her face looking bruised, beaten-up, the way *their* faces must have looked, she can't stop herself from thinking, when he'd done his dirty work.

Nothing in the papers again this morning. She'd bought an early *Echo* in Paddington Station, opened it up right there, and scanned the front page. The headline told of victory not murder: 'English Team Routs Welsh Contenders in Final'. She had turned through all the other pages, even though she knew the sandwich boards around the newsstand would have roared out the news of another killing had one occurred.

Mari rubs a cotton wad over her green and purple cheek and the bruise turns into a livid scar that slashes down to her jawbone. She sighs and dips a new wad into the cold-cream jar.

Well . . . she hadn't been searching the paper only for murder at home. News of assassinations and executions across Europe she'd looked for too, catching her breath when she read, on a centre page, 'Anarchist Taken in Barcelona'. But it wasn't Antonio, another feller with an unsayable name, caught in the act, the police coming up right behind him and snatching the bomb before he could light the fuse and toss it into the crowd, nearly 1,000 people the paper said, watching a Corpus Christi procession (whatever that was). The captain of the police was praised for his courage and swift action. There was a photo of the Anarchist, but too dark to make out his face clearly. With his black hair and black eyes, he could have been Antonio using a false name, but then she had read that his age was 25 and that he had been born in VillaFranca, a town outside Barcelona, where his mother wept now and lit candles in the local church and told the reporter her son was a good, quiet boy led astray by violent times and wicked men.

'We have no work and no money here,' a neighbour said. 'Empty hands and empty pockets fill up with discontent,' he told the reporter, 'and that's what *Los Anarquistas* make their bombs out of. Print this in your paper so the world will take notice.'

Empty hands and empty pockets... With a vicious swipe, Mari eradicates the vile make-up scar, and one side of her face is cleansed at last. What about empty hearts and empty arms then? What did they lead to? Lighting candles and saying prayers if you're the mother of a Spanish Anarchist, crying in the dark and keeping your chin up in the daylight if you're Mari Prince, with no faith in the love of God and too much in the love of men.

Mari works on the other side of her face where rouge has mingled with glitter to create a shiny contusion, a bright fresh wound. Ever since she said goodbye to Percy at Paddington, she has felt a vast space, like a wide deep pit, in the place where her heart should beat. It's not like last time, when Antonio left and she was all too aware of her heart and its painful swelling.

Even when the swelling subsided, not fatal after all, the region around it remained tender, inflamed, raw, until she met Percy and he slapped his rough-and-ready poultice on it. Too much lust and too much admiration oozing like goose-grease, she should have seen that, should have known he offered a quack remedy not a real prescription. And yet, why hasn't her heart-sickness come back, now that Percy's salve has proved a fakery? Why this hollow where a poisonous wen should be growing?

Cleaning up her room that morning, she had found among the debris – wrappings from their pie-and-pastie supper, the empty wine bottle – two mementoes of Percy, a crumpled green rosette and his little battered book of poetry. She had made herself a cup of tea, sat down at the table, and flipped through the book to see if it would help her make anything of the enigma that was come-and-gone Percy. She had read:

> The lovely lady, Christabel,
> Whom her father loves so well,
> What makes her in the wood so late,
> A furlong from the castle gate?
> She had dreams all yesternight
> Of her own betrothed knight;
> And she in the midnight wood will pray
> For the weal of her lover that's far away.

The language is strange, almost foreign in the way words come in different places than where she expects them, but she understands the feelings, all right. Love is a 'midnight wood', that's sure, and the all-night-long dreams she knows about, too. But with that emptiness inside her, she had felt more impatient with the poem than moved by it.

She had lain down on the unmade bed and thought, unexpectedly, of them all — her father with his fiddle, Antonio with his knife, Percy with his suitcase, all pausing to greet her, to blow her a kiss, as they went on their way towards one of the many exits in her life.

'An entrance and an exit,' she had said, 'that's what I've been. And in the middle, I've been the stage, too, where they could play their part.' Without sentiment or self-pity, she had said this, as if only to hear herself say it; and without trying to make sense of it either — as if she were an actress reading a script, or herself reading the lyrics of a new songwriter whose work she would reject, telling Alf, 'It's not my style, sorry.'

Alf Ramsey crosses the stage, too, but stops in the middle, looking bemused, as if he didn't know that simple fact of life, that where there was a way in, there was also a way out.

Upwards of fourteen years she has known Alf, and for many of those years he has been begging for her company, promising to cherish and protect her if she'll favour him.

'Go on,' Doris has urged. 'He's all right, Alf. He won't let you down. It's not just a fling he's after.'

If she'd gone with Alf in the first place, when she was a green girl in London, he might have given her some happiness, spared her a lot of pain. She'd never have loved and lost Antonio, or Percy either, and she might not now be in this worst-of-all state, the bearer of a dead and useless heart. Yet, what a mystery, now that she's lost all feeling, she does, at last, consider Alf, telling herself, 'Tonight maybe I will.'

She had drifted off to sleep, she remembers, slept until early evening, waking with no dream memories, only a sense of rising up out of a darkness she did not want to leave, as out of the arms of a kind parent or lover, and forced herself to get up, light the lamp, get dressed, make a cup of tea.

Before leaving for the Palladium, she had stood by her bed in contemplation again. And she had thought, there's no such thing as a bank for good and bad deeds. No one sits up there with a ledger, keeping stock of our deposits and debts, making checks in credit and debit and loans columns. It don't work like that.

No, it's all chance and circumstance, and who you happen to bump into on the street. And so it doesn't matter what you do. Some will always pay more than they can afford, and treat others as well . . . and some will get away with murder.

Thinking thus, she had left her room and made her way, on foot and by tram, across London to the Palladium, as she has done countless times, six nights a week, for the last ten years. She could do the journey with her eyes closed now. Tonight, in a way, she did, looking into the window of the tram, into the window of Nan's Pantry as she passed, as if into mirrors that threw back her own empty-eyed reflection, London and its busy, variegated life invisible to her.

On stage, too, she had performed all the parts of her act (to a half-empty house, emptier than usual even for a Sunday) as if by rote, telling herself silently, 'Sing "Pretty Flowers" Do the scarf trick . . .' and the audience had clapped and cheered and failed to notice, apparently, that there was a zombie on the stage masquerading as The Infamous Princess Marie.

Mari's face is clean now, and pale as an unbaked pastry. Her brown eyes are lightless and heavy, like sedge on a winter's lake:

> O what can ail thee, knight-at-arms,
> Alone and palely loitering . . .

Those are lines she read in Percy's book and recalls now, looking at her mirrored face. Her hair is untidy, split ends and frizzles sticking out like bits of twigs from a bird's nest.

'I'm a sight,' she says, pulling out the pins. 'A fright, a nightmare, something escaped from the cells at Holloway. I should get my hair cut, give it a new go before it dies on me.'

Well, if she's going to say yes to Alf tonight, she'll first have to give him a halfway decent reason to ask the question. She opens a flowered cardboard box and fluffs the powder puff it contains over her face, creating a smooth, matt surface for the artificial light and colour she will apply from other boxes and jars, a purchased glow and zest that Alf won't be able to tell from the real thing . . . she trusts.

As she spreads pale green shadow, a more muted shade than her stage colours, over her eyelids, lines from another poem come into her head:

> She only said, 'My life is dreary,
> He cometh not,' she said.
> She said, 'I am aweary, aweary,
> I would that I were dead.'

But who would be coming for her now? It doesn't make sense that this line should rise up from the others, like an airy phantom, and repeat itself.

> 'He cometh not,' she said.

As she is stroking rose-pink rouge over her cheeks, Doris appears in the doorway. 'Rotten house tonight,' she says.

'Not much of a turn-out,' Mari agrees. 'But we never do draw our best crowd on Sunday.'

Doris comes in. She sits in the basket chair beside Mari's dressing table, places her silver-topped cane between her thighs, tips the chair back and swings her black-slippered feet up on to the edge of the table. 'I tell you what,' she says. 'Just between you and me and this table, I think music hall is going down the drain.'

Mari takes up her tortoiseshell brush and begins to work on her tangled hair. 'You been talking to Alf?'

'I don't have to. I got eyes and ears. The cinema's the thing of the future, Mari. Besides, there's a war coming. Even if the

Bioscope don't take all our customers, the Kaiser will. What'll you do if the Palladium shuts down?'

Mari's brush has caught in a clump of knotty curls. She uses both hands to separate the bristles from her hair. 'I haven't given it much thought,' she says. 'Should I get my hair cut, Doris?'

'Never! How could you do that, love? Your hair is what makes your act, ain't it? I mean, 'course you got heaps of talent and all, but . . . I can't see it, a lady magician with cropped hair–'

'I'd wear a wig till it grew again.'

'You'd never get a wig as good as your real hair. It's your crowning glory, Mari. It's the heart of your mystery, see, what the men love about you. With that hair – here, go easy with the brush, love – you're an angel and a witch both. Men like that, a mixing up of two opposite things.' She runs a hand up her thigh, stroking her black diamond-patterned tights. 'It's why they like to watch *me*. 'Cause they can't make out if I'm one sex or the other.' Doris sniggers. 'Queer bastards, men. They're never happy with women unless they're confused. Confusion's what excites them.'

Well, Doris is right about herself, her own mystery, at any rate. Mari looks at the long shapely legs in black fishnet, the knob of the cane sticking up between the lean thighs, the boyish hips and waist, and then the cleavage, the white throat and platinum hair.

'You'll land in trouble if you're not careful, Dor,' she can't help saying.

Doris widens her mouth into a real smile and tosses her head, brazenly, as she does on stage. 'With who? I know how to manage men, which is more than you do, love. When have you seen me heartbroken over a feller, Mari? Not bloody likely! I don't care about men enough to get in that state.'

Mari turns away and begins to wind up her hair. 'Heartbreak's not what I meant.' She slips in a hairpin.

'I won't fall into any other sort of trouble either,' Doris says. 'Don't you lose sleep over that. Why, I'm even safe from the Gardener. He likes his women to look like women, don't he? No confusion in that feller!'

Mari waits for the shivering, heart-sliding panic to possess her . . . but nothing happens. Her hands, picking up hairpins, remain steady, her body unflinching, as unfeeling as if she were assembled from mortar and brick. Only a line of poetry drifts through her head, as clear as if it were printed on the mirror in front of her:

> 'He cometh not,' she said.

Doris swings her legs off Mari's table and leans towards her, her hands on the knob of her cane. 'I'll tell you what I'm planning. You'll be the first to know. I'm giving up music hall and getting married.'

Mari drops her hands from her hair and stares at Doris. 'Are you having me on?'

'Honest truth.'

'Who to?'

'Feller I told you about . . . the one I've been knocking about with since January. He's smitten with me proper. Asked me half a dozen times already, and last time the question made sense, so I said, "Don't mind if I do."'

'Do you love him?'

Doris looks at Mari from under lowered eyelids, a sly, foxy look, as if there's a joke and Mari's not getting it. 'Times are changing,' she says. 'We got to move with the times. You ought to be thinking of settling down yourself. He's got a friend wants to meet you—'

Mari shakes her head. 'I couldn't do it, Doris.'

Doris shrugs. 'What about that feller you went with last night then?'

'Just a flash in the pan. He went back to Wales this morning.'

'Not coming up to see you sometime? Gone for good?'

'For better or worse,' Mari says, but she doesn't feel like telling Doris the whole story. She knows what her friend would say.

Doris says it anyway: 'See, Mari, I told you so. And you thought he was in the palm of your hand. You said that, didn't you?' She sighs. 'You're the one needs to watch out, love. With everything else you got plenty of, you got no common sense.' Rising, she rests her hand briefly on Mari's shoulder before striding, on her strong suggestive legs, to the door. 'Ta-ta, then. You'll come to my wedding, won't you?'

'I hope you'll be very happy,' Mari says to her friend's reflection in the mirror.

Doris grins, gives her a thumbs-up sign, and vanishes.

Mari, her hair pinned and almost tidy, puts on her skirt and blouse, buttons her jacket and leaves the dressing room.

'Different house from last night, Miss Prince,' Rudolph greets her, pushing his bucket out of her way with his foot. 'Floor's wet. Mind you don't slip. Left your bottles with Mr Ramsey as usual. Got you a half of Black and Tan, too – my treat.'

He ducks his face out of view, presenting her with his shiny bald crown instead. 'It's to congratulate you for last night's feat. I never did see the like of it, all my days in music hall.'

Mari feels a slight stirring of her comatose heart. Here's her most loyal admirer, bowing before her as he is wont, and he's brought her a present, too, not in the hopes of getting one back, but simply because he's a good man.

Looking at the top of his head, another good man comes to mind, also bald – Ernie Frith the publican, saying to her, 'There's a home for you here, Mari.' Fifteen years ago that was. Fancy! He could be dead now for all she knows. Or perhaps he has married, a nice widow, young enough to give him children. Yes, she'd rather think that . . . that he'd had a second chance. Like her mother. Whom she can never bring herself to visit in Yarmouth, but who writes from time to time to say they're all well. Her sisters are happily married. Except Lily, Mari's favourite, whose cough wasn't cured by the sea air after all and who never reached an age to be wed. Mari sighs. Funny how she's haunted by ghosts since Percy left; old ghosts not recent ones – Ernie, her mother, her sisters, saying 'There's a home for you, Mari . . .' and her father, best-loved, saying 'What'll you do, darling, after I'm gone?' Antonio seemed to rob her of her future when he left; Percy has stolen her present, as well.

Mari pulls herself out of this, puts her hand on Rudolph's shoulder, her lips, briefly, on his forehead. 'It's yours,' she says. 'That part of my act is dedicated to you, and I'll say so on stage, too–' She steps back and lifts her right hand with a flourish. 'Ladies and gentlemen, I will now perform the death-defying Rudolph's Rise. How does that sound, eh?'

The janitor tilts his head back between his shoulders; it's a long way for him to look up into Mari's face. 'I'd be honoured,' he says.

'And when I'm too old for the stage, I'll start a school for apprentice-magicians–' as she speaks, it strikes her that she *could* do this '–and I'll tell my star pupils, the ones who put their heart and brain and arse into learning the trade, "You've earned the right to my best trick," and I'll teach 'em Rudolph's Rise. And so your name will live forever, you see, passed on from one generation to the next, like a family treasure. There now, what do you say about that?'

'Grand. I say that's grand.' In their deep pouches, his blue eyes are blurred, and his voice cracks with unsteady pleasure, as if she's taken his name not just for her act but for always. 'Your heart's in the right place, Miss Prince. Top notch, it is.'

'Ah,' Mari says on a sigh, 'well, it's slipped a bit lately – but I thank you anyway.' She smiles for him. 'Toodle-oo, then. Better be on my way. I'll look forward to a glass of Black and Tan at the other end. I'll toast you, Rudolph.'

'Watch how you go outside,' he calls after her. 'It was getting a bit foggy when I came in.'

At the end of the corridor, Alf's door is open. Mari steps into the opening and says, 'Just stopping by for my bottles.' Her voice is abrupt, and she knows it, bites her tongue, as if to punish it for misbehaviour, for this is not how she meant to greet him. But shyness, a feeling she's never had with him before, makes her maladroit, and she can't say anything to undo the harsh-sounding words.

Her body, too, feels shy, awkward, her face stiff as a plaster cast, so she can't let him know by a smile or a gesture either that tonight, if he repeated – for, it must be, the three-thousandth time – his offer, he'd get a different answer, hear a word that dissented from the army of three thousand nays that have marched out of her lips.

Alf lays down his pen, takes up his cigar, sits back in his chair and looks up at her. 'What's wrong?' he says.

She manages a shrug: nothing, what do you mean?

'You look worked up about something,' he says. 'Anyone spoken out of turn?'

Only me, Mari thinks, and shakes her head.

Why is it so hard, when it's always been simple before, a thing she's never given thought to, to lean in the doorway, one hand on her hip, and exchange a bit of pleasant banter with this man she's known for years?

'You're looking very glamorous, love. Got a new beau, have you?' His smile is a sad, weary one.

'She only said, "My life is dreary,"' . . . and his must be, why has it never struck her before? Bills to settle, employees to mollify, patrons to court, competitors to fight . . . and no loving arms to welcome him home at the other end of a long night. ('Mary doesn't care.') She hardly ever thinks of Mary Ramsey; two years since she's seen her, after all. A sweet-faced, girlish, shrinking creature, Mari recalls, with night eyes and a rapturous manner, entranced by the music hall and by Mari afterwards. She remembers draping her magician's cloak over Mary's shoulders. Yes, she had taken to her, but still . . . Alf's a decent sort, as Doris says, so whatever's wrong in his marriage must be half his wife's fault.

Alf sits there, smiling at her, his strong teeth showing through grey bristles, a wolf's teeth she has been wont to think, but tonight he looks more like a pantomime bear, big and strong, capable of great comforting hugs. Why should Mari be frightened?

Well, it's not from fear of him that she's as rigid as the props that crowd his office. Of what then? . . . '"He cometh not," she says.'

'Not telling, eh?' Alf says. 'You're a close one, Mari.'

At last, she says, 'It's not what you think.'

'How do you know what I'm thinking?' Then he takes a hard, sucking drag on his cigar and says, ''Course you know. I've been telling you for years. I wish *I* was your new beau, that's the long and the short of it.'

Luck favours her. Gives her another chance. All she has to do is open her mouth and say, 'Yes.' A nod, even, will do. Her tongue, her head, refuse to stir.

'It's foggy out tonight, Mari. Hard to see your way. A lot of rapscallions about, too, using the fog as a cover for dirty deeds. I hope you have a reliable escort. If not . . . allow me?'

She *must* speak now. He's looking at her, his eyebrows tilted hopefully, his grey eyes fixing her with the longing he never tries to hide. He's always managed to stir her, tempt her with that look. Tonight, it's a cold, contriving response that touches her brain only: let him take care of you. He will, for the rest of your life. You can see in his eyes he's not a fickle feller. Go on, say the word. Quick!

Alf puffs again on his cigar. Seems like he's willing to wait all night for his answer. She knows why, too, can tell by his face he expects, at last, to hear what he wants to.

Smoke rises between them from his Havana, curling up wraithily, slender and graceful, like a certain type of woman . . . a dead woman, shriven of all flesh and substance, pure spirit. More smoke, more cloud-and-air creatures, flimsy, flighty things . . . like her wishes at this moment. For how can she go through with this intention, change in a moment the habit of a lifetime?

'Cat's got your tongue tonight.' His voice is low, teasing. He believes he has her, sure. He puffs, exhales, and now the semi-circles of smoke are the spirits of *his* dead, the Gardener of London, rising, free from pain and shame – but dead, nevertheless.

To go with Alf, she, too, would have to murder a woman.

Mari's tongue loosens. Her mouth is dry, thick with fuzz, as if after a long sleep, but she can croak out the words. 'You're married, Alf. Would you pass me my bottles, please?'

His face alters, his grey eyes narrowing, darkening, like the horizon at Brighton that day she walked on the prom – only yesterday! It seems like years. He's holding in his eyes the storm she's brewed, shilly-shallying, giving him hope then dashing it . . . but on a firm rock not on shifting sand. He can bear anger and pain. He gets up, lifts her paper bag from the shelf, holds it out to her.

'Tonight, I thought for once you'd –'

She shakes her head. 'Never.'

The bag of bottles in the crook of her left arm, her right hand pressed firmly on the clasp of her shoulder bag, she leaves his office and strides the few steps to the stage door.

'Mari!' he calls.

She turns back. It's all right to linger now. Her hold on herself is as staunch as the grip she has on her possessions, her holdall, and her bottles of whisky and stout.

He comes down the corridor. 'Mary . . . my wife.' For a moment she thinks he's going to press his suit even now, but, 'She's not well. Hasn't been for a long time, but she's getting worse, I believe. It's . . . a mental condition.'

'You should take her to a doctor.'

He flicks his left hand, his cigar dropping its ashy tip. 'She's too much on her own, that's the whole thing, no friends, no children to occupy her. I'm wondering . . . she liked you. That night in your dressing room, you put life into her—'

'That was years ago, Alf.'

'I'm wondering . . . would you pay her a visit, Mari?'

He's given up on her then, finally. Whatever woman he woos in the future, it won't be her again.

'I'll be glad to,' she says.

'Thank you.' He presses her arm, drops his hand swiftly. 'I'll tell Mary. She'll be pleased. Maybe she can come to the show, too, once in a while. When she's up to it.'

'Good-night, Alf.'

Mari opens the door and steps into a fog as thick and grimy as an old workhouse blanket. The gas lamps in the lane are pale circles, holes in the blanket, and when she reaches Leicester Square, though there are more lights, visibility is not improved.

People on the pavement fumble their way along, their hands pressed to the wall or stretched out in front of them, as if this were the Kingdom of the Blind. Six young men pass her, hands on each other's shoulders, in single file behind a leader who gropes the murky blanket. The silence is profound, as if the fog has clogged the mouths of the passers-by.

As Mari hesitates, trying to get her bearings, a child of seven or eight appears in front of her. She has red-brown hair, frizzy like Mari's own, and sad brown eyes in a pale face . . . ashen, really, like . . . like Lily's after a coughing bout! In her right hand she holds a long-stemmed flower, the petals no whiter than her face, the stalk hardly more slender, it seems to Mari, than her body of skin and bones. It can't be . . . but it is!

'Lily!' Mari breathes.

The child holds out the flower and says, 'There's a home for you, Mari.'

No, that's not what she said! Mari, seeing the wicker basket on the child's arm, other flowers drooping over its edge, gets a grip on herself. In her pocket she finds a couple of pennies and pushes them into the child's left hand, already open. 'Here,' she says, 'you shouldn't be out on a night like this. Get on home! Where do you live then?' As she says this, she reaches out to grasp the child, but the little girl evades her and slips away, wordless, into the furry night.

Mari, trembling, stares into the fog. Is it an omen, the child appearing like that, the spitting image of her dead sister when she last saw her? Ah, it's a night for dead things to walk if ever there was one, a night like the one on which Antonio vanished, slipping through her fingers just like that child, only a ship's hooter to mark his departure, everything else holding its silence, even her breaking heart.

Bloody hell! Don't stand about reminiscing, you ninny! It's not a night to loiter!

She peers into the road. It's as dark and empty as a drained pond, no traffic risking travel tonight. Her tram won't be coming then. The tubes will be running though. She sighs. It's a longer journey, with a change of trains. But she has no choice, so she starts out, moving close to the wall, close enough to feel the stone against her shoulder, and thrusts her right arm out in front, opening her palm.

It's not far to the tube, just the other end of the Square. Mari inches along the wall, jolting a bit when stone gives way suddenly to air. Only a shop entrance. Here's the window, the shutters down. She can't remember which of several shops this is. The newsagent's, the tobacconist's, the fancy jeweller's? Funny, she can rattle off the names of all the establishments in order when she conjures up a picture of Leicester Square in her mind. Walking through the fog, she hasn't a clue what she's passing. She might as well be in Rome or Paris.

She'll have to watch out she doesn't miss the entrance to the tube, for she has no idea either of how little or how far she's come. Distance and time are eaten up by the fog, too, just like the buildings. Her shoulder signals another opening in the wall. Mari pauses and peers in. It's not the tube station, just a doorway.

Out of the grey cavern a darker shape emerges. A man in an overcoat, muffler, and homburg blocks Mari's path. He's about her height, well-built, and a gentleman, velvet lapels on his coat, the muffler white silk, neatly trimmed whiskers, a gentrified voice when he speaks: 'Forgive me if I startled you.' He raises his hat. 'I was waiting for the fog to lift—'

A white silk muffler!

'Excuse me,' Mari interrupts him, and tries to dodge past.

He side-steps too, as if they are dancing partners, and her way is still barred. 'Have you far to go? Are you lost?' His voice is kindly . . . oh, but that's part of the hoax, the bait. His eyes and lips are narrow and sharp as razor blades. Or is she imagining this? Does *he* engage his victims in chit-chat first? Unlikely. This is just a feller trying to get off with her. No, it's not! His eyes cut, slicing through flesh and bone – she feels it – to her insides, to her panic and revulsion. And cut past her, yes, as if he were the one wanting to get by and she the obstruction. He looks into her and through her at the same time, and his forehead creases, as if he's considering how to remove her.

'Let me pass!' Mari cries.

'I'm afraid I can't do that,' he says. 'You got in my way, you see. So you owe me an apology . . .'

His voice is so reasonable, that's what shocks her more than his cut-throat, darting eyes and the teeth that seem sharpened on a whetstone. His eyes, as if by accident, fix on her again. 'You see how it is, don't you? You understand why I can't simply allow you to pass on?'

Mari musters her strength, makes a dive to get round him, but again he's too quick for her. His left arm whips out, she stumbles against it, and reels back, the breath knocked out of her, for he has thumped her in the ribs.

'Now that won't do,' he says, breathing a bit harder himself, but keeping his voice low. 'If you forget your manners, I'll have to forsake mine, won't I?'

'I know who you are,' Mari says, her voice coming in gasps, 'and you're not going to do me in like you did those others –'

'*Pardon?*' He lifts his chin, as if she's insulted him.

'I'll do worse than Rose Doyle if you try –' But she can't finish. The look on his face wipes out the little bit of defiance she's conjured.

His lips curve away from his teeth and, for the first time in her life, Mari hears a human being snarl. The sound amazes her, it's so horrid, so blood-curdling, a werewolf or a vampire might make such a noise, a rabid dog or a wild boar . . .

Her heart responds with a shriek. A sleeper waking from a

nightmare to discover the menace is real, her heart leaps up and cries, 'Oh, beware! Oh, defend yourself! Words are no use! To arms, Mari!'

Mari slides her paper bag out of the crook of her arm and down along her body to where her hand can grasp it. As he reaches for her with one hand, dipping the other into his coat, she has closed her fingers on the neck of a bottle. Before he can draw his hand out again, she swings. Inside the bag, the bottle she grips cracks across his face, the other bottles breaking the paper and smashing to the pavement.

He staggers, his arm raised to shield his face. But he does not drop. He stumbles to the wall and leans his back against it, groaning, cursing. She waits for him to go down, waits to see blood spurt from his head. Surely she's given him a death blow. Concussion at least?

He lowers his arm. She sees blood trickling from his nose, a rapidly swelling right eye, but – but he's not incapacitated. Enraged, wounded, shocked, but – she can't get over it – nothing worse.

Suddenly he bellows like a bull and lunges for her.

Mari runs. She can't see where she's going, can't see what's in front of her, but these things are of little matter now. What she feared before, tripping over a paving-stone, banging into a lamppost, are as nothing compared to what threatens behind her, the lumbering, roaring shape that pursues her. A wild and maddened brute, disguised in human skin and a gentleman's overcoat, if he catches her he will rip her limb from limb, as he has others before.

She must not trip, she must not falter, she must not run too far. A single mistake, her heart warns her, and she'll never have the chance to make another.

Capisco! So where the bloody hell is the tube station?

She's passed it, she must have; racing headlong, she must have dashed right by it, for it couldn't be this far from the Palladium. In fact, is she still in Leicester Square, or has she strayed into another street? And if so, which one, and what to do?

Not slow down, not turn around. Those options are out. She can't hear him any more, but she knows he's coming after her, quiet as a hunter now, to throw her off his scent.

Sod the fog! She thought she knew this part of London blindfolded, but it isn't so. She doesn't even know if she's still on the pavement or in the road. Where's the wall? Where's the kerb? And where, sweet Jesus, are the people? Is it so late, everyone's gone home, the tube shut down for the night?

A sob rises in Mari's throat. Her feet hurt, her chest hurts, her head throbs – but her heart in its panic flings her on.

All at once, behind her, out of the dense fog, comes a sound so unexpected, she almost collapses, her legs almost giving up.

His voice, again, not more than a few yards off, singing, for God's sake, a music-hall song:

> I'm Henery the Eighth, I am,
> Henery the Eighth, I am!
> I'm a bit of a nob, you see,
> Belonging to royalty!

He's got the words all wrong, Mari's brain, quite calm, informs her.

Out of the fog, a laugh to chill the marrow, and then:

> The Undertaker called to say,
> Got any orders, sir?
> We're rather slack today!

Why fancy, her brain remarks, he's not even out of puff. He's enjoying himself. A bit of malarky, it is, before the snatch. And then her brain conks out and gibbers like a lunatic. Over its senseless prattle, the voice of another lunatic rises:

'I've got you, my beauty. You may as well give up.'

And now Mari finds obstructions all about her in the fog. Out of its whirls and clouds, the murdered women rise, all his victims, closing in on her, their faces and hair bleached of colour, their eyes turned up to show the whites, their hands opening their clothes to display their wounds, their insignia, sisters of the rose.

Like children playing ring-a-ring-a-roses they circle her, these poor ghastly shades, and hem her in. Mari knows her will is flagging, her feet failing – how far and for how long can she run like this? And now she must fight the murdered women, too, who show her their torn flesh, as if to welcome her into their secret circle, the circle of those who have known the Gardener and his deadly embrace.

'Even I couldn't get away, Mari . . .' Rose Doyle wafts before her, her modish hat askew '. . . even I. Women can't escape.'

Ah, but here's her heart leaping up again. Ever rash, unstoppable, when risk rears up, it pumps blood bravely, snaps orders to the rest of her, musters her weary limbs, pushes her on through the ghostly fray, and –

At last, shouts a loud hurrah! For there, to her left, a bright light at the bottom of the grey pit, and when she staggers towards it, steps for her to hurtle down, and here she is in the Charing Cross Underground with other human beings.

Ah, her heart loves them! She wants to embrace them all, make them a speech like Lloyd George, sing them a song, give them free tickets to the Palladium. But if she did, someone would call the law and she'd be bundled off to the lock-up.

Instead, she buys her own ticket and goes through the barrier.

Sitting on the train, safe, rescued, homeward bound, Mari wonders what action she should take. Should she, first thing tomorrow, get herself down to the local police station to give an account of the attack, a description of her attacker? Surely, it's her duty as a citizen, as a woman, as the only victim who has escaped the Gardener and can identify him? She owes it, doesn't she, to her fellow-citizens, to the murdered women, and to all the other women in London who, like herself, walk in fear of murder?

All well and good, but her spirit balks at such a venture. To thrust herself forward in this way, into the public eye – her picture in the papers, perhaps, and her name. Just thinking of it, she's frightened all over again. It's tempting fate, to draw attention to herself, to let him know who she is and that she knows him . . .

And doubt creeps in, too. Could she describe him? That's to say, describe him so accurately that the law could pick him out from the thousands of men on the streets of London?

He was about my height, Officer. In heels, that is. And well built. Not fat. He had whiskers . . .

'Like most men, Miss Prince. Like myself. Hair colour? Eyes? Distinguishing marks? Age?'

'It's hard to remember. It was dark, you see, and foggy – and quick. One thing I do recall. He had such sharp eyes and teeth, they cut right into me—'

'Colour?'

'Beg your pardon?'

'What colour were his sharp eyes?'

'Like I said, I'm not sure. Black? Grey?'

Ah, it's hopeless! The only description she can offer would fit tons of men, including her imaginary officer, who now tosses his pen down, clears his throat, stands up, holds out his hand, says, 'Thank you, Miss Prince,' but in a tone that tells her she's wasted his time. Worse . . . he doesn't believe she had a brush with the murderer. To his way of thinking, she was accosted by a feller with nothing more on his mind than getting off with her. And why shouldn't he have hoped for that, a woman on her own, so late at night? Yes, he'd ask her that, too, the policeman, why she was abroad in such times, in such weather, without an escort, and when she told him her profession . . .

Mari's train arrives at Tottenham Court Road where she must change lines. She gets off, crosses the station, gets on the next train, arrives at her destination, her mind made up. She'll do nothing. There's nothing to be done. She's not a useful witness.

When she comes up out of the tube station, the fog has lifted a bit, enough so she doesn't have to feel her way down Holland Park Avenue, enough to give her fair warning of anything, or anyone, a dozen feet in front of her. She's tired, her calves and ankles aching from running in high heels, but she forces herself to walk briskly, for now that she's away from well-lit places and people, fear rises in her again.

What if he has followed her all the way from Charing Cross to make a second try? No, she'd have seen him. Or would she? Plenty of men who look like him, she's just decided that, plenty of camouflage available. She looks over her shoulder. Only gloom and silence behind her, more of the same in front. Of course he hasn't followed her. He wouldn't take that risk, come out of the night into a public place, into the tube station, where she could scream for help and point her finger at him. Still, she breaks into a trot despite her complaining feet. When she arrives, out of breath, at the turning into her own street, her right foot stumbles on a crack in the pavement and the heel of her shoe snaps off. She lands on her behind on the damp flagstones.

'Damn it all!' she says, and gropes for the missing heel. At least she landed on a well-cushioned part of her body and hasn't hurt herself much. 'I'm used to it now,' she mutters, 'Always landing on my arse, one way or another.' She finds the two-inch wooden block and slips it into her bag, takes off her shoes and puts them in the bag, too, and proceeds along her route, the pavement so cold, so clammy, under her stockinged feet.

She hopes she won't meet Constable Dawes tonight, for what a freak she must look, all in disarray, shoeless, her hair like a briar patch, the way it always gets in fog or rain.

Her hair!

A new thought occurs, and it hits her with the force of a fist. As if she had truly been bashed on the chin, she reels toward the low wall that fronts the gardens and sits on it, robbed of her ability to stand upright again, though this time it's not a broken heel but the snapping of nerve that clobbers her.

From now on, he'll be looking for her. Not knowing that she can't distinguish him from John Doe or Mr Smith, he'll have to fear her, a woman who could put handcuffs on him, send him to the gallows. He'll have to find her, put a stop to her, before she stops him. And he'll know her by her flaming torch, her flaring beacon, her brightly burning bush, her hair, the like of which, she has prided herself, is possessed by no other woman in London.

God help me. What am I to do?

Well, get up for one thing, and get out of the street, you fool. She rises, totters to her gate. Should she leave London? Should she quit the Palladium and get herself a day job, one where she'll come home at a decent hour? Take up with a man, a fair-and-square, unmarried man, a grocer, a baker, a candlestick maker?

As she opens the gate and enters the garden, something moves in the shadows at the corner of the house where a gully leads around to the back . . . some*one* it looked like, jumping for cover. Mari stares hard into the space between the house and the fence that separates it from its neighbour. Only remnants of fog drift there, yet she'd swear on the Bible . . . and now it seems as if the garden is crowded with invisible presences, lurking behind walls, crouching in the shrubbery . . .

'All my ghosts!' she mutters. '*They've* followed me home, nothing worse.'

Up the path she goes, fits her key in the lock, enters the house. Light under Mrs Perkins's door. Ah, she'd like a cup of tea and a bit of company tonight . . . especially as she won't have the company she expected, her bottles of stout and Black and Tan. Mrs Perkins doesn't come out though. Mari taps on her landlady's door.

'Who is it?' Mrs Perkins calls from within, her voice strangely high, as if she's speaking through her nose, trying to put on a posh accent. Why does she do that? She knows it's Mari outside, not the bloody King.

'It's me,' Mari says. 'Can I come in?'

'Not tonight, dearie, I'm ever so sorry,' Mrs Perkins says in the same hoity-toity voice. 'It's not convenient.'

Mari stares at the door, amazed. Hurt, too. She's about to say something sharp when, suddenly, inside the room a man coughs – and she understands all. Mrs Perkins has found herself a companion. Wonders will never cease! Is this the latest fashion, the latest miracle, or what – first Doris, now her landlady?

'Sorry to bother you,' Mari says. ''Night.'

'Goodnight, dear. Be careful, mind.'

Be careful? What's she talking about? Mari's only going up to her room, not out on the town. Has love knocked Mrs Perkins's brain askew? Probably. That's what love does. Mari's glad if some worthy widower or single gent has made her landlady as dizzy as a girl . . . but why tonight, when she needs company herself?

On the landing, Mari notices the bathroom door ajar. Well, nothing strange about that. In fact, Mrs Perkins often leaves it half open, 'so air can circulate'. Tonight, though, it seems sinister, that slice of deeper black, as if . . . Did she hear a breath? Was it her own, catching in her throat? Get on, do! You're timid as a sparrow tonight, jump at your own shadow, wouldn't you? Move now, a cup of tea will put you right.

She reaches her own door and unlocks it. Pauses on the threshold . . . for something's not right within. How she knows this is a mystery to her, for with no moon at the window and no light on the landing, the room's as black as a cave. Yet, it overwhelms her, the sense that someone is in there, waiting. Percy? Antonio? Or is it . . . Steady now. No one's here. Who could come through two locked doors, or a window thirty feet up? Besides, didn't she lock the window?

Nothing's stirring inside, no breathing, no movement. What it is, she feels Percy's recent brief occupation of the room . . . or is it Antonio's presence? Some ghost, anyway, of a lost love. Only natural, when she's so worked up, so in need of comfort . . .

Go on, go in and light the lamp.

Don't! her heart cries.

Mari ignores her heart, enters, clicks the lock behind her, fishes out her matches, reaches up and lights the Japanese lantern.

The first thing she sees is the thing she tells herself is merely a spectre, merely a whiff of memory. And, indeed, the brief glimpse she has of it confirms that it can't be human – a tall, slender figure, its face framed by a woman's long black hair, its body clothed in a man's black evening suit, stands in front of the window, one of Mari's silver candlesticks in its raised right hand, another silver object, sharp and pointed, in its left fist.

Mari opens her mouth. No sound comes forth. Swift as a knife thrust, the creature leaps. Mari feels the searing pain of the candlestick cracking across her temple, sees mad, black eyes staring into her own . . . and passes out.

23

Mary: Sunday Night

The fog has lifted and the moon's full face shines out of a sky like grey satin. The moon is our mother, the mother of women. I have read that in one of my father's books, some old treatise penned by a patriarch of the church, doubtless. Like the moon, women wax and wane, the author declared, the workings of their bodies and their emotions (he did not mention our minds) governed not by the laws of science and reason as men's are (he was a doctor of medicine, perchance), but by nature. Unlike men, women were therefore inconstant, he averred, unsteady, and as proof, he listed the ailments we are subject to: the floating womb, hysteria, fainting-sickness, the menstrual cycle which, he explained, occurred in part to rid us of our bad blood, blood infected by emotional excesses, poisonous effluvium that, were it not drained regularly, would cause an early demise. I believed this when I was seventeen, and since my own cycle was irregular then, I feared imminent and agonizing death. A winter chill or a spring fever alarmed me, for I thought it was the poison killing me off.

The learned doctor warned his readers of the dangers of lying with a menstruating woman. Fever, impotence, incurable genital disease, blindness, could result. Self-control, abstinence, were recommended at these times. But, a wise and tolerant practitioner, he conceded that not all men possess control in the same degree. For the over-lusty, or the weak, he had this advice: it would not be wrong for a husband to request his wife, during her contagion, to pleasure him by other means, by hand or by mouth. The doctor provided instructions for how this pleasure might be most fully, and most hygienically, obtained. He cautioned, however, that if his instructions were faithfully followed, such ecstasy would occur that a man might come to prefer these means of gratification. That would be wrong and perverse, for the foremost Christian purpose of the marriage bed was to produce offspring, and the Bible warns that a man should not 'spill his seed upon the ground'.

Foul book! Reading, I thought of my father savouring its lasciviousness disguised as learning, approving its vainglorious and crushing masculinity. I saw him forcing my mother to the acts described therein, and I tore the pages out and ripped them to shreds before replacing the volume on a high dark shelf.

But now I remember something else . . .

This room where I lie has a long narrow window, domed at the top, like a window in a church. I can see the moon, like a painted icon, and the drifting clouds. Tonight the moon looks old, fatigued, sucked dry, her face cracked and jaundiced, a grey-haired whore, one eyelid closed in a lecherous wink.

She is no mother of mine!

This is what I remember. Once, after she had served him on her knees, he pulled her up into his wild, bestial embrace. I, peeping at the window, saw her face over his shoulder. She was smiling, a smile like a drunk's, like the grins on the faces of the opium-eaters and gin-swillers I have seen in London's gutters. I wiped her face from my memory so that I would not have to know what here I confess: She, too, took pleasure in that act. Hers was the smirk of satiety.

They have brought me into a small bare room and put me in a narrow bed beneath this tall window. Whatever place this is, I am very high up, for I see nothing but sky . . . and the moon, winking at me.

On the other side a woman sits knitting in a basket chair by the light of an oil lamp placed on a rough, wooden night-stand. She is middle-aged, robust, and wears a nurse's starched uniform. But I am not ill. Why am I confined to bed, with an attendant, in a room that smells of antiseptic, behind a barred window?

'Where am I?' I say to the nurse.

'Awake are you, dear?' She does not look up from her work.

'Where is this place and how did I get here?'

'Hush,' she says, not unkindly, 'I'm not supposed to speak to you. The doctor'll be up shortly.'

'Am I ill?'

'Yes, very. Hush now.'

'No I am not ill!' I cry, and I sit bolt upright, pushing the covers off, thrusting out my arms. 'Look, I am strong and healthy!'

I startle her. She drops her knitting into her lap and a look of fright comes to her face, a broad face like the moon's but ruddy. 'Don't turn violent now,' she says. 'It won't go well with you if I have to call for help. They'll put you in a straitjacket, most likely.'

I am frightened, too, and to show her I mean no harm, intended no mischief, I sink back on the pillows and fold my arms across my chest.

'That's better.' She picks up her knitting again. 'No point getting craxy, is there?'

I know what sort of place this is, and why I am here. I have lost neither my memory nor my mind . . .

They put handcuffs on me, the policemen, and held me, two of them, their grip as tight and chafing as the manacles, and carted me down the stairs and into the Black Maria as if I were baggage, or violent – but I was not resisting them. I *wanted* them to take me away from that room, away from the sight of her . . . what I had done to her.

There was a detective, too. He sat with me in the black van and asked my name.

I said, 'My name is Mary.'

'I am Inspector Vulcan,' he said. 'What is your last name? Where do you live?'

But I would not answer. I was thinking of Alf, the shame to him.

'Don't be afraid,' he said. 'No one means to hurt you.'

'They have hurt me.' I held out my wrists. 'These hurt me.'

And he ordered a policeman to remove the handcuffs. 'Will you tell me who you are?'

'My name is Mary. Are you going to lock me up in a cell?'

'No, I have told them to take you where you can rest,' he said. 'Tomorrow I'll come to see you.' And then he bid me good-night most civilly, as if I were not a murderess but simply a woman sorely afflicted.

Here, they took off my man's suit and put me in a shift. A doctor came with his little black bag and I submitted, docile, to his stethoscope and spatula. I did not ask what the state of my tongue and my chest had to do with the crime I had committed. To his questions, I only said, 'My name is Mary.'

'Drink this then, Mary,' he said. 'It will refresh you,' and I did, and knew no more until I awoke in this bed, with a nurse beside me.

I stare out of the window at the moon and think, revenge is like this: it is the most voracious of demons, ever craving food, sustenance, so that it can grow to monstrous size. It consumes its progenitor, and its siblings – nostalgia, desire, despair; it eats up kindness, reason, and mercy, and stalks abroad in human guise in search of more victuals, its bread, flesh, its wine, blood. I, who birthed it, then nursed it, spawned a dreadful progeny who devoured its mother and set forth in her skin, just as I put on my husband's suit and thought it was I who had accomplished the *coup d'état*. But my malformed child, my freak, my monstrosity, expired, choked on its own greed. Or rather, I killed it, vomited it forth, when I saw what it had done to Mari Prince.

'I have aborted my only child,' I say, 'and I am glad of it.'

The nurse gasps. Then she says, softly, 'Nonsense! Try to sleep again. It's the best thing for you.'

My father had other books in his study besides those dry tomes he compelled me to read and those heinous, misogynistic works he himself perused. Novels, he possessed – which were forbidden to me. Nevertheless, he was not always at home, and from what activity had *his* injunctions ever deterred me? In all things, I did as I wished, and many wet or wintry afternoons when he was abroad in his parish, to chasten the backslider, to chide the sick or the impoverished, to put the fear of Hell into the dying, I, a silent, scavenging mouse, mounted his step-ladder and lifted down a real book, *Jane Eyre*, *Wuthering Heights*, *Tess of the d'Urbervilles* (what characters within to stir me, seeing as I did my own unhappy lot in theirs!). One day I took down Mary Shelley's *Frankenstein* and read of the lonely, loveless monster and the destruction it wreaked. I wept for the creature, I recall, understanding well its rage, its envy, its self-loathing. I felt no sympathy for the human characters. Already, I was growing inhuman myself, for how else could I have borne my father's cruelty, my . . . I balk still, yet it must be said . . . my mother's complicity, her preference for him? Between them, they raised a freakish, heartless thing.

'But you were a monster, too, Mother! A two-faced monster, one face for him and one for me. But *he* had all your heart. Your soul, too. He had your soul, did he not . . . ?'

'Hush, oh hush, for heaven's sake!' the nurse cries. 'You are raving.'

'I was never more sane,' I tell her. 'I should have killed *her* when I did him in.'

'Would you like a glass of water?'

I nod and she pours from a pitcher beside the oil lamp, offers the glass, but my hand shakes, and she props my head, holds the glass to my lips. I drink every drop, and then I know at once that she has slipped in a sleeping-draught. My limbs grow heavy, my eyelids are an insupportable weight.

I dream of a nightmare landscape. As I trudge over desolate wasteland women rise all around me, all identically dressed in shifts like mine (or shrouds, perhaps?). Their faces are woebegone, haggard, jaundiced like the moon's, and some of them thrust bottles, or their empty hands, toward me. Others . . . others carry dead babies. One shows an infant whose head rolls off like a ball, its neck spurting blood, and one of them has my mother's face, and I reach out to slap her. For she is smiling at me with one eyelid closed, the way she smiled perpetually after he died, roaming the house in her petticoat, her hair matted and wild, ignoring my pleas, refusing to acknowledge me. She had ever one destination, his study, the place of their abomination, where she ran her hands over the furniture, over objects on his desk, and imitated obscene acts on brass, on wood, on air, until she was taken away to the place where she swiftly expired, unable to survive without his ghastly nurture.

Remembering, I swing my palm at her face, but when my hand touches her she changes into Mari Prince, and I have a bright, sharp object in my fist.

'Mary, what did I do to you?' Mari says, and blood flows from her mouth, and somewhere, far off, another woman is screaming.

I open my eyes. The dream women vanish, but the screaming is real, harrowing, tortured, and I say to the nurse, 'For the love of God, what is that?'

'Just a patient in the ward,' she says. 'Don't fret yourself. She has these fits. They'll give her something in a minute. Are you feeling better after your sleep?'

'How long did I sleep?'

'Less than an hour. I thought you'd be out longer. How are you feeling?'

'My mother is dead,' I tell her. 'She died soon after my father of heart failure.'

'I'm sorry to hear that, dear. It's a terrible thing, I know, to lose a parent.'

And I have been writing letters to a dead woman for ten years or more, and tonight I murdered another woman because I thought my mother lived.

I must be mad then.

'This is an asylum,' I say. 'I was brought here because I am insane.'

The nurse stares at me. She doesn't know what to say. Before she can compose an answer, frame a half-truth to fob me off, another nurse opens the door and says, 'She has a visitor. Is she fit to see anyone?'

I sit up. 'Who? Who is visiting me?'

'She's a bit agitated—' my nurse begins, but Alf thrusts aside the woman in the doorway. 'Mary!' he says, and they cannot prevent him, my guards, he pushes them off to come to me, sits on my bed and takes my hands in his. 'Mary.'

And I am weeping like an abandoned child, like one damned, or sentenced to die, on his breast, on his maroon waistcoat, the fanciful embroidery, the links of his watch-chain pressing into my cheek, and his arms hold me fast.

'Sir, don't distress her,' my nurse says. 'She's already—'

'It's her husband, Jenny.'

'Does he have the doctor's permission?'

'Mary,' Alf says against my hair, 'Mary,' as if he can't say my name enough (and once that was true), 'I've been out of my head with worry. I've walked the roads. I've been to four police stations, and then, when they had no news of you, in a cab to Scotland Yard . . .'

And is that where they told him? Or . . . does he not know yet? If he knew, would he hold me like this, and stroke my hair, and speak to me kindly? My tears cease. I make no effort, they stop of

257

themselves, water turned to ice. For a killing frost has penetrated my body, and I feel as I did long ago, when my father put me out, a child, into the wintry garden, without hat or coat, to punish my misdeeds. Soon Alf, too, will thrust me from him, call me vile names as my father did, and look at me with revulsion in his eyes. I prepare for this, detaching myself from his embrace, pressing my palms against his chest to hold him off. 'You don't know,' I say. 'I have committed . . .' but I can't shape my tongue to the word when his eyes are so soft on me, '. . . a crime.'

His face does not alter. His voice is not changed when he says, 'How do you think I found you at last, Mary? My description of you fitted . . .'

He cannot speak the words either. 'The woman who murdered Mari Prince,' I say.

Behind Alf, the nurses mutter. I hear their words in snatches . . . 'delusion' . . . 'said she killed her father' . . .

Alf takes my hands from his chest and holds them, one in each of his. His hands are like gloves, warming my numbed fingers. 'Is that what you think? You didn't, Mary. You didn't murder Mari. Though you hurt her, it's true—'

'I had a knife—'

'No, Mary.'

'A candlestick in one hand, and a knife in the other. I meant to put her out first, you see . . . for she is much stronger than I . . . and then to plunge the knife—'

Alf chafes my hands. 'You meant to hurt her, and you did, but you never meant to murder her. The inspector who was there, who was at Mari's house, told me so.'

'The knife—'

'There was no knife, Mary.'

I am bemused, distressed, like a child who knows she is the subject of her playmates' hoax but cannot fathom the gist of it. Except that Alf would not trick me, would not tell a cruel lie that would soon have to be untold. It must be so then. I had no knife. Yet, I slipped the knife into my pocket when I left the house. I had it in my hand when Mari Prince came into her room, I know that. But I also know that they have brought me, not to prison, but to an asylum. For I am subject to delusions and dementia, writing letters to a dead woman, dressing as a man to wreak revenge . . . So, then:

'There was no knife, and she is not dead.'

'That's right.'

'But she is hurt? How badly did I hurt her?'

'A bruise on the forehead.'

'A bruise! Surely! What more, Alf? I know there is more! You are holding back. Ah, don't, for I must know!' My voice has risen, and I am writhing in his grasp. 'Let me go! I must go and see for myself—'

'Ah, you are distressing her. I must call for the doctor.'

'Mr Ramsey, we must ask you to leave.'

'One moment, please,' he says over his shoulder, and to me, 'Mary, calm yourself or they will send me away. I promised the doctor and the inspector I'd not speak of it with you tonight. I did so only because you thought . . . the worst. Tomorrow, they will tell you everything. Ask me no more now.'

And I pretend to be calm, pretend to submit, for it is not to be borne that they should take Alf from me. 'Only tell me how badly I hurt her,' I say, and hear how steady my voice is, 'and I will be quiet.'

'She will be very well, Mary,' Alf says. 'As well as ever.'

Relief I feel for the deed not done, but married, inextricably, to shattering regret that my rival, undiminished, undimmed, still stands between me and Alf.

'She will never forgive me, however,' I say. 'Nor do I deserve forgiveness.'

'She may,' Alf says. 'We will have to see. Mari has a good heart, that's sure.'

I look into his eyes. 'You love her,' I say.

He does not answer. And his eyes do not flinch.

'She is your . . . mistress.'

His heavy eyebrows lift. His eyes are bright, as they were in his youth, but not with joy. Pain, too, can glow. 'No,' he says, 'that she has never been, nor ever will be.'

'Ah, tell me the truth, Alf,' I say. 'I know you have feelings for her.' I speak in a whisper now, though passion has seized me. I do not want the nurses to hear this.

'The truth,' he says, his head close to mine, so that he can murmur in my ear, 'is that I asked her many times but she always refused me. Mari won't go with a married man, Mary.'

'A married man . . .'

'That's the whole truth.'

'Then I have wronged her.'

'Yes, sorely.'

'And you have not been an adulterer.' My heart lifts when I say this. For the first time, I glimpse the possibility of happiness, blossoming, oddly, out of error not veracity.

'Not with Mari,' he said.

My heart plummets like the fledgling bird that leaps too soon from the nest. 'But with another? There is another then, is there?'

He shakes his head. I feel the movement against my cheek, for we are very close now, conferring like lovers, though not on those matters of which lovers speak. 'Not in the way you think. I have had carnal thoughts . . . often . . . of Mari, of other women, and . . . less often . . . I have indulged my wishes.'

Ah, why the pain? I have known this for ten years, seen the evidence of those brief infidelities in his face, in his demeanour, late at night, smelled his body when he lay down beside me. So why should my heart ache now? 'But you don't,' I say, 'have such thoughts or wishes about me.'

'Mary, have you forgotten?' he says, his lips so close to my ear, it seems not his voice I hear but a voice in my head. 'You would not come to me. You warned me, did you not, forbade me . . . and in such a way—'

'Ah hush, don't!' I say, for I do not want the image, the memory, that rises now between us, that divisive knife that ripped and killed after all, though then I knew it not.

'Let's not speak of it more tonight,' Alf says. 'It's not on my mind, Mary. You are on my mind. I'm thinking . . .' he draws me closer yet, gathers me into a tighter embrace, '. . . we should have a holiday, go up North—'

'My mother is dead,' I say. I must – to hear myself say it, aloud, to another. But Alf misunderstands.

'Yes, you have no family to visit, but the country is still there, and you loved the country—'

'More than I ever loved my family.'

'And so . . . ?'

'First, Alf, I must see Mari Prince. If she will see me.'

'Yes, that's the right thing. I had planned for you to meet her again, Mary, but differently from this.' He sighs. 'I don't hold myself guiltless. I don't want you to think I do.'

I draw away from him a little, enough to place my hands on his whiskered cheeks that were once clean-shaven and fresh of complexion. A passionate young man, he was once, my husband, his passion all for me, but I denied and thwarted it, denying myself also. And now his hair is grey and he has aged early. And it is true, he has wronged me, as I have him, and what might have been can never be.

Still, this is the man I love, and so I dare, as I have never dared in my life before, though I was a wilful and reckless girl (but the daring that springs from hatred and rebellion possesses none of the danger, none of the risk that the daring of love carries). Once, Alf hesitated. If he hesitates this time, I will lose all – him, myself, my newfound, hard-won sanity. But if he does not hesitate, I might win the world again. So I, ever and never a gambler, take Fortune by the hand.

I say, 'Kiss me.'

24

Mari: Monday Morning

Someone is holding a parade for Mari, and she is borne along on a high, buoyant seat above cheering crowds. A brass band marches in front of her. She can see their scarlet tunics and the golden flash of the trombones and trumpets. She can feel the throb of the music, too, oom-pah-pah, oom-pah-pah . . . and it's giving her a headache.

Fireworks fill the sky, cascades of coloured stars, an astonishing display. But it does hurt her eyes. I must get off, she thinks, and exerts a great effort to rise from whatever floaty vehicle is bearing her along. Her body lifts, she feels herself rise and soar, up into the far reaches, until she seems to pass into the sky and skim through layers of azure, and she wonders, am I dead? Am I going to Heaven?

Her eyes, which she did not know were closed, open, but it's not the pearly gates of the Illustrious City she sees, just a cluttered room . . . her room . . . and she is slumped in her Turkish chair, an almighty pain in her temple, and an incredibly light feeling about the rest of her head, as if it's not fastened properly to her neck. A bewhiskered gentleman in a dark grey overcoat sits at her little claw-foot dining table, writing in a notebook.

Mari opens her mouth and croaks.

The whiskered gentleman turns in his chair. He has a face that calms, in her, the stirrings of anxiety, a sixtyish face, deeply lined and strong-boned, a good grandfather's face. And he's smiling at her as if she were a favourite grandchild.

'How are you feeling, Miss Prince?'

'Like I died and went to Hell,' Mari says.

'Well, that's appropriate in the circumstances. You have been through a bit of hell tonight. But you're far from dead, I'm glad to say. In fact, a cup of tea will have you in top form again.' He shifts his eyes to the door behind Mari and calls, 'Constable!'

A blue uniform moves into Mari's field of vision. Painfully, she tilts her head. The young policeman is smiling at her, too, not a grandfatherly smile (he's no more than thirty-five), but a warm, delighted grin, as if . . . well, it's the smile a man gives a woman when . . . Mari swerves from the thought, as she might sidestep a manhole in the road.

'Constable Dawes!' she says.

'Morning, Miss Prince.'

'Morning?' Mari slides her eyes to the window. It's still dark outside.

'You had a long sleep,' the man at the table says, 'after Constable Dawes woke you up the first time. Be so good as to put the kettle on, Constable . . . I daresay I'll soon be calling you Sergeant after the events of this night . . . Miss Prince could do with a cup of tea.'

'My pleasure,' Constable Dawes says, and gives Mari another fond, lingering smile before busying himself with her teapot and gas ring.

'Here,' Mari says, 'what's going on then? I was attacked, wasn't I? Hit with my own candlestick . . . ?' She looks at her mantelpiece, sees the candlestick back in its place, opposite the other one, and lifts her hand to her forehead. Gingerly, she moves her fingertips over a swelling there, which someone has covered with a gauze poultice. She's been given a whopper, all right – a lump the size of a tennis ball. No wonder her head throbs like a tom-tom. Yet . . . this is not the worst of it. She knows without having to touch and confirm that her attacker, whoever he was, has done her greater harm than this crack on the head. He has taken from her as well as given, committed an appalling robbery . . . Her fingers begin to trace a tentative path from the lump on her forehead towards the other crime scene . . . and halt at her right earlobe. No, she dare not discover it yet, dare not admit what the lightness about her neck must be attributed to. Her dear old dad the fiddler used to say, 'Never face the music, darlin', till you're sure you can jig to it,' advice on procrastination and evasion that doesn't serve in the end, she's well aware, but she heeds it now, craving the comforts of denial. Mari drops her hand. 'Who did it? And what for?'

'Before I tell you your story, Miss Prince, let me introduce myself. Inspector Vulcan, Scotland Yard. I'm assigned to the case involving the Gardener, as he's popularly known. You don't need to be told who he is, of course. And that's why I'm here. We thought at first it might be that personage who attacked you. No, don't distress yourself. It wasn't, we've ascertained.' Inspector Vulcan takes out a graceful-stemmed rosewood pipe. 'May I? Thank you.'

As he pauses to fill the pipe, Constable Dawes crosses to the window and thrusts his hands through the aspidistra leaves to open it a crack. 'With your permission, sir. The smoke will go out now. Miss Prince could do with a bit of fresh air, I expect.'

He has nerve, Mari thinks. He'll probably go far.

'Quite right, Constable.' Inspector Vulcan lights his pipe. 'To fill you in on the details then, Miss Prince: Constable Dawes here had noticed, for the last month . . . early March it began, yes, Constable? . . . a suspicious individual frequenting your neighbourhood, your street, to be precise. A young gentleman, he thought, at first, always dressed in evening clothes. Now, we can't arrest anyone for looking suspicious. Got to have more of a case than that. So the constable kept close watch, and tonight–'

'Thank you,' Mari says as Constable Dawes hands her a cup of tea. It's just the right strength, she can tell by its colour, and he hasn't spilled any in the saucer either.

'Sugar, Miss Prince?'

'Two spoons, please. Level, not heaped.' How nice to be waited on like this, and he spoons the sugar into her cup so neatly, with a delicate turn of his wrist, though he's not a delicate-looking man by any means. She's always had a soft spot for men with feminine accomplishments.

'Have a cup yourself,' Inspector Vulcan says when the constable hands him his tea. 'No need to be on watch now. We have a man outside. Be so good as to close the door, too. Don't want the landlady coming up.' He winks at Mari. 'I've already had the pleasure of Mrs Perkins's company tonight.'

'It was you I heard coughing behind her door!'

'Indeed. I wanted to deter you from coming in. Let me explain why. Earlier, about ten o'clock, wasn't it, Constable . . . ?'

'Ten minutes past, sir.'

'At ten past ten, Constable Dawes observed the appearance of the suspicious personage again. Your safety, and catching that person, has been his first concern recently. Though you didn't know it, you've been under the protection of the law, Miss Prince.'

Mari turns her head. It hurts to move it, and pain slices through her smile when she says, 'Thank you.' Constable Dawes licks his lips and says, 'All mine . . . the pleasure.'

'He dived behind a rhododendron bush and saw the suspect enter your garden, climb the larch tree, and gain access to your room by the window here. You don't lock up at night, Miss Prince! Constable Dawes acted swiftly then. He knocked on the door of a neighbour's house, requested the use of the telephone, rang me at the Yard and then rang your landlady to inform her that, in a few minutes, a policeman (himself, of course!) would be making a routine safety check of houses in her street. This, so as not to alarm her. An alarmed person can make a lot of noise, and he didn't want to alert the intruder. Good work all round, Constable.' Inspector Vulcan pauses to nod approvingly at Constable Dawes. 'Quick thinking. Definitely a promotion in this.'

Mari turns again to look at the constable, a pleasure worth the cracking pain, for he's certainly dazzling tonight, something of the hero in his mien. When he returns her gaze, he seems to be saying, 'I did it for you not the promotion.'

'To continue,' says Inspector Vulcan, who's been watching them both, Mari sees, one eyebrow cocked, his lips twitching. 'In your landlady's parlour, the constable explained the situation to her, calmed her down, and kept watch at her window for my arrival. I came post-haste, of course, with several men. We couldn't dismiss the idea that the intruder might be the Gardener, though it wasn't his method, breaking and entering. In any case, by the time you got home, the house was surrounded (all the men hiding, naturally) and Constable Dawes was stationed in the bathroom adjacent to your room.' (So all my ghosts were policemen, Mari thinks.) 'We intended to prevent any harm coming to you, but we had to catch her in the act. She was faster than we'd anticipated, however. Right, Constable?'

'Like a streak of lightning. Couldn't have been more than twenty seconds between the time you entered, Miss Prince, and *my* entry. Of course, you'd locked your door, so I was hampered by that. Had to break the lock, I'm afraid.'

'Hold on,' Mari says. '*She*, did you say?'

'Your attacker was a woman,' Inspector Vulcan says. 'A woman known to you. You are acquainted, are you not, with Mary Ramsey, the wife of your employer, Alfred Ramsey, manager of the Palladium?'

Mari gawps. 'Never!'

'You are surprised. You had no sense of her antagonism then? You can't suggest a motive?'

'I haven't laid eyes on her,' Mari says, 'in nearly two years. Are you positive . . . ?'

'There's no doubt about her identity. It's the motive we can't discover. What is your relationship with Mr Ramsey?'

Mari bridles. 'Steady on!' Inspector or no, she won't have this. 'There's no reason down that road. He's my employer, that's all. You can ask him, too. Anyway, what does *she* say she did it for?'

'She's in no condition to explain at the moment. Sorry if I gave offence. It's a routine question. Constable Dawes has already attested to your unimpeachable character. We know you're respectable, Miss Prince.'

Mari gives the constable another smile. The smile he gives her back is an elixir.

'Is Mrs Ramsey in the lock-up?' Mari says. 'Does Mr Ramsey know about this yet?'

'She's in St Bartholomew's, a hospital for . . . for the mentally disturbed. Her husband is with her. He'd reported her missing and that's how we identified her, for she wouldn't say boo to us.'

'I can't take it in. I hardly knew her.'

'Well, insanity itself is often sufficient motivation, as you can understand from this other case . . . the Gardener. I'll be going to the hospital later on to talk to Mrs Ramsey. If she is certified insane, it will complicate the procedure of pressing charges.'

'I don't want to press charges,' Mari says quickly. 'Her husband would be dragged in, and he has enough on his plate.'

(No wonder Alf wears that worn-down look. Living with a madwoman. 'Mary's not well!' Talk about understatement.)

'That's generous of you.' Inspector Vulcan rises, brushes ash from his overcoat. 'In the circumstances, I won't argue. She's not likely to trouble you again. I must be going.' He offers Mari his hand. 'Goodbye, Miss Prince. The constable here will take care of you. You can give him a formal statement when you're up to it.'

'Goodbye and thank you,' Mari says. 'I'm glad you're on that other case.'

Should she tell him? No, not now. She's not up to the questions that would follow. He's a man she *could* tell though. Well, tomorrow . . .

'A word with you downstairs, Constable.'

Constable Dawes touches Mari's shoulder as he passes her chair. 'I'll be right back, don't you worry,' he says, and he is. In a very few minutes, he's standing over her again, rubbing his hands, saying, 'Another cup of tea then?'

'Wonderful,' Mari says. 'Will you have one with me, or do you have to get back on your beat?'

'My beat's over for tonight.'

'I expect you're dying to get home to bed.'

'I'm wide awake. Couldn't sleep tonight after all that's gone on. I'd be glad to join you in a second cup.'

Mari begins to rise. He thrusts his palms out in front of her. 'Don't you move now. I'll do it. You have to be the convalescent for a bit.'

Mari sinks back. 'I do feel a bit weak.'

'No surprise. A blow on the head like you've sustained.' He moves towards the gas ring. 'I'll tell you, I was worried when I saw you, Miss Prince.'

'Won't you call me Mari?' she says to his bottle-blue back, a long, strong back; he's as tall as Percy, but with Antonio's shoulder girth.

'I will,' he says, pottering with the tea things. 'I'll be happy to, if you'll call me John in return.'

'John,' she says. 'That's a good name.'

It is. Straightforward, no nonsense, solid and reliable-sounding, with a nice softness in the middle of it . . . a name from the Bible, too. 'There are digestive biscuits in that green tin.'

She likes watching his back, watching him make tea in her room, but the angle at which she must hold her head makes her temple throb, so she turns away and looks at the aspidistra instead. The plant seems to have perked up since she remembered to water and dust it. Its leaves have lifted and their surfaces reflect the sheen of the lamplight. Mari winks at the plant to encourage it further. She, too, is feeling surprisingly perky considering the shocks she's received, and her throbbing head . . . not to mention, not to think of, the other thing, the thing that she's lost . . .

She's heard that knocks on the head can lead to other harms . . . possible brain damage, she's heard.

'I suppose I should see a doctor about my bump,' she says.

'Doctor's already seen you,' Constable Dawes . . . John says. 'I rang him on your landlady's phone soon as they'd removed the assailant and I'd carried you to that chair where you're now sitting.'

Oh, he carried her, did he? That sounds nice. She's never been carried by a man before. What a pity she was out cold and has no memory of what it felt like. 'You've thought of everything, I must say,' she says. 'You've been more than kind.'

'Anything I can do for you is a pleasure, Mari.'

Yes, that aspidistra's really in fine form. Hasn't looked so well since Antonio tended it.

'What did the doctor say about me?'

'Said you'll have a nasty lump and a headache for a week or two, but right as rain after that. 'Course, he wants to check you in a few days.'

'I *am* giddy,' Mari says, 'but I have a nastier feeling than that. Something more horrible has happened to me . . .'

His golden eyes, watching her, seem to darken, turn the colour of burnt umber. 'I blame myself, Mari,' he is saying in a sad, grave voice. 'If only I'd been quicker—'

'No, no, don't say that!' Mari cries. 'You came in the nick of time—'

'Well, your life was never in danger, as we know now—'

That's not what she meant, but never mind.

'—but giving you a crack on the head wasn't all that woman did, as you've realized. She had a pair of scissors, you see, and before I could break your lock – I can't get over how swift she was – she cut off . . .' He gestures towards her head.

Mari slowly she lifts her hands, places her palms on the back of her head, as gently, as fearfully, as she touched the swelling on her temple. Her hair's gone all right. She can feel her skin under the rough crop.

'Help me to the mirror,' she says, rising.

John puts his arm around her, his hand under her right breast. He supports her across the room, her head drumming violently, stars exploding in front of her eyes again, to her dressing table. In the swing mirror Mari confronts herself, a self she's never seen, a self she can't contain or feel. Is it me, this woman with the ragged hair of a street urchin, and a gigantic disfigurement on her forehead?

'Oh, ugly!' she cries. 'Vile! What a guy she's made me. I could kill her for this! I can't go out in the street, let alone on the stage. I'll be a laughing-stock–'

'Steady on, steady on.' John's hand strokes Mari under her breast. 'It's not as bad as you're making out.'

'It's worse! Because I can't find the words–'

'Hush, stop.' His left hand appears on her shoulder. Gently, he presses her back to lean on his chest. 'Listen, I know it's a shock, but take a good look. It's cut very rough, but imagine it trimmed a bit by a hairdresser. If you want my honest opinion, that's a very fetching and out-of-the-common style you have there.'

Mari stares at him. Is he serious? Or is he loony, after all, under all the good sense he gives out? Doris's words come to her unexpectedly: 'Men like a mixture.' Ah, surely not . . . not John Dawes!

'Look properly,' he says. 'Do yourself that favour.'

So she does. She looks like a boy. In the face, that is, not her body, of course. Her face, in fact, looks years younger, as if a decade has fallen off with her shorn locks. She can see how, when the horrible lump goes down, she might look quite dashing, quite flirty, with such a haircut. She's no longer a dead ringer for Aphrodite, though, or any of that illustrious crowd.

'My hair was my glory,' she says.

'You're the glory,' John answers. 'Nothing to do with your hair.'

Ah, he's nice. And it really must be herself he likes, for he doesn't mind the loss of her aureole . . . which *was* hard to live up to offstage. A bit of a relief really, to know no one will, in future, mistake her for a goddess.

'I'll have to wear a wig for the Palladium.'

'That's up to you. Personally, I think you'll be an out-and-out hit, a bigger success than you are already, you look so smashing. And your patrons will be entranced—'

'They won't recognize me!'

As she says this, it strikes Mari that there's another who won't recognize her now. A weight heavier than her hair once was lifts off her shoulders. She needn't creep about in fear of *him*, the Gardener, knowing her by the glaring billboard on her head.

So . . . it's not all bad then.

'Where is it now then, my hair? Not thrown in the dustbin, I hope?'

'It's up at Scotland Yard. Evidence, you see. But you can claim it in a day or two. Fetch a nice price, if you care to sell it—'

'I *was* thinking of cutting it,' she says, 'but I just couldn't bring myself to. Maybe I ought to thank Mary Ramsey, eh?'

'I wouldn't go that far,' John says, 'but I'm glad to see you looking on the bright side again. You've been through a lot. Never mind. It's a green world after a storm, I like to say.'

'You have a touch of the poet in you.'

John shakes his head. 'Not me. I'm a down-to-earth feller. In my job a man has to be.'

His words make her glad. She doesn't want another poet, another dreamer, a make-believer, a feller cockeyed with visions. 'Down to earth' has a nice sturdy sound like his name, solid as the chest she's leaning on. What he's doing with his hand just under her breast is nice too.

'You know, I'm thinking,' John says, 'that you shouldn't be on your own for a bit. Would you like me to stay and keep you company?' His thumb has lifted and now he strokes the underside of her breast.

'Are you married?' Mari says. 'Or engaged? Or attached in any way?'

'I'm free and single, Mari. If I wasn't, I hope you don't think—'

'Just getting the facts, as you policeman say.'

'I'm living with my sister on Rosemary Street. They make me welcome, but it's a bit cramped. I share a room with her two oldest sons. Cramped,' he says again.

'Well, you're welcome to—'

'Thank you, Mari.' He presses his lips to the short, springy hair on the crown of her head.

'I'm so dizzy! I can't think straight.'

'Let me help you,' John says, 'to the bed.'

On his arm, she crosses the room. Side by side, Mari leaning on her new friend, they look down at the rose coverlet and lacy, scattered pillows.

And there, looking up at her, smiling cocksuredly, lies Percy . . . or is it Antonio . . . or this John, this new suitor of hers, an hour or two hence?

'Now this is a fine bed,' John Dawes says. 'Wouldn't want to get up from it once you've laid down.' He presses her close, his thumb finding its place again.

Mari steps briskly out of John's lovely embrace and moves out of arm's reach. Leaning on the Turkish chair, she says, 'I'm sorry, John, but I shall have to withdraw my invitation.'

'Pardon?' His lion's eyes are wide with shock, as if someone had poured cold water on his head.

'I know it's sudden, but so was our agreement. And it won't do, you see. People have to proceed with caution in these matters, that's what I believe.'

(I do, too, she thinks, with a little caper of her heart. I do believe it, at last.)

'I'm robbed of words,' John Dawes says.

'I'll tell you what. Come round for a cup of tea tomorrow.'

'A cup of tea?'

'I'll get in a cherry cake and a loaf of madeira. We'll have a nice long chat.'

'A chat,' he says.

'If it appeals to you to come, of course. No obligation. I must say goodnight now though. Or good morning, rather.'

For a moment he stands immobile, staring at her, as if she had plucked him out of the Palladium audience and put him under hypnosis. He opens his mouth as if to speak, emits a sigh, and shuts his lips. It's a blow to a man, naturally, she understands that, to have his hopes raised (as well as that other part of him) then dashed. But she has to find out if he's worthy of her, and that takes time. If he is, she needn't pity the sorrow on his face, for it's only temporary. If he proves a sticker, she'll raise him up again ... oh, endlessly, and with the greatest of pleasure. 'Good morning, John,' she repeats, primly.

He crosses the room and picks up his helmet. By the time he has it on, Mari is at the door.

'I'll bring my tool box,' he says, 'and mend that lock for you.'

He's a handyman as well! Could fix up a little house maybe, bought cheaply because it needed repairs. Mari stops herself: We'll have none of that, thank you!

'Till tomorrow then,' John Dawes says. 'Will four o'clock suit?'

'Perfect,' she says.

'We could go to the Bioscope after, and have a spot of dinner if you're in the mood.'

'Sounds lovely.'

'I'll let myself out. You shouldn't chance the stairs yet. With your permission ...' His lips brush her cheek.

She waits while he goes down the stairs, to give him the light from her room. From the darkness at the bottom, his voice rises. 'Do you prefer flowers or chocolates, Mari?'

Mari smiles down into the dark well. 'I like either, John, but please don't trouble yourself.'

'No trouble. A great pleasure.' She hears the door close.

Mari bounds across the room to her window. Parting aspidistra leaves, she watches John Dawes stride down the street. She does feel a pang, seeing him walk away. But he'll be back, and back again. She has a strong, sure feeling she's going to be courted this time. Because she hasn't done it arse-backwards for once.

She bounds from the window, and cavorts about the room, her new-shorn hair putting a spring into her step, as if she were a lamb or a foal or some other newborn creature instead of a woman soon to be thirty-six, suffering from dizziness, headache, and nausea. She collapses on to her bed.

'Ah, I shouldn't have done that. I'll pay for it now. I'm in no condition to jig about.' She giggles all the same. Flowers or chocolates? A solitaire or a cluster? Now, stop it! Can't you mind when you're told?

Mari looks up at the ceiling and sobers, the cracks and bulges in the plasterwork reminding her of life's ups and downs. She nearly died twice tonight. And what about John Dawes . . . is *he* merely a coincidence? Ah, there's more mystery in life than can ever be dreamed or imagined . . .

Mary Ramsey, of all people! Alf has his worries added to now. The Palladium will surely be dark for a while. Will it close down as Alf and Doris have been saying?

And the Gardener . . . he won't be looking for the new person she's become, but he's still out there, isn't he?

And . . . and . . . what if she and John don't hit it off after all? For there's no telling . . . can't rely on intuition, who knows that better than she?

A vast drowsiness is overtaking her. She can hardly keep her eyes open. In the first rays of morning sunlight the ceiling takes on a sheen like the surface of a frozen pond, like the rink at the Crystal Palace. . .

Mari is skating on the ice. Round and round she goes, very confident, very dashing, on the narrow blades. Fancy! she says to herself. I'm an expert and I've never skated in my life!

Then she sees someone else on the ice. It's John Dawes in his bottle-blue uniform and a sergeant's cap, his hands full of flowers, a big beribboned box tucked under one arm. She waves to him, blows him a kiss, but she doesn't join him yet.

Instead, she glides off alone, far across the ice, performing leaps and bounds and perfect figure eights, to the left, to the right, forwards and backwards. She twirls like a waltzer, shimmies like a fan dancer, pirouettes, dips, arabesques. It's all very daring and complicated, but the funny thing is, she never trips, never slips, never falters, and she knows she can keep up this fancy footwork as long as she likes. This time, she's not going to land on her arse.

Also available from Mandarin Paperbacks

ROBERTA MURPHY
The Enchanted

All her life, Olwen has lived in the small village of Pont Ysaf. Her childhood has been one of happy make-believe as John, her beloved grandfather, has taught her all he knows of the magical world of Welsh legend in their daily walks through the beautiful Cwm Woods. But when, after a long and painful illness, her grandfather dies, Olwen has no-one to warn her against the supernatural figure he most feared – the all-powerful creature who preys on human desire – the enchanter. And as Olwen reaches the full maturity of womanhood, she is tormented by a maelstrom of dreams and visions which draw her inexorably closer to the darkness of her family's past . . .

THOMAS HARRIS
The Silence of the Lambs

The Silence of the Lambs is razor-sharp entertainment, beautifully constructed and brilliantly written. It takes us to places in the mind where few writers have the talent or sheer nerve to venture. I confess it, I'm addicted.' Clive Barker

A killer is attacking women across the United States. His methods are horrifying, his motives unknown. Only Dr Hannibal Lecter, a homicidal genius incarcerated in a hospital for the criminally insane, can help Clarice Starling, FBI trainee, to prevent the murder of another young woman.

'A virtual textbook on the craft of suspense, a masterwork of sheer momentum that rockets seamlessly toward its climax.' *Washington Post*

'It's marvellous, the best I've read for a very long time. Thank heavens for a novel with a real plot at last, subtle, horrific and splendid. It is infinitely superior to any novel published this year.' Roald Dahl

JUDITH KELMAN
Someone's Watching

Six-year-old James Merritt has been dropped off by the school bus. He is waiting for one of his parents to help him cross the busy road and take him home for lunch. But his mother is held up at the hospital with a patient, and his music producer father is in a recording session, so no one comes. Then he sees a familiar figure beckon him across the road, and as he starts to run a car suddenly accelerates towards him . . .

In the past few years in the fashionable suburb of Tyler's Grove, several children have been severely injured, some even killed, in hit and run accidents. But were they accidents? As James fights for his life, a sinister presence hovers at his hospital bedside; even his distraught mother surely cannot maintain her sleepless vigil, and the police have alarmingly few clues to go on.

FRANCES FYFIELD
Trial by Fire

The sleepy backwater village of Branston in Essex seemed an unlikely spot for a crime of passion but what else could account for the naked, hastily buried body of a woman found overnight in the woods?

For Helen West and Detective Superintendent Geoffrey Bailey, his transfer to Branston seemed an ideal opportunity: a borrowed home, neither his nor hers, to experiment in living together; a simple move for Helen in the Crown Prosecution Service; the chance of a slower, more civilised existence.

For Bailey's staff, the trail led all too easily to Anthony Sumner, local English teacher and lover of Christine Summerfield, Helen's only friend in the district. Sumner could not deny having had an affair with the dead woman. Neither Bailey nor the Crown Prosecutor who was Helen's superior was in much doubt of his guilt.

Barred from the case for being too personally involved, Helen began her own surreptitious digging. She was nagged by a feeling that the evidence against him was just too pat. And behind the closed country doors of Branston, she found a hidden world of envy, lust and murderous rage that threatened to consume her in its fiery embrace ...

A Selected List of Fiction from Mammoth

While every effort is made to keep prices low, it is sometimes necessary to increase prices at short notice. Mammoth Books reserves the right to show new retail prices on covers which may differ from those previously advertised in the text or elsewhere.

The prices shown below were correct at the time of going to press.

☐	416 13972 8	**Why the Whales Came**	Michael Morpurgo £2.50
☐	7497 0034 3	**My Friend Walter**	Michael Morpurgo £2.50
☐	7497 0035 1	**The Animals of Farthing Wood**	Colin Dann £2.99
☐	7497 0136 6	**I Am David**	Anne Holm £2.50
☐	7497 0139 0	**Snow Spider**	Jenny Nimmo £2.50
☐	7497 0140 4	**Emlyn's Moon**	Jenny Nimmo £2.25
☐	7497 0344 X	**The Haunting**	Margaret Mahy £2.25
☐	416 96850 3	**Catalogue of the Universe**	Margaret Mahy £1.95
☐	7497 0051 3	**My Friend Flicka**	Mary O'Hara £2.99
☐	7497 0079 3	**Thunderhead**	Mary O'Hara £2.99
☐	7497 0219 2	**Green Grass of Wyoming**	Mary O'Hara £2.99
☐	416 13722 9	**Rival Games**	Michael Hardcastle £1.99
☐	416 13212 X	**Mascot**	Michael Hardcastle £1.99
☐	7497 0126 9	**Half a Team**	Michael Hardcastle £1.99
☐	416 08812 0	**The Whipping Boy**	Sid Fleischman £1.99
☐	7497 0033 5	**The Lives of Christopher Chant**	Diana Wynne-Jones £2.50
☐	7497 0164 1	**A Visit to Folly Castle**	Nina Beachcroft £2.25

All these books are available at your bookshop or newsagent, or can be ordered direct from the publisher. Just tick the titles you want and fill in the form below.

Mandarin Paperbacks, Cash Sales Department, PO Box 11, Falmouth, Cornwall TR10 9EN.

Please send cheque or postal order, no currency, for purchase price quoted and allow the following for postage and packing:

UK 80p for the first book, 20p for each additional book ordered to a maximum charge of £2.00.

BFPO 80p for the first book, 20p for each additional book.

Overseas including Eire £1.50 for the first book, £1.00 for the second and 30p for each additional book thereafter.

NAME (Block letters) ....

ADDRESS ....

....

....